PRAISE FOR LIZ TALLEY

"There is no pleasure more fulfilling than not being able to turn off the light until you've read one more page, one more chapter, one more large hunk of an addictive novel. Liz Talley delivers. Her dialogue is crisp and smart, her characters are vivid and real, her stories are unputdownable. I discovered her with the book *The Sweetest September* when, in the very first pages, I was asking myself, How's she going to get out of this one? And of course I was sleep deprived finding out. Her latest, *Come Home to Me*, which I was privileged to read in advance, is another triumph, a story of a woman's hard-won victory over a past trauma, of love, of forgiveness, of becoming whole. Laughter and tears spring from the pages—this book should be in every beach bag this summer."

—Robyn Carr, *New York Times* bestselling author

"Liz Talley's characters stay with the reader long after the last page is turned. Complex, emotional stories written in a warm, intelligent voice, her books will warm readers' hearts."

—Kristan Higgins, *New York Times* bestselling author

"Every book by Liz Talley promises heart, heat, and hope, plus a gloriously happy ever after—and she delivers."

—Mariah Stewart, *New York Times* and *USA Today* bestselling author

"Count on Liz Talley's smart, authentic storytelling to wrap you in Southern comfort while she tugs at your heart."

—Jamie Beck

Come Home
to Me

OTHER TITLES BY LIZ TALLEY

Morning Glory

Charmingly Yours

Perfectly Charming

All That Charm

Prince Not Quite Charming (novella)

Home in Magnolia Bend

The Sweetest September

Sweet Talking Man

Sweet Southern Nights

New Orleans' Ladies

The Spirit of Christmas

His Uptown Girl

His Brown-Eyed Girl

His Forever Girl

Bayou Bridge

Waters Run Deep

Under the Autumn Sky

The Road to Bayou Bridge

Oak Stand

Vegas Two-Step

The Way to Texas

A Little Texas

A Taste of Texas

A Touch of Scarlet

Novellas and Anthologies

The Nerd Who Loved Me

"Hotter in Atlanta" (a short story)

Cowboys for Christmas with Kim Law and Terri Osburn

A Wrong Bed Christmas with Kimberly Van Meter

Come Home to Me

LIZ TALLEY

Montlake
Romance

Published by Montlake Romance, Seattle

www.apub.com

Amazon, the Amazon logo, and Montlake Romance are trademarks of Amazon.com, Inc., or its affiliates.

ISBN-13: 9781503900998
ISBN-10: 1503900991

Cover design by Shasti O'Leary Soudant

Printed in the United States of America

This book is dedicated to the CCU staff at Willis-Knighton North, in thanks for saving my father's life, not once but three times. Special thanks to his nurse, Summer Urban, and the best boot-wearing cardiothoracic surgeon I know, David Mull. I used your names in the book, but I can never repay you for the care you gave my father . . . and my entire family.

CHAPTER ONE

California, present day

Standing in his garage, Rhett Bryan elbowed the door of his Maserati Gran Turismo the rest of the way open, juggling a leather messenger bag, a banana, and the protein smoothie that would get him through a production meeting, dress rehearsals, and a quick lunch with Skye Lauren, his soon-to-be next conquest. Or at least he hoped it would swing that way. The up-and-coming actress would look good on his arm for the Emmys in a few weeks. *Variety* had named her the "it" girl last year. Her star was on the rise . . . and her legs weren't bad, either.

"Mr. Bryan, should I drop off the dry cleaning?" his housekeeper, Marta, asked, appearing at his side while drying her hands on the scrubs she wore in lieu of a traditional housekeeper's garb. He liked that she didn't wear the fussy uniforms some wore.

"Please do. Oh, and make sure the new dark-gray suit goes out. I need it for a meeting early next week." He'd had the Italian suit made for him that spring when he'd taken a train to Naples from Cannes. The solitary sojourn had helped him decompress from the film festival he'd attended with some studio execs who he hoped would finance his new venture. He liked the way the suit, crafted by a wizened, fourth-generation tailor, made him feel—impeccable, powerful, rooted. That was the image he wanted to cultivate, a much different one from the loveable goof he played on his late-night talk show.

"Yes, sir. Have a good day," Marta said as he climbed inside his car.

He gave his usual salute, glad he'd hired the unflappable woman last year. His house sat in the Hollywood Hills, an excellent example of a midcentury modern built by a disciple of Wright. The four-bedroom house was modest for someone who had two Emmys and a late-night show on a major network, but Rhett loved the clean lines, the white-oak built-ins, and the louvered windows that opened to an incredible view of the canyon. Sometimes he rolled his bar cart out to the patio, made a martini, and turned on Sinatra, re-creating a time when the Rat Pack reigned with their fedoras and undone bow ties.

Yeah, he had a vivid imagination, but it had served him well over the past fifteen years he'd lived in LA. He was number one in his market and positioning himself to enter the world of feature films with a new production company.

His phone buzzed as he wound down his street, tossing a wave to an older couple walking their Afghan hound. The dog wore a fuzzy pink collar with rhinestones. Only in LA.

"What's up, Stevo?"

"JT can't make it for the rap video bit. Got a bad summer cold."

"You're shitting me."

"Nope. Thank God we didn't promo it. I can try to tap someone else, but it's short notice." Steve Ermine booked the talent for *Late Night in LA with Rhett Bryan*, but even Steve couldn't do anything about sick celebrities.

"Sucks he got the flu 'cause that bit was gold. Viral material. Wait, what about doing it with Bieber next week? Let's switch the sketches and do the karaoke thing with Melissa McCarthy. She's good at improvising. Put in a call to her assistant and see if we can clear it."

"On it," Steve said.

"Anything else?"

"Nah, we're good."

"I'll be there in thirty. Maybe forty, depending on if I run into delays. Call back if Melissa can't do the sketch, and we'll put a writer on sub material. Someone's gonna earn his paycheck."

"Or hers."

Rhett smiled, remembering Steve had three daughters. "Right."

Steve hung up and Rhett sighed. He liked working with Timberlake because the dude was straight-up cool and knew how to play off Rhett, but Bieber had matured enough to recognize that self-deprecating humor endears an entertainer to a broader audience. After a period of screwing up, the pop star had finally gotten his shit together.

Rhett tapped the navigation screen and clicked on his preferred music for the drive into the studio. Retro country.

No one would guess that the slick and funny Rhett Bryan liked to sing along with Barbara Mandrell and Merle Haggard, yet Rhett knew you could take the boy out of rural Carolina, but you couldn't take Carolina out of the boy. Something about singing along to the music that had poured from his grampy Pete's tinny radio centered Rhett. He lived in California and rubbed elbows with the grossly rich and too famous, but his audience wasn't made up of Beverly Hills socialites. His audience was made up of mechanics with grease beneath their nails and housewives who'd left a sink full of dishes to watch him tell jokes and interview people who'd forgotten what it felt like to scrub a toilet or drink a non-craft beer. It served him well to remember who he'd once been—just a South Carolina small-town boy with big dreams and his radio tuned to Garth Brooks.

The late morning was typical of a Southern California summer—bursts of hibiscus and green palms against an Easter-egg-blue sky. He wound through the streets, leaving his quiet neighborhood to join the battalions of shiny convertibles and Smart cars marching toward purpose. He slid on his aviator sunglasses and opened the sunroof. Days like this, he could hardly remember sultry southern nights with biting no-see-ums buzzing around his head. He could almost forget the thick palmettos and the Spanish moss dripping from the interlocked oaks. But the country music reminded him.

God, he loved California.

No, he loved his life. He was living a dream—the one he'd set his eye on during his freshman year of college, when he'd tried stand-up and found out he was pretty damned good. He'd studied classic Carson and dissected Leno and Letterman. Interning, writing, then performing on other late-night shows and in comedy clubs were stair steps to the dream offer that had come three years ago. Rhett Bryan was the young-est guy on late night . . . even if Jimmy Fallon looked younger.

He braked as he came to a red light, picked up the banana, and peeled it. He had worked out before showering and dressing for the day. He always had a smoothie and a banana on the way in. Once he made it through meetings and a brief rehearsal, adrenaline would see him through the rest. After the show, he'd have a bigger meal. Maybe a steak. Or rare tuna.

The light turned green and he took off, roaring down Franklin, heading toward the studio that sat on Hollywood Boulevard. Patsy Cline crooned about weeping willows as a blinking yellow arrow warned of construction ahead.

"Damn it," Rhett muttered under his breath as he shifted lanes, doing a quick survey of the area. If he hooked a turn to his left, he might be able to circumnavigate the construction and save precious time. The neighborhood was a collection of lower-income apartments and over-priced duplexes but would kick him onto Hollywood Boulevard in a few easy turns. If he was lucky and didn't run into a lot of other people doing exactly the same thing.

Rhett had a good sense of direction and kept the blur of the ele-vated 101 in sight as he wove through the narrow streets. *Please don't let me get stonewalled by a dead end. I need to review the script and talk to Bonnie about audience participation. I need to remind an intern to screen a few guys, find the perfect person who won't get bent out of shape if he gets a little green slime in his hair.*

Reaching down to the cup holder, Rhett grabbed his protein drink and gave it a hard shake. Sliding a glance toward the carton in his hand, he grimaced. "Ah, crap. Effing strawberry?"

His sigh of disgust amplified into a yelp of surprise as something darted toward his car. A blur of red, a flash of brown.

"What the—" He stomped his brakes, making the car squeal and fishtail. The sound of his car thumping into whatever the blur was made his heart lurch, his stomach immediately cramp.

Whatever he'd slammed into, his front tire had rolled over. His car rocked to the left before his seat belt jerked him back into the smooth leather.

Rhett slammed the car into park with hands that shook so hard that they couldn't be his. His legs flushed hot as a thrum of adrenaline vibrated his body. Darting a glance toward where the blur had come from, he met the stunned face of what looked to be a ten-year-old boy. Their gazes locked, and something cold slithered into Rhett's stomach. "Oh God."

Only a second had passed, but an eternity stretched in front of him. What had he hit? A dog?

God, please let it be a dog. It had to be a dog. Or a cat. A cat would be good. Or not good. But better than—

The boy's mouth opened and closed. Then abject horror flashed on the child's face, relaying that what lay beneath the car wasn't a dog. Or a cat. Hot acid boiled up into Rhett's throat. He was going to vomit.

He pressed a hand against his mouth, begging his body to obey the dictates of his mind. *Hold it together. Get out of the car. You're an adult. React. Deal.*

Yet his body wouldn't move. The only sound he heard was his heart beating in his ears and the muffled something beneath his car.

A piercing scream jarred him from his trance, forcing him to unlock his frozen body. Somehow, he opened the car door. He wasn't conscious of climbing into suffocating heat, but suddenly he stood outside.

"*Dios mio,*" a woman screamed, running toward him, passing him. "My baby. My baby."

Rhett rounded the car and nearly fell to his knees.

He couldn't unsee the sight that met him. Pink high-tops with glitter laces. Legs encased in tight jeans jerking beneath his car.

"Oh Jesus no," someone said.

Rhett realized it was his voice.

The boy who'd locked eyes with him reached down and picked up the soccer ball that bumped against the curb. Then the child sat down hard, his thin arm falling helplessly beside him as he turned away, clutching the ball to his gut like a pillow.

A rush of movement came from his right—the woman falling to her knees, pulling at the child beneath his car, sobbing. "Josefina, *meu bebe, meu bebe.*"

Blood bloomed from beneath his tire, crimson ribbons unchecked by the small brown hand curled into a fist, a fist that fell open. Little brown hands with pink fingernails.

Rhett began to shake harder. What should he do?

911.

Call 911.

More yelling. Sobs. Screams. Horror.

Rhett lurched toward his open door and grabbed the cell phone sitting in the door pocket.

"911. What's your emergency?" The dispatcher's voice was nasally.

"Send an ambulance. Now. Hurry." His breath came in spurts. He couldn't breathe. The air was too thick. And his heart banged too hard against his ribs. It wasn't supposed to do that. Maybe he was having a heart attack. Or maybe he was about to pass out.

"Sir, what's your emergency? Can you give me an address?"

"I'm not at my house. I'm at . . . where is this?" he yelled at a man running toward his car.

The man's eyes rolled wildly as he advanced. "Oh my God. Sweet Jesus. What have you done?"

"I just turned off Franklin. By the . . . oh shit . . . where is this?" Rhett said, panicking, searching for a clue about where he was. Several yards away he saw a street sign. "North Kingsley. It's North Kingsley. Hurry. Please, God, hurry."

He heard riffling on the other end, clicking and stuff rattling. The dispatcher made another call and then said, "Sir, can you give me your name? Are you calling from your number?"

"My name's Rhett Bryan. Please hurry. There's been an accident. A child ran out in front of my car."

"Rhett Bryan?"

"Yes. Please hurry."

"I have someone en route, sir."

"Thank you," he said, feeling a small measure of relief. The initial shock tumbled into absolute horror.

He'd hit a child. He'd run over a child. Oh God.

"Rhett, can you tell me more details about the accident?" Her voice softened, as if she could sense what had happened. As if she could see the blood, feel the thud of a body against his car. Maybe she was sincere, or maybe dispatchers practiced stuff like this. It was a weird thing to wonder in such a terrible moment.

On wobbly legs, Ryan shuffled toward the side of his car. The wailing woman, who wore shorts and a paint-splattered T-shirt, pulled at the child's legs, sobbing and muttering words in a language he couldn't understand.

"I was driving down the street and something came at me. She was chasing a ball. A soccer ball." His voice cracked on the sob that tore from him. "A little girl. Oh God, it was a little girl. I didn't see her. She came out of nowhere. I don't know what to do. She's under my car. I don't think we should move her. I think my car's on her."

His legs buckled and he crumbled to the hot asphalt. From the corner of his eye, he saw someone with a phone aimed toward him. It wasn't uncommon. People filmed him all the time, taking covert pictures or asking for autographs. But not in a moment like this. Never during something like this.

"What do I do?" he asked the dispatcher. "I don't know what to do."

"Can you tell if the child's breathing? Is she conscious?"

"She's under my car. There's blood and . . . I can't look. Please, it's bad."

"Okay, sir, paramedics are on their way. Stay calm."

Sirens sounded in the background as more people clumped together, speaking rapid-fire, stunned words he couldn't understand. He'd never felt more alone.

The dispatcher was silent for a moment, but he could hear her tapping on her keyboard. Finally, she asked, "Sir, can you see the ambulance?"

"I can hear them." His throat closed up and he could feel panic close in on him. Breathing was hard, darkness skated in . . . then back out.

"Good. Just a few minutes more, Rhett." Apology shaded her voice.

Seconds later, a police car arrived, pounding feet, baying sirens, wails of grief. The dispatcher hung up. He stared at his phone, refusing to look at his car. At the broken headlight. Bent fender. Life bleeding onto the asphalt.

Someone pulled at his arm. "Sir?"

"I can't. I can't move," he said.

"Sir, stand up. I need to move you," a policewoman said. "Over here, please."

He told his legs to move. Tilting forward, he crawled, eventually getting his feet beneath him. When he stood, his legs shook so badly, he could hardly support his weight.

He should have done something. He should have helped. Maybe CPR. Something.

But he knew. God, he knew. CPR wasn't going to work. He knew this the same way he knew the sun would set that evening.

Sobs shook his shoulders. "Oh God. I'm so sorry."

The policewoman tugged his elbow. "Sir, let's get someone to check you out."

"No, help her. I'm not hurt. I'm okay."

But he wasn't okay.

Rhett Bryan would never be okay again.

CHAPTER TWO

Mangham High School
Moonlight, South Carolina
April 2003

Summer Valentine watched Mr. Wilson, her AP Calculus teacher, discreetly pick his nose before wiping whatever he found under his desk.

The man was totally disgusting.

Not only was Mr. Wilson hygienically challenged, but he'd sprung a calculus pop quiz on the AP class twenty minutes ago, earning a huge groan, if not a push for all-out anarchy, from the class. He was not a well-liked man, especially that day. Lucky for Summer, she had reviewed the material last night. She was the first to hand in her quiz, and Molly Dorsett shot daggers of hatred at Summer as Summer nearly tiptoed back to her desk.

Summer and the head cheerleader were locked in a dead heat for top of the senior class. Molly had spent last night decorating for prom rather than studying. Summer had first-period physics with the bouncy blonde and had heard all there was to hear about the miles of shimmering fabric and etched lanterns festooning the gym. Molly also had other attributes besides being smart going for her—like curly hair, a tiny waist, and the heart of the Mustangs' star pitcher, Hunt McCroy.

So, shouldn't Molly let Summer have something in life? Like the title of valedictorian?

Summer knew she should work on the rough draft of the five-paragraph essay due in AP European History, but Rhett Bryan sat two desks over from her, and if she pretended to be drawing on her notebook and held her head just so, she could covertly watch him bite his clickable pencil and frown at the quiz.

Rhett was M. T. Mangham High School's hottie patottie.

With sandy hair that curled at the tips, a strong jaw, and baby-blue eyes that netted him extra fried chicken from the lunch ladies, Rhett was at the top of the high school food chain. And to make matters even worse, he was actually nice.

Yeah, most popular guy in the school, and Rhett did things like talk to the special education students when their aides brought them out for break and smile at plump girls like Summer. The guy deserved a medal—the "decent to rejects" award.

If he'd been remotely nasty, she wouldn't waste her time mooning over him, but Rhett was . . . every girl's ideal. Even dorky Summer's.

"Pencils down." Mr. Wilson interrupted her study of Rhett's perfect lips wrapped around his pencil. How could lips be so pretty? On a guy?

Another collective groan from the class.

"I've told you young people that your job every night is to review the material. I will elect to give periodic checks to see if you're doing as instructed," Mr. Wilson continued, knocking a knuckle on Rhett's desk and motioning for the rows to begin passing the quizzes forward. Summer eyed the hand Mr. Wilson had used to pick his nose. She hoped he didn't touch Rhett with it.

"While I waited on many of you to deliver what I'm sure will be rather uninspiring computation, I glanced at Miss Valentine's quiz. She got all five problems correct. Studied the material last night, eh,

Summer?" Mr. Wilson's bushy eyebrows danced like twin caterpillars as he turned his regard on her.

She immediately bloomed a vicious pink.

"Summer?" Mr. Wilson prodded for an answer.

She managed a nod.

"All right, then, let's move on to derivatives. Again."

More sighs. Summer pulled her eyes away from Rhett, but not before he caught her eye and gave her a smile, making her turn the shade of ripe strawberry. She cursed her fair complexion and smattering of freckles before turning her gaze to gross Mr. Wilson. God, she had to stop being such a goober every time Rhett smiled at her. After all, the guy smiled at everyone.

Thirty minutes later, the bell sounded and everyone started shoving books into their bags. Summer liked to leave the classroom last—she hated getting trampled—so she took her time packing up.

As she made her way toward the busy hallway, she noted Rhett stood at the door . . . waiting on her?

"Hey, Summer," he said, cute-as-a-button grin in place.

She stutter-stepped and tried to ignore the butterflies thrashing in her stomach. "Hey, Rhett."

"Man, rough quiz for me. Guess not for you, huh?"

Summer lifted a shoulder and lied. "I had to guess on a few."

"You're trying to make me feel better about bombing it. Senior year's supposed to be easy. What happened to that?" Rhett made a face and Summer tried not to focus on his lips. Instead she zeroed in on that little dip at the base of his throat. There had to be a name for it. She couldn't recall what it was, though.

"So I wanted to see if you had some extra time to help me out in calculus. I'm not doing so hot, and Coach told me to get a tutor."

Summer's butterflies fainted. This was it. The classic plot to count-less movies she'd vegged on for years. The hot guy asks the smart, geeky girl to help him with a hard class and then once he gets to know her, he sees beneath the bad fashion sense and subpar haircut to the special girl beneath the frumpy sweatshirts. There were half a dozen of these plots floating around, so there had to be some universal truth to them, right? "What did you have in mind?"

Lord, she even sounded more sophisticated. She might as well be dangling a champagne glass and blowing cigarette smoke from the side of her mouth. *What do you have in mind? Derivatives or me, big boy?*

"I have baseball practice until seven o'clock every night. Can't blow that off if we're going to make a run at district, but I can skip out on prom committee. You free tonight?"

"Tonight?"

"If you can't—"

"No, I can. I just have to figure out what to do with Maisie, uh, my sister. My mom and dad have church leadership tonight." She could get her next-door neighbor, Gretchen, to watch her ten-year-old sister while she helped Rhett. If she promised to clean Gretchen's kitchen or something. Gretchen was an opportunist.

"I can come to your place if that helps," Rhett said, taking her elbow and moving her out of the way of the onslaught of freshmen pouring out of the gym.

Summer felt tingly where he touched her. That totally meant something. She knew because she'd read every romance novel in the Vaughn Memorial Library last summer.

But she didn't want him at her perpetually cluttered house, which was decorated in last-decade harvest gold. With her parents coming in from Bible study and wanting to chat with him. Lord have mercy. "How about we meet at Butterfield's Grill? It's quiet there after the early-bird rush."

"It's a plan," he said, tossing her another grin before adding, "You rock, Summer."

Then he was swallowed up by the students hurrying to their next class.

"Hold. The. Phone. Were you just flirting with *the* Rhett Bryan?" Vanessa Clair Rafferty asked, skidding to a stop right before she slammed into Summer.

"Flirting? No. Talking. Yes," Summer said, ripping her gaze from where Rhett had disappeared and focusing on the girl who'd been her BFF since sixth grade. Nessa was small, almost elfish, but could eviscerate even the most confident underclassman with her acerbic tongue. She wore a skater dress and high-top Converse. When she could get away with plopping a porkpie hat on her inky locks, she did. Nessa said it made her interesting, like the Winona Ryder of Mangham High. Nessa had a thing for *Reality Bites* and *Mermaids* . . . and any other Winona Ryder movie.

"What did Boy Wonder want?"

"To meet me in the back booth at Butterfield's at seven o'clock tonight."

Nessa pinched her. Hard.

"Ow." Summer slapped at her friend's hand, noting that Nessa wore the black polish her preacher father railed against.

"I'm just making sure you know you're not dreaming," Nessa said, moving toward the art class they both had.

"For tutoring, Nessa," Summer clarified. "Just for a little calculus tutoring."

"Which *could* be code for stick your tongue down my throat," Nessa teased, riffling through her backpack and pulling out her portfolio. "Or maybe that's what he uses with Graysen . . . 'cause his tongue is always down the pageant queen's throat."

"I know," Summer said, trying to ignore the rude reality that Rhett had a girlfriend that looked like Britney Spears, only prettier. Deep down, Summer knew she didn't have a chance with Rhett. All those movies she'd watched and romances she'd read were fiction for a reason. A hot guy falling for a girl like her—a girl whose own mother said she was "pleasant to look at"—happened once in a trillion. Or maybe not even that often.

"Wear the new plaid shirt over the tight tank. You actually have boobs. Accentuate the positive. Isn't that a song from a Disney movie?"

Summer made a face. "*The Jungle Book*? *Mary Poppins*? I don't know. All I know is that this is for math only, Ness."

"You so lack vision," Nessa said, pushing into the art studio. "And for heaven's sake, wear your hair down. The braid thing has to go. You're not seven years old."

Summer pulled the brown braid over her shoulder. "I don't want him to think I'm trying too hard."

Nessa dropped her portfolio on the big table where she sat next to Peyton Wilton, a redheaded obnoxious junior who liked to do stupid things like pull chairs from beneath people and talk about the size of all the football players' penises. Nessa hated him. So she shot him a warning when he started leering at her like a lopsided jack-o'-lantern. "Just trust me. For once."

Summer closed her eyes and issued a sigh before heading to the back table.

So she was challenged when it came to style? Wasn't for lack of trying. She scoured fashion magazines, even spending her hard-earned babysitting dollars on purchases at the trendiest stores, but when she tried to wear what other girls were wearing, she looked stupid. Inevitably she'd rip off the necklace that had looked so cool in the store, or the flared jeans that seemed like they'd flatter her, in favor of her standby—dark T-shirt and well-worn Levi's. Wearing her hair in a braid was sensible and suited her. But maybe Nessa was right. Perhaps tonight she should be a little bolder. Just in case.

Their art teacher took roll and left them to their final projects, which were due in a few weeks. Summer had been working on a poetry collage mounted on canvas. She figured it would be perfect for her dorm room at the University of South Carolina in the fall. Two birds, one stone.

But as she worked on painting the sunny rays to frame the Edna St. Vincent Millay poem she'd picked out, her mind drifted to the song she'd been working on for the past month. The second verse about the horse and crumbling trail didn't match the intensity of the first verse. She needed to rethink the ending of the song, about how the cowboy never goes back for the girl. About how he plunges to his death. Or not. She still wasn't sure.

Her grandmother had given her a guitar for her twelfth birthday, and Summer found she had a gift for composing and picking out tunes. When she wasn't studying or babysitting, she spent her time with Nessa talking her out of various insane ideas (like sneaking off to Columbia for a punk concert) and playing around with writing songs. Sometimes her dad sat with her and picked his own guitar, adding chords and suggestions. Those were her favorite times. In those moments, she wasn't super-smarty-pants Summer. Or chubby, invisible Summer. In those moments her words swelled with life—stretching, growing, becoming something wonderful . . . something she could pin her dreams on.

Which was the dream she usually didn't allow herself to think about.

Writing music and singing was a pipe dream. She'd never been one to sparkle, shine, or have the guts to sit in front of a crowd of people. Still, a piece of her wanted to chuck aside her college scholarship and give it a whirl. She'd spent hours reading about Nashville, studying her favorite songwriters, and imagining her transformation into a country music star. And then after three Grammys, she'd marry Rhett and have two children.

When she accidently dipped her brush into a pot of green paint, she forced herself to focus on her project and stop daydreaming about singing at the Ryman Auditorium or kissing Rhett Bryan.

When the period was over, Nessa appeared beside her like a pesky mosquito. "I'm going to my locker. Meet me by the tennis courts and we'll plan what you shouldn't say tonight to Rhett."

"I'm tutoring him, *not* going out with him," Summer clarified. "He has a girlfriend."

"But it's probably your only chance," Nessa shouted before she disappeared into a herd of sophomore boys slapping each other on the back of the neck.

Boys were so stupid.

Summer rounded the corner heading for her locker and nearly slammed into Graysen, Rhett's aforementioned girlfriend. Speak of the devil.

"Summer." Graysen's annoyance faded into a grin. "Rhett told me you're going to help him with math. He's been so stressed."

"Happy to help," Summer said, tugging on a smile.

Graysen wore a shirt with strategic cutouts highlighting her thin shoulders. Her layered and highlighted hair framed a square jaw and bright-blue eyes. "I'd totally come hang with y'all, but I gotta help with prom decorations. Only one more week. Are you excited?"

"No worries. We're going to work on derivatives. They're boring."

"That's why I don't do all that upper-level stuff. I told Rhett not to take it senior year, but he thinks it will look better on his transcript." She released an exaggerated sigh. "So who are you going to prom with?"

Dreaded question of the week. "Prom's not my thing."

"What?" Graysen stopped midstep, looking like someone had smacked her. "But you're a senior."

"Correct," Summer said, not wanting to have yet another conversation about her electing to skip prom. She'd already endured her mom's woebegone eyes for the past month. But no one had asked her to go, and the thought of going by herself like some pathetic loser, or as her mother called it, "a confident girl," didn't appeal to her. Nessa was going with the saxophone player in the school jazz band. They both had a penchant for bad music.

"But you have to."

"It's not required, Graysen," Summer joked.

The blonde stopped in the middle of the hall, and the other students veered around them as if they were rocks dividing a stream. Graysen's eyes narrowed, then her eyebrows lifted. "Oh."

Nice. Even a dim bulb like Graysen could figure it out.

"I can totally get you a date, Summer. And I have a ton of dresses. You can borrow one." Graysen's eyes widened. "You know what we could do? We could do a makeover. I would love to do you."

And I would love to do your boyfriend.

Summer shook her head. "I'm good. I don't even dance."

"Prom's not about dancing. It's bigger. You can come with me and Rhett. Everyone's going."

Summer felt panic well inside her. She wasn't a charity case who needed the popular girl to get her a date. Uh, much. "Truly, it's fine. I got to run. See you later."

And with that, Summer did a fast run-walk thing away from Graysen like Ms. Thomas made them do in PE. Because she wasn't going to stand there and argue with the Shrimp Festival Beauty Queen over not going to prom. What was the big deal with prom, anyway? The whole thing was an excuse to buy an expensive dress she'd never wear again, drink vodka mixed with fruit punch, and stagger around in high heels that pinched her toes. So not her thing.

But Graysen's words were almost the same ones her mother had uttered three nights before over a Weight Watchers enchilada casserole.

"Come on, sweetie. It's your senior prom. If you don't go, you'll always regret it. I can still remember my dress. I wore this long, flowing dress with a big ruffle across my bosom. It was lilac. So pretty. But your dad. Lord, he wore a powder-blue leisure suit." Her mother laughed, sliding a glance over to Summer's dad.

"That was the style. And you weren't complaining when I worked it better than John Travolta under that disco ball."

"You were the bomb diggity, Jer," Carolyn said, reaching out to clasp her husband's hand.

Summer's dad wasn't much for smiling, but the memory of him doing the Disco Duck or whatever it was they did in the 1970s caused a crack in his stoic veneer. He looked over at Summer as she eyed the casserole her mother had dished onto their plates. "You really should go, Sum. Your mother's right about regrets. I, for one, will never forget that night."

Her mother gave her father an intimate smile. Summer so didn't want to know what it meant, but she suspected. Something gross, no doubt.

Summer flipped an onion ring off her cheesy potatoes. "I won't regret it. All kids do now is get wasted and get hotel rooms. That's not me. Y'all know that's not me."

"Not all kids drink alcohol and have s-e-x," her mother said.

Maisie took that moment to pipe up. "I know what that spells, but I don't know what it is. When are you going to tell me about this stuff?"

Saved by the kiddo and her questions about s-e-x, Summer excused herself . . . and tried to avoid similar conversations every time her mother brought up prom dresses. She also tried to ignore the *Seventeen* magazine Prom edition that landed at the foot of her bed one afternoon. Her mother was anything but subtle.

"Hey, Sum, wait up," Nessa called, jarring her from her contemplation of proms, mothers, and stupid dresses with sequins.

Nessa fell into stride with her. "What did Queen G want?"

"To make me her pet."

"Come again?"

"Obviously, Graysen has watched way too much *Clueless*. She wants to find me a date for 'One Thousand and One Arabian Nights' and loan me a dress to—I don't know—fit around one thigh?" Summer pushed out into the chilly spring day. They'd had a few warm days, but early April often demanded a hoodie.

"Let her. I know prom's lame, but I want you to go. How else will you conquer learning to pin on boutonnieres and doing the Tootsie Roll? Do people still do that dance?"

Summer glanced at her friend. "How would I know? And if I did, I don't want to do it with some scrub Graysen digs up for me. Wait, doesn't she have a brother who's a sophomore?"

"Yeah, but he hasn't gone through puberty yet. He's my height."

"Exactly. I'm not going with Graysen's kid brother. In fact, I'm not going at all." Summer made her way to the benches by the tennis courts, digging out her peanut-butter-and-honey sandwich and the **vitamin**-water she'd tucked in her bag that morning.

"Summer," someone called.

She turned to find all six-feet-one inches of Rhett jogging toward them.

"Wow," Nessa breathed.

He stopped and set his hands on trim hips, making his shoulders broader. Rhett had such an ease about him, like Justin Timberlake from *NSYNC, possessing a magnetism that made him a guy's guy and a girl's ideal.

"Glad I caught you," he said, not even out of breath. "I have to change our time to seven fifteen tonight. I told Hunt I'd give him a lift since his truck's in the shop. He lives out on Vermillion Island so it'll take an extra few."

"No problem," Summer said.

"Cool." His smile grew even bigger. "Gray tells me you're coming to prom with us next weekend."

"Uh," Summer said, trying to decide if she should tell Rhett she thought prom was a waste of time . . . or play along.

"She is," Nessa said, drawing Rhett's attention.

Summer shot Nessa a look. "Actually, I'm not sure—"

"Awesome," Rhett interrupted. "It'll be cool hanging with you."

His words hit the mark. *Thunk.* Rhett wanted to hang with her. What did that even mean? Was that different from when they worked on the world history project together sophomore year? Or better than the time she rode shotgun with him while delivering canned goods to the food bank? If Rhett wanted her to go, she probably should. Prom couldn't be that bad.

But it probably would be.

She'd spend all night watching Rhett and Graysen play tonsil hockey and wishing she'd just said no.

She'd learned in world history (after she moved to the front of the class so she didn't spend all period staring at Rhett) that it was acceptable to lose a battle. Just don't concede the war. "So . . . I'll see you tonight?"

Rhett smiled. Angels sang. "Yeah, it's a date."

Except it wasn't. And never would be.

He jogged back toward the gym, where Hunt McCroy and a few other guys with lean bodies and jacked-up trucks loitered and put out the "cool people" vibe. Some of the kids were rich, like Hunt. Some were good-looking, like Rhett. Most were just assholes who wanted to be rich and good-looking but didn't make the cut.

None of them had ever shown any interest in Summer.

So why now?

She didn't have a good answer, so she sank onto a bleacher and pulled the crusts from her sandwich to feed to the blackbirds stalking around the tennis court.

CHAPTER THREE

South Carolina, present day

Summer dug her toes into the sand and watched her son drop the skim board on the beach and leap upon it with a natural grace she envied. To her right, the evening sun hovered over the horizon as if reluctant to accept its watery fate.

"Watch, Mom," David called out, picking up the board that had slipped from beneath his ever-growing feet. He tossed it back onto the water rushing to and fro on the hard-packed sand.

"I am," she said, shielding her eyes against the dying rays.

He rode the flattened water pushing onto the beach, his brown body tight, arms spread out, before leaping nimbly off.

"Nice," she called because he expected a compliment. Like every man. Her brown-eyed boy with his too-long shaggy hair and beautiful white smile lived for the applause, no matter who it came from.

"Dad said he has a surfboard I can borrow," David said, picking up the skim board and jogging her way. His tongue hadn't tripped over the word *dad* this time. Her son was getting used to the fact that he had a father in his life now. Summer was not . . . even though she'd moved back to Moonlight, where his father lived, and tried to accept what was best for David.

"I'm not sure I want you out surfing, honey. There are plenty of sharks—"

"Mom, don't be moronic. More Americans get injured by toilets than attacked by sharks," David scoffed, catching up with her as she started back toward the parking lot, where her car sat under the shadow of the Hunting Island lighthouse. She'd already packed up her beach chair and bag containing the remainder of their snacks and the near-empty bottle of sunscreen. The beach was David's Sunday afternoon choice nine times out of ten, but now that November had arrived, bringing cooler temps and more school activities, their times frolicking in the waves were drawing to a close.

"How does one get injured by a toilet?" Summer asked, wrapping her arm around her son's neck.

He promptly ducked beneath her embrace. "I don't know. Fall in?"

"Or trip and hit their heads on it?" Summer tried not to feel miffed that the boy who had once snuggled next to her at every opportunity now ran from her embraces. This was what fourteen-year-old boys did. They pulled away.

David tucked his board beneath his arm and dug for his cell phone in the bag she'd shouldered.

"Don't get it wet," she cautioned.

"Dad got me a LifeProof case," he said, head down, thumbs moving on his phone as he tuned her out.

"David," she chided, tapping his forearm. "At least wait until we get in the car."

"I'm just checking something," he said, nearly walking into one of the palm trees that had fallen across the beach.

"You're always just checking something," she said, trying not to sound like a nag. It grew harder and harder to have patience with her son. He'd started at Mangham High School that fall, something she found tough to believe. When had her chubby toddler become a freshman? When had watching YouTube videos and Snapchatting his friends become more important than her?

David didn't have the problems she'd had as a teen. Her son, with his good looks and athletic ability, never lacked for friends or, as she'd found out recently when checking his social media accounts, admirers. She so wasn't ready to have a kid that all the girls were crazy about, but it looked like that's what he was becoming. God help her.

"What's for supper tonight?" David asked, still not looking up.

"You're going to trip if you don't look where you're going," she said, pulling his elbow as he nearly hit the beach rules sign. "I'm picking up something from the Shrimp Shack. Didn't get by the store this morning like I thought I would."

David had gone to church as he did almost every Sunday with her mother. It was an easy concession to make since she wanted her son to have a good moral foundation, spend time with his grandmother, and, if she were honest, give herself a few hours to sleep in.

"I love their gumbo. I'll have that. And some fried shrimp," David said, still tapping at his phone but with a smile. Feeding a teenager broke the bank, but dinner tonight was on Pete Bryan, their irascible landlord.

Summer had been back in Moonlight, South Carolina, for almost a year. After struggling to make ends meet in Nashville, having little success at a songwriting career and losing her father to a massive coronary, it had been a no-brainer to come back to where her mother and Maisie lived. Her mother, for all her protests that she was fine, liked having Summer and David back in Moonlight. And then there was Hunt McCroy, David's biological father.

Hunt was another link in the chain that had pulled her back to South Carolina. David needed a father in his life, which was something the child had made clear last fall, when he'd bought a ticket to South Carolina and left for Moonlight while she was at a late-night gig. When she'd finally swallowed the fear clogging her throat and gotten past the desire to beat her son within an inch of his life, she'd gotten the message—if she didn't let David have his father in his life, she'd cement a wedge between them she'd never chip away.

After she'd completed community college with a degree in business administration, she'd passed up going to Columbia and the University of South Carolina for a chance to grab her dream. She'd taken David and climbed on a bus to Nashville. There she worked hard managing a restaurant during the day while playing three or four gigs a week. With a child at home, she didn't have much time for friends or dating. And it had been enough. Or so she'd thought.

But David's misadventure paired with some less-than-savory friends he'd started hanging with had convinced her David needed some male influence in his life . . . in spite of the huge issues she still had with Hunt.

She'd not forgiven the man for their past, but she wouldn't deny her son a relationship with the man who fathered him, even if Hunt had treated them both horribly in those early years. She shook off her thoughts, wanting to live in the present. The past was too damned murky.

Loading everything into her secondhand Toyota RAV4, she made sure David buckled up and then started the winding drive back to the Nest, Pete Bryan's ancient house that sat right outside the luxurious gated community of Seagrass Island. Pete had five acres on Rowen's Creek he could sell for several million, but the old coot refused to budge from the land that had been in his family for generations. Summer wasn't complaining, because Pete let her and David live in the adjacent cottage for half the rent in exchange for her running his errands. Of course, she did much more than pick up Pete's prescriptions or take him to the doctor. Summer paid Pete's bills, organized his medications, and made sure the older man ate something decent every night. She wasn't exactly his nurse, but she tried like heck to look out for the eighty-year-old rascal who still went out crabbing in storms and refused to use a walker when he probably should have done so years ago.

"Mom, can I spend Christmas with Dad? Um, not like the whole holiday or anything. But Mamie and Mitchell are having all my cousins over on Christmas Eve for dinner and then we're going to church in the morning. After that, I can come back and spend the rest of the day with you." David put his phone down and zeroed in on her.

Her heart lurched. She'd known this day would come. David and his father had grown closer over the past year, but she hadn't expected her son to want to abandon her for a major holiday. "What about the Christmas Eve party at Coco's? You love making gingerbread with Maisie. I was going to ask Pete to come to Mom's house since Rhett never comes home, and he doesn't want to go to his cousin's house in Columbia this year."

David looked out the window. "Yeah, I like that, but Dad sorta asked if I could come with him. He's kind of lonely."

Summer repressed a sigh, wishing for a few seconds she'd kept Hunt at arm's length. So what if Hunt was lonely? "Let me talk to your father and we'll see what we can work out."

"You're saying yes?" David sounded shocked.

"I'm saying 'we'll see.'"

"Cool."

As she drove over the Harbor River Bridge, she tried to let go of the aggravation that seized her every time Hunt's name came into the conversation and instead admired the beauty of the evening. Living outside Moonlight had its pluses. Coastal South Carolina could compete with any place in the world for natural beauty. The grass marshlands, carved up by natural waterways and shaded by mossy oaks, were breathtaking in the orange glow of the fading day. She never thought she'd come back, but on days like today with a salty, windblown boy beside her trying to find rap music on the radio, she was glad she'd come home.

Of course it hadn't been easy returning to a place she'd left in, well, not disgrace, but something different from what she'd envisioned as a child. Summer was no longer that nice, smart Valentine girl. It had been easier to leave Moonlight than it had been to come back. Currently, she taught after-school music lessons and worked part-time at her sister's flower shop. Refusing to totally give up on her past life, she'd joined a band and did a few gigs around the county. Between that and Hunt's child support payments, she made ends meet.

"Mom, you're going to miss the turn," David said, jarring her from her thoughts.

"Thanks," she said, making a tight turn and waving to the man at the guard shack before turning down the old dirt road that led to her tiny rented house. Pete had sold the real estate development company a thin stretch of land as long as he could have right of access to his place. To her right, she passed million-dollar homes with their big columns and fancy outdoor kitchens facing the Rowan River. It took only four minutes to reach her tiny cabin situated to the left front of Pete's house, which sat on pilings. The wide porch of his house jutted out onto the river, and that's where she found Pete on most afternoons, reading crime fiction and swatting at the mosquitos.

Instead of parking at her place, she pulled into the horseshoe in front of Pete's house. "Go ahead and take the food. Pete likes to eat early and I know you're starving. Just save me some shrimp and coleslaw. I'm taking a quick shower."

David jumped out, gave her a salute, and grabbed the plastic bags with their Sunday-night dinner. Her son and Pete would watch the *Sunday Night Football* game on TV while she played on Pinterest and read the magazines stacked up on Pete's coffee table. It was a nice end to one week and beginning of the next.

Summer drove around and parked in the makeshift driveway beside the cabin. The two-bedroom house was painted dark brown and had a potbellied stove, a tiny galley kitchen, and old hardwood floors that needed refinishing. Still, it was cozy and just big enough for her and David.

Climbing out of the car, she grabbed the beach bag and her guitar case from the trunk. She'd need to hurry if she wanted dinner. Both Pete and David were bad about "forgetting" to leave her some food. Each blamed the other, but that didn't help her empty belly. Summer pulled out her key to the back door but then realized the door was already unlocked.

"Jeez, Sum," she chided herself. She rarely forgot to lock her doors. When she'd moved to Nashville years ago, she'd learned that lesson the hard way. It only took three months and a stolen guitar to learn the important habit of locking up her stuff.

She nearly tripped over David's book bag as she headed toward the small table sitting in the corner. She spent most of Saturday working for Maisie, and since David had spent Friday and Saturday night with Hunt, she'd gone to her mother's house and helped her hang a new ceiling fan. After struggling for hours on that not-so-small feat, she'd stumbled home exhausted and had slept nearly to noon, which left little time to pick up the week's junk that had collected in the living area and kitchen. She knew from living in small spaces that being diligent with picking up was the key to being able to find her keys, the phone bill, and her sanity.

After dumping everything on the cluttered table, she headed back to her room, pulling off the white swimsuit cover-up and kicking off her flip-flops. She felt the sand in her suit, and the sunscreen made her sticky, but it was nothing a quick, hot shower wouldn't cure. She untied the bow behind her neck holding up the halter top of her one-piece and pushed into the bathroom . . . and right into a man.

"Oh shit. Oh shit. Oh shit," she chanted, backing from the bathroom.

The man stumbled backward, the towel at his waist dropping to reveal a lean backside as he scrambled, knocking into the toilet. "Oh fuck, that hurt."

Summer didn't stick around to see what happened next. Fear tearing through her, she ran into the living room, her mind racing as she tried to think. A man in her house.

Oh God, she needed a weapon. And her phone.

Where had she set her phone?

The living room, still cloaked in darkness, held nothing she could use to defend herself. Lurching toward the kitchen table, she scanned the table for her purse. Damn. It was on the front seat of the car. If it came down to it, she was prepared to fight. Multiple personal safety classes paired with martial arts workshops ensured she wouldn't go down easy.

Whoever had been naked in her bathroom knocked around, saying curse words.

Screw putting up a fight—she needed to get out. Holding the ties of her suit together, she scrambled for the back door.

"Wait, wait," the man said, rushing into the room, holding up a hand. "I'm not trying to—"

"Who are you? What're you doing in my house?" Though she stopped, her hand stayed on the knob as her heart pounded in her ears.

"Your house? This is my grandfather's house," he said, sounding confused. He moved into the faint light streaming from the kitchen window.

"Wait, Rhett?" Her pounding heart dropped to her toes. "What the hell? Why are you in my house?"

"Huh?" he said, holding the edges of the towel together, looking confused. "You *live* here?"

"Yeah. I'm renting the place from Pete and helping him out around here." She dropped her hand from the doorknob and flipped on the kitchen light. Harsh fluorescent light flooded the room, making them both blink.

"Guess that explains the pink hairbrush and tampons. I thought one of the cousins left them over the summer. Grampy didn't tell me someone was living here."

"He wouldn't. Stubborn man likes everyone to think he needs no one." She wished she hadn't noticed how splendid Rhett Bryan looked with a fluffy rubber-ducky towel looped about his trim hips. He was brown as a berry, a virtual postcard for California beach life. His wet hair was plastered to his forehead, somehow making his boyish features more masculine, almost craggy.

Rhett grunted. "Sounds about right. Sorry I scared you. I'm Pete's—"

"I know who you are," she interrupted. Then it dawned on her. Rhett hadn't recognized her. Of course, the last time he'd seen her, she'd been in pajama bottoms and had puffy eyes from crying. The past fifteen years stretched like a galaxy between them. "You don't recognize me."

"You're not one of my cousins, are you?"

"No. I'm Summer. Summer Valentine."

"Summer? From Mangham High?" His baby blues widened as he took her in. At that moment she was very, very grateful she did daily yoga and watched what she ate. She'd gone from a pudgy size twelve in high school to a svelte size six. Her highlighted hair framed her square jawline. She still wasn't much for makeup, but she had developed a natural, Bohemian style that suited her personality . . . not that Rhett could tell from her simple, navy, one-piece swimsuit.

His eyes moved over her body, rising to her face. "You look . . . uh, great. Not that you didn't before or anything. You've always been a pretty girl, but . . . wow."

Summer stifled the blush that threatened to rise. She wasn't that stupid girl who'd found excuses to watch boys like Rhett anymore. Life had changed her, made her tough, made her into a woman who didn't blush or stammer. Hell, she'd been hit on while singing at bars by more charming, better-looking guys than Rhett Bryan.

Rhett smiled. "It's good to see you, Sum."

Okay. Not as hot as Rhett. Damn, but there was power in that man's smile. "What are you doing here?"

Rhett hadn't been back to visit his grandfather in over four years, instead electing to fly the older man out to California last December. Pete had vowed he'd never fly out there again, even if it had been on a private jet. Said California and all the fruit-eating nuts weren't his cup of tea when it came to celebrating the holidays. Summer had gotten a big kick out of his stories of movie stars and Rhett's weird house, though she noted Pete liked all the soft cashmere cardigans and fancy monogrammed robe he'd received as gifts.

"I wish I knew," Rhett said, giving her another smile but unable to hide the shadows lurking in his eyes. She knew the past months hadn't been easy for the Hollywood celebrity. His star burned brightly, but the accident with the girl last summer had dampened it a bit. Pete hadn't talked much about it . . . or the pending wrongful-death civil suit. Or the breakdown Rhett had on the show a few weeks back, when he'd interviewed Bev Bohanan, the reality star of *BEVerly Hills Blondes*.

"Pete didn't say anything about you coming home. Usually he tells me things like this."

Rhett looked guilty. "Actually, he doesn't know. I got here about thirty minutes ago. I hadn't showered since I left LA yesterday, and after the long drive south from New York, I thought I'd clean up. I knew where the key was hidden."

"Where's your car?"

"Around back. I didn't want to . . . to be honest, I wasn't even sure if I would stay. I wasn't sure if I would even let Gramps know I was here." He shook his head. "It was a last-minute decision I don't know why I made. When did you move in?"

"In March. Your grandfather goes to church with my mom and mentioned he wanted to rent the cabin out. It just worked for both of us. You *do* know there are easier ways to get to South Carolina. LaGuardia's not the closest airport."

31

Rhett's laugh was dry. "Well, I had planned a much-needed vacation at a Catskills spa, but when I neared the exit toward I-95, I just turned south." He held his hands up like he couldn't fathom how he'd ended up where he stood.

Summer stared at him, wondering about a man who would make such a spontaneous decision. Pete was going to be both ecstatic and irritated his only grandson had shown up without warning. Her perusal seemed to unnerve Rhett. He pushed a hand through his wet hair and avoided eye contact. "Let me grab my bag and get dressed. Then I'll clear out so you can. . ." He looked at her hand grasping the ties of her suit. " . . . take a shower."

She nodded, realizing it wasn't her son's bag she'd tripped over earlier but Rhett's overnight bag.

Rhett passed her, smelling like the vanilla bath gel she liked. Funny how it smelled different on a man. Or maybe it was just Rhett. He'd always been larger than life, a quintessential Carolina golden boy, a guy she'd built up in her mind as the ideal.

But Rhett wasn't perfect.

He was just a man . . . a man who seemed to have shadows dogging him.

"I'll be quick," he said before closing the door.

He didn't even lock it.

Summer sank onto one of the dinette chairs.

Rhett Bryan had come home to Carolina.

But he wouldn't stay. Pete constantly complained, or rather made excuses, about Rhett's failure to visit. Rhett hadn't even made it in for Pete's big birthday celebration that past June. Summer had been disappointed in Rhett for not coming, instead sending a huge cake that exploded to reveal a buxom redhead dressed in a bunny costume. Summer had not been upset about the silly prank, but because she'd known Pete's feelings had been hurt. Rhett had excused himself with commercial shoots and production meetings, but she found none of those good enough reasons to not show up for the eightieth birthday celebration Pete's buddies at the Elks Lodge had thrown.

Five minutes later, Rhett emerged wearing a pair of designer jeans and a tight, light-blue T-shirt. His feet were still bare, but he'd tamed his locks. "Okay, she's all yours."

Summer stood, wrapping her arms about her midriff before realizing she looked uncomfortable in her own place. She dropped them. "So are you staying?"

He shrugged. "I'm here. Might as well see my grampy."

"Pete would like that. Why don't you go on up to the Nest? I picked up dinner, but if you want some, you better hurry. My son's fourteen and he has an empty leg."

Rhett opened the front door and stepped out into the fading day. At her last words, he turned. "You have a fourteen-year-old kid?"

How could he not remember all that had happened? "His name's David."

His expression grew cloudy. She could almost see the wheels turning in his mind, trying to remember, trying to catch hold of the wisps of memory. "I remember now. You and Hunt. You two getting together always surprised me."

Summer felt something cold slither down her back. "Together? Hunt and I were never together, Rhett."

His smile flickered before he tried to capture some lightness. "No. I remember. You hooked up at prom. I had forgotten about the pregnancy. God, I . . . that must have been rough."

Summer stared at him for a second . . . two seconds . . . . three.

"Yeah, something like that. Welcome home, Rhett," she said, walking toward the front door and pulling it closed.

CHAPTER FOUR

November, present day

Hunter "Hunt" McCroy tapped the pen his father had given him when he'd joined the company five years ago against the desk calendar and stared out the window at the baseball field. A few guys threw batting practice, horsing around like kids who didn't have anything better to do on a nice Sunday afternoon often did. The crazy inclination to climb out the window and join them struck him. God, how he longed for the satisfying slap of the baseball hitting the pocket of his glove. Like a drug to him. Yet his love for baseball hadn't been enough, had it?

Hunt shook his head. His baseball dreams were over.

His father had once bragged about building his office complex near the baseball field at Mangham High so he could walk out the door and into the stands to watch Hunt play. One time the man had even raised the window and yelled at Hunt when he'd missed a hot shot that zipped toward him on the pitcher's mound. Hunt had nearly died of embarrassment, and his coach had growled about Mitchell McCroy keeping his own damned nose in his own damned business and let him do the damned coaching. A common plea back in those days.

Now the ball field sitting right outside Hunt's office was lemon juice dripped onto a paper cut. A stinging reminder of what he would never have again. A deep, painful gash of failure haunting his life.

Hunt sighed and tried to focus on the bid his father had put together for the property near Fripp Island, but just as he started reading the first page, his cell phone buzzed.

His son.

"Hey," Hunt said, leaning back in the squeaking chair. "How was Hunting Island?"

"Cool," David said.

"Good." Hunt's gaze found the picture of David on his desk. New frame. New part of his life. Sometimes he still didn't know how to feel about the kid. Until last year, he'd only seen his son on rare occasions, but it wasn't until Hunt got cut from the San Diego Sand Vipers five years ago and slunk back to Moonlight that he'd pulled on the full responsibility of being a parent. Or at least as much as he could with Summer and David then living eight hours away. "I used to go out and catch a few waves there. Don't forget I have that old surfboard, if you want to try sometime."

"Sure. If Mom will let me. She started in with the whole shark thing," David said, not trying to hide his disgust with Summer. "But she did say I can come for Christmas Eve. I wanted to tell you so you can tell . . . Mamie."

Hunt ignored the kid's hesitation when it came to the nickname his sister's kids had given his mother. Diane McCroy was David's grandmother, too. "That's awesome. I didn't think she'd let you. Your grandmother will be happy. She's been sewing you a stocking to put with all of ours on the mantel."

"Really?"

"Yeah, really." Because Hunt had commented on David not having one yet. Guilt had filled his mother's eyes, and she'd gone to the fancy fabric store in Charleston to pick out materials for David's stocking.

"Okay, then," David said, something sounding in the background. "Guess I better go, then. Pete's trying to eat my fries."

"Hey, have you given any thought to the pitching lessons?" Hunt asked, part of him hoping the kid said no and part of him longing to share that bond with him. Baseball could be common ground. He'd held off buying the kid a glove for Christmas until David decided if he wanted to try out for the freshman baseball team. The kid had played ball when he lived in Nashville and had even made all-stars, but since moving back, he'd been slow to get involved in sports. Hunt had encouraged him to join in a team activity. It was good for a kid to be part of a team. Hunt's best moments had come surrounded by his team.

"Yeah. I think that sounds okay."

"So I can schedule you with Don?"

"Yeah. I talked to Mom. She said if that's what I wanted. I used to be good, so maybe I'll still be able to—"

"Of course you will." *You're my kid.* But he didn't say that. No use in putting pressure on David the way his dad had pressured him all those years ago. He could still hear Mitchell strident in his ear. *You're a McCroy. This is what we do. Give it our all. Do what needs to be done to make things happen. Be the best.*

He didn't want to do that to his kid.

His kid.

The thought he was a father still startled him sometimes. Almost as badly as the day fifteen years ago, when Summer had delivered a baseball bat to his head.

"I'm pregnant," she'd said, her voice sounding hollow.

"Who is this?" he'd said, tossing his gear into the passenger seat of his truck, wondering who'd gotten someone to prank him.

"Summer Valentine."

Summer? His date to prom months ago? "Wait, how are you pregnant? You said you were on birth control. Is this a joke?" He stood next to his truck outside the practice field on the University of Florida campus. The team wasn't supposed to be working yet, per NCAA rules, but Hunt had wanted to keep his arm loose.

"I wish it were," she said. He could hear people behind her talking. "I told my parents about that night. They're going to talk to your folks. I just wanted to be the one to tell you."

"Wait," he said, slumping against the frame, glancing around at people biking to class, people drinking coffee while they walked across campus. "Look, this can be fixed. You can't be that far along. Like, four months. Isn't an abortion still an option? 'Cause we're like too young for this. I'm in college. Aren't you at college, too?"

There was a long pause. "I'm not having an abortion, Hunt. That's not what my family or I want. I'm just being decent and letting you know. That's it."

And then she'd hung up, leaving his head spinning and his gut churning.

After he'd climbed in his truck and cranked up the air conditioning, Hunt had done what he always did—he called his dad and told him what had happened. His father had screamed at him, but Mitchell had fixed it . . . eventually.

But not before everyone in Moonlight had a fun week of gossip.

The anger he felt at Summer simmered deep inside, twisting around the resentment he felt against parents who made him feel like a huge fuckup. It had been easy to stay away from Moonlight. Easy to tell no one in his new life about the baby born in January. Summer had sent him a small picture of a fuzzy-headed, gummy-smiling baby, and he'd taped it under the pitching schedule in his locker. He'd tried to summon an emotion other than regret for the kid. Even back then, Hunt knew he should try to love his son, but he'd been too stuffed with self-importance and consumed with making it to the Show to worry about a life he'd never asked for.

David's voice jarred him back to the present. "But, Dad, I might not be as good as I once was. It's been a little while since I've picked up a bat."

"You'll do fine," Hunt said.

"Yeah, okay, I gotta go," said David, not sounding certain. Hunt knew the kid wanted to please him. Ever since David had moved back, he'd tried to be the perfect kid. David never spilled anything on the carpet, always asked for things politely, and feigned interest in anything Hunt liked. On one hand, his son's eagerness to please warmed Hunt's heart, but on the other hand, he hated that the kid felt like he needed to be perfect to mean something to him.

Maybe you shouldn't have ignored him for most of his life.

Hunt squashed the persistent thought that pecked at him.

"Have a good day tomorrow. Be your best." As soon as the words left his mouth, he wanted to snatch them back. They were his own father's words, and he'd sworn he wouldn't do to David what had been done to him.

But telling a kid to do his best was what parents did. Perfectly acceptable. Even if Hunt hadn't seen that in the parenting books hidden in his bedside table. He'd bought the books the month after he'd left rehab, telling himself it was time he took responsibility and made better decisions in his life. Time to grow up . . . and then show up for the son he didn't know.

Hunt hadn't been there for midnight feedings or irritable teething. He'd not seen the first wobbling steps or celebrated the first word tumbling from the child's mouth. He'd not held the limp, fever-stricken body to his chest, praying for respite. But he was trying to make up for his initial absence. He'd been late to the party, but he was there, damn it.

He'd be a good father because he'd promised himself that was something he could do right in his life. It was the one thing he could do right in his life.

"Hey."

He looked up to find Jenny Carson standing in the doorway. He'd almost forgotten he'd brought her with him to the office. "Hey, sorry about taking so long. I'm almost done here."

Jenny smiled, reminding him why he'd asked her out. She held genuine warmth in her eyes. "No worries. I've just read all the magazines you have in the reception area, which is, by the way, not very many. I need to pick up my daughter by five."

Hunt looked at his watch. "Let me run some copies of these specs and I'll take them with me. For all his insistence that the company be technologically advanced, my dad is still a dinosaur. Wants hard copies." He rose and moved into the darkened room with the copier.

"I could help you," Jenny said, her smile turning a bit naughty for a kindergarten teacher. They'd been seeing each other for only a few weeks now, and Hunt liked the tall blonde well enough to consider taking her to the company Christmas party. In the last five years, he'd failed at relationships, too. As soon as something turned serious, he shook the dust off and moved on to the next woman. But he liked Jenny. She made him feel normal, and she liked David to do things with them.

"You know, I'm good at pressing buttons," Jenny drawled. The little twinkle in her eye gave her intentions away.

"Are you now?"

They'd spent the weekend having hushed sex because David was in the guest bedroom. But no one was around on a Sunday afternoon, and a little office sex might be the best medicine for the guilt that plagued him when he thought of David . . . of failing so miserably at so much in life.

But it's getting better.

He brushed away the thundercloud above his head, the one reminding him he hadn't been good enough to make it in the big leagues. He pushed away the second dark cloud, the one that jeered at him for slinking home to Moonlight to work for his dad. Other little dark puffs fought for their space—a failed marriage and brutal alimony payments, the Percocet he'd stolen from his mother's medicine cabinet, a father who looked at him with abject disappointment. The clouds formed a towering stack that threatened to implode and rain shit down upon him.

But standing before him was a happy little umbrella.

"Oh yes. I'm very good at button pushing. And kissing. And stroking," Jenny said, pulling the hem of her shirt over her head. She had soft blonde hair, small breasts, and narrow hips. She had a few tats in hidden places he liked to kiss, and she brought him chocolate-chip cookies when she made them for her five-year-old daughter. She'd been divorced for only two months and was hungry for the sex she'd missed out on while her husband had been overseas doing something with the marines or the navy. Whichever. Didn't matter. All that mattered was that Jenny protected him from cold, wet failure.

Her pants joined the shirt.

And then Hunt didn't care so much about his crappy life.

He was content to be out of the rain with Jenny.

CHAPTER FIVE

April 2003

Summer ran her finger around the rim of her Diet Coke and tried not to stare at the door of Butterfield's like a total freakazoid. *Play it cool. Don't think about it being ten minutes after the appointed time. Rhett will be here. You haven't been stood up for tutoring.*

Because that would be beyond pathetic.

Like miles and miles beyond pathetic.

She sucked in her stomach and tried to look nonchalant. She'd worn her hair down in looping curls that sat fat on her shoulders. Heeding Nessa's advice, she'd worn the navy tank beneath the soft, flannel, plaid shirt she'd bought on a trip to Charleston after Christmas. She didn't like the way her stomach pooched out, but her boobs looked good. Her jeans had flared bottoms that just hid her worn Merrell slip-ons. Nessa had argued for her wearing wedges, but it was a tutoring session. Hair down and tight tank were the only concessions Summer was willing to make. Oh, and light lip gloss. A girl had to have lip gloss when tutoring Rhett Bryan.

The bell on the door jingled, but it was just Dr. White coming to eat the midweek patty melt. Everyone made jokes about the cardiologist's diet. He told everyone to cut out butter and fried foods, but visited Butterfield's for chicken-fried steak and hamburgers at least once a week.

The bell jangled again, and this time there was payoff.

Rhett's hair was mussed, a few tendrils clinging to his forehead. His eyes swept the diner, smiling at a few adults he obviously recognized, before finally landing on her. She felt heat slide into her stomach and her heart squeeze when he headed her way.

"Hey, Rhett Bryan," Joe Butterfield brayed from behind the counter. Joe wore a stained apron and a Gamecock ball cap. "Ain't seen you in a while. How's the team looking for district, kid?"

"We're gonna take state this year, Mr. B. I feel it in my bones." Rhett wore a clingy athletic undershirt and tight baseball pants. It was like scoring the Rhett Bryan jackpot because he looked beyond hot. Miles and miles beyond hot.

"McCroy's looking good. Hear he's throwing ninety-three," Joe continued. The owner of Butterfield's had an addiction to every sport at Mangham High.

"That's what Hunt says," Rhett said, skirting a table of older ladies eating pie. They all smiled sweetly at him. "Hey, Mr. Joe, can I have a burger? No onions, extra tomato."

"Coming your way, kid," Joe said, holding up a metal flipper.

"Sorry I'm late," Rhett said, sliding opposite her. He smelled like outdoors—that boy-mix of wet dog, sunshine, sweat, and maybe some kind of cologne. It should have been gross, but it wasn't. "Hunter's dad spent ten minutes trying to talk me into going to Florida with Hunter. He just wants someone there to keep Hunt out of trouble."

"Trouble?"

Rhett lifted broad shoulders. "You know Hunt. He's a great guy, but . . . you know."

42

She didn't. Hunter McCroy was someone she'd had little opportunity to know. His family had money, and thus Hunter had attended some fancy private school through his freshman year. He'd shown up sophomore year, making girls' hearts flutter with his dark-brown eyes, gorgeous tan, and ability to whip the baseball past a batter at frightening speed. He drove a big truck, wore the most expensive clothes, and had taken his rightful place among the upper hierarchy of Mangham High School by the end of school that first day. Summer had shared a few classes with him, but he'd had little cause to talk to her, much less look her way. "Everyone makes bad decisions."

"Except you. You're a good girl," Rhett said, unzipping his book bag and pulling out a binder.

"I'm not a good girl."

"It's not a bad thing. Don't be mad."

"I'm not. It's just not true."

"What's one bad thing you've done? Turned in homework with ragged edges? Left teeth marks on your pencil? Forget to recycle your milk carton?" His teeth flashed and dimples appeared. Holy hell. The Dimples.

"No." Summer felt flustered, mostly because she couldn't think of anything bad she'd done. Okay, so she was a rule follower. Big deal. She didn't have a family with money who could fix things for her or smooth her way. She had to make good grades, follow the rules, and keep her head down. "I'm just not perfect."

"I think it's sweet."

Sweet? That was the kiss of death coming from someone like him. "I'm glad my ability to follow rules and make good decisions gives me 'sweet' status."

"You're mad. Don't be. I like that you're different from other girls. You don't flirt and bullshit people."

"I don't know how to flirt." God, she'd said it before she could think better. Why had she said that? Who says something like that?

"It ain't hard. Just bat your eyelashes and touch a guy's arm every chance you get. Maybe squish your boobs together," he said, his eyes doing that twinkle thing that made her thighs warm. Then his gaze lowered to her boobs. "First time I've seen those out. Should I feel honored?"

Summer turned the color of the tomatoes on the plate heading their way. "Uh, no . . . I just . . ."

Rhett grinned. "You're too funny, Valentine. Hey, that's a song. Maybe I'll call you my Funny Valentine. You got some ketchup around here, Mr. Joe?"

Joe set the plate down, reached to the table behind Rhett, and slapped the half-empty bottle beside him. "Paige made a lemonade pie this morning. Think there's two pieces left. They'll be on the house."

Joe left before Summer could protest. Last thing she needed was a piece of pie. While Rhett doused his fries with ketchup, Summer buttoned her flannel shirt.

"What're you doing?" Rhett asked, watching her.

"I'm . . . cold."

He smiled knowingly. "That was flirting."

"Huh?"

"You said you didn't know how to flirt. I was showing you how." He took a bite of burger and chewed, closing his eyes briefly. "Oh man, I was starving."

Summer didn't know what to say. It was as if she'd entered some twilight zone where the best-looking guy in school was flirting with her (albeit for a lesson) and calling her a special nickname. What in the heck was going on?

Rhett ate half the hamburger, washed it down with the water, and looked at her expectantly. "Well?"

"Well, what?"

"Are we going to get down to business? I gotta get an A in Wilson's class. I got goals, Funny Valentine."

Summer gave herself a mental shake. "Right. Let's get to it." She pulled out the first worksheet Mr. Wilson had given them on derivatives and the notes she'd taken with the practice work. Better to start at the beginning so she could clarify any errors he'd made.

Rhett finished his burger and both pieces of pie while she showed him what he was doing wrong. She'd just given him a few problems to work on when the bells jingled again.

Graysen pushed through the door with her best friend, Katie B, shadowing her. Both girls wore cutoff shorts and thin hoodies that fit snug against their waists. Like a uniform. Their ponytails bobbed back and forth as they headed toward Rhett and Summer.

"Hey, y'all. We had to take a break from making paper lanterns. My fingernails are destroyed." Graysen glanced down at the French-tipped manicure and frowned.

"Still making them?" Rhett asked, scooting over to make room.

"There are only, like, a million of them," Graysen said, sliding into the booth beside him and laying her head on his shoulder. "I missed you. Come help me."

Gag.

Rhett kissed her head absentmindedly and refocused on the page in front of him. "I gotta finish this first."

Graysen's gaze went to Summer. "So Summer helped you?"

"Yep." Rhett didn't look up.

Graysen delivered a smile that was perfect, thanks to braces and Crest Whitening Strips. "You look pretty, Summer. You should start wearing your hair down."

"It gets in my way," Summer said, trying not to be annoyed that Rhett's girlfriend had crashed her fantasy. She glanced at Rhett's worksheet. He'd made two mistakes already, but she didn't want to point it out in front of Graysen.

Katie B scooted in beside Summer, nudging her with a hip bone that doubled as a rapier. "Gray says she's making you over for prom."

"I don't know ab—"

"She should wear her hair down, don't you think?" Graysen said, narrowing her eyes critically as she assessed Summer. "You'd look good in red. I have the perfect dress."

"I don't think we're the same size, Graysen," Summer said, wishing the two girls would go back to doing whatever it was popular kids did on things like prom committee. Still, one tiny sliver of her ego felt bolstered that she sat in Butterfield's with three of the most popular kids in their school. Hey, she was human.

"Don't worry. It's stretchy. Besides, you can wear Spanx."

"Spanx?" Summer echoed, wondering if she should be offended. Wonder how much babysitting money those puppies would take.

"You know, those girdle things Oprah wears," Graysen said, snagging a french fry off Rhett's plate and popping it into her mouth. "I'm so starving. I forgot to eat lunch today . . . and dinner."

Who the hell forgot to eat?

Obviously, skinny girls.

Then Summer remembered the way her stomach poofed over the jeans . . . and the fact Graysen had suggested she wear a girdle. Maybe Summer should forget a meal every now and then. Maybe two meals.

Rhett winked. "Why you girls gotta talk about underwear? You aren't supposed to do that around guys. We can't handle it. Turns us into raving sex fiends."

Graysen giggled. "I'm not talking about lingerie, dumb butt. I'm talking about figure support. Get it straight."

"But I like your figure." He leered at her.

"I know." She wiggled her eyebrows and gave the same grin Summer's father had given her mother when they'd argued about prom. It was the "we were naughty and we liked it" grin.

Summer wanted to throw up. Not just because Rhett and Graysen were so damned cute together, but because Graysen was still fixated on Summer going to prom. And now she'd told everyone Summer was her makeover project. The whole thing was getting bigger and bigger by the moment, and if Summer didn't relent and go, everyone would think she was weird or petulant or . . . ungrateful for the charity. She could just hear people in the halls. "Graysen is so sweet. She wanted to help that pathetic fatty and that bitch didn't show up. Let's nominate Graysen for sweetest, prettiest, most wonderful girl in the whole of South Carolina!"

Rhett and Graysen were an inch from locking lips.

"Get a room," Katie B said, picking up a french fry and launching it at Graysen. Summer averted her eyes from the almost PDA and looked at Rhett's paper. He'd totally screwed up the problem he'd worked. He'd need more than a few tutoring sessions to make an A in calculus.

"Hey," Graysen laughed, throwing the missive back at her friend.

"So who are you going with, Summer?" Katie B asked, brushing the fry onto the floor.

"Uh, I don't exactly have a date. I'm not even sure—"

"I'm finding her a date," Graysen interrupted, planting her index finger in her own chest. "I'm in the process of making a list and trying to see who already has a date. It's kind of last minute, so it's a short list."

"What about Hunt?" Rhett interrupted. "Molly broke up with him today and she's already asked some guy from Hazelwood Prep. I had to listen to Hunt vent all the way home this afternoon. He's so pissed. He said he might just go to Hilton Head with his parents and blow off the whole thing." Rhett gave Graysen a meaningful look.

Graysen's blue eyes widened. "We can't let that happen. You're so brilliant, baby. Summer's perfect."

"*Her?*" Katie said, looking at Summer with horror.

Summer didn't have time to be offended. She was trying to wrap her mind around the idea that Rhett wanted her to go to prom with Hunt McCroy.

"Hunt?" Summer squeaked before clearing her throat. "Uh, no way. We have nothing in common."

Rhett made a face. "You don't have to have anything in common. You're just going to a dance. Plus, he needs a date."

"Wrong. I've been told it's more than a dance," Summer said, looking pointedly at Graysen, whose eyes were literally sparkling with excitement. "It's an event you look back on and wish you'd gone with someone else or wore a different dress or hadn't cut your bangs."

Katie B drummed her fingers on the table. "She's right. It's kind of a big deal. You have to go with the right person."

"Girls are so weird. Dudes don't care," Rhett said, chewing on his eraser tip. Summer tried not to goggle at his beautiful lips wrapping around the rubber end because that was, again, weird. But she couldn't help herself. Everything he did was so provocative . . . sensual . . . hot.

Okay, maybe she needed to lay off reading the Harlequins.

"So you don't care about who you go with?" Graysen said, her words carrying a pinprick of hurt.

"Well, of course *I* do," Rhett said, wrapping his arms around her and pulling her close. "You're my girl."

Appeased, Graysen refocused on Summer. "Don't worry, Summer. I'll take care of everything."

Summer took a sip of her watered-down Diet Coke and wondered how in the hell she was going to get out of what had snowballed into a possible date with the ubercool Hunt. How could she stop all this from happening? It would be her very own Grinch-like mission. She briefly envisioned her dog, Herman, with an antler bound to his head, but then she remembered there was no way in hell Hunter McCroy would agree to go with her to senior prom. On his list of girls to ask, she'd be way down at the bottom in teeny-tiny print. A footnote. In fact, Summer was certain he didn't even know her name. They'd spoken exactly three times. Maybe four, if "excuse me" counted.

"We need to roll, Gray," Katie B said, looking at her watch. "I'm working for another hour and then going home to watch *American Idol* . . . if my mom recorded it. Last time she forgot."

"Okay," Graysen said, grabbing Rhett's chin and turning him to her for a kiss. Luckily, it was of the quick variety. "Later, gator."

"After a while, crocodile," Rhett said.

"See ya soon, you big baboon," Katie B said, joining in on the fun before sliding out. "Bye, Summer."

"Bye, y'all," Summer said, as the two girls hustled from the diner before Joe could deliver the two glasses of water he carried. On seeing them depart, he did a 180-degree turn and went back to behind the counter.

"Sorry about that, Valentine. She just can't stay away from me," he said, doing an eyebrow waggle.

"So I see," Summer said, tapping problem number three. "You did this one wrong. Go back and rework it."

"Why don't you want to go to prom with Hunt?" Rhett asked, his blue eyes fastened on her. Not an accusation. More like he was curious why anyone wouldn't want to go to prom with his buddy.

Because he's not you.

"He's not going to want to go with me. I'm not his type," she said.

Rhett made a face. "What type? You're a girl. You're nice and pretty."

"Ha," Summer said, nearly choking on the ice cube she moved around her mouth.

"I think you are."

His words coated her like honey on a biscuit. She almost closed her eyes and sighed. "Vision already going, huh?"

"Valentine, get a clue. You're pretty, and even better, you're easy to talk to. Not to mention, you're smart. And you don't spend all day talking about *NSYNC and getting your nails done. You've got substance."

And this was why she was head over heels for Rhett Bryan. He'd never point out that she was twenty pounds overweight and a social pariah. No, Rhett found the things most didn't look for. "You're a good guy, Rhett Bryan."

"Shhh! You'll ruin my bad-boy rep."

Summer twisted the pretend key at her lips. "Your secret's safe. Now, work problem number three again. You need to figure out what you're doing wrong."

"You like to crack the whip, don't you? Ol' Hunt may be getting more than he bargains for."

"I'm pretty sure I'm not going to have to worry about Hunter McCroy." She tapped the problem. "Back to calculus."

"Fine, but so you know, this calculus is giving me indigestion."

Rhett Bryan could always make her smile.

CHAPTER SIX

November, present day

Rhett shifted on the old tweed couch, feeling like he'd been dropped onto a movie set. That being home was oddly familiar didn't make it any less strange. Four years had passed since he'd come home to South Carolina, and even then, he'd rented an isolated place on the water. He'd not sat on this couch since the night before he'd left for college in California.

Weird.

And even stranger was the kid sprawled in his grandfather's recliner, tapping on a phone. Pair that with Summer Valentine, who currently licked her thumb and flipped through a *Southern Living* magazine, and the older, stooped man who'd aged into someone he had to blink at to register was his grandfather, and Rhett was in *The Twilight Zone.*

His only comfort at that moment lay in the bottle of Four Roses bourbon he'd found in the back of the pantry. He currently jiggled the melting ice and watched Grampy Pete shuffle around the kitchen.

"Where's that goll-danged bottle opener?" his grandfather growled from the doorway.

"You've had your one beer," Summer said, not bothering to look up. "And you ate my shrimp dinner, so I'm not inclined to find the bottle opener I hid half an hour ago."

His grandfather shot Summer a hateful glance. "Damn women. That's why I didn't marry Sally McCorkel. Women want to manage everything a man does. Hell, you can't even take a whiz without them criticizing your aim."

"Which, judging by your powder room, is the floor," Summer said, a ghost of a smile around her lips.

Summer Valentine had grown into a looker. Gone was the baby fat and dimpled cheeks and in their place was a wily woman who obviously managed his grandfather quite well.

"I don't go on the floor," David piped up.

"Of course not. I'm training you to be an accurate shot. Unlike Pete, who is like a fireman with a rogue hose."

Rhett laughed. "Are you sure you're Summer Valentine?"

She glanced up. "What?"

"The Summer I remember was too sweet to harass an old man with a bad prostate."

"I ain't got a bad prostate," Grampy Pete said, giving up on the beer and reshelving it in the fridge. "She's exaggerating about my aim."

Summer snorted. "As the head head-cleaner, I can assure you I'm not."

"Bah," Grampy Pete said, shuffling into the living room. He regarded Rhett. "Still, boy, can't believe you showed up without a call. I didn't raise you right, I guess. You probably whiz all over the toilet, too, but I bet your maid don't harp on you."

"I'm not your maid. I'm your assistant who sometimes wipes up after you." Summer turned another page, her pretty eyes firmly fastened on the article within the magazine.

"I will make every attempt to hit the mark while I'm here. I'm sorry I didn't call. It was an impulse I still don't understand, but I can rent a place, if that's better for you. You don't have to worry—"

"Why would you get another place? Last time you came with that washed-up actress. What was her name?"

"Scarlett Ro—"

"She had the longest legs and fingernails I'd ever seen. But anyway, I was insulted you rented a place. Never hardly saw you. This is your home."

Something about those words comforted him, even as he knew them to be untrue. He hadn't made his home in South Carolina for a long time. *You can never go home again* was a phrase he'd often repeated when people asked him if he ever thought about where he grew up. In his mind, Rhett had always been meant for the sunny West Coast. Still, there were times when the tang of the ocean hit him just right. The fecund smell reminding him of dying marsh grasses laced with briny grit, mornings when he rucked around the tidal plains looking for treasure. He'd close his eyes and instead of the California beaches, there was marsh, low-hanging oaks brushing against the lapping tidal push and pull onto the shores of Carolina. Shrimp. Grits. Low Country life—all would tangle into an intense longing for a simpler time.

But those moments were rare and fleeting. He was Rhett Bryan. He was California personified. A mover and shaker. On his way up. Until he took a detour.

But he'd get past the sleepless nights and nightmares. He'd rebound. Just had to get his head straight. Sleep. Revive himself so he could press forward toward his goals. Something inside him told him staying at the Nest, named by the grandmother he'd never met, would be the best place to find what he needed. He'd first come to the Nest when he was a three-year-old, right after the funeral of his parents. They'd been killed in an automobile accident in Michigan, and Grampy Pete had brought him home to South Carolina. Home had healed him then; surely it could heal him now.

Besides, renting a house meant he'd be alone with his thoughts and the nightmares that denied him sleep. "As long as I don't cramp your style, Grampy."

His grandfather fastened his beetle eyes on him, thick eyebrows drawing together. "You ain't crampin' me none. But you'll have to bunk in your old room. Summer's got the cabin. And this here boy who better get his skinny butt outta my chair in three . . . two . . ."

David looked up with a lazy smile that looked so much like Rhett's old bud Hunt McCroy, he felt a flash of . . . something. Irritation? Fondness? Mere acknowledgment that Hunt had fathered a kid with someone who'd professed she disliked him?

"Move it, kid. I'm serious," Grampy Pete said, lowering his bony ass toward the lanky teen.

"Okay, okay. I don't want your old balls touching me," David said, holding out his hands to prevent Grampy from sitting on him.

"David Matthew Valentine!" Summer barked, slapping the magazine shut. "I don't want to hear that talk."

David laughed and slid from beneath Rhett's grandfather. The look he shot toward Rhett was pure imp. He loped over to the couch and dropped beside Rhett. "You don't look the way you look on TV."

"I don't?"

"No. You look older."

"Thanks. That's what every talk show host wants to hear."

David's lips curved and Rhett noted the kid had his mother's eyes. "You're my dad's age. He said y'all used to be good friends."

Rhett lifted a shoulder. "We were. Haven't seen Hunt in a while."

"Because you're famous?"

No. Not because he was famous. Or maybe that was true. He'd moved away and made a different life, one that he'd loved until . . . well, until he'd made the biggest mistake of his life. His impatience, his preoccupation with his career had led to . . . He dashed the bad thoughts away. "No. We just drifted apart, I guess. Hunt went to Florida, I went to LA. Different places, different paths."

David's gaze was as intense as his mother's once was. Rhett would be willing to bet a hundred-dollar bill that David had inherited Summer's smarts. "My dad played baseball with you. He was good, huh?"

"Good enough to win 4A pitcher of the year and a scholly to Florida." What more was there to say? Rhett knew about the performance-enhancing drugs, the sanctions, the bad press. Hunt's career had tumbled down a flight of concrete stairs. His friend had landed hard at the bottom. Rhett had stayed away. Maybe that was wrong. Perhaps he could have stopped Hunt's fall with a well-placed word or something. But fear of getting dragged into his former best friend's cesspool of bad choices had kept him silent. "Hunt and I had some good times together."

"He wants me to play ball. I'm going to start lessons with some guy who trains pitchers."

"Yeah?"

David shrugged. "I guess. My dad says it's important to be part of a team. Builds character, and he said baseball's the best sport. Takes patience."

Rhett glanced up and caught Summer watching them. Something in her gaze was unsettling. "That's true. Have you played baseball before?"

"Sure. When I was a kid. It was in Nashville, though. We lived there before we moved here."

"Nashville?" Rhett asked, looking questioningly at Summer. He had no idea she'd lived in Nashville, and then he remembered her singing. That one day when he'd gone to her house. After prom. Before she stopped speaking to him.

"David, stop boring Mr. Bryan with the details of our lives. Don't you have homework or something?" Summer said, sending the pointed glances mothers were so good at giving. Not that Rhett would know. The only looks he'd gotten came from teachers. And Grampy Pete.

"I already did it."

Summer lifted an eyebrow.

"I swear. Dad won't let me play Xbox until I do it. He read that on some parenting website."

"The game's about to come on. Y'all are going to have to stop all your yapping," Grampy said, picking up the remote control and turning on the TV Rhett had bought him four years ago when he saw the man was still using the one they'd had when Rhett was in high school. The old man had begrudgingly agreed that the HD picture was better than the old set. But Grampy Pete wasn't one to quit on a piece of equipment because it had some years on it. He was a living testament to not quitting on anything.

Rhett set the empty glass on the scarred end table and rose; his body was stiff from the long drive south. He moved toward the French doors that led out onto the wide deck. Beyond the windowpanes, the night sat quiet on its haunches.

With a jerk, Rhett pulled open the door that still stuck at the bottom.

"Don't let in the skeeters," his grandfather yelled.

One thing for certain—his grandfather didn't believe in the kid glove treatment. That Rhett rubbed elbows with superstars meant beans to Pete Bryan. Rhett closed the door and walked to the cedar rail. Frogs barked in the distance and the moon shimmered in the water. Outside of nature and the hum of the television inside, there were no sounds. No traffic, no loud K-pop from his teenage next-door neighbors, no fluffy Pomeranians yipping at a leaf turning over (his other neighbor). Serenity should be settling upon him.

But it wasn't.

For the past five months, he'd been a condemned man swinging at the end of a rope, someone holding onto his feet, pulling him down hard. He couldn't kick free from the shadows. Therapy had helped for a while. He'd done all the exploration of his feelings he could do. Still, something he couldn't name had him by the throat and wouldn't lessen.

The door opened behind him. He didn't need to turn around to know it was Summer.

"Strange being home?" Her voice parted the night as she halted a foot from him, setting her hands on the aged wood railing.

"How'd you know?"

"Because I've only been back for a year now. It's quiet, huh?" Her voice was like whiskey.

"Yeah," he said, studying the marsh, the way the shadows moved, the way the light divided into distinct dark and light. Summer's scent reached him—honeysuckle or some other sweet flower that bloomed on southern summer nights. "Just thinking about how quiet it was. Almost makes me uncomfortable."

"Why are you here, Rhett?"

He turned to her. She stood with fists braced against the railing, the moonlight painting her in the same relief as the marsh. He couldn't remember what color her eyes were, but they looked dark. Mysterious. The Summer he'd once known had been as obvious as red paint on a front door. "Why are *you* here?"

"Oh, so we're going to do that, huh? Answer a question with a question?" A ghost smile materialized on her lips.

"Turnabout's fair play. Or so they say."

"I came back because there wasn't a good reason not to."

"That's not an answer."

"It's all you'll get. I'm not one of your Hollywood pets with secrets."

"Pets? That's harsh coming from someone like you," Rhett said.

"You don't know me anymore."

"Or maybe I never did."

She turned back to the night. "True."

"You did Nashville?"

Summer nodded. "It was harder than I thought. Yet somehow easier."

"Again, cryptic." He curled his fingers around the banister, thinking about how true those words were for many things in life—easy yet hard. Some things were harder than others, though.

"I put Nashville on a pedestal, but I shouldn't have. Anyone can go. Wasn't hard to pack the car, get a place, or find someone who wants to make you a star. Unfortunately, the people who take advantage of dumb hicks in Nashville are a dime a dozen . . . as long as you pay 'em. Most are full of crap. I wasn't willing to bow, scrape, or screw my way to success, so . . ."

Rhett made a face. "Sounds like LA."

"You had to screw a slimy record exec to get your job?" she asked.

"Almost. I did a lot of tap dancing. You can lose sense of who you are out there." Maybe that was why he was in South Carolina. He needed to remember who he'd been. Try to get back that brash, cocky son of a bitch who'd blazed a path to stardom. Because right now he was tired. So fucking tired.

"It wasn't all bad. When I first got there, I got a recording contract. We went on the road. I drank champagne . . . until my manager made some bad decisions, ripping that bottle from my hand and smashing it on the ground. Not sure I ever recovered from the mismanagement of my career. It's hard to have something and then watch it disappear."

It felt insincere to agree with her. He'd been golden from the start. Lots of empty champagne bottles that someone else took away while he basked in the limelight. He'd been lucky. Didn't mean he hadn't worked hard for his success. There were many nights he never went to bed, many times he'd prostrated himself at the feet of power, many hours of worry, sweat, and pinned hopes. "But you're not done."

"I am for now. Sometimes dreams . . . change."

"Why?"

"Because some things are more important." Heaviness shaded her voice. Perhaps even defeat. He didn't like to think of Summer as defeated. He remembered the way she'd played that guitar, how haunting her voice was. "My turn. What are *you* doing here?"

Rhett dropped his hands and stepped away. He eyed the Adirondack chairs that looked on the verge of collapse. The Nest needed some attention. Like an old warrior, it held too many scars and bruises. Perhaps Rhett should hire someone to make repairs and wield a paintbrush. Or maybe he could get his own hands a bit dirty. Once upon a time, he'd known how to swing a hammer and repair a simple engine. Occupying his hands would keep his mind from straying to things it shouldn't. "I don't know."

Summer watched him test the chair. "That might not be a good idea."

"What? The chair?"

"Yeah. It's wobbly. So are you here because of what happened?"

"Don't." His word was a warning. He wasn't going there with her. Hell, he wasn't going there with anyone. No more talking about the accident, drinking, depression, survivor's guilt, the breakdown he'd had on national TV.

Her gaze stayed on him, and for a moment he felt as naked as he'd been earlier when she'd barreled into the bathroom and knocked him into the toilet. A jellyfish stranded by the tide, quivering, craving the protection of the sea. "Oh, Rhett."

His name was an exhalation, filled with things she wouldn't say. He could hear everything she felt in that simple sigh and he hated it. "Let's go inside."

Because then he wouldn't have to talk about why he'd taken that exit and headed south.

"Okay." She extended her hand. He took it, noting how capable she seemed. Her grip was firm, like an answer to an unspoken prayer. "But you were right to come here."

He rose but didn't drop her hand. Instead he turned it in his hand, cradling it. Her fingertips were calloused, likely from the guitar strings. At that moment, he heard her voice the way it had sounded that night fifteen years ago—throaty, sultry, unexpected. She'd had talent for finding the right words, eliciting the perfect emotion. A plucked string of regret reverberated inside him at the thought she'd let that dream go. "Was I?"

She turned her hand over, giving his a squeeze. "I think you were."

For a moment they held hands. It was one of those narrowed-in moments, when the camera catches something unexpected. A oneness. An understanding. A simple human touch. A special must-see episode.

"Pete has pie in the fridge. I picked it up for him at the Sweet Cheeks Bakery. Want some?" she asked, dropping his hand.

"I don't eat sweets." Sugar was the enemy of everyone who appeared on TV.

"It's lemon. I'll let you have my piece," Summer said with a quirk of her lips, like she knew something he didn't.

"Well, maybe just a small slice."

Summer headed toward the weathered doors that hadn't seen a good coat of paint in too many years. And then he remembered those nights studying at Butterfield's Grill. The old guy—what was his name?—always brought him pie on the house.

Maybe he'd been wrong. You can go home again. At least when you needed to remember who you were and where you came from. Nothing wrong with a visit . . . or a small sliver of lemon pie.

CHAPTER SEVEN

November, present day

Summer closed her son's bedroom door and then immediately bent over and picked up an errant sock.

There was *always* an errant sock.

She took the offender to the stacked washer and dryer and made a deposit into the laundry basket. Then she took a few minutes to tidy up the kitchen, stacking dirty dishes for washing in the morning and riffling through the stack of mail she'd left on the counter on Friday. She couldn't remember a time that she hadn't spent the moments after David had gone to bed cleaning up the day's messes. Maybe when he'd first been born and her mother had been there, but that was too long ago to recall.

Finally, she sank onto the secondhand couch and dangled a glass of chardonnay as she stared into the darkness.

Rhett Bryan was back in Moonlight, South Carolina.

Odd how difficult it was to reconcile the witty, polished, late-night host with the man who'd stood outside that evening in such obvious pain. Most nights she couldn't catch his *Late Night in LA* show because that would mean a *really* late night in SC, but sometimes, when she got home late from a gig, she would catch some of the show, and even though she'd known him once, he had evolved into an A-list star—not accessible and, therefore, not real to her.

But tonight he'd been real to her . . . maybe too real.

How long would Rhett stay?

According to celebrity gossip rags, NBC had ordered him to take a break, which was understandable after he'd gone ape-shit crazy on Bev Bohanan. Poor woman. The controversial reality star had stumbled into a conversation about her show *BEVerly Hills Blondes*, sparking Rhett's ire.

"You think it's okay to belittle people who work for you?" he'd barked after she'd laughed about her housekeeper watching Hispanic soap operas and not picking the peppers off her pizza.

Bev had assumed a deer-in-the-headlights pose. "Uh, no. I was just joking. I like my housekeeper."

"Being a celebrity doesn't give you the right to act like an ass. Who makes other people pick crap like peppers off her pizza? What? Are your fingers broken?" Rhett slammed his palms on his desk.

"No. But I pay her to do her job," Bev said, frowning, obviously growing annoyed.

"See, that's the problem with people in our society, the problem with people in *this* town. They want to blame other people for their issues. They want to shit on people who they think aren't as good as they are. Just a bunch of shallow, vapid opportunists occupying space. That's what your reality show is. A bunch of nothing. A bunch of stuff that doesn't matter. Shopping at Louis Vuitton and getting your nails done. Like that's fucking life."

The network had gone to commercial break, fading from a livid Rhett Bryan and a gawking Beverly Bohanan. When it had come back on, Rhett had apologized to the viewers and proceeded with his interview with some guy from the local zoo. The next day, the morning shows were abuzz with the Rhett Bryan–and–Bev Bohanan fiasco. Memes of his meltdown on the arrogance of celebrities had popped up on social media, and even *Saturday Night Live* had spoofed him.

The consensus was that the pressure of the accident that summer paired with the recent wrongful death suit had pushed Rhett toward the disdainful judgment of the very world he occupied. Some called him a hypocrite, but Summer thought his diatribe on Hollywood's shallowness had been both horrifying and beautiful.

Her phone buzzed, drawing her from her thoughts about Rhett's pseudobreakdown. She struggled from the depths of the couch to find where she'd left it, which was the normal place: on the catchall kitchen table.

Hunt.

Scheduled D with Don Marris for Tuesday afternoon. This good with you?

Summer stared at the text. She hadn't had a chance to talk to David about taking pitching lessons. David had mentioned the possibility a few weeks back, and she'd halfheartedly agreed that going out for baseball might be a good way to bond with his father. But they hadn't talked about the commitment it would take to play baseball if David made the team. Not to mention David playing baseball would be another grappling hook anchoring Hunt to her life.

She sighed and texted **Sounds fine. THX.**

Tossing her phone back onto the newly cleared kitchen table, she returned to her wine and muttered her recurring mantra, "It's not about you. It's about the kid."

That had been her guiding thought from the moment she'd discovered she was pregnant and knew she would keep the baby.

Nothing more horrifying than facing your third day as a freshman in college while praying for your period . . . and knowing it wasn't coming. She'd woken that morning, tiptoed from the dorm room so she didn't wake her not-even-close-to-a-morning-person roommate, and rushed to the bathroom. Jerking down her pajama pants, she'd stared once again at the totally white crotch of her Victoria's Secret bikinis and felt like she might vomit. Her boobs were heavy, her period totally absent for over three months. She'd told herself it was the strain of working two jobs that past summer, dieting like a madwoman, and moving to Columbia. Stress and nutrition affected a woman's cycle. She'd looked it up in a few magazines and knew female athletes often missed their cycles.

She'd had sex only once. And it hadn't even been sex. It had been something altogether different. A girl didn't get pregnant from something like that. One time?

But in that exact humbling moment in the women's bathroom of Hogarth Hall, she'd known the truth. She was eighteen, pregnant, and her parents were going to freak.

Not to mention she was going to have to tell Hunter McCroy that he was going to be a baby daddy.

At that thought, she had actually spun around and vomited into the toilet.

The girl in the stall next to her had yelped and vamoosed, but Summer hadn't cared because what dignity did she have left? What future remained? If her calculations were correct, she'd make it through this semester before she had to leave . . . unless she had an abortion.

But she knew she wouldn't.

Her parents would never let that happen. They were deacons in the church, and even though they'd be horribly embarrassed by Summer being pregnant, they'd never forgive her if she had an abortion. An abortion would be much easier than carrying a baby, stretching out her stomach, making her look fat and gross. She knew a girl who'd had an abortion. Summer hadn't been able to understand how someone did that, but now she understood perfectly. Erase the mistake. Don't ruin two lives. Make it all go away.

Summer couldn't do it, though. She just . . . couldn't.

She'd wiped her mouth, padded back to her dorm room, fell into her narrow bed, and cried huge, gulping, almost quiet sobs into her pillow with the eyelet lace and purple monogram, cementing the fact that Hunter McCroy would always be in her life. She'd never be able to forget him now.

Draining the wine, she glanced at the closed door to her left.

Never had she regretted keeping David.

In her mind's eye, she saw his heart-melting grin, his clutched fist grimy with baby food, and the joy that had swept her heart when he babbled "mama." Her parents had pleaded for her to put the child up for adoption. They'd begged her to put her mistake behind her. But Summer stubbornly refused. Because deep down she knew she would dedicate her entire existence to making sure this poor child wouldn't get hurt. That she could ensure. Everyone thought her insane. They'd whispered about how she'd had so much potential, a full-ride scholarship, a chance to give another couple a child they so desired. But she'd dropped out of the University of South Carolina, put together the baby bed that would sit crammed between her small twin and the too-bright-purple wall she'd painted as a fourteen-year-old, and registered for community college.

The day they'd placed him in her arms, she'd vowed to protect him with her everything.

He was hers, and she had a mission—to love, protect, and fight to the death for her son.

End of story.

He was worth every tear she'd cried.

Right as Summer lifted the glass to drain the last of her chardonnay, she heard something outside. A thump. Or maybe a scratch.

Alarm prickled her neck hairs, and she set the glass on the narrow end table, rising and creeping toward the window. After her earlier scare in the afternoon, her senses remained on high alert.

Likely it was the raccoon that had been plaguing her garbage can. The bastard was crafty and had figured out how to pry off the lid, causing her to spend money she didn't have on a bigger, more secure can. Then again, there had been a rash of burglaries a few communities over. They lived far from the gatehouse, and Pete slept like a dead man, disproving any claims he made about being a light sleeper. The man couldn't hear thunder.

The porch light illuminated the cement stoop but not much beyond. The Carolina palmettos and lacy Spanish marsh melted into the inky darkness, but the open door of Rhett's rental car provided enough light for her to see him sprawled on the edge of the crushed shell drive, rolling back and forth on his haunches.

What the hell?

Summer slid the chain from the front door and stuck out her head. "Rhett?"

She heard a string of curse words that would make a whore blush. She shoved the flip-flops waiting beside the worn mat onto her feet and inched onto the stoop. "Rhett?"

"What?" His voice was sharp. Or maybe holding pain?

She walked outside, fanning away moths, and made the journey to the horseshoe loop in front of Pete's house. The Carolina golden boy with his perfect body and too-white smile now lay on his side, clutching his big toe, hair stuck to his forehead, a horrible grimace on his face. "Stubbed my fucking toe on that fucking stump. Shit, it hurts."

She squinted at where he cupped his big toe. "Is it broken?"

"I don't fucking know."

"Can you please stop using that language?"

"Why?" He removed his hand and stared down at his toe.

"I have a fourteen-year-old." Maybe they cursed like that in California, but in Moonlight, it was still considered crass and unnecessary . . . unless you broke your toe. Maybe breaking your toe earned a person three— maybe four—choice words.

"Sorry, it just hurts like a son of a bitch."

"What were you doing out here?" she asked, squatting beside him and drawing his hand from cradling his toe. She couldn't see much in the scant light. "I can't tell how bad it is. Come inside and let's take a look. Can you walk?"

"Of course I can walk," he said, dropping a knee and rising. But even as he rose, she could see he wobbled. Made her wonder if he'd had too much of the bourbon he'd been nursing earlier. Or maybe it was something stronger. Pete had worried about his grandson living in that "godforsaken land of bad choices." Of course, Pete thought no place compared to South Carolina—every state was inferior, whether it was full of those goll-danged tree huggers, weirdo liberals, or dumbass rednecks. But she couldn't see Rhett having an addiction problem. He'd never seemed the sort to rely on booze or pills to get him through.

Summer clasped his elbow to steady him. "Okay?"

He nodded, dangling the offending foot and hopping toward the car where he'd left his other moccasin. Looked like the pair she'd given Pete for Christmas last year. The older man had never worn them, electing to wear the raggedy ones he'd had for too many years. "Except for my damned foot throbbing like a son of a—"

"Yes, everyone on the island knows. Now, hush so we don't wake up David or Pete. I'll get you some ice and something for the pain."

Rhett did as suggested, hopping toward her open door, where no doubt mosquitos and moths were migrating inside by the dozens.

Once in her living area, Rhett collapsed on the couch, plunking his big foot down on her coffee table. Summer stifled her frown and went to the freezer for a bag of peas. Covering the Jolly Green Giant with a thin dishcloth, she went back to the living area, perched on the edge of the couch, and peered at Rhett's swollen right toe. The man had his head back with eyes closed. He looked out of place, and she felt a crazy inclination to shove him out the door, hurt toe or not.

Gingerly, she ran a finger over the top of his toe. "Does that hurt?"

"The whole damned thing hurts." He cracked open a bleary blue eye, and she wondered if he were talking merely about his toe or . . . everything.

"We need to stop the swelling. Let's try this." She carefully set the makeshift ice pack atop his foot. "I have aspirin. Can you take that?"

"I have something stronger in my shave kit. That's what I was after when I ran into that damned stump."

"I'll get it for you," she said, starting for the door.

"Don't bother. I can get it when I leave. I'm better now."

She hesitated. "You sure? You seem like you're in a lot of pain."

Truer words had likely never been spoken. If anything was certain, it was that Rhett's toe was the tip of the iceberg when it came to the pain in his life.

"Come sit by me. I'd like that." His voice sounded somehow seductive.

Danger. Danger.

"Rhett," she said, caution in her tone.

"Just sit by me. You know how long it's been since someone sat beside me and didn't want something from me? You don't want anything, do you, Summer?"

"I want a lot of things, Rhett, but none from you." She meant the words when she said them. Or maybe she lied to herself, because who looked at a gorgeous man sprawled on a couch, a man she'd once loved to near distraction, and not want a damned thing from him? Summer had always been good at telling herself what she shouldn't want. Actually doing that was quite another thing. Her judgment wasn't always the best. She'd learned that the hard way.

"Then sit by me. It makes me feel better. Tell me about Nashville. About David. About anything other than me probably breaking my toe or any of that shit that went down in California." His voice carried weariness shaded with a dash of desperation.

Summer sat. Not too close, but close enough to smell a mixture of bourbon and expensive men's cologne. Close enough to feel his warmth. Close enough for him to reach over and take her hand. "You have calluses. I noticed them on the deck earlier."

"From the guitar."

The pad of his thumb stroked the side of her hand and did utter magic. She couldn't lie about the pinpricks of heat in her belly, the lava flow of desire sliding into her pelvis. Summer could chalk it up to a lack of a man in her life for the past year, but truth lay in the fact it was Rhett Bryan stroking her hand.

To her, he was the guy she'd fallen in love with senior year and couldn't shake from her heart because his smile, his bluebonnet eyes, his very essence had clung to her like stink on a dead oyster. No amount of scrubbing had erased her desire to have him. This was why he was so dangerous. This was why her words seconds ago were an absolute lie.

In that moment she remembered the way he tasted—spearmint and shame.

"My sister owns a floral shop," she said, because she couldn't handle where her thoughts headed. "The old House of Flowers, but Maisie changed it to Crazy Daisies. She liked that it rhymed with her name."

"She was younger than you, right?" He hadn't let go of her hand, but he'd stopped stroking it. Thank Jesus.

"By seven years. She has two four-year-old boys—twins. Recently divorced from a dirtbag."

"Always a dirtbag, huh?"

Summer sighed. "In this case, absolutely. Cheated on her with his dental hygienist."

"Cleaned more than his teeth, huh?" Rhett joked, before clearing his throat. "Everything around here has funny names—Crazy Daisies, Sweet Cheeks. I forget that's how small towns are."

"Don't forget the Kum and Go. Whoever thought that was a good idea for a gas station?" Summer said, wondering if she should pull her hand away from his. They were essentially holding hands.

"A horny commitment-phobe?" Rhett asked.

She chuckled. "Now I remember why you're so good at what you do."

His smile faded, and the strange melancholy Rhett had displayed on the back deck returned.

"Rhett, are you okay?" As soon as she asked, she knew she shouldn't have. Hadn't she learned anything from parenting a male? *Don't press. Let them come to you.* But here she went, treading on dangerous ground like a moron.

"Yeah, except for this toe."

"I didn't mean your toe," she murmured.

His eyes fastened on the remote control. "Sure. I'm fine. Nothing a little rest won't cure."

"I don't think so, but I'm sure you believe that." *Shut up, Summer. Why are you poking a stick at him?*

Rhett's eyebrows drew together, his mouth flattened. "What are you saying, Summer?"

"That you can get rest in California. Or at that spa. I think you're looking for something more. You're hurting."

He shook off her hand, blue eyes snapping. "Who asked you what you thought?"

"No one." She curled the abandoned hand in her lap, studying fingernails that needed filing before they got in the way of playing the guitar. She wished she'd kept her damned mouth shut. What was wrong with her? She didn't have to fix everyone around her. Rhett was not hers to fix. "I'm not trying to pry."

"You don't know me anymore. Just like I don't know you."

"So why are you sitting on my couch?" she asked.

"You told me to come in. My toe was hurt."

"I'm just trying to be your friend."

"So that means you can stick your nose in my business? I thought I made it clear earlier that I don't want to talk about why I'm here or if I'm okay. I just wanted a fucking normal conversation." He jerked the bag from his foot and tossed it onto the table with a splat.

He was right. He hadn't asked for her to pry. Rhett wasn't ready to be honest with himself about why he'd come home. Summer knew he'd come back to the place where he'd once been whole and untouched, seeking to put Humpty Dumpty back together again.

But there were pieces of himself he would never find. But he didn't know that yet.

"You're right. I don't have any business asking you anything," she said.

"I need to go," he said.

Why had she taken a simple moment and made it complicated? Maybe it was because earlier that evening, when he'd sat in that broken-down chair, she'd felt a kinship. She knew how it felt to pull on a mask while inside you curled into a fetal position. For a moment in the moonlight, she'd believed she could be part of his journey toward healing. But Summer couldn't help Rhett. To believe that was to believe he was somehow like her . . . and he wasn't. "I hope your toe feels better."

He jabbed the moccasin he'd tossed on the floor on his foot, wincing as he did so. They were definitely the ones she'd bought Pete last Christmas. Maybe they'd been too big for Pete and that's why he'd not worn them. They looked too small for Rhett.

"Thanks," he said, standing. He wore baggy shorts and a worn T-shirt, nothing like the dapper man who spewed witty monologues and ate lunch with George Clooney. Again, she was taken aback at how familiar he felt. Which was weird because they'd been friends for only a short time those years ago. Or maybe they hadn't. She still didn't know what they'd been.

Rhett hobbled toward the door, his shoulders hunched in protection. Summer felt a prick of guilt at driving him away with things too difficult to discuss. Sometimes she pushed too hard, oftentimes not enough. Her timing had been off tonight.

"Good night, Rhett."

He turned but didn't meet her gaze. "Thanks for the peas."

"Always good for it," she said, wishing the moment had not been ruined.

Rhett passed through the door into the darkness, lurching toward his rental. He didn't turn around or say good night. So she shut the door, slid the chain in place, and went back to her wine, thoughts of the past and present tangling into a dry knot of regret.

CHAPTER EIGHT

November, present day

Hunt sat in the stands, watching his former pitching coach show David exercises he could do to strengthen his legs. They were the same exercises Hunt had done years before. Don was old school, but he knew pitching. Many people thought a pitcher's skill was in his arm. That was important, but the legs and full-body motion were what gave a pitcher power. Teaching David exercises to strengthen his thighs and butt would take his already natural delivery to new heights. Hunt knew his son had the potential to be good, but the kid was behind. Pitchers started young these days, maybe too young. But if Don could work with David enough, the kid could potentially make the JV team as a freshman. Deal was, unlike Hunt, his son was a left-hander. That bode well for being useful to a team, so Hunt liked David's chances.

Occasionally, David would look up and catch his eye. The kid's smile was so damned hopeful, it did weird things to Hunt's gut.

Or maybe his heart.

It was harsh to even admit he hadn't automatically fallen in love with his son, but at least he was truthful. Hunter McCroy was a lot of things, but he wasn't a bullshitter and had never been one. He shot straight. Or at least that's what he told himself.

"Hey," Summer said, sliding onto the bench beside him, keeping her distance like she always did. She treated him like he had a stomach virus she didn't want to contract.

"Hey," Hunt returned, not taking his eyes off David. Summer made him uncomfortable, mostly because their relationship was tenuous at best. She'd not forgiven him for knocking her up and not taking interest in the kid during his early years. Of course, it wasn't his fault she'd gotten pregnant. She'd claimed to be on birth control. He didn't know why he had to bear all the blame for the wedge that sat between them. "I could have brought him home. No need for you to pick him up."

Summer shrugged. "I was in town. I had a late lesson at the school, so it seemed needless for you to run him all the way out to our place. How's he doing?"

"Good. He's a natural."

"Well, that makes sense," she said, her lips twitching into an almost smile. "He was excited this morning. I don't think I realized how much he missed playing sports. Moving here midsemester last year was tough. All the travel-ball teams were full, and he didn't know anyone to get on a Little League team."

"I should have been better about procuring that for him." Hunt felt guilt tug at him. Last October, when Summer called him to tell him she and David were moving back, he'd been pleased . . . but then anxiety crept in. He'd spent four years wishing David were closer, but when faced with his kid living in Moonlight and having the responsibility of being a father day in and day out, he'd grown nervous. What if he sucked at being a dad? He knew he probably would. A guy who didn't feel anything for the picture of the toddler in his locker had to have something wrong with him. Still, he was trying and doing okay. David seemed to like spending time with him, and Hunt could honestly say he looked forward to their time together.

"It's not your fault. This past year has been a big adjustment for us all," Summer said, her eyes following David as he hustled toward the visiting dugout. The kid ran with a loping, graceful stride. He looked like a baseball player, even flashing a thumbs-up at his mother when he caught her watching. Summer's smile was immediate.

At that moment it struck Hunt how attractive Summer was. Back in high school, she'd been pleasant to look at, nothing spectacular. But then five years ago, he'd seen her again. She'd turned into a confident, stunning woman. When she'd moved back to Moonlight, he'd tested the waters with her, thinking maybe the universe had known all those years ago who he was supposed to be with. They could be a normal family and buy into all the bullshit everyone constantly sold—picket fence, Christmas cards, vacations in Disney World. But Summer had rebuffed any attempt at his getting to know her better.

He remembered saying something casual. "Want to have dinner . . . uh, me, you, and Dave?"

She'd looked at him like he'd served a cockroach in her soup. "No. The time you have is for you and David. I'm not part of that."

"Come on, Summer. I'm not asking to hook up. Just have dinner. Try to be friends."

"After what your father did to my parents? After ignoring me and David for years? That's a stretch. I'm good with you being in David's life, Hunt. But not in mine."

"My parents?" he'd repeated in disbelief. "They paid for everything."

Her expression hardened like Alaska in winter. "Yeah, they did. Stellar people."

Okay, so his parents' attempt to throw money at the pregnancy had been a craptastic mistake, but Summer's parents had put his father on the defense. Not a good place to relegate Mitchell McCroy. When someone pushed his father, he laid them out and then stepped on their throat. Not many had the nerve to go up against him. Summer's parents had.

And they'd paid. Hunt wasn't proud of what his parents had done, but he ignored the goings-on because the most important thing in his life back in his freshman year of college was earning a spot on the mound with the Gators. What had happened back in Moonlight with the Valentines—custody agreements and all that other bullshit—had been easy to ignore. He'd been freaking nineteen, so he'd done what his father told him to do. He signed on the dotted line and tried to live his life.

His decisions had been wrong, but he'd been a kid himself. Wasn't like he had intentionally set out to hurt anyone. He'd been as lost as any kid who'd made a stupid mistake.

"You're right. Things have been challenging, but I think this new chapter in all our lives is going all right," Hunt said, refocusing on the present discussion about their son. Hey, Summer was actually holding a conversation with him. Sometimes she refused to talk about anything with him in a genial manner.

Summer nodded, sliding her gaze briefly his way. "I think so, too. David asked about spending Christmas Eve with you and your family. It surprised me that your parents wanted him to come to their family Christmas."

"They're trying, Summer." He didn't want to argue with her, but she made it damned hard.

"And you're good with taking care of Christmas morning?"

"Yeah, I never got to do the Santa thing. I mean I know he's too old, but it would still be cool. We're all trying to set things right, Summer." The words were thick on his tongue. He'd never addressed the fact that his father had essentially gotten her mother fired from her job all those years ago or that his family had implied Summer was a desperate girl looking for a cash settlement. Everyone in town had believed his parents. After all, no one would naysay the McCroys. Things had been bad between the Valentines and McCroys for years, but things were better now. Hunt was determined everyone would accept his son and forget about the past.

"Hmm," Summer said, her voice doubtful. She still wouldn't speak to his parents, but he gave her credit for never blackening their name in David's presence.

"They *are* trying. They feel bad about everything that happened. They were hasty in their judgment and cut off their own noses to spite their faces. They admit it and want to make it right."

"To you," she said.

"Yeah, to me. To David."

"But not to me."

He had no words because her conclusion was true. Perhaps if Summer actually spoke to his parents or graced them with her presence, they would have the opportunity to repair the gaping maw between the two families. Hunt had done what he could to repair his mistakes. He'd reached out to Summer about having more of a role in their son's life, and she'd finally relented. He didn't know what else he could do to make things better other than try to be a good dad to David.

"Don said David has really good mechanics. Did he have lessons in Nashville?" Change the subject. Don't wade into murky, potentially soul-sucking waters.

Summer shook her head. "Actually, he never pitched. He played catcher and first base. I bought him a cheap catcher's set, and he wore the mitt out."

"Think he would rather catch?" Hunt didn't want him to catch. He wanted him to pitch, like he had. Something about his son carrying on the McCroy pitching tradition pleased him, but then again, teams always needed good catchers. That was what had earned Rhett a place on the baseball team his sophomore year. Hunt and Rhett had gotten together and strategized how they could both make the varsity squad, and those two positions needed a steady supply of backups. Their hunch had paid off.

"I don't think so. He seems to like pitching," Summer said. "I think he wants to please you. Share that connection."

Hunt couldn't stop the smile that came at her words. "I can't say it doesn't make me happy watching him on the mound. I think he'll be good, but I don't want him to do something because of me."

"I don't think that's the case, but we'll see how it goes."

"I heard Rhett's in town. Shocked the hell out of me that he came here. Thought he hated Moonlight."

"I don't think he hates it, but, yeah, he surprised Pete . . . and me. He went to the cabin first to shower. Nearly scared me to death when I came in from the beach. Pete never told him I lived there."

"Or Rhett never listened. I get the feeling he's too busy for details out there in LA. Wonder why he's here?" Hunt asked.

Summer's face shuttered, and he remembered how much she'd always liked Rhett. Back during high school, it had been as obvious as the nose on her face. "I don't know why he came to Moonlight."

"Probably trying to escape all the rumors. Didn't the network make him take a break after he had the meltdown? Man, he tore that actress a new one, huh? It was pretty funny."

"Most people seemed to think so," Summer said, sounding like she'd rather not talk about Rhett.

Which made Hunt want to talk about him, for some reason. "Rhett's a little hypocritical, if you ask me. He chose to live out there and make his bread off celebrities. Come on, they're all shallow. I think they fake being concerned with things like the environment or child abuse or other crap just so they look like they're human."

Summer whipped her head around. "That's a bit jaded, even for you."

Hunt didn't like her having any insight into who he was. She hadn't wanted to get to know him, so she didn't get to judge him now. "What? It's probably the truth. Besides, there's no disputing Rhett makes his living off the drama and shallowness of that world."

"Maybe he does, but Pete raised Rhett to be compassionate. Rhett has a moral compass. Maybe he came home so he could figure out what direction to head next."

Hunt grunted. "Yeah, 'cause that works."

He felt her perusal. "You aren't happy in Moonlight?"

Pulling his gaze off the field, he zeroed in on the woman beside him. "Are *you* happy in Moonlight?"

She didn't speak for a moment, making him wonder about her happiness. He hadn't really thought about why she'd agreed to move back. He'd been preoccupied with the monumental task ahead—being a father. "As happy as I was in Nashville, I guess. My mother and sister are here. David's happy here and that's what's important."

"But you? Are you happy? You had a band in Nashville and a better job."

"Sometimes we make decisions for the betterment of others, Hunt." Her gaze met his and he saw conviction there. "David wanted a relationship with you, and I was unwilling to put my selfish goals before his. He'll eventually go to college and claim his own life. I can wait for mine a few more years. The only bad thing about Moonlight is the memories. They hide around every corner and I can't really escape them."

She slid off the bleacher and picked up the keys sitting on the metal bleacher below her. "The sunshine was nice, but I need to make a few calls."

Conversation over. But they'd actually had a fairly meaningful one, so that was another step in the right direction. He and Summer didn't have to be friends, but if they could strike some semblance of accord, it would be better for David. Her coldness had a way of throwing a damp blanket on any kindling of something more than politeness between them. "I'll be in touch about the frequency of the lessons. Still have to talk to Don and see what David needs. Don't worry. I'll foot the bill."

Summer paused and then nodded. "That would be helpful. I've picked up a few more clients, but with the holidays coming up, I'll need every penny."

"I got it."

"Tell David I'm waiting in the car. Have a good evening, Hunt."

"You, too," he said, watching her as she made her way back to the parking lot. She wore trim pants that clung to a nice ass, and a stretchy cotton shirt highlighted her toned shoulders. David said Summer ran and did yoga. The exercise had paid off. A stab of hunger hit him, but he dashed it away. *Friendship. Aim for friendship, if that.*

"Hey, Hunt, got a minute?" Don called, jogging toward him.

David stood in the dugout, packing up the old gym bag Hunt had found for him. He'd also given David his old glove, but the kid would need his own, eventually. Maybe they could drive to Charleston and visit a sporting goods store. Probably get a better deal online, but the idea of taking his kid to look for baseball gear was more attractive. Bonding time. They still needed lots of that.

"What do you think?" Hunt asked as Don crashed onto the metal bench Summer had abandoned minutes ago. "And don't bullshit me."

"I wouldn't," the man panted, out of breath from the jog. "He's got plenty of potential. Need to correct a few bad habits and work on widening his stride, but he's a natural. Like you were. He needs to do the strengthening exercises daily. But I can work with him twice a week. No more than that. Don't want to wear his arm out."

Hunt nodded, eyeing the boy who kept nervously looking over at them. "Sounds good."

"I'll text you my schedule," Don said.

Hunt slid off the bleacher and motioned for David to join him. The kid shouldered the bag and headed toward him. Though it was cooler that afternoon, sweat plastered the kid's dark hair to his forehead and neck. Hunt could never deny the kid was his. Didn't need a paternity test, though his parents had insisted on one before they paid any money to Summer.

"Did I do okay?" David asked Hunt.

"You did great, bud. But I want to make sure you want to do pitching lessons. This isn't about me. If you don't want to pitch or even play baseball, it's fine."

"No, I want to . . . unless you don't think I'll be good enough." Doubt shadowed David's voice, doing something to Hunt. He didn't want David to wonder.

But wasn't that always what Hunt wanted to be? Good enough? His own father had been an All-American at Virginia Tech but had injured his throwing arm working on his family farm. That's why Hunt had never had a summer job and had to sneak out to surf or skateboard. His father had wanted to protect Hunt's arm. Mitchell had sat through countless practices watching Hunt, grading his technique and noting any laziness on the mound. Hunt had never felt good enough for his father, and he damned sure didn't want David to worry about being good enough for him. "Baseball's a sport, Dave. It's played for fun. Sure, you have to put in work, but at the very heart, it's a game. You'll always be good enough to play a game."

His words were a lie, but he sold it anyway. It wasn't a game. It was life . . . or it had been for Hunt, until he didn't cut it in the big leagues. But to the fourteen-year-old standing in front of him, baseball needed to be a game.

Conviction carved a place inside Hunt. He wasn't going to do to David what his father had done to him. For his son, things would be different. Hunt hadn't done much in life that he could feel proud of, but he would feel good about this decision. His son would know it was okay to mess up. Hunt would give him space to make mistakes, to learn from them and to hold on to the dreams *he* wanted . . . not the ones his father had for him.

"Thanks, Dad. I want to pitch. I like it and if I practice enough, I can be good at it. I think."

"Absolutely," Don said, slapping his hands together. "You're Hunter McCroy's boy and that says something. We're going to have people talking about you just like they did him."

Hunt felt that old pressure squeezing at him. "He's not me, Don. No pressure, okay?"

Don's face crinkled in thought. "But he could—"

"Your mom's waiting in the car for you, David," Hunt interrupted, shooting Don a silencing look. He slapped the kid on the back and jerked his head toward the parking lot.

"Okay. I'll see you later, Dad."

Hunt watched David walk toward Summer's car and turned to Don. "Look, Don. I want you to work with him and give him confidence, but he's not me and I'm not my father. End of story."

And Hunt believed those words.

CHAPTER NINE

April 2003

Summer Valentine had never had the occasion to visit Graysen Hadley's house. Why would she? The blonde cheerleader had her own friends who complemented her like good accessories should. Or maybe that observation was Summer's smart-girl cattiness coming out to swat at the perfection that was Graysen. Still, on that Tuesday afternoon before junior-senior prom, Summer wished she'd never given in to the crazy makeover. Because everything felt too much . . . and was way outside her comfort zone.

Graysen had insisted Summer come over that afternoon because it was the absolute only time she could do it. Her schedule was so slammed. The pageant queen's words, not Summer's.

"Hello, girls," an older version of Graysen cooed when they came through the back sliding glass door by the pool. Pauline Hadley stood in the kitchen, cordless phone pinched between her shoulder and ear, highlighted hair artfully arranged around a face that had seen light-handed plastic surgery, if the rumors were to be believed. She wore a tailored pantsuit and looked like the successful realtor she was. "Y'all want a snack? I have some yogurt or granola bars around here some-where. If your brother hasn't eaten them all."

"Prom is, like, five days away, Mama. I'm not eating anything but salads. Let Grant have all that crap," Graysen said, tugging Summer out the door toward the sweeping staircase. The living room had mint-green carpet, soft butter walls, and Oriental runners. The glittering chandelier tied the formality together. The décor was a far cry from Summer's liv-ing room with its two La-Z-Boys and mounted ten-point buck survey-ing the microfiber couch with the jelly stain on the left arm.

Graysen's room extended the quiet affluence with cream carpet, a soft-pink, minky dot comforter, and pooling curtains of toile. It didn't look exactly like a princess threw up in Graysen's room, but a tasteful Victorian lady may have belched.

"I love your room," Summer said for want of something to say as Graysen closed the door, dumped her L.L. Bean backpack on the window seat, and collapsed on the fluffy bed with at least twelve needle-point pillows piled on it.

"I hate it. My mom had a decorator do it for the parade of homes right before Christmas. Like, who cares if it's something they might put in *Southern Living*? That's, like, my mom's entire goal in life. Get in that dumb magazine." Graysen opened her bedside table drawer and withdrew a bag of peanut M&M'S. "Want some?"

"No, thanks," Summer said, wondering what had happened to the salad plan. Actually, Summer wanted to wolf down at least half the bag of candy, but she wouldn't ruin what little success she'd had on her diet. She'd tried over the past week to avoid her mother's fattening casseroles and stick to fruits and veggies, but those peanut jewels of wonder were a particular weakness. She'd nearly cried when she tossed out the remain-der of her Easter basket candy last week.

Graysen popped a few candies in her mouth and chewed thought-fully. "I told Katie B to bring over some dresses, but she's so much smaller than you. I have this red dress that's sorta stretchy, and my mom has a lot of dresses 'cause she goes to conferences and awards crap all the time. But some of her dresses are so . . . eww. But first we do your hair." Graysen removed a folder from the feminine desk between the two transom windows.

A folder?

The tab read "Summer Valentine 2003" with a heart bubbled in before her name.

"I'm scrapping the updo because your hair is pretty down. Have you thought about highlights? Nothing brassy, maybe some soft brown and warm red," Graysen said, studying Summer as she sat awkwardly on the end of the bed. "I can do them today."

"You're really into this, huh?" Summer asked, fingering the end of her braid, marveling that the girl had spent so much time thinking about how Summer should wear her hair.

"One day I'm going to own a salon, so I'm already developing a portfolio. I did highlights on Katie B before Craig Mooney's Halloween party, and everyone thought she looked great. You're victim number two, and I'm determined you're going to rock it."

"But I can manage my own dress. My mother wants to do that whole shopping thing. You know moms. We're going to Charleston tomorrow. I'm checking out of school." She hated missing class. Her focus, to date, had been on holding on to being number one in her class. She wanted that scholarship, that honor, but she couldn't tell her mother no. Buying a stupid dress was obviously more important than taking notes in AP European history.

Her mother had been beyond ecstatic when Summer had mentioned possibly going to prom. After a near-deathly hug that may or may not have cracked a rib, Carolyn Valentine had danced a little jig. Summer had rolled her eyes, but she couldn't stop the smile. Seeing her mom happy . . . and dancing . . . was always a treat.

"Come with me," her mother had said, pulling her into her parents' bedroom. Flipping on the light, her mother shifted the full laundry basket onto the floor and pulled the afghan off the chest that her grand-mother had given her before she'd died. Summer's mother unlocked the button lock and raised the lid of the cedar chest.

Inside the chest were memories—tiny baby clothes, stained pin-afores, tarnished cups, and a set of Peter Rabbit cups and bowls. Photo books stacked three deep and other assorted "treasures." Her mother pulled out a plastic container. "Here's my corsage."

Inside the clear container was a shriveled brown grouping of roses with yellowed ribbon. "You kept your corsage?"

"Yeah, I kept it, and here is the prom program. Look, I was a class favorite. Most likely to marry my high school sweetheart." Her mother laughed before tossing the program atop the vacation album.

Summer smiled. "Well, you made that happen."

"Never say I don't have goals," her mother said with a sheepish smile. "Here are some pictures—this is Lucy Orgeron. She was my best friend. Her date, Charlie, wore cowboy boots, which looked hideous with that powder-blue tux. We had such a good time. Stayed out until the sun came up."

"Why are you showing me all this? I mean, why keep this?" Summer lifted the dried-up corsage.

"Because that's the night your daddy told me he wanted to marry me. We danced under those stringed-up lights and . . ." Her mother's words faded. "I know it's silly to hang on to my old corsage, but those were the first flowers I had ever received."

"They look like they were pretty," Summer said, feeling like an ass for not understanding. If Hunter McCroy asked her to prom, he might bring Summer a corsage, too. Like her mother, she'd never received flowers from anyone before, outside of her grandmother bringing her some after her first and only dance recital. Maybe she'd keep her cor-sage, too.

"They *were*," her mother said, taking the container and smiling at the remainder of a night she obviously treasured. "I thought you might like to see some of my things from high school. Hard to believe but I used to be young once."

"You're not old, Mama," Summer said, looping an arm around her mother's plump shoulders.

"Oh, sugar, but I sure feel that way most days." Her mother stacked her treasures back inside the chest and closed it. "We'll go look for a dress next week. And shoes. Pretty shoes. It will be such fun."

After seeing her mother's excitement, she couldn't blurt out the fact one of the more popular senior girls was going all *Clueless* on her, and the only reason she had agreed to go was out of guilt or whatever had made her agree to the madness. "That will be cool, Mama. I have a friend who's helping me with my hair and makeup."

"Who?" her mother asked.

"Graysen Hadley." Felt weird to even say her name.

"Pauline's girl? The Shrimp Queen?" Carolyn looked confused. "But you're not friends with her."

"I know," Summer said, but couldn't explain how she'd tripped and fallen into prom hell . . . or the fact that she'd likely be the star pitcher's frumpy backup date. Throwing Hunter McCroy into the mix seemed a bad idea. Her mother might get notions, and the whole thing was too humiliating. Especially if he refused to ask her. "It's just . . . it's a fun senior-girl thing."

"That's cool," Graysen said, drawing Summer back into the pink room and her new reality. "But no gray or yellow. You need a dress with brighter colors. Now let's practice your makeup. Rhett's bringing Hunter by so he can do the official ask."

"Wait. Today?"

"Sum, prom is in four days." Graysen started pulling various bottles out of a drawer in her en suite bathroom.

Panic swept through Summer at the thought of having to endure Hunter asking her to prom in front of Rhett and Graysen. Part of her was ecstatic she'd have an actual date. The other part wanted to crawl under a rock and make a home there. "Uh, he's coming here?"

Graysen leaned back. "Chill. It's not that big a deal. It's just Hunt."

Just Hunt.

"I don't know him all that well."

"Well, study up on baseball. That's all he freaking talks about. That and some booze will get you through the night. The after-party is at Hunt's beach house—his parents said we could use it as long as it doesn't get trashed."

An after-party? Dear Lord, she not only had to go to prom with Hunt, but now she had to go to a beach house and party with all the popular kids?

Graysen motioned her toward the open bathroom door. "Okay, let's make you pretty, Mama."

Summer spent the next half hour with Graysen all up in her face. She worried about the zit on her chin, but Graysen had "awesome" concealer. When Graysen wiped spit from the corner of her mouth with a tissue, Summer turned the color of the lipstick. Still, something about the dedication with which Graysen attacked her role as transformer of nerds was heartwarming. Finally, after she bit her lip and brushed gloss on Summer's bottom lip—just the bottom lip—Graysen said, "There."

Summer had been sitting on the stool borrowed from the desk, so she couldn't catch her reflection until Graysen drew her to her feet. The reflection in the mirror that met her was her . . . but not her. "Wow."

Graysen faced Summer's reflection, tucking an errant strand of hair behind her ear. "I know. Still think some highlights would be good."

Summer twisted a finger around a brown curl, noting her hair color was sort of flat. "Nothing too blonde, though."

Just as Graysen was about to say something, the doorbell rang. "Oh, good, they're here."

Summer swallowed. "Damn it."

Graysen laughed. "You're so nervous. It's cute."

Then she disappeared, opening her door and yelling down the stairs to her mother. "Mama, tell Rhett and Hunt we'll be down in a few minutes. We're not dressed."

"Not dressed?" Summer repeated to the girl in the mirror who looked kind of like her.

"Come on," Graysen ordered, tugging Summer from where she stood. "We need to get you something decent to wear."

"What's wrong with what I have on?"

"You're joking, right?" Graysen said, casting her baby blues down the jeans and Pearl Jam T-shirt Summer wore. Summer thought she looked like she wasn't trying too hard. Which was the point. But Summer let Graysen steer her across the hall to a much larger room with a huge walk-in closet.

"This is my mom's but she still tries, you know? You have nice boobs. You should be accentuating them."

"That's what Nessa always says."

"The preacher's kid?" Graysen asked, raking through the hangers. She pulled out a light-pink blouse and held it up to Summer before shaking her head and returning it. "Well, she's right."

"Shouldn't we go down? They're waiting," Summer said, praying Graysen didn't try to put her in something super tight. She still had baby fat that poofed out over her waistband, though she had noted that morning things were feeling looser. Eating blueberries and nibbling celery had paid off.

"Always make them wait, Summer," Graysen said, selecting a light-blue, short-sleeved sweater. The material wasn't fuzzy or tight, but rather a nice polyester blend that wouldn't cling to Summer's tummy. "Try this."

"It still has tags. Your mother—"

"—won't know it's gone. Trust me. Look at all this shit." Graysen lifted a hand à la Vanna style. "Hurry, I need to adjust your hair before we go down."

Summer didn't want to take her T-shirt off in front of Graysen, but the girl wasn't moving. Turning her back, she quickly pulled the tee off and tossed it toward her feet. She always wore a soft cotton jog bra and suddenly that felt wrong. Graysen probably wore pretty underwear, not plain Hanes cotton ones from Walmart. She shimmied into the blue sweater, noting it was a little tight on her arms, but overall it seemed to fit.

"Turn around," Graysen commanded, her eyes narrowed in critical-assessment mode. "Not bad."

Summer sucked in her tummy and looked down in dismay at how wrong the Converse sneakers looked with the sophisticated top. "What do I do about my shoes?"

"Take them off," Graysen said.

"Off?"

"Guys love a barefoot girl. It's sexy."

"Barefoot? You're kidding. You just did all this to my hair and face."

"Trust me. It projects confidence, a sort of caught unaware but that's cool because I'm comfortable in my skin."

Summer had no idea what Graysen talked about, but toed off the sneakers anyway.

"Please tell me you have toenails that are painted and feet that don't stink," Graysen said, eyeing the plain white socks.

"I painted them last weekend," Summer said, peeling off her socks, inhaling deeply to ascertain if she did indeed have stinky feet. She couldn't smell anything, but the lines pressed into her pale feet weren't super attractive. Her toes were painted an orangey pink her mother called Cajun Shrimp. It looked good when she had a tan, but the spring had been cool, so she'd not spent much time in sandals.

"That's fine. Now let me look at you," Graysen said, tipping Summer's chin up. "You look great. Just let me take my shoes off so we match, like we were doing homework or something, and put on some lip gloss."

Summer figured the guys had been waiting for at least ten minutes, which seemed kind of rude, but Graysen's knowledge of guys was probably 200 percent better than her own, so she scooped up her discarded T-shirt and shoes and padded behind Graysen as she headed back to her room. Butterflies—or maybe it was bats—thrashed in her stomach, making it gassy and crampy. Oh God, what if she had to fart or something? She sucked in deep breaths and told herself she was being ridiculous. What Hunter McCroy thought about her, which had to be very little, shouldn't matter to her.

Five long minutes later, Graysen emerged from the bathroom, smelling like perfume and looking slightly trussed up in a skintight shirt and jeans with holes in the knee. She was barefoot, and her toes were painted a sparkling blue. She looked thin, hip, and gorgeous.

Damn it.

"Okay, little butterfly, time to spread your wings," Graysen said, looking excited at the prospect of debuting her work of art, which frankly paled in comparison to the artist herself.

Graysen skipped down the carpeted stairs without a backward glance. Summer followed, concentrating on not falling as she went down and on the tiny chip of polish on her left big toe. She tried not to think about how seriously weird this all was. She didn't belong here, wearing a borrowed shirt from a fortysomething-year-old woman and eye shadow that made her eyes look smoky. Why did people want smoky eyes anyway?

"Hey, babe," Graysen said, entering a room behind the living area Summer hadn't seen yet. It was a big family room with a fireplace and fluffy-looking sectional. Graysen went immediately to Rhett and looped her arms around his neck. "How was practice?"

"I hit a double off Hunt," Rhett said, dropping a light kiss on Graysen's lips.

Rhett wore almost exactly the same thing he'd worn the last time Summer had tutored him—athletic shorts and a compression T-shirt that molded to his chest and nicely toned arms. He wore a backward ball cap, which made him look both boyish and absurdly hot.

"Got lucky," Hunter McCroy said from where he sprawled on an overstuffed chair. His dark gaze flickered over Summer before returning to the golden couple in the center of the room.

"Hey, Hunter, this is Summer Valentine. You've known her forever, right?" Rhett said.

Summer felt as if she hung in between two alternate realities and couldn't move. She placed a steadying hand on the door frame and reminded herself she would not throw up. She needed to project a cool vibe. If not cool, indifferent. Something other than about to barf on the cheerful patterned rug in the Hadley family room. On the TV, a reporter from *Inside Edition* stood on a red carpet yapping about something only a few people cared about. Or maybe it was merely that Summer didn't care about it. She only cared about breathing and not spazzing out . . . and that chip of polish missing from her left toenail.

"Yeah, I think we had Spanish together."

They hadn't had Spanish together but Summer nodded anyway. "How's it going?"

She'd asked a question! Boom! She was almost normal and hadn't thrown up.

"Cool. Done with practice," Hunt said, suddenly looking a little unsure. That was likely because Graysen was making a face at him. It was the face that said, "Do what I told you to do."

Summer clasped her hands behind her back. "Well, are we going to do this or not?"

She had no idea why she said that because as soon as she did, Graysen got a constipated look, her eyes opening wider. Hunt looked annoyed. But Rhett laughed.

"That's my Funny Valentine. Right to the point. And you look really nice, too," Rhett said.

Something in his voice made her feel calmer. "All due to your girl-friend's skill."

Graysen stopped looking constipated and glittered appropriately.

Hunt rose. "Uh, so, Summer, you want to go outside and see the, um, pool?"

"The pool?" She glanced at Graysen, who gave a barely perceptible nod. "Uh, sure. I haven't seen the pool yet."

"Cool," Hunt said, opening one side of the French doors. Beyond his shoulder she could see the aqua water and the lush green palmettos. He walked out, not even waiting on her, but she forgave him because it was a very uncomfortable situation. In fact, she would rather face a proctologist . . . or not. Maybe facing the popular, talented, rich boy studying the leaves in the bottom of Graysen's pool was better.

"So, like, I guess you know why I asked you out here," he said, turning to her. Hunt had an inch or two on Rhett, which meant he was almost a foot taller than Summer. His skin was beautifully golden, his movements almost lazy as he glided toward the pool. His dark hair curled above his ears, and a pointed chin gave him a decidedly preda-tory look. He reminded her of Scar from *The Lion King*—talked slow, walked slow, and was a consummate smart-ass. If girls weren't falling all over Golden Boy inside, they were chasing after Hunter McCroy. So the fact he was about to ask her to prom felt like a big joke.

Oh God, what if it was a big joke?

Like in the movie *She's All That*. The artsy chick, a bet, and every-one popular smirking behind their hands at her naïveté. The nausea came back as she searched the fronds dangling over the gorgeous pool. Maybe Graysen's brother lurked behind one, capturing the prank on the chubby geek on film.

"You don't have to do this. It's really stupid," Summer managed.

Hunt lifted his brows.

"I mean, we don't even know each other, and I know you have a girlfriend—"

"Had," Hunt said, walking toward her. "I *had* a girlfriend. Molly's not my girlfriend anymore."

"Right," Summer said, wanting to step away from the guy advancing on her. "Had."

"So, you already know what I'm asking. You okay with it? Last minute and all?" He looked like he ordered a pizza. Like it wasn't about prom. It was about getting a task out of the way.

"I guess."

"You guess?" He sounded annoyed at that.

"I know you don't want to go with me. I'm me and you're . . . you."

"So? It's just a dance, but I'm not going alone. That would be fucked up. And if I don't go, no party. Everyone's up my ass about the damned party. Someone already bought the keg. Let's just go together and not make it such a big deal. Just as friends."

Except they weren't friends. "Okay. Sure. Senior year and all."

"That's right. Senior year." He held out his fist.

She looked at it.

"Fist bump," he said, looking at her like she'd sprouted leaves from her ears.

"Right." She bumped her fist against his.

"I'm out. See you this weekend. Gray's making all the plans. I'll just show up when she tells me to."

"Oh, okay," Summer said, following him into the house.

Graysen sat in Rhett's lap. Her hair was messed up and he had a slight sheen of lip gloss on his mouth. Both lifted their eyebrows in a universal question.

Hunt said, "Yeah. It's cool."

"Yes! This party's going to be epic," Graysen said, laying a hard, fast kiss on Rhett.

Rhett smiled at Summer. "Thanks for doing this, Summer."

Summer felt a hand reach in and squeeze her heart. This wasn't some charity, feel-good thing. There was motive. A party was at stake, and Summer agreeing to go with Hunt to prom had placed the "epic" throw down back on the table.

They were using her. Even Rhett.

"Sure. Glad to help," she said, the words ash in her mouth. "Anything for a party."

Rhett grinned at her. "That's the spirit. Prom 2003. We're going to make it a night to remember."

"No, an Arabian Night to remember," Graysen joked, before kissing Rhett hard . . . and a bit longer than appropriate in front of guests.

At that moment, Summer hated them all.

CHAPTER TEN

November, present day

Rhett shouldn't have come to Moonlight. He didn't know what he'd been thinking when he drove onto that ramp and headed south, but he certainly hadn't counted on Summer Valentine pushing his buttons, his agent freaking out because he'd couriered papers to the Catskills and now couldn't locate them, or the fact he'd be driving his grandfather to his doctor's appointment. But it was too late now. He was locked in.

"You carry the stool sample," Grampy Pete said, handing him an envelope before thumping out to Rhett's rental.

Rhett shifted the envelope so he held it pinched between his finger and thumb. "You're joking, right?"

"Naw, that's got poop in it. They gotta check my prostate or colonrectal or something."

"Uh, I think you're supposed to mail this somewhere, Grampy." Rhett didn't want to stand there holding his grandfather's poop, and he really didn't want to drive the old coot to the doctor, but since he had nothing better to do, he couldn't actually say no. Grampy said Summer usually drove him, but she had to go help her sister at her shop.

"Dr. Meyer will mail it. Stop standin' around. I gotta be there by ten o'clock."

"It's only a little after eight," Rhett said, unlocking the car, reluctantly climbing in, and setting the envelope on the back seat. "What are we going to do for an hour and a half?"

"All you California types are always in a goll-dang hurry. You're on Carolina time, boy. We're going to have some coffee. Etta Washington makes the best."

Rhett made a face. He wasn't prepared to go into town. The whole point of coming home to the Nest was to lay up and lick his wounds, figure out what was wrong in his head, and maybe take a few naps. He didn't want to have people in town staring at him, asking for his autograph. He didn't want to have to play Rhett Bryan, lovable charmer. "You don't have to have a blood test or anything? You have to fast for those, you know."

"Nope," Grampy said, lowering himself into the passenger's seat and fumbling for the belt. "Just getting the usual."

Rhett had no idea what the usual was, but he supposed he was about to find out.

Ten minutes later, Rhett pulled into the downtown parking area. Gulls crisscrossed through stately oaks, looking for tourist leftovers. In the marina, boats bobbed, much too happy for an early Wednesday morning. The taste of the sea greeted Rhett when he stepped from his car and shoved his credit card into the parking meter.

"You could have parked on Third Street for free. Dr. Meyer's office is not a block away. Spending good money on a parking spot when there's plenty of free ones."

"I wanted to park by the water. Haven't been here in a while," Rhett said, moving his gaze over the waterfront park. Big front porch–style swings nestled into the lush azaleas that skirted the brick walkway, offering southern hospitality to those who needed to sit a spell and watch the bay for the sight of dolphins. Hardwood trees draped gracefully against the dark-green of the oaks, festooning the gardens with cheerful autumn color. He'd forgotten how pretty and quaint Moonlight was.

"Well, look your fill. I need coffee. And cake," Grampy said, slamming the door. "Make sure you lock it up. Got my stool sample in there."

"We wouldn't want that to walk away, would we?" Rhett drawled, following his grumpy grandfather up the steps toward Front Street, where one could buy antiques, fishing gear, and a great egg salad sandwich at Whetstone's Deli. A few people moved about, exiting the Knit and Needle shop or entering Bailey's Barbershop with its traditional barber's pole spinning red and blue on the corner. Sweet Cheeks Bakery seemed to be Grampy's destination, so Rhett fell into step and cast occasional furtive glances around the area, hoping like hell no one had leaked his whereabouts.

But he knew that was wishful thinking. Social media pretty much rendered the ability to hide out null and void. If he had to take a guess, he'd bet five or six Moonlight residents had already posted on Facebook that he was in town. Probably ready with cameras. Maybe he was being suspicious . . . or maybe the paranoia was a result of so little sleep.

Last night Rhett had woken in a cold sweat, the screams of someone he couldn't save ringing in his ears. Every night, he lay awake, praying for a good night's rest. He watched reruns of shows like *The Andy Griffith Show* or silly sitcoms like *The Simpsons*, hoping to escape into dreamless sleep. But peace eluded him, and once his body succumbed to exhausted slumber, he found himself imprisoned in a personal hell. Total catch-22.

"Here we are," Grampy said, jabbing a bent finger at the bakery on the corner. Sweet Cheeks had a blue-and-white striped awning and curlicue script advertising treats for everyone.

Rhett thought about LA and the pursuit of health and things like tofu and sprouts. Maybe it should say, "Treats for everyone . . . except crazy, narcissistic health nuts." The thought made him smile . . . mostly 'cause he fit that bill. Even the narcissism. Because being trim, young, and flawless was expected of him.

"Why you smiling?" Grampy said, side-eyeing him suspiciously.

"Because I'm happy," he lied.

What a load of crap, but if anyone could sell it, it was Rhett Bryan. Welcome to *Late Night in LA*, motherfuckers. Smile at camera three. Say, "We've got a great show for you." Commercial break.

Grampy frowned. "Right. Sure. You coulda fooled me when you woke up hollering last night."

Rhett pulled open the door so he didn't have to respond.

"Looka, here comes my Pete bringing a handsome boy with him," a large lady called out from behind the counter. She wore a traditional Gullah headdress, had a smile as wide as her bosoms, and huge hoop earrings that brushed her shoulders. Her dark skin looked luminous and smooth. She could have been thirty or seventy.

"Morning, Etta. Brought my grandson."

"Well, I'll be. Mr. Rhett Bryan himself coming up in my place. I'm gonna see an uptick in sales now. I'm set."

Rhett gave his trademark smile. "Hi, nice to meet you . . ."

"Etta," she said, grabbing a ceramic mug, filling it with coffee, and handing it to his grandfather. "You want coffee, too, Mr. Rhett Bryan?"

"Um, just Rhett. And please."

"You ain't sold out of those carrot muffins, are you?" Grampy Pete asked, eyeing the display with the fluffy iced cupcakes, layered napoleons, and large, saucer-size cookies.

"Sure am, but I saved you one, you old goat," Etta said, fetching a plate.

There were a few others in the bakery, sitting at the cute café tables. Local art adorned the walls, and fresh flowers sat on each table. The overall effect was cute and comfy. Small town at its best.

Grampy shuffled over to a table, and Etta set the coffee and huge muffin down in front of him. Seconds later she brought Rhett's coffee and lifted an eyebrow. "What you want to eat, Mr. Rhett Bryan?"

"Just coffee is fine."

"You skinny as a scarecrow. Have a muffin, darlin'." Etta bustled back to the display case. Rhett figured he was getting a muffin whether he wanted it or not, so he sank down next to his grandfather and tried to pretend the soccer moms in the corner weren't totally absorbed by him sitting at the table in the middle of Moonlight. He should smile, play the part. But he wouldn't, because he was tired of playing parts. At least at present.

Etta plopped down a blueberry muffin in front of Rhett and then took a seat with them. "You get your stool sample, Pete?"

"Yep. Thanks for sending me home with some of that high-fiber bread. Took a day but got my sample out in the car."

"I knew that would work. You gotta take care of yourself. Summer said your cholesterol was too high. Now, you know you gotta eat better than what you're doing. One carrot muffin a week. That's it. I'm going to have to cut you off, Pete."

"The hell you are. It wasn't that high. Summer's always exaggerating. When you going dancing with me? I wanna take a good-looking woman out one more time before I die. Plus, I need the exercise. It's your civic duty."

"Oh, pshaw, you old rascal. You too old for me."

"I still got fire in my blood, woman," Grampy said, taking a big bite of the muffin, washing it down with black coffee.

Rhett sat there, marveling at his grandfather discussing his bathroom business with Etta and then flirting with her. It had been a long time since he'd been in South Carolina, that was damned certain.

"What you doing here, Mr. Rhett Bryan? You taking a break from show business?" Etta didn't look to be nosing into his business. Just general Wednesday-morning conversation.

"Not really. A little vacation. I haven't been to Moonlight in a while so . . ." He still didn't have a good reason for why he was here, but he figured it was okay for everyone to draw their own conclusions.

"Make Pete take you fishing. He's always catching good eating. That's the thing about those waters—they'll give you what you need. Now, me, I like oysters." Etta eyed the women behind them now tapping on their phones.

"You know what those are good for, don'tcha?" Grampy waggled his eyebrows and then stuffed another hunk of muffin in his mouth.

"You ladies want some more coffee? I made a fresh pot right before Pete came in to harass me," Etta said to the women behind them.

"That ain't harassing, that's flirting. Think you could tell the difference," Grampy said, giving Etta a wink. The women waved Etta off.

"Lord, Pete, you bad at flirting. Take that stuff down to Garden Park Retirement Center and see if any of those old biddies will bite what you're throwing out. 'Cause I ain't." Etta smiled in spite of her words and rose.

Rhett turned his attention to the delicious muffin while Etta poured coffee and nattered on about the upcoming holiday and the treats she could bake for customers' Thanksgiving tables.

Thanksgiving was next week. He hadn't really celebrated the holiday in any other way than a random dinner here or there. Once he'd hosted the Macy's Thanksgiving Day Parade and had turkey with the camera crew before heading to some trendy restaurant in Tribeca for good sushi. Would he be in Moonlight for Thanksgiving?

He glanced at his grandfather, who looked more stooped, more gray, more feeble. Maybe staying awhile longer was a good idea. After all, he had several weeks of forced break. *Take some time, Bryan. It's been a hard end of year for you and the show. The network wants to put some time between you and the event. Come back at the beginning of the year better and stronger.*

The chimes pealed and he cast a glance at the door.

Summer.

His gut lurched and the coffee in his empty stomach churned. He'd been an ass a few nights before. Justified but still an ass.

"Morning, sugar," Etta called out, a wide smile splitting her face. "Pete's here harassing me again."

"Well, Etta, you know he can't resist you. Or those delicious muffins," Summer teased.

"I refuse to hide my candle under a bushel, so I'll have to deal with old hound dogs sniffing around for what they can get," Etta said, pulling out another cup. "You want something to eat, sugar?"

"Nope. Just coffee. Black."

Summer plopped down into the chair Etta had abandoned. "Pete, I want you to talk to Dr. Meyer about switching your blood pressure medicine. What you're taking now doesn't seem to be working as well."

"And good morning to you, too," Grampy grumped, shoving another hunk of carrot muffin in his mouth. Crumbs scattered the table and Summer casually swooped them off into her hand, deposited them into the trash can, and reseated herself.

She glanced over at Rhett. "Force of habit."

"Cleaning up after kids?"

"No, cleaning up after Pete." She smiled and it punched him in the solar plexus. Damn, but Summer was a pretty woman. He'd always thought her pleasant to look at, even when she was baby fat and uncertain. Both of those traits were gone, leaving behind a square jaw, and soft lips that could narrow into disapproval and exacting questions that made him wriggle. Her eyes held both intelligence and compassion. Something about her tugged at him, the way the moon urged the waves on the oceans.

"How's your toe?" Summer asked, accepting the coffee from Etta.

"Better."

Grampy lifted a bushy eyebrow. "What's wrong with your toe, boy?"

"Nothing. Just stubbed it when I went out to my car Sunday night. I scared Summer to death. Again," he said, relieved she wasn't holding a grudge. He knew she'd felt bad about nosing into his affairs. And he felt bad for acting so childish and stomping off.

"He's making it a habit," Summer said, accepting her coffee and giving a small wave to one of the women behind them. She refocused on him. "They're taking your picture."

"Yeah, I know," Rhett said, pinching off a piece of muffin and popping it into his mouth. Sinfully good and not what he needed, but he ate it anyway. Part of being home was accepting the comforts it offered. "Hope we don't get too many amateur photographers around looking to make a quick buck from the rags."

Grampy leveled dark eyes at Rhett. "I seen them vultures on the television. Won't leave you alone, will they? Got that little girl's mother being interviewed. Like they're wallerin' in her tears. Those reporters love the tears. And now I hear they're puttin' on some kind of race to bring awareness to something or other. What do they think you did? Run her over intentionally?"

His grandfather's words caused him to flinch, something Summer seemed to notice. A hard flash of pain, awareness of what he'd done, of what everyone now thought of him spun around inside him, chewing him up. "It's a 5K to bring awareness to inattentive driving. It's not aimed at me. Just a campaign."

"Bullshit. That kid ran out in front of you. Plain ol' accident but folks gotta make it into something. Never an accident, right? Always someone's fault. They dropped the criminal charges, didn't they? The goll-danged state knew it was an accident. That family's just trying to get some money from you with this civil suit. Probably had those buzzard lawyers circling before the ambulance got there."

Every time he heard an ambulance, he wanted to vomit. Just the thought now made him want to get up and leave. Just run like a fucking coward. Grampy didn't know how horrible that day had been, how the images seared his memory, clotting into something he couldn't shrug off. The child's mother haunted his dreams, nightmares tangled in blood, screams, and an inability to move. "Can we not?"

"Not what?" Grampy barked, warming up to the subject at hand. Grampy loved a soapbox and he'd climbed aboard, creaking knees and all. "Not talk about all the people trying to throw you under the bus on this? Why's the parents trying to blame you for what their kid did?"

"Grampy, please. I don't want to talk about this. My attorney is handling it. My publicist, too." Rhett focused on a painting of a chicken hanging over his grandfather's shoulder. The composition was off. Something about the eye placement. But of course, he was no expert on art or chickens, so maybe the artist had been correct.

Rhett hated what his attorney and publicist were doing to manipulate public opinion in his civil case. On one hand, he knew this was how the game was played, but on the other, he couldn't stand smearing the family of the child he'd accidentally killed. They were claiming that his inaction during the accident proved complicity. They accused him of speeding, not paying attention. The boy who'd retrieved the soccer ball had been deposed and claimed Rhett had been looking at the radio . . . that he hadn't even tried to stop. In defense, Rhett's agent had hired a spin doctor publicist to go after the family with private investigator reports, interviews with neighbors, financial investigators—whatever it took to cast the family in a dubious light and prove parental neglect. His team planned to use the court of public opinion to destroy the Tavares family.

"You know, we should order a pie for Thanksgiving while we're here," Summer said, thankfully changing the subject and drawing his thoughts away from his troubles.

Summer wore an embroidered tunic shirt and Birkenstocks. She'd used to wear Birkenstocks back when they were in high school, too. This woman was such a mystery to him. Practical, whimsical, chilled, and intense. Maybe she was like every woman he'd been around . . . or none he'd ever met.

"We gotta have a pecan. That's my favorite. David's too," Grampy said, seemingly giving up on haranguing the people suing Rhett. Thank God.

"David is actually why I came in. Saw y'all from down the street. Maisie has a funeral tomorrow morning and Shelia has to teach Bible study tonight, so I told her I would help out at the shop. I need someone to take David to pitching lessons this afternoon. It's the only other time the pitching coach can fit him in this week. Hunt can bring David home, but he has a meeting in Hilton Head and won't be back in time to run him to the field. I was hoping you could do that for me, Pete."

"I can do it," Rhett said, surprising himself.

Summer raised her eyebrows. "That's asking too much of you. You're visiting."

Ah, the polite way to say thanks, but no thanks.

"It's no bother. I have nothing to do this afternoon," he said, giving her his most direct stare. *I'm responsible enough to drive your kid to the ballpark.*

She met him with a stare of her own. "Thought you were trying to keep a low profile."

Rhett swept the café with a gaze. "Too late, don't you think?"

"Probably. But, I don't want to impose—"

"I don't have anything to do." *In other words, I need some damned distraction. If I nap, I dream. If I dream, I wake shaking. Let me have something worthwhile to do.*

Grampy brushed the last of the carrot muffin from his finger. "He don't have anything. Already fixed the railing on the deck. Rhett ain't forgot how to use a hammer. David got lucky. The kid was supposed to help me over his break, but since he's gonna be a star pitcher . . ."

"Let's not give him star pitcher title just yet," Summer warned Grampy. Then she set those enigmatic hazel eyes on Rhett. "Thank you, Rhett. I'm sure David will grill you about the celebrities you know. He particularly likes Lil Wayne, much to my delight."

Her words were light, but he knew it was hard for her to give up any control, especially to a virtual stranger. "I'll let Dwayne know he has another fan, but no problem on taking David. I'm happy to do it. He's a cool kid."

"Okay, I have to run. Call me when you're done, Pete," Summer said, rising.

"I don't need to give you a report on my prostate or blood sugar. You already make me eat wheat germ in my oatmeal. I don't even like oatmeal, neither. Having you around is like being married without the good benefits like biscuits and gravy . . . and sex."

Summer rolled her eyes. "David needs to be at the field by four thirty."

As Rhett flashed her a thumbs-up, he caught the soccer moms watching Summer depart with sharklike interest. Sexy, single Summer probably didn't have many fans among the PTA crowd. She likely drew the eye of husbands and boyfriends alike.

"Is Summer dating someone?" he asked.

Grampy knocked a knuckle on the table. "Nope. Don't even think about it. She's not like those women you gad about with. Leave her alone."

"I didn't say I was—"

"You don't have to. I see that spark in your eyes."

"I'm not interested," he lied, taking an angry bite of muffin. "I just wondered."

"She's new to town and too busy to mess around with the bums around here. Summer's a good girl, and she deserves better than what she's had." Grampy's gosh-darn demeanor was gone. His grandfather could be as congenial as a little wren, but get his dander up, and he went cold-blooded raptor on a guy. A warning had been delivered.

And received.

Rhett should probably pack up his crap and get the hell out of Moonlight. Wasn't like the place was a magic pill that took away nightmares and restored calm. To even contemplate dragging someone like Summer into his damaged existence was ridiculous. He had no clue why he had the inclination.

"I'm not into Summer, Gramps. Just merely curious. I'm going to hang with her kid today. Just thought I'd get the lay of the land," Rhett said, wiping the remains of the muffin from his fingers. He rose and took his plate and cup to the counter, smiling at the soccer moms in their lululemon pants and matching jackets. He had a role to play even in his small hometown. "Morning, ladies."

"Hi," one said, smiling broadly. "Welcome home, Rhett."

"Thank you. It's good to be back in Moonlight."

But was it?

Rhett hadn't been part of this life for too long, and being here, while it gave him some measure of comfort, felt like squeezing into a shoe he'd found in the back of his closet. *Get out. Go to the spa.*

"Let's get going, boy," Grampy Pete said, scooting his chair back. "Can't wait to introduce the doc to my boy. I ain't much on sentimentality, but I'm glad you came home, Rhett. Don't worry. We all got your back."

Maybe he should put that phone call to the spa on hold.

Felt nice for someone to have his back . . . and Gramps wasn't getting any younger.

CHAPTER ELEVEN

November, present day

Hunt pulled into the high school baseball field and parked next to a rental car. He knew Rhett Bryan had come home to lick his wounds. So did the rental belong to his former best friend, or was it merely a soccer mom getting her transmission fixed?

But why would Rhett be at the high school field? Then he remembered Summer's unread text. Something about a funeral. Probably helping her sister. Of course, the Boy Wonder would step up to give the kid a lift. Rhett had always enjoyed the role of good guy.

Climbing out of the truck, Hunt brushed a hand through his shaggy hair, trying to cover the thinning area. He'd spent the morning in meetings with architects before joining a few potential investors at Sea Oat Plantation, an exclusive golfing community, for a quick nine. He'd bullshitted about his handicap and had one last beer before realizing he wouldn't make David's full practice. Maybe if he hadn't stopped to flirt with the beer cart girl, he would have made it in enough time to watch David throw some pitches.

Sure enough, the pride of Moonlight sat spraddle-legged and loose next to Hunt's father, who never left the house without a crease in his trousers or a collared shirt. Hunt couldn't recall seeing his father in his undershirt and boxers but a handful of times, mostly when they went on hunting trips and Mitchell had to shuck out of his waders and wet thermals. Mitchell had a certain standard he held himself to . . . and everyone close to him.

Hunt's father sat erect, leaning slightly forward, eyes fastened on David, who stood listening to Don show him the proper way to grip the ball for what looked to be a curve or a slider.

"Dad," Hunt said, as he walked up. Then he shifted his gaze to Rhett. "Long time, man."

Rhett gave the lazy smile that, no doubt, sent many hearts into a quick trot. "Doesn't seem like it, though." He held out a hand.

Hunt gave it a hard, fast shake and slid onto the bench. "Yeah, time flies whether you're having fun or not." Again, the bitterness. Wouldn't do to let it leak out too much.

"True enough. Good to see you," Rhett said, glancing back at Don positioning David's arms. The kid looked focused on the task at hand and hadn't seemed to notice Hunt had arrived. For some reason he wanted David to see him, to smile, to want to please his father. If only because the thing he had that Rhett didn't was a kid. God, he was reaching for a way to beat Rhett, the way he always had. Rhett probably hated kids. After all, it was a kid who'd fucked up Rhett's life last summer. Guess that was another thing he had on Rhett—Hunt had never killed someone.

"What brings you back to Shitville?" Hunt asked.

Rhett issued a chuckle. "That's what they call it now? No longer 'America's backyard'?"

"We still have all those godforsaken no-see-ums, so it's kinda like a backyard . . . next to a dump."

"Hope you're not trying to interest Rhett in investing in his home state. If so, you're going about it the wrong way." Mitchell McCroy's lips seemed frozen in perpetual downturn.

"I'm joking, Dad. Rhett knows that. Don't get your shorts in a twist."

"My shorts are never in a twist," Mitchell said, jabbing a thick finger toward the pitcher's mound. "I don't like the way Don has him addressing the batter. He needs a wider stride for more power."

"Don knows what he's doing," Hunt said.

"Maybe we need to look around for someone who knows new techniques. Don's getting on up there." Hunt's dad narrowed his eyes in that critical manner that made Hunt's dander rise. Mitchell had no business here. He wished to hell he'd never mentioned David taking pitching lessons to his dad. The practice field mere yards outside their office was too much a temptation for the old man.

"Good pitching hasn't changed, has it?" Rhett asked, doing what he'd always done—defusing the situation between Hunt and Mitchell.

His old friend wore a Rolex on his tanned wrist. His clothes looked casually rumpled, but Hunt would be willing to bet they'd come out of some Rodeo Drive shop priced at what most people paid as a mortgage. Jealousy pecked at him despite his best efforts to not give a damn about how successful Rhett was. The dude had come home because his life was fucked up. He'd run over a kid and then went ballistic on television. Obviously, he had issues.

Hunt didn't. Or at least nothing of that proportion.

"Sure it has," Mitchell said, clasping his hands between his knees. "Or don't you watch baseball out in California?"

"Sure. When I'm not getting my junk waxed or having Pedro bring me martinis at the pool," Rhett said.

Hunt gave a bark of laughter, but his father frowned. "Wax your junk? What's that code for? Doesn't matter. What matters is that Hunter get that boy the best coach possible. Anyone can see the potential he has. He's big, strong, and athletic. He could probably be better than Hunter with a little work. Maybe David will be the one to make it."

The unstated words fell hard, crushing Hunt. He didn't want to give a shit what his old man thought about him and his failures, but the words left unsaid weighed heavy on him. *Because Hunter here couldn't cut the mustard.* "I'll take care of David. I'm his father."

Mitchell crooked an eyebrow. "That's what the blood test said."

"Cut it the fuck out, Dad," Hunt said, anger finally inching up his back, flushing him with heat. His father had to bag on him in front of Rhett. Of course.

"Language, son," Mitchell said, easing up from his seated position. "I'm going to walk out and speak to Don. I won't interfere. Just want to say hello."

Rhett was silent as Mitchell made his way toward the dugout and eventually out toward the mound.

"I can see your father hasn't changed," Rhett said.

"Nah, he's still a son of a bitch." Hunt gave a tight laugh.

"How are things with you?" Rhett said, polite as ever. That was Rhett. Never confrontational, always the peacemaker. And fucking lucky in life, like a shiny penny that was never passed over.

"Good. Just put together a big deal out on Bohicket Island." God, why had he done that? Pissing match with an effing millionaire Hollywood hunk? He sounded defensive. Trying to be important in some small way.

"I'm surprised at how things have built up. Hardly recognized the town."

"Yeah, it's growing. Perfect location for vacationers. Who would have thought?"

Theirs was an awkward conversation. Two guys who'd once been good friends who'd drifted into different currents, and now they found themselves surprisingly beside one another again. Wasn't like Hunt could come out and say, "Why didn't you ever call me? Why weren't you there when things were too hard to face alone? When I needed a friend?"

'Cause that would have made him a little bitch, whining about feelings and all that shit. But Hunt resented the fact that Rhett had gone away and erased the life he'd had like it hadn't mattered. He'd deleted Hunt. In fact, Hunt would probably have trouble getting tickets to Rhett's stupid late-night show. He'd have to call and say, "Um, I'm this guy he had his first beer with. Uh, we used to climb the water tower, watch porn, and shoot crows together. Think he can get me some tickets?"

Stuck in his damned craw that he was so unimportant to everyone. He hated feeling like that, too. He didn't want to need other people's approval . . . but somehow he did.

"I had forgotten how pretty it is here," Rhett said, looking out at the woods showing off fall color. "Sorry I didn't do a good job of keeping in touch. I wasn't a good friend."

"No big deal. People move away. I did. I was on the road and stuff." Hunt hoped Rhett couldn't hear the emotion in his voice. He didn't want Rhett to know his casual dismissal of their friendship had hurt him. "It's whatever, you know?"

Rhett frowned. "Yeah, whatever, but I'm sorry."

"It's cool."

Silence stretched a cold shadow between them.

Hunt turned his attention to his father, who demonstrated a motion to David. His son's gaze found Hunt and the kid smiled. Hunt couldn't stop the pleasure that bloomed inside him. Here was a person who thought Hunt important.

"He's a good kid," Rhett said.

"Yeah, he is."

"So much like you. It startled me when I first met him. He looks more like you than Summer."

Hunt nodded, pride joining the pleasure inside him. He'd not had much cause to feel such an emotion. Yet the kid out on the mound watching his grandfather with hungry eyes evoked it. "David has her eyes. Her stubbornness."

"Never remembered Summer being stubborn back in school. She was pretty easygoing, but she's changed."

"She's different. I didn't see her for a while after high school. The whole pregnancy thing was . . . awkward. Shouldn't have happened and then . . . suddenly I was a father. I wasn't ready for that. I didn't do right by David."

Rhett didn't say anything.

"I'm trying to change things," Hunt said, wondering why he admitted this to Rhett.

"I don't think anyone is really ready to be a father, huh? Or that's what I've heard." Rhett's tone wasn't accusing. Just conversational. It occurred to Hunt this was how Rhett got all those movie stars to say things they didn't mean to say.

"Definitely not at nineteen. I don't know how Summer managed to be a mom and go to school at the same time. She could have, you know, skipped it all and no one would have known."

"Mm," Rhett murmured. "That's true."

"Sometimes I wish she would have. It's wrong, because David is great, but that one decision molded the rest of my life. Sometimes . . . nah, never mind." God, what was he saying? Why not just get out a blade, open up a vein, and bleed out? Rhett wasn't even trying to get him to say these things, but yet they were spilling out. Dark, ugly truths he'd never want anyone to hear.

"You resent her for having the baby?" Rhett asked.

"Not anymore. But back then, I did. But, hey, it was her choice, right? Isn't that what all the women libbers say?"

"I don't think they like being called that. Maybe go with *feminists* or *pro-choice advocates*." Rhett said it with a smile.

"Yeah, I'm politically incorrect, I guess. Dumb redneck. Sorry." Hunt tried to remember what they'd been talking about. He didn't want to admit to the mistakes in his life. "I was just commenting on Summer's stubbornness. She's like the ocean. Finds a path no matter what you erect against her. But I can't complain. Summer never asked for one damned thing from me."

Rhett didn't respond. Instead he stared out at the field, his face reflecting an indiscernible emotion. In the dying light, a golden hue bathed the field, a rarity seen only in November when the orange and reds of the hardwoods lining the outfield greedily pulled at the last rays, desperately soaking in the remaining warmth before darkness covered them. The setting was poetic, the emotions between him and Rhett not so much.

Rhett looked back at Hunt. "I know about how one decision can fuck you. One simple veer off the path and everything changes."

"Yeah. I'm sorry about that, man."

"Thanks, but that's how life is, right? Tons of people make those seemingly simple decisions every day without knowing how quick life can change. They buy a lottery ticket with the rent money and become millionaires. Or they buy the last ticket on the *Titanic* and get a watery grave. We can never predict the ramifications of a simple decision. I took a shortcut to avoid traffic and a child died. A simple, split-second decision that on any other day would have saved me a few minutes to the studio."

"Is that what happened? They said you'd been texting, not paying attention."

Rhett stiffened. "Who's *they*? The press? You think they know what happened?"

"You saying that's not true?"

Rhett's face narrowed. "If *they* say it is, it must be, huh? Where there's smoke and all that crap."

Hunt latched his hands together and trained his eyes on David and his father. Don looked up and shot him a look. Hunt knew that look. *Come do something with your old man.*

Sliding off the bleacher, Hunt stood. "I need to rescue Don. Mitchell's obviously trying to hijack the lessons."

"Like I said, same old Mitchell," Rhett said, a wry grin twisting his handsome features as he relaxed his posture. Water off a duck's back. Nothing truly bothered Rhett. He rolled with the punches, handled whatever came his way, and came out smelling like a petunia. But maybe this time his old friend couldn't undo what he'd done, any more than Hunt could undo what had happened between him and Summer all those years ago. Sometimes mistakes stuck with you despite your best effort to shake them loose. Hunt knew, because he'd spent nine years trying to pretend away his own son. He regretted he'd done that. More than anyone could know.

Hunt made his way through the dugout, marveling at how familiar and yet foreign the squat concrete bunker seemed to him. He'd spent too many years sitting on that bench, awaiting his call to the mound. Somewhere near the third screw, he'd carved his and Molly's initials into the plank. Probably painted over now.

"If you'd just get the ball back *here*, see?" Mitchell said, jerking David's arm at an awkward angle. "You'd be able to put better rotation on the ball."

"That's not exactly true, Mitch," Don said, shaking his head.

"The hell it ain't," Mitchell said, maneuvering David's hand. "See? Let your elbow come slightly toward your ribs when you start your forward motion and then whip—"

"Dad, stop," Hunt said, taking his son's arm. "David's had enough for today."

"He's still got plenty of pitches in him. Gotta work on the curve. The kid can't even throw a curve!"

"It's okay. I can try, Dad," David said, his voice growing solemn at the obvious tension between Hunt and his father.

"No, you don't need to wear out your arm. You're not used to throwing a lot of pitches and need to work on arm strength. The curve will come. No need to rush it. Why don't you go check out what Rhett's doing? Maybe he can prank call some celebs or something. Scoot."

Had he just said *scoot*? Jesus, he sounded like his mother.

David shifted his gaze between a grandfather who looked ready to blow and Hunt. Hunt winked. "Tell Rhett to tell you about the monkey."

"The monkey?"

"Yeah, go on."

David tucked his beat-up glove under his arm and loped back to the dugout. As he entered, Hunt turned on his father. "Don't start, old man."

"Start what?"

"Doing to David what you did to me. It's not happening," Hunt said, crossing his arms, trying to tamp down the anger creeping into his gut.

"What did I do to you? Give you every opportunity to succeed? Don bought a boat with what I paid for your opportunity. And look what it got me."

"Got you? I'm not a fucking investment, Dad. I'm a person. You took the one thing I could do well and mined it. You ignored all the other parts of me. It was all baseball all the time. When I wasn't practicing, you made me watch games and break down pitchers' movements. I couldn't even be normal. You're the reason I didn't make it."

"Bullshit," his father said, jabbing a meaty finger his way. "Same old song and dance from you. Always someone else's fault. You had an opportunity in front of you on a silver platter and you pissed it away to chase skirt and feel good. Don't put this on me. Your failure is yours."

Hunt curled his fist and thought about decking his father. He wanted to for all those years his father had ridden his ass, made him throw a ball over and over until he got it right, and refused to let him make any excuses. Mitchell had pushed and pushed Hunt until he broke . . . and when he did, his old man would berate him for his tears. Sometimes he hated his father . . . with a passion that exceeded all other passions.

"Dad?" David called from the bleachers. "Did you really kiss a monkey?"

Rhett called out, "Never make a bet with your father. He'll do whatever it takes to win."

Hunt swallowed the anger and pain before walking away from the source and toward the one thing he could do right in his life—David. No way he'd be like Mitchell McCroy. Hunt wouldn't ride his son's ass every day, pointing out every flaw, making him feel not good enough for him. A father wasn't supposed to control his kid, nor was he supposed to build the kid up only to let him fall down a concrete set of steps, crumpling at the base like a cheap suit. Hunt wouldn't ignore the parts of David that weren't so good. He wanted to love all of the boy and be the father he wished he'd had growing up.

"Where are you going?" Mitchell called. In his father's voice he heard the anger. The old man wanted to fight, wanted to bring up all Hunt's shortfalls. It was as if the man reveled in Hunt's failures.

"I got better things to do," Hunt called, ducking through the dugout and heading back toward the benches.

Rhett still grinned and David's eyes danced with amusement.

"The monkey's name was Lily and she smelled like old shoes, but I wasn't letting Rhett win the boom box, so I did what the DJ at the radio station told me to. He said I'd have to kiss Lily. He just didn't tell me she was a chimp."

"You're joking," David said, his eyes alight with laughter.

"You guys want to head to the Rib Hut for dinner? I'm in the mood for barbecue," Hunt said.

David nodded. "Will you come, too, Rhett? I want to hear more stories about you and my dad."

Rhett's gaze met Hunt's. Again, he couldn't read his old friend. "I'd like that, but we better call your mom. You know how moms get."

"Yeah," David said, disgust edging his voice. "They're crazy."

Hunt gave a bark of laughter. "Come on, don't rag on your mom. You know how much she loves you."

David rolled his eyes. "Yeah, they're good for that, too."

CHAPTER TWELVE

April 2003

"You look so pretty, Summer," Carolyn Valentine said to her daughter's reflection in the mirror.

"Thanks, Mama," Summer said, staring back at the girl in the mirror. She couldn't believe how good she looked. Seriously. How could a little makeup and some highlights in her hair make her glow? Though she'd lost only seven pounds, she looked thinner.

The size-twelve cerulean dress fit her perfectly and sat slightly off her shoulders with small seed pearls dotting the placard below her breasts. The cut hid the slight pooch of her tummy and fell like a Grecian waterfall to her ankles. A cluster of pearls and rhinestones on the strappy sandals just matched the ones on the placard. Half of her hair was twisted into a knot with a small beehive bump and the rest fell in pretty curls to brush her neck. Her eye makeup made her look slightly like Cleopatra, but her soft, pink lips kept it from being over the top. Her mother had splurged on some chandelier earrings that felt too heavy but looked perfect.

"Wowsa," her dad said from the doorway of her bedroom. "You look . . . you know, I'm not sure I want to let that punk waiting downstairs take you to the prom."

"Hunt's here already?" Summer asked, her nerves amping.

"Yep, him and two others out in a limo on the street. They've been posing for pics on the hood of the car. The driver is taking pictures with one of the kids' flip phones. Can't believe those kids have cell phones. And a limo."

"A limo?" Summer repeated, swallowing hard. Suddenly prom felt bigger than what it was. She stood here sparkling in her mirror, looking strangely pretty, and downstairs her date awaited her. She'd never dreamed she'd be going to prom with a popular guy . . . with popular kids. A sweet longing for pajamas and her recorded copies of *Gilmore Girls* emerged. She wasn't the girl staring back in the mirror. She was plain ol' nerdy Summer pretending to be something she wasn't.

Still, Rhett was in the limo, and that was a game changer.

Because she wanted to please him, even if she knew she was merely a means to a party for the senior class. They were using her, but even so, she couldn't stop wanting to be near Rhett. She was a compass. He was a pole. She turned toward him.

Summer supposed she shouldn't be thinking about Rhett when she had a date with Hunt McCroy, but over the past two weeks, she'd fallen even harder for her study buddy. She'd told herself not to, but he made her heart trip every time she looked at him.

"Mom, where's the boutonniere? You picked it up, didn't you?"

Her mother patted an errant strand of Summer's hair. "Relax. It's on the table."

Maisie stuck her head under their dad's arm. "There's a boy downstairs. Oh, Sum, you look pretty. Like a movie star."

Summer moved toward the doorway and rubbed her sister's head. "Thanks, kiddo."

Maisie swatted at her hand. "Don't."

Summer tried to calm the butterflies assaulting her tummy. God, she hoped she wouldn't get diarrhea or something. Who knew being social was so terrifying? Maybe she should have had something to eat instead of skipping lunch so she'd look thinner in her dress. Sucking in a deep breath, she released it. "I'm so nervous, Mama."

Her father was the one to reach out and brush her temple with a kiss. "Sweetheart, you have no need to be nervous. It's just a dance. You look incredibly beautiful. That guy down there's lucky to have you on his arm."

She bet Hunt wouldn't think so, though she had to admit, she looked much better than she expected. Maybe he wouldn't be so ashamed to be with her. Maybe she didn't look like such a charity case. "I'm pretty sure I can't look any better than this."

With that last affirmation, she descended the stairs.

Hunt stood in the middle of her living room, studying the collection of bass that hung on their walls. Her father entered tons of fishing tournaments and loved to display the fruits of his labors, whether it was a bass, a deer, or that one hog that sat in the corner. Summer jokingly called it the "Room of Death," and she wasn't far off.

"Hey," she said, aware that her parents were right behind her.

Hunt turned and his eyes widened. "You look great, Summer."

Her date looked pretty dang good in his tux, too. Hunt wore a classic tuxedo that had probably never seen a rental. No doubt, he owned one to attend the social events his parents were known to attend in Charleston. They did cotillion and that sort of stuff. Hunt's bow tie was a pretty shade of blue that almost matched her dress. She wondered how he'd managed to get a matching one so quickly. She supposed rich people had ways. "You look very handsome, Hunt."

His answering smile looked almost genuine. "Thanks. So, here's the corsage. My mom picked it out. I hope it matches. You said baby blue, right?"

Technically her dress was cerulean, but close enough. "Right."

Carolyn brushed past them, grabbing Hunt's boutonniere off the dining room table. "And here's yours. I'm Summer's mom. That's her dad." Summer's mom waved toward her husband.

"I'm going to take a picture of y'all pinning it on," her father said.

"Sorry," Summer breathed under her breath to Hunt. "I've never gone to a dance before. They're going to take pictures."

"Sure," Hunt said with a smile in his voice. No doubt, her country-bumpkin parents amused him. But she wasn't denying her mother the chance to revel in Summer's prom pictures. That's all her mother had talked about for the last week. Prom this and prom that. Summer was glad it would be over by tomorrow . . . and that her mother hadn't insisted on going up to the school gym to snap photos like some of the mothers did. Summer had drawn that line early on. Her mother had sulked, but she'd eventually agreed when Summer threatened to call the whole thing off.

After five minutes of awkward pictures, Summer finally eased toward the door. "We have to go, Mom. I'll be home around midnight."

"You can stay out longer tonight if you want. It *is* senior prom," her mother called.

"I don't know about—" her father started.

"Hush, Jeremy. She can stay out late tonight," her mother said, guiding Summer toward the door. Her mother gave a quick wave to Rhett and Graysen, who stood by the limo looking at Graysen's flip phone. The two looked up, and Summer's breath caught at how gorgeous they both were. Total golden couple.

Graysen wore a slinky dress of gold that hugged every angle and curve. The bodice molded to her breasts, making them look somehow perfect, and the dress skimmed her taut stomach and the flare of her slim hips before swishing around her feet with a small train. Her hair was piled upon her head, and dangling yellow-diamond earrings twinkled at her ears. Her makeup was flawless, and she looked like she could grace the cover of *Seventeen*'s Prom edition.

Suddenly Summer felt dowdy, like a fat girl trussed up for slaughter. She'd seen *Carrie*. Was there a bucket of pig's blood waiting for her somewhere?

Rhett looked like the man he'd been named after—Rhett Butler. Suavely cutting quite the figure in the black tux that cut at the waist and dropped to a traditional tail in the back, he took her breath away. His burnished hair was coiffed perfectly, and she could swear she saw the twinkle in his blue eyes from the front porch stoop. The angelic opposite of her brooding date.

"Wow, look at our Funny Valentine," Rhett called, his smile big, making her feel both calm and nervous at the same time.

Graysen clapped her hands. "Oh, Sum, you look so pretty. That dress is perfect on you."

Summer smiled. "You look gorgeous, Gray."

Graysen gave her a hug and pulled her against the car. "Take a pic of us, Rhett."

Rhett took her phone as Summer pasted a smile on her face. "Prettiest girls in this town."

Graysen beamed. "Yeah, this is what happens when you stop wearing Birkenstocks and hoodies."

Summer tried to ignore the tug of hurt at Graysen's words. She liked her Birkenstocks and hoodie. Okay, so maybe she used them like a security blanket, but they were comfortable. And her.

"Can we jet already?" Hunt said, looking impatient. "I'm tired of pictures. Jesus."

The driver opened the back of the limo with a flourish and the four of them climbed in, Summer being extra careful not to snag her dress on her heels. Her parents had sacrificed to get her this dress and shoes. She wasn't about to pull the first thread. She double-checked her pretty white rose corsage, too. White roses, looping satin, and little seed pearls. Like her mother, she would let it dry and pack it into her memory box.

"Whew, thank God that's over," Hunt said, reaching into the fancy center console and bringing out a bottle of vodka.

"Ooh, let's do shots," Graysen said, grabbing two crystal glasses from the gleaming shelf.

Summer's eyes widened. Hunter had two bottles of vodka on ice along with a six pack of beer.

"Not for me," Rhett said, grabbing a beer and wrenching it from the plastic holder. He cracked it and lifted it. "A toast to senior prom 2003!"

Graysen handed Summer a glass and Hunt poured a shot of vodka inside. Summer didn't want vodka. She had never drunk, well, outside of a wine cooler once. Even that had made her light-headed. But she didn't want to look like a prudish loser, so she clinked her glass against Graysen's and then Hunt's.

Hunt grinned like a gator. "Well, well, little Summer knows how to party."

The blush that covered her face was answer enough, but she murmured, "I've drunk before."

Graysen and Hunt slammed back the shot so Summer did the same.

Dear God, it burned. Bad.

And it was terrible.

She tried not to choke as the liquor burned a path down her throat, but she couldn't help herself. "Oh God."

Graysen laughed. "Okay, lightweight."

Hunt steadied Summer's glass and poured her another shot. "If you're going to do it, Valentine, do it right."

Rhett took the glass from her hand. "Hey, now, let's not get too loaded before we get to the dance. There could be a Breathalyzer. Save it for the after-party."

Hunt made a face and took the glass from Rhett, tossing it back. "That's total bullshit. They say that every year."

Relief flooded Summer because she hadn't wanted a second shot of vodka, but she also didn't want to look scared of drinking. Saying no was a whole lot harder than everyone said. Especially when you were the resident nerd hanging with the cool kids.

The vodka had already warmed her stomach, taking the edge off her nerves. One shot wouldn't register on a Breathalyzer, would it? She didn't think so, but she also didn't want anything to jeopardize her shot at valedictorian. That was her ticket to the school's two-thousand-dollar alumni scholarship. Bad choices led to bad consequences. She heard those words in her head . . . in her father's voice.

The limo pulled up to the high school gym, where two huge lanterns perched on the aged stone flanking the entryway. A canopy of colored clothes lined with lights stretched atop the doorway.

"Wow," Summer said, peering out the window. "Y'all really did a great job."

"Thank you," Graysen said. She looked well pleased with herself. "It was my idea. The whole Arabian Nights thing. Wait until you see the inside."

The driver opened the door and gestured with his hand. "My ladies and gentlemen."

It all felt so grand—the limo, the flickering lanterns, the sequins on the dresses of the girls streaming into the entry with their tuxedoed dates. Summer paused, lagging behind, enjoying the thrill of prom. Graysen had been right—prom was more than just a dance. It was an experience.

"Oh my Lord, look at Addison Meeker's dress. Totally the wrong color for her, and that ruffle over her boobs? What the hell was she thinking?" Graysen said, leaning in conspiratorially. Graysen's breath smelled like mint and alcohol.

"Well, she has a big chest. Sometimes girls who are well-endowed feel like they should cover it up, I guess." Summer liked Addison, who was at least a DD in cup size. The girl always slumped like she was trying to minimize her assets. Summer felt bad for her.

"That's true. Come on, time to party," Graysen said, looping her arm through Summer's and dragging her toward the steps, where Hunter and Rhett conversed with a few other guys. Everyone was smiling . . . except Mrs. Miller, the vice principal, who was eagle eyeing everyone. At one point the woman leaned close to Hunt and took a deep breath. Was she actually trying to smell alcohol on him? And was there a Breathalyzer?

"Hi, Mrs. Miller," Summer said, donning the good-student smile she always used around teachers.

"Oh, Summer, don't you look . . . different."

Summer's face must have reflected her confusion.

"Oh no, dear. You look beautiful. I didn't mean you didn't. Just not like yourself. And who are you here with?" Mrs. Miller looked around, her gaze skipping over Rhett and Hunt and going out to the space beyond. "Or are you here alone?"

"No. I'm here with Hunt," Summer said, nodding toward her date, who seemed to be deep in a conversation about someone's truck and a fight after a baseball game. He glanced over at Summer and smiled, acknowledging her perusal.

"Hunter McCroy?" Mrs. Miller said. The incredulousness in the older woman's voice was both hurtful and amusing.

"Yes, ma'am."

"Huh," was all Mrs. Miller said before taking the group's tickets and telling everyone how nice they looked. Then the four of them walked into the draped tunnel covered in twinkling lights that led to the darkened gym. Just before they entered, Summer glanced at Rhett. The lights glinted off his golden hair, and his strong jaw seemed to invite little kisses along its length. He epitomized gorgeousness. Catching her gaze, he gave her a wink and a smile.

Just like the song her grandmother used to play. A wink and a smile. Dang, if those two things together weren't a dangerous combination.

Rhett placed his hand on Graysen's waist and looked down at her. She smiled and Rhett kissed her.

Okay. Slap of reality.

Hunter stood behind her and she could feel him close, smell his cologne. *Stop longing for Rhett and pay attention to the guy who awkwardly placed the corsage on your wrist, nerd girl. Rhett belongs to Graysen. You're with Hunt . . . at least for tonight.*

Summer stepped into the noisy gym. Lights crisscrossed above them, holding alternating colored lanterns. Gauzy fabrics covered the collapsed bleachers, and filigreed panels completed the exotic theme. Small tables holding flickering lanterns surrounded the dance floor, where couples were writhing and shaking to the band on the raised platform. No more stinky gym and faded mural of a buccaneer. Instead, the space had been transformed into something magical.

"Whoa, this is incredible," Summer said, turning a circle.

"I told you," Graysen said, laughing as she twined her arms around Rhett. Her Boy Wonder smiled down, his gaze adoring.

Summer wanted to gag but instead, she turned to Hunt. "Should we get a table?"

Hunt shrugged. "Yeah, let's get one in the back."

Rhett and Graysen headed toward the back right corner. As Summer moved to follow them, Hunt grabbed her elbow. "Hey, put this in your bag. None of the teachers will check you. They're already all over me."

He opened his jacket and tapped the top of a pint bottle.

"I'm not sure if I—" Summer stuttered, stepping back.

Hunt pulled her closer. "Come on, Sum. They won't even think to check you. You're such a good girl." His arm twined around her shoulders and he pulled her close, an almost hug.

Hunt smelled expensive, and he radiated warmth beneath his jacket. She'd never been this close to a guy before, outside of her father, and she found it heady. Of course, it was Hunt, a guy who didn't like her, but his voice was soft and pleading. And he was her date.

"My clutch isn't that big. I'll have to take out my lipstick."

"Good girl." He smiled, looping his arms around her, pulling her into a hug. "Be cool about it."

Summer slipped her hand between them, feeling for the bottle. Hunt dropped a kiss on her forehead. It was soft and dry, and it made her slightly tingly.

But you have nothing for Hunt. You don't like or respect him. Stop being silly over a covert operation. His hands on your back mean nothing. The hot breath he's blowing against your hair is a ruse.

Still, Hunt was a good-looking guy with a lean body, wavy hair, and expensive cologne. Plus, he had his arms around her . . . and Rhett had his arms around Graysen. Sometimes a gal had to be grateful for what she had at hand rather than what stood several feet away from her . . . in love with another girl.

Hunt wasn't that bad. In fact, he was a pretty good catch for any girl. Even a discerning geek like Summer.

With her finger and thumb, she twisted open the clasp of her borrowed clutch and jammed the pint bottle inside. "Okay. I got it."

"Good girl," Hunt said, releasing her.

She found she missed his arms, but then she shook herself and followed her date to the table farthest from the teachers clustered around the refreshment table. A few other of the popular kids who she knew only from class or the occasional club meeting joined them. A few of the guys eyed her and lifted their eyebrows. Summer jerked her chin up and went to stand by Graysen, who was oohing and aahing over Katie B's slinky dress and the shoes Ashley Goodwin wore. They were Manolos borrowed from her NYC cousin who was in town for a family event. Summer thought they looked painful and strange, but she nodded when everyone declared them to die for. Then Molly walked up with a swaggering guy in a black tux.

"Hello, everyone, this is Joshie. He's from Cedarwood Prep in Charleston." Molly beamed at the boy who stood almost as tall as Hunt. "He plays lacrosse."

Joshie frowned at the nickname. "It's just Josh. What's up?" He held his hand out to Rhett, who took it and gave it a quick shake.

"I'm Rhett. This is Hunt, Shawn, and Jamie."

Hunt glowered at the guy and didn't offer his hand. He merely jerked his head in acknowledgment. Josh didn't seem to take offense. Instead he surveyed the gym. "Been a while since I've been to a dance in a gym. I'm digging the old-school vibe. Cedarwood's is held at a downtown hotel. Which makes it convenient."

He didn't elaborate, but Summer assumed he meant the hotel was centrally located. Or maybe he was thinking about the minibar in each room? Or the queen-size beds? She wasn't really sure. Maybe all three.

"Prom in this gym is a tradition," Hunt muttered, crossing his arms. He looked defensive. Pissed. Kinda hotter than normal, and at that moment Summer was glad she'd said yes to prom. Even if he'd used his soft brown eyes and pretty words to get her to hide liquor in her purse.

Molly narrowed her eyes and then turned to Graysen. "You look pretty, Gray. The dress is perfect."

Graysen smiled, like the queen bee Nessa had dubbed her. "You, too, Molly."

Molly turned her attention to Summer. "Wow, you look different. I didn't know you even wore dresses."

Harsh. "Thank you, Molly. I actually have another in my closet. Hanging right next to my power pantsuits."

Molly's lip curled into a pseudosmile. "And you tell jokes. Winner, winner, chicken dinner, Hunt."

Hunt took Summer's hand and pulled her to him. Then he patted her rump and eyed her boobs. "Yeah, that's what I was thinking."

Summer knew her eyes were googly but Molly didn't seem to notice as she sniffed, took Josh's arm, and tugged him toward the dance floor. "Come on, Joshie. I want to dance." She looked back at Hunt. "I want to feel *your* arms around me."

Hunt's body tightened beside her and she felt his anger.

"Don't worry about it, man," Rhett said, sinking onto a chair and pulling Graysen onto his lap. "She's trying to goad you. Ignore her and pay attention to your date. And the way she fills that dress out."

Rhett winked at Summer.

Hunt dropped his arm from around her waist and sat down next to Rhett. "Yeah. Whatever. Shawn, you and Jamie go grab some punch. I'll hook you up. Bring that purse over here, Summer."

He patted the chair next to him as his minions went off to do as he bid.

Summer surveyed the dance floor. Molly had disappeared into the crowd with her prep-school trophy. Out of sight, out of Hunt's mind. She hoped.

Just as she set her purse between her and Hunt, she caught Nessa coming toward her with her geeky clarinet player in tow. Nessa wore a fitted bustier with satin ribbons that streamed down and a tulle skirt. She'd paired a glittery pair of black Chucks with the ensemble, making her look a bit like a deranged ballerina on the run. The look was fashion-forward, cool, and very Nessa.

But obviously Graysen didn't think so because the face she made when Nessa parked her hip on the table and studied Summer sitting beside Hunt was almost comical.

"Wowie, wow, wow, look at you. Are you showing shoulder, Summertime?" Nessa drawled, her green eyes twinkling in the low lantern light.

"Who are you?" Hunt asked.

Nessa delivered a withering glance at Summer's date. "Your worst nightmare, Romeo."

Hunt did his glower thing and then rose. "I'm going to get punch."

"Thought Jamie and Shawn were fetching your refreshments." Rhett's voice held laughter.

"I need some air. I'll be back, Summer." He tossed her a backward glance before drifting toward the two tables holding iced cookies and stacks of punch glasses.

Well, at least he remembered his manners.

"You look cute, Nessa," Summer said, leaning over to say hello to her date, who looked appalled as he stood there with all the jocks.

Nessa grinned like a naughty nymph. "I'm channeling Madonna meets Tinkerbell."

"And succeeding," Summer said, patting the chair Hunt had vacated. "Sit down."

And this was how prom went. Summer spent the night sipping vodka-laden fruit punch, chatting about dresses with Nessa and the other girls, and making one appearance on the dance floor after Graysen insisted that Hunter dance with her. Summer would give the magical entrance to prom a 9.5, the actual dance a 4.5, and the slow dance with Hunt a firm 6.7 only because he didn't step on her feet and didn't look at Molly dancing with Josh more than ten times. So when they finally crowned Rhett and Graysen prom king and queen, respectively—as if everyone didn't already know they'd be the bejeweled monarchy of Mangham High—and Hunt downed the last of the contraband booze, Summer was happy to see the back end of "Arabian Nights."

"Time to party," Graysen crowed as they piled into the limo, each of them listing slightly more than when they had first emerged at the gym.

Summer's thighs felt oddly heavy and warm. Her head swam a bit, and she had the absurd inclination to giggle. Maybe drinking vodka and beer and whatever else Hunt had in his liquor cabinet at the beach house wasn't such a bad idea after all. Liquid courage, that's what they called booze, and Summer understood why. She felt free . . .

and pretty . . . and young. Ready to have some fun and be normal. Not nerdy and lonely and . . .

Rhett pulled Graysen into his lap and kissed her as the limo pulled away from the curb. Graysen wound her arms around Rhett and shifted so she fell onto the soft leather seat, pulling Rhett with her. They were all hands, legs, and lips.

Summer glanced over at Hunt. He cough-laughed before saying, "Get a room."

Rhett and Graysen both laughed, but they didn't stop making out.

Hunt shook his head, poured a shot of vodka, and tossed it back. Then he grabbed Summer's hand and jerked her toward him. Not expecting him to pull her toward him, Summer sort of fell into him. Hunt smiled and said, "When in Rome."

She didn't have time to think before Hunt's mouth covered hers. Hunt took advantage of the gasp she issued, his tongue invading as his hand came up to clasp her head and hold her to him.

Summer didn't know what a good kiss was because she'd never had the pleasure . . . or the displeasure. Either one. But Hunt's mouth on hers wasn't unpleasant. He tasted like Big Red gum and medicine, and she liked the way he curled an arm around her, bringing her breasts to the hardness of his chest. Just like in the Jude Deveraux books she'd read. Skin on skin, lips on lips, desire curling around her. The whole thing was strangely intoxicating. Or maybe she was intoxicated from the spiked prom punch and it felt better than what it should.

Because in her awakened a hunger for something. For being normal. For kissing a guy. For Hunt McCroy.

The least likely boy.

"Well, look at that. Our good girl may not be so good after all," Graysen said, interrupting Summer's first kiss.

Hunt ripped his lips from hers. "Well, I'm just the guy to teach her how to be a little bad."

"Yeah, you are," Graysen said, reaching for a beer. "Hope you have more booze at your house. You only live once."

Summer lifted her fingers to her lips. Her first kiss and it had been with the superpopular, not-so-nice star pitcher. Who would have thought Summer had it in her? Maybe Hunt was right. Maybe she needed a guy to teach her to be a little bad.

But then her gaze met Rhett's. A question lingered in the depths of his baby blues. Did she want this?

Summer licked her lips and pressed the material of her dress to her thighs. Maybe she was in over her head? Kissing Hunt was a bad idea. Drinking too much was an even worse idea. She couldn't do something stupid. She didn't even like Hunt.

But just as she had that thought, Graysen slid back into Rhett's lap and jerked his head toward hers.

Right.

Exactly so.

Summer placed her hand in Hunt's and gave him a smile. He smiled back.

Exactly so.

CHAPTER THIRTEEN

November, present day

"Pass me that spool of ivory satin," Summer said, pinching the base of the orchids she was making into a corsage. She hated making corsages because they took an enormous amount of time for such a small reward. Summer much preferred helping her sister create big, lush bouquets designed to grace pulpits or casket tops.

"So what's he like?" Maisie asked, jabbing a wire between her lips and tossing the spool toward her older sister.

"Who?"

"You know damned well who," Maisie muttered around the floral wire.

"Rhett? Oh, he's fine."

"I'll say," Maisie said, managing a smile around the wire. Or she had gas.

Maisie took the wire and wrapped it around the base of a white rose. Summer hated white roses. They made her think of death.

Summer's sister may have been seven years her junior, but she didn't look it. The recent divorce had weighed heavy on Maisie, and the young mother looked tired and worn. Which was why Summer was quick to pitch in when Maisie needed help. Her sister had someone who ran the front of the shop and handled deliveries, but when there were multiple big events like homecoming or a large funeral, she needed an extra set of hands. Summer wasn't necessarily talented at creating floral displays, but she could trim stems and make bows.

"He's not like he is on television," Summer said, not wanting to talk about Rhett, mostly because, like years before, she couldn't seem to get him out of her mind, but if she avoided the fact that late night's favorite son was staying next door, Maisie would be suspicious.

Yeah, he'd been on her mind too much. So what?

Lord, the sadness in his eyes haunted her, and, God help her, she wanted to make that better for him. Problem was, she didn't know how, and she had no right to want anything when it came to Rhett. She'd learned that long ago. There had been something between them even back then, but it was not romantic in nature. More of an understanding, an acknowledgment that each could see through the bullshit life shoveled their way. Had nothing to do with the erratic beating of hearts or breathless kisses . . . at least not on Rhett's behalf. "I mean, he's charming and funny, but he's not dazzling. Eh, I take that back. He's dazzling but real. That's it. Rhett's still a golden boy, but not so shiny you can't look at him."

"Wow, you've really thought about this," Maisie said, tossing a quizzical glance her way.

Crap. She'd overshared, and now Maisie might glimpse the former longing that had made a strong comeback. Fine. She could admit it to herself—she'd never really gotten over the crush on Rhett. He had always been her ideal, but she was also reasonable enough to understand that she'd built Rhett up in her head. Sure, he was a good guy and a Hollywood celebrity, but he was just a guy. He scratched himself, forgot to recycle, and probably didn't tip the bag boy at the grocery. Everyone had flaws. "No. I'm just saying."

"'I'm just saying' is everyone's cop-out when they don't want to admit something."

"You sound like a therapist."

"That's because I'm seeing one," Maisie said with a grin. She then jabbed the rose into the large spray, making it look somehow perfect. Summer's sister was definitely talented and had become the go-to florist in town. There were a few other florists, but none had as artistic an eye as Maisie. "Can you date your therapist? 'Cause I think Dr. Weaver is really doing it for me."

"I think that's against some law or something."

"Damn."

Her sister's teasing was almost enough to make her forget about her nosing around about Rhett. Maisie hadn't laughed much over the last year.

"You think you're ready to date?" Summer asked.

"Maybe. No. I don't know. It's still weird that I'm single again. With kids. No, two little demons. Isn't that the kiss of death on dating sites?" Maisie asked.

"I don't know. I only tried a dating site once. Had my profile up for a month before I realized I didn't have time to date. What about Brad? Is he still with the bimbo teeth cleaner?"

Last fall Maisie had left the twins with their grandmother in order to surprise her husband at his dental implant conference in San Diego. She'd left him a sexy note at the front desk, put on a slinky dress, and waited at the bar for him. But the surprise was on her when she got tired of waiting, knocked on his hotel room door, and Brad's hygienist answered wearing nothing but a robe. Then Brad walked out from the shower, wearing a towel around his hips.

"That's what I hear from the kids. Noah and Paul like her. Which pisses me off. She's an effing home wrecker and they're all, 'Geena let us make pancakes,' or 'Geena bought us a new movie.' I want to say,

'Geena is a two-bit skank who got you kids a broken family and a father only every other weekend.'"

Summer watched her sister grow agitated. Then do some breathing exercises. "It might be time for you to focus on you. Get a profile up on Match.com or something. Try online dating. Hell, ask the shrink out."

"Nah, I'm laying off anyone who calls himself 'doctor.' Maybe a football coach or an accountant?" Maisie picked up the "Thinking of You" ribbon and attached it to the arrangement.

"Don't football coaches have a bigger ego than dentists? Try the accountant. Surely people who deal with the IRS don't have egos . . . but lots of patience. The right kind of patience for twin four-year-old boys," Summer joked.

"I know some nice football coaches," Maisie said, putting her hands on her hips, "but I'm not ready to be out there. But you are. Like beyond time to get back into the dating world."

"My life feels pretty full."

"But you're not getting laid," Maisie said.

"Neither are you. Besides, sex is overrated. I have a kid, a life, and a gig tomorrow night. And I have a really good vibrator."

"You do? I mean, you use one?"

Summer rolled her eyes. "Guess I know what to get you for your next birthday."

"Oh my gosh, Sum. But don't give it to me in front of Mother."

"Who do you think recommended the one I have?" Summer couldn't help it. Joking around with her sister felt good.

Maisie recoiled, her eyes wide. "You're joking. Please tell me you're joking."

"I am," Summer finally conceded with a giggle. "Couldn't help it. Your reactions are priceless. Don't enter any poker tournaments."

"Oh yeah? You think you have a poker face? Let's talk about Rhett Bryan some more. And that giant torch for him you're toting around."

Bull's-eye.

How did Maisie know? She thought she'd gotten better at hiding the longing for Rhett. "I don't have a torch for him. And if I did, who cares? Half of America has a thing for him. He's cute."

"But it's more than that for you. I mean, Nessa once told me you were totally in love with him in high school."

"I had a crush on him in high school. So did every other girl. And when did you see Nessa?"

"She came home a few weekends ago. You had a gig in Columbia, remember? She's doing good. Nominated for preschool teacher of the year in her district, and her twin girls are so cute."

"I missed Agnes and Bess?" Nessa lived in Charleston and came home a few times a month to see her parents. She and Summer's sister had become good friends when Maisie lived in Charleston while Brad was in school. That they both had a set of twins bonded them even further.

"Don't try to change the subject. I'm just saying every time I bring up Rhett's name, I can tell. You're still into him," Maisie said.

Damn it to hell. "Fine. Once upon a time, I had a thing for him. But that torch has been extinguished. What you're sensing right now isn't about having a thing for Rhett. It's just he's an easy guy to like, and we've always been friends."

"Okay, I believe you." Maisie lifted a thin shoulder and flattened her mouth. "But if the opportunity arises to, uh, skip the vibrator in favor of a real live man, go for it. Those Hollywood types sleep with anyone, right?"

"Thanks." Nothing like being "anyone" to a man.

"You know what I mean. You won't have to worry about, you know, him bringing emotion into the equation."

"I'm pretty sure everyone feels emotion, even celebrities." Summer turned toward the collection of blooms resting in metal buckets and selected a pale-pink flower to bring depth to the rose. She didn't want to have this conversation, mostly because Rhett tempted her in ways she couldn't explain. The rational part of her knew there was no way Rhett would see her in such a light, and even if he did, having sex, letting herself fall back into love with him, would leave her with nothing but a memory. Somehow having Rhett and then losing him would be worse than never having him at all.

"I'm not saying he's a robot or incapable of love. I guess I've read too many tabloids over the years. Celebrities seem to switch their partners around frequently. Still, why not? You deserve something good. You always put yourself last. It's like you don't think you deserve good things."

"That's not true."

Maisie's eyes held doubt. "You carry around an inferiority complex."

"Do you want to do this psychoanalyzing thing? I know my flaws, but I like the way I'm living my life. I'm not a martyr, but I'm not going to jump Rhett Bryan's bones."

"Why not?"

"Because." Because her sister had dug a needle into the painful blister of rejection that plagued Summer. Not being good enough. Hell, she'd dragged that notion with her all the way from her high school days. She knew her propensity for doubt, she fought it, but somehow her self-confidence flagged when it came to grabbing the brass ring.

Maisie snorted but didn't say anything more. She knew she'd crossed a line.

"Look, I know myself. But, first, Rhett would have to be interested. He's not, Maisie. We're friends. Besides, he's a celebrity and going back to California. I don't want to . . . it's just not going to happen." She understood what her sister thought about Rhett. Maisie saw a gorgeous, charismatic host. She hadn't seen him on Summer's couch, looking so lost. The clouds in Rhett's eyes made Summer want to take away the pain, give him comfort and peace. To her, he wasn't just a lay to brag about. He was Rhett.

Maisie also didn't know what had happened the night of senior prom. The ship carrying the thing she'd wanted most had sailed, and Summer wouldn't turn the boat around. She didn't want to spend time thinking about the past—what had happened, what could have happened, what should have happened. Summer had grown accustomed to not getting what she wanted, and that was okay. She accepted her life as it was and loved it in spite of the disappointments.

"I think you're being closed off. Don't bind yourself with an expectation of failure. Don't hold yourself back from joy." Maisie narrowed her eyes and moved a piece of something that looked like a weed to a new position. Again, it made the arrangement look ten times better.

"I'm not closed off. Or joyless. I'm a realist. There's a difference." Summer shoved the corsage into a clear plastic container and took it to the giant walk-in fridge. "Besides, if you were really worried about my relationships, you would accept the goodness Mr. Happy brings me."

"Mr. Happy?"

"My special friend who has three speeds," Summer said, desperate to take their conversation back to lightness. She didn't have a vibrator, but teasing Maisie deflected talk of Rhett.

"TMI," Maisie squealed.

"I'm kidding. I don't call him Mr. Happy. I call him, 'Oh, yes.'"

Maisie threw a clump of sunflowers at her. "Stop it, weirdo."

Summer jumped back and nearly tripped over the fan Maisie used to keep the work space cool. "I better jet. As fun as this sex talk is, David will be home soon, and I have to nag him about homework, taking a shower, and staying off social media. That's part of the job, you know. And I have to Skype Jim. Greyhound Blue has a gig at the Sundown Tavern tomorrow night."

"How's that, by the way? You've been getting more and more gigs. Jim's wife's been bragging about how y'all are going to be the next big thing."

"Jim's wife is delusional. We're doing fine for a local band. That's it."

"I hate to see you wasting your talent."

"I'm not. I'm working on new songs. Just finished one that Jim's tweaking the arrangement to. We're going to play it tomorrow night. Why don't you come by? Maybe Mom can watch the kids. It would do you good, and I can tell the bartenders to keep the losers away from you."

Maisie brushed back the ginger locks that had escaped her clip and looked self-conscious. "For all my talk about doing my shrink, you know I'm not ready for that scene."

"What scene? It's the Sundown. Nothing fast about that place, though occasionally someone gets a little bent out of shape over fantasy football. I've seen one punch thrown, and that was by Fred Frye, who thought Ben Pringle was looking at his wife's dumpster."

"That's understandable. You can't avoid looking at her ass. It's so big it envelops the organ bench at church. In fact, Paul asked me one Sunday if 'that woman ate that bench.'"

"He's so adorable. But, really, there's no scene at the Sundown." Summer washed her hands in the big metal sink and dried them before riffling through her purse for her phone. She had several texts. Hunt. David. And a number that was probably Rhett, if her knowledge of area codes still held up. They were eating barbecue and would be home in an hour.

Summer should stay and help her sister, but Maisie looked to have everything under control. Besides, a hot shower, a glass of wine, and some Netflix sounded like heaven. If she left now, she could at least have the wine and shower.

"I'll see you later, Sum," Maisie said, drying her hands against her apron. She moved around the worktable and gave Summer a half hug. "Thank you for helping me . . . and making me laugh. Sorry if I got too personal. I just love you and want you to be happy."

Summer bussed a kiss against her sister's head. "Ditto, kiddo. And vibrator jokes are what big sisters are for."

When Summer slipped out the back door of the shop, inky darkness met her. Stars winked overhead, and she could see the outline of her breath in the air. Thanksgiving was upon them, and Christmas would arrive on its heels. Holidays had always been a nonissue when it had been just her and David. Sometimes they'd drive in to go to church with her parents and pick at her father's overly dry turkey. But many times, they'd stayed in Nashville because Summer had to work. She'd worked damned hard to get nowhere. Okay, not exactly nowhere, but not where she wanted to be.

One of her friends had joked at her Nashville going-away dinner that Summer had cashed it in and was giving up. Sometimes it felt as if that were true. Years ago, she'd put all her eggs in one basket, banking on a manager who'd driven her to near bankruptcy. He'd mismanaged her band, ignored decent offers in pursuit of ridiculous producers, and stolen money from other clients. His reputation became her reputation. Wasn't long before she felt like the guys in the mockumentary *This Is Spinal Tap*, playing backup to puppets at state fairs. And she didn't even have an amp that went to eleven to save her.

She'd sold some songs to get back on her feet, but by then she'd been making more as the manager of the Branding Iron Steakhouse than she did playing gigs. A few band members escaped to greener pastures, and it seemed silly to hire replacements when opportunity had dried up. But in the end, she'd walked away because of David. Because he'd started hanging around the wrong kids and sneaking out to do God knows what. He needed guidance and a parent home at night.

Parenting wasn't for egomaniacs. Putting her child's welfare above her own was pretty much a standard clause in the parenting contract she'd signed the moment she became one.

The moon played peekaboo through the trees as she drove the bay highway toward where her boy waited, barbecue-heavy and no doubt too tired to study for the civics test he had the next day. Occasionally, when her car pierced the thick oaks and palmettos and met a clearing, the reflection of the moon on the water invited deep, twisty contemplations. Song lyrics wove in and out of her head, always flirting with her, begging her to make them into something more.

Summer had been henpecked by melodies and lyrics her entire life. Much like she'd been haunted by Rhett Bryan. Seemed silly to allow an adolescent crush to follow her, raising its head every time she caught his show, every time Pete mentioned his grandson had phoned. Wasn't as if she hadn't had successful relationships with other men. Okay, not totally successful, or she'd be with someone right now. But good. Mostly. Rhett Bryan was a fantasy she'd hidden from the world, with no real hope of ever having him.

Summer rocked down the pitted road to the Nest and rounded the bend that would take her to the snug cabin. As she swung into her drive, her headlights caught Rhett in the beams. He stood on her stoop with his hands in his pockets, a T-shirt clinging to his lean torso and a smile that suggested possibility.

Hadn't someone once said, "Nothing is impossible?"

Um, yeah. The Bible. *All things are possible through Christ who strengthens me.*

But as impossibly angelic as Rhett looked with his golden glow and sugared smile, he could probably lead the most reverent down a slippery slope of unobjectionable sin. If *Us Weekly* was to be believed.

Summer rolled her eyes at her thoughts and put the car into park.

Rhett opened her door like a valet. "David's studying for civics. How about a moonlit walk?"

What was his motive? Did he truly want a walk? Or was there something more? Maybe he needed advice. Maybe he merely wanted to have company. Maybe it didn't matter because Rhett was asking her to walk with him. She contemplated the dark road toward the gated community. "You know there are gators and snakes out there."

"I like a challenge."

She laughed. "I had a glass of wine and a bath in mind, but I guess I'll risk losing a limb to walk with you. Sacrifices must be made."

"Hey, you'll still look pretty with only one leg."

"Thanks. And it will save me money on shoes."

Rhett's smile made all the angst over everything in her life melt away. Such power existed inside this man—the ability to make her let go of practicality and pursue what she could not have. That made Rhett dangerous.

More dangerous than alligators.

CHAPTER FOURTEEN

November, present day

After taking David home to the small cottage on his grandfather's property, Rhett sent the kid inside and hung around outside, telling himself he was merely enjoying the night air. But he'd been waiting on Summer.

They'd not ended things well several nights before, and Summer had been tactful enough not to bring it up in front of Grampy. Rhett knew he ran from the answers to the questions she'd posed. In fact, he avoided his problems like a barefoot man skirting a thorn patch.

After the accident, he'd tried to pretend what had happened didn't affect him. He was a professional. He could soldier on. But after the nightmares started, the incessant bouts of racing heart and clammy palms, he'd gone to a therapist. The breathing exercises and the anti-anxiety meds had helped some. But he still dealt with nightmares and lack of sleep, which came to a head when he'd had Bev Bohanan on the show. Her cavalier manner and ingrained sense of privilege had made everything boil over. He couldn't seem to control the anger . . . couldn't stop the things he'd said.

Summer wasn't a substitute for therapy, but when he was around her, things felt easier. She'd always done that for him, even back in high school. She possessed a genuineness, an earnestness, a sincere warmth that permeated the outer mask he felt he had to wear to be liked.

He felt like a normal person with Summer.

Feeling normal. Why couldn't he attain that anymore? He felt like the world sat and watched and waited for him to crack.

Sometimes he forgot about who he was now. Like when gnawing on barbecued ribs at the Rib Hut with David and Hunt. After initial awkwardness, they'd fallen into their old ways. Of course, something still sat between him and his old friend, something intangible and laced with hurt. Or maybe Rhett still felt guilty about bowing out of Hunt's life so easily. Things had gone well for Rhett. Not so much for Hunt.

"Been a while since you've drunk a Bud Light, I bet," Hunt had said, nodding at the bottle at Rhett's elbow. "Got all those fancy craft brews in California?"

"Probably. Organic beer." Rhett cracked a smile. "The West Coast is notorious for being picky about quality ingredients and food sourcing. I don't usually drink beer. A martini every now and then hits the spot, but I'm constantly having to watch my diet," Rhett said, licking his fingers. He'd forgotten how good the barbecue was at the Rib Hut. Couldn't remember the last time he'd eaten so much. Felt good to be full.

David's gaze hung on Hunt, adoration glistening in his eyes when his father wasn't looking. "I've had a beer before."

Hunt looked sharply at his son. "When?"

"I snuck one of Pete's. I didn't like it, though," the kid said, almost too quickly. The constant push and pull of awkward emotions on display was fascinating. Hunt didn't seem to know what to do with David, and the kid didn't seem to know how to take his father.

But at least Hunt had stood up to his own father and protected his son. Hunt had spent much of his youth being ridden by Mitchell McCroy. The man never let up, whip in hand, urging Hunt toward whatever he deemed the appropriate destination. When Hunt had failed to step on a major league field, the man had taken Hunt's failure as an insult.

It would have been a shame for history to repeat itself.

"Nice job out there on the field, David. You, too, Hunt," Rhett said, noticing Hunt had gone with sweet tea rather than alcohol. He wondered if that was because of rehab. Hunt had been addicted to painkillers, but maybe he stayed away from booze, too. Or maybe he didn't want to drink in front of his kid.

"Yeah, you remember how that was. My dad is a force," Hunt said with a wry grin.

There were many times Rhett envied Hunt his involved parents, but he'd learned quickly to be relieved he had a grandfather who stayed out of his business. Grampy Pete believed in keeping his mouth shut about things he knew nothing about, which meant Rhett never got tips about his swing or his sliding technique. Mitchell had tried to step in and "help" Rhett, but Rhett had shrugged him off and stopped going to Hunt's house to hang out. Mitchell seemed to get the hint, but that never stopped him from riding Hunt's ass.

All. The. Time.

"Some people never change and some do," Rhett said.

"I think we know which category Mitchell McCroy's in," Hunt joked, glancing at his son. In David's face Rhett could see the hunger for more time with his father.

"Um, my grandfather was just trying to help, I think," David said with a shrug.

"Your grandfather likes to have control over everything, Dave," Hunt said, shooting Rhett a look. He knew Rhett knew exactly what he meant. "Don's the person teaching you how to pitch. If your grandfather tries to undo things you've learned or run roughshod over you, let me know. He means well, but he can be hard to say no to. I know. I lived with him for half my life."

David's forehead creased. "It's okay, Dad. I'm good."

"I'm just saying," Hunt said. "Rhett can attest to your grandfather's overinterest. He tried to get Rhett to pitch, too. And go to Florida with me. Didn't work, though. Rhett's whole happy-go-lucky bullshit hides a stubborn SOB. He doesn't get backed into many corners."

Hunt saw beneath his shtick to the calculating, intent man he was . . . or used to be. Maybe that was his issue. Rhett Bryan had been backed into a corner and he couldn't figure out how to fight his way out. How did a person fight sadness, guilt, accepting he couldn't control the things he wanted to control?

David looked tired of the contemplative things. "Tell me about more things y'all did growing up here. That monkey story was crazy."

So they'd talked and fallen back into old times. Over brisket, ribs, and cherry pie, time had fallen away, and Rhett remembered why he'd liked Hunt. Hunt listened to others, didn't hog conversation, told a good joke, and tipped the waitress too much when he paid for dinner. Rhett had tried to pay, but Hunt wouldn't let him. He sensed his old friend wanted to prove that he was successful enough to handle the check. On second thought, maybe that tip was about more than good service.

Summer's headlight beams swiped over him as he moved off her front stoop.

He needed a reason for skulking around her house, so he suggested a moonlit walk, which sounded kind of strange if not slightly romantic. He'd felt even more stupid when she'd remarked about the gators. The island was home to deer, osprey, aforementioned alligators, and several poisonous snakes, but the moon was full and invited contemplation. Creepy crawlies be damned.

Summer wore a cardigan that should have made her look dowdy, but didn't. Her brown hair had been confined in a low ponytail, and she wore tight pants that tucked into brown boots. Not practical for walking down a gravel road, but she'd come with him anyway. For a few minutes, they didn't speak. The South Carolina island closed in on them, winnowing the road such that it resembled a tunnel. Big oaks dripped moss onto the moonlit path.

"How was the barbecue?" Summer asked, interrupting the chirrup of insects.

"Better than sex," he joked.

"You're probably having the wrong kind, then," she said.

"Sex?"

"Barbecue," she said with a smile in her voice. "David okay?"

"He's a cool kid. He liked the old stories about baseball tournaments, the time Hunt and I sabotaged the town Christmas lights display—"

"That was *you*?" Summer asked.

"Yeah. We stole a bulb from a new display every night. Poor old Danny Laborde. About went crazy trying to figure out why the lights wouldn't stay on. I feel bad about that now," Rhett said, shoving his hands into his pockets so he wouldn't reach for her hand. For some reason, he wanted to hold her hand.

"But it makes for a good story," she remarked.

"That it does. Just so you know, I overheard Hunt giving his father hell about trying to ramrod pitching lessons. Surprised me to hear him being so vocal. Mitchell didn't take it too well."

"I'm relieved to hear Hunt was protective of David," Summer murmured, her hands jammed in the pockets of her sweater as they crunched down the road. "I've been worried that Hunt might put too much pressure on David. I wasn't sure David was ready to climb onto a pitching mound with his father."

"It actually surprised me because Mitchell always ran roughshod over Hunt when we were growing up. Like father, like son. But maybe not. Maybe Hunt will break that chain of whatever that is. Abuse? Or just impossibly high standards."

"Hunt didn't have a choice. Mitchell held all the power." Summer sounded like she'd surprised herself with that observation. "I used to envy people like Hunt. Like you and Graysen."

"Graysen. I wonder how she is," Rhett said. "She was pretty peeved when we broke up. She wanted a long-distance relationship. I knew that couldn't work. She never spoke to me again. Just cut me off."

"Actually, she's doing good. She's married with three children. She married Chip Henry. He was three or four years older than us, I think. They live outside of Columbia, where she owns a salon where I'm sure she turns the plain into fabulous." Self-deprecation with a touch of humor lay in Summer's voice.

"How do you know all this?"

"Facebook. It's pretty much how anyone keeps up with people these days."

"I wouldn't know. Mostly I try to stay off social media these days." Rhett didn't want the conversation to tilt into his reasons for avoiding tweets. "Good for Graysen. And why would you envy me . . . or Graysen . . . or Hunt?"

"You seemed to have had everything at your fingertips. You were the Golden Boy, she was the beauty queen, and Hunt had more money than sense. Still, I've come to understand that beneath the glitter can lay darkness."

Her arrow found its mark.

She continued. "The good thing is that Hunt's trying to do the right thing by David. That's why I agreed to move back here and let him spend time with David. David needed a father, and Hunt wanted to be part of his life. It's taken some time, but he's getting there."

"You don't like Hunt much." It was a statement.

"I don't know him. Not really. We were never together. We just happened to make a kid." Her words were like stones dropped on cold tile, making Rhett wonder if he should stick to lighter topics. Talk about puppies or baking apple pies or her favorite new country artist.

"But you were together. At least for a night," he said.

Summer's glance toward him was cryptic as the shadows clustered around them. Frogs sang, an owl flapped in the near distance. "We weren't together. You know what happened. I was his date. Things happened. I got pregnant."

He should have stuck to puppies. The displeasure in her voice wasn't unexpected. He'd known things weren't good between her and Hunt the day after prom. He'd felt bad enough about it to stop by her house and check on her, to try to issue some sort of apology for the role he'd played in getting her tangled up with Hunt. Even back then he knew why she'd slept with Hunt. And he knew why Hunt had slept with Summer. None of the reasons had been good ones. David had been conceived out of two hurting teenagers looking for some kind of comfort.

"After I found out I was pregnant, and not just overly stressed about starting college, things were hard between Hunt and me. He didn't want to take responsibility. What nineteen-year-old does? I get it, and even then, I understood, to a degree. He was in college and didn't want to think about a girl he never truly liked carrying his baby back home. Then he got drafted by the majors and went on the road. Got married. Got divorced. Lived his life."

"But denied David?"

"He didn't deny him. He ignored him. For too many years."

"How does David feel about that?"

"Curious. Hurt. Resigned but glad to have him in his life for more than an occasional visit."

"When did he come back into the picture?" Rhett asked, not sure if he should be prying into her life, but he wanted to understand her better.

"I've had full custody of David from birth, but I never stopped Hunt from seeing his son. About five years ago, Hunt left baseball behind and came back here. He e-mailed me, told me he'd screwed up by not being more present in David's life. He said he'd been scared and now he wanted to rectify his mistakes. Hunt asked if he could come to Nashville to see David, and he asked me to consider letting him build a relationship with his son."

"And you said yes? I mean, obviously you did."

"I didn't want to. Not really. David was nine at the time and starting to need some male guidance in his life. Honestly, I wasn't sure Hunt was the right person for that. But he *is* his father," she said with a harsh laugh.

Bitterness was hard to hide, and Summer didn't seem to be good at hiding much. She never had been. Back in high school he knew she had a thing for him. And he knew he should have stomped on her crush, but hadn't. Selfishly, he liked the way she looked at him. She never asked anything from him. Instead she'd given him something almost pure, almost spiritual in nature. Sounded hokey and stupid, but he'd been drawn to her even then. So he hadn't squashed her interest. He'd reveled in it, content to have no obligation to her other than being the guy she tutored.

The moonlight through the trees dappled her face, making her suddenly not the Summer he'd always known. He recalled Hunt's words—that Summer was like the ocean. Would she push and pull, giving him little reprieve before sucking him back into her depths? Or would she be a gentle wave washing over him, cleansing him of all the bad? He'd only know if he waded in. Common sense said he should stay his ass on the beach. She was a single mom . . . and he'd be going back to who he used to be. As soon as he figured out just how to do that.

He shouldn't have asked her on a moonlit walk like some moron. He should keep his distance. Yet, here he was. Walking beside her. Uncovering the rawness in her life.

They'd continued their walk in silence, each wrapped in thoughts too heavy to express. Still, it wasn't uncomfortable. Perhaps because each of them knew the intentions of the other. Or thought they knew. Or were afraid to uncover them.

When they got back to her front porch, he stood in the yellow porch light and studied her. "Thank you for the walk. Sometimes a walk helps me sleep better."

"Sure," she said, her hand on the front door handle. "I don't take enough walks. I usually have wine to help me sleep."

"I'd need probably two bottles for that," he joked, realizing he revealed more than he wanted.

Her eyes softened. "Maybe you'll be able to sleep tonight. Something about going back and sleeping in your childhood room feels so safe. My mom kept my purple walls and the poster of 98° on my wall. I sleep like a baby every time I stay there."

"Grampy still has all my trophies and team pics on the wall. Plaid wallpaper. Even found a pair of cleats in the closet."

"I know. I sometimes vacuum your room. It's like going back in time and meeting the boy I never really knew." She opened the door and fanned moths away. "Gotta go. See you later, Rhett."

Then she slipped inside.

The boy she never really knew . . .

Rhett wished like hell he could find that boy again.

CHAPTER FIFTEEN

November, present day

Thursday afternoon, Rhett had a conference call with Townsend Public Relations, the firm his agent had hired to handle the civil suit the Tavares family had filed against him.

"We have three witnesses who will testify the Hispanic girl was unsupervised most of the time. One said her brother nearly got hit last year. The boy sustained some scrapes and was taken to a clinic. We can get those records, and I have some friends in social media who can get this information in circulation. Maybe even an article on the family, casting them in a greedy light," Jane Townsend said, excitement in her voice.

"What boy? The one who witnessed the accident?" Rhett asked, remembering the child's face. He saw that face in his dreams. Sometimes the boy took off his own head and kicked it like a ball. Last time Rhett had dreamed that, he'd not been able to sleep for two days.

"No, the Tavares family has a boy younger than the girl. He's five years old, I think. This proves neglect pretty easily. Pair that with the fact that they don't have much money and you're a celebrity, and they'll look like they're opportunists. We'll make it look like they're trying to capitalize on their daughter's death. People hate that shit. Oh, and the father has a bad temper and a record. Aggravated assault and some bad checks."

"I'm not sure I want to go that low. This feels low," he said.

"Do you want to lose? Pay them three million dollars? You hired me to do a job," she said, her voice growing stern.

"Bruce?" Rhett asked.

"I'm here," his agent said, clearing his throat. "Look, Jane. We hired you to help manage the talk around this suit, but Rhett's not the kind of guy to destroy a family."

"We're not destroying anyone, Bruce. We're casting doubt on this family. They're playing hardball and have the edge. They lost their kid. They're dragging out the traumatized friend who saw it happen, neighbors who swear Rhett refused to help the child. They're using big guns. At present, public opinion is that Rhett is a callous, entitled white millionaire who killed an underprivileged minority child. We have to cast aspersions on the character of the family. We have to make them look like desperate opportunists."

"Or we can settle," Rhett said.

"And look guilty," Jane said.

They'd ended the discussion at an impasse, with Jane continuing to gather more for her campaign to smear the Tavares family. Bruce seemed certain this was the way to handle everything, and Rhett felt like a pile of dog shit.

So, after hanging up, Rhett went out in the boat and tried to forget the stupid lawsuit.

But being alone didn't work.

He needed distraction, and luckily there was one to be found on the outskirts of Moonlight—the infamous Sundown Tavern, home of the shrimp buster and coldest beer in town.

Rhett pushed through the door of the Sundown Tavern, already berating himself for going out in public where people would recognize him, want to take pics with him, and beg for stories about what Beyoncé is really like. All he wanted was a drink and a place to brood. His efforts to get his production company off the ground were stalled. Seemed running over a kid and getting sued for it made investors nervous.

Goddamn it. Why had he taken that shortcut that morning? Why had he looked down at that stupid smoothie? Maybe if he hadn't, he would have had enough time to swerve or something. If he'd just been patient or satisfied for once in his life, Josefina would still be kicking the soccer ball and painting her fingernails with sparkle polish.

His chest clenched and his gut churned. *No thinking about the girl. No thinking about that day. No thinking period.* The need for a whiskey on the rocks clawed inside him. He'd have one drink. Maybe two. He'd still be fine to drive, and it would blur the edges enough for him to sleep . . . if he could sleep.

Rhett wore a pair of jeans and an old flannel shirt he'd found in his grandfather's hunting closet. Haute couture jeans and two-hundred-dollar T-shirts didn't work in Moonlight. He needed to blend in and look normal.

A few people turned to look at him when he emerged from the foyer pasted with band posters from years past. The country band playing commanded everyone's attention, so he was able to slip into a table tucked at the back of the bar. He hadn't adjusted himself on the stool before a buxom waitress with hair too red to be natural pulled up next to him.

"Whoa, hey, I know who you are. What are ya doing *here?*" Her question implied he was slumming. It wasn't like he always wore a tux and swilled champagne 24/7. Even in LA he liked to find dives and soak up local culture.

The redhead tucked the round serving tray under her arm and waited.

"Just looking for a good bourbon on the rocks. What do you have?"

"The usual. Maker's, Wild Turkey, um, maybe some Booker's." She lifted a shoulder.

"Double of the former." He wasn't even going to ask about the batch or year. Whatever she brought him would be warm, wet, and give him reprieve. Good enough.

"Um, can I . . . maybe get your autograph or something? I'm Jenn, by the way."

"Sure, but can it wait until I'm ready to pay the tab?"

She wrinkled her nose like she was slightly offended, but then her dark eyes registered what he'd not said. If he gave her one now, everyone would want one. Normally he didn't mind taking selfies with fans or signing grocery receipts, but tonight he needed some solitude.

Then why did you come to a bar, dumb ass?

Because you really don't want to be alone. You just want to be alone in a room of strangers.

"Gotcha. And don't worry. I won't let folks pester you." With a smart salute, Jenn disappeared.

He felt the other patrons' curiosity, which he ignored so he didn't invite an approach. Instead he turned his attention to the band rocking a cover of a Shania Twain song.

The singer was surprisingly good.

He squinted. She almost looked like . . .

Realization slammed into him. *Summer.*

He'd forgotten she was in a band. Had she said the name? His gaze scanned the room and found a flyer nearby with the calendar for November. Tonight was Greyhound Blue.

The name didn't suit. Her band should reflect who she was. Something sincere and soft. Like a homecoming or a downy quilt. Like warm bread from the oven or sun-kissed daisies. Summer *was* her name—hazy, warm, and sweet. Being with her dragged him back to a simpler time, a time when everything felt possible and not so damned hard. When he was with Summer, he could almost forget he'd killed a child.

No. Do not go there, dumb ass. Let it go for a while. Leave it behind.

Jenn set the tumbler of bourbon on the table. "Start a tab?"

"Sure." The glass caught in the neon light—a beautiful anesthetic atop wood worn-out by hundreds of forearms. Rhett knew the danger in allowing alcohol to numb the pain. Not a crutch he wanted to use. Even so, he picked up the glass, finding pleasure in the clink of ice against the side, enjoying the anticipation. Rhett took a sip and felt his body sigh.

Jenn watched him. When he set the drink back on the table, she said, "We got wings and cheese fries if you're hungry."

His stomach growled. He hadn't had cheese fries in a good ten years. But he couldn't. Not after barbecue, not with the knowledge that he'd be back on the air in just over a month.

"Better not."

"All right. Enjoy the show . . . and being alone."

Rhett frowned as Jenn sashayed away. Because that made him sound lonely.

And why was lonely bad? Everyone needed downtime. Okay, so every vacation he'd taken over the past ten years had had an angle. Either he was working a deal, maximizing face time with someone who could help his career, or designing his presence at the right place at the right time for whatever reason. Rhett was a workaholic. He knew this and had always been okay with it. This was who he was—a guy who had a plan, who knew exactly what he wanted, who liked making the deal, hustling his career. Which was great . . . until it wasn't.

He sucked on an ice cube, trying to extend the life of the drink. He wanted to down the honey elixir. Order another. Down it. Another. And another. Until there was nothing but blessed blackness. Instead, he focused on Summer strumming the guitar and allowed her husky voice to become the substitute for the liquor.

Summer looked somehow sexier in her tight jeans and off-the-shoulder shirt. Cowboy boots completed the look, along with her hair in a soft braid that reminded him of Meg Ryan in the nineties. But most impressive was how good she was. She maintained rapport with the band, smiled at the audience, and at times lost herself in the music.

After the rollicking cover of a Janis Joplin song, she pulled up a stool and sat down with her guitar.

"Thank y'all for being such a great audience. We're going to take a break, but before we do, we wanted to debut a new song we've been working on. It's a little slower, but I think y'all will like it. It's called 'Carolina Boy.'"

A rousing smattering of applause and then the lights lowered. Summer tilted her head and positioned her fingers, her face softening. She plucked the first few chords and then the band joined in. Her voice was husky and sweet as she sang about love, back dirt roads, and sunset on the marsh. And a boy. And a dog. And loss. The song was hauntingly beautiful in that way that made a person hold his breath and sit mesmerized by the depth of emotion rising within. The last few words of the song, "Come back to me, my Carolina boy. Don't throw our love aside for her. Oh, my Carolina boy, come home to me," trailed off, and Summer looked up, her eyes filled with tears.

The place went nuts.

Why wouldn't they? It was good, like Carole King, Carly Simon, and Alanis Morissette had had a baby and it was Summer. Sweet, husky, powerfully poignant.

Summer looked up and smiled her thanks before setting the guitar on a nearby stand and unhooking her mic. Several people stopped her on the way toward the bar. Rhett watched as the girl he once knew stepped into being the woman he longed to know. He studied the curve of her cheek, the tiny wisps of hair escaping her braid, the light laugh when people complimented her. Maybe they weren't compliments, but whatever they were, Summer smiled. And Rhett figured that should be a mission in every person's life—make Summer smile.

She turned toward the bar and caught his stare. Tilting her head, she made a surprised face and started toward him. As she neared the table in front of his, Jenn stepped in front of her and said a few things. Summer shook her head and pushed past the waitress. The feisty waitress frowned at Summer's back.

"What are you doing here?" Summer asked.

"I could ask the same, but I just found out what you're doing. Man, that was incredible, Summer."

He couldn't tell if she blushed or not, but pleasure seemed to blanket her. "Well, it wasn't perfect. Still have a few kinks to work out, but since it was the first time for us to try it live, I don't expect perfection."

"Join me?" He gestured toward the stool opposite him.

"You sure your guard dog won't bite me?" she said, glancing back toward Jenn, who still looked perturbed that Summer hadn't obeyed her dictate of not disturbing Rhett. "How'd you get her to do that, by the way? Jenn's . . . uh, difficult."

"I promised her an autograph and sex in the bathroom if she'd keep people away."

"What?" Summer's eyes went wide.

"Just kidding. On the sex. I still gotta do the autograph-and-picture thing. But she's got a nice ass. Maybe I should see if she wants to meet me—"

"Only if you want to fight Randy, her boyfriend. He's a trucker and six foot four." Summer slid onto the stool. "I have fifteen minutes before I have to go back. One more set tonight."

Jenn appeared beside them. She gave Summer a flat stare but asked, "Get you anything, Summer?"

"Just ice water. And Rhett wants to ask you something." Summer's eyes sparkled with humor.

"I just wanted a water. Just a water." Rhett really wanted another bourbon, but having water in between drinks was a good idea. Safe. Responsible. Showing control over himself.

People gawked at him and Summer sitting together, but no one infringed on their space. He redirected his attention to the woman across from him and away from the lookie-loos. "Thanks for trying to get me killed."

"Randy wouldn't kill you. Maim you? Yes. Kill? No."

"Why didn't you say something last night about playing here? I would have come tonight. I mean, I did, but you know what I mean."

"It didn't come up, and I didn't think you'd come out in public like this," Summer said, accepting a glass from Jenn and sliding it to Rhett before taking hers.

"Rough day and I just needed to get out."

"You okay?" Concern shaded her eyes.

"Yeah, just business stuff. Things I don't want to think about. Tell me about the band."

"I joined them five months ago. They were pretty much a group of pickers who messed around doing American Legion dances and nursing home gigs. Joe Carmichael, the drummer, plays in the praise band at my mom's church. She mentioned I was looking for a band, and he invited me to come play with them one night. The rest is history. They love having a front woman. Lester Earl wasn't exactly the best vocalist, so he was happy to step aside."

"Why Greyhound Blue?"

Summer laughed. "They wanted to rename the band when I joined. Seemed The Floor Stompers wasn't the tone they wanted, so we brainstormed. One day I said something about getting the bus blues when I was out doing tours with my former band, and Joe joked about how he'd had the Greyhound blues when his wife divorced him and he had to ride one from California back to Moonlight. Then Lester said we'd all had the Greyhound blues one time or another and"—she snapped her fingers and grinned—"that sounded right."

"Good story," Rhett said, gulping the water he didn't want.

"Yeah, maybe one day we can tell it when we win a Grammy," she said, sipping her own water and tucking an errant strand of hair behind her ear. "I'm joking, of course. The guys are good players but they aren't really motivated, if you know what I mean. They like to play, not perform. There's a difference."

"So why are you with them? I know some people in the industry. One word and—"

"No, thank you," she interrupted, her smile fading. "I don't need someone to use his influence to get me something I'm not sure I want."

"Why not? You know someone who has some . . . sway in the entertainment industry. I know producers, people who can help you. Why wouldn't you use that?"

"Because I don't use people to get ahead. I could have done that a dozen times in Nashville. Step on others to climb higher. I don't do that. That's not who I want to be. For David. For myself."

Rhett paused and studied her. "You wouldn't be using me. I offered to share your name and your talent with someone who might help you. That's not stepping on someone."

Summer's expression shuttered. "I don't need your charity, Rhett." She made to scoot her stool back.

Rhett caught her by the wrist. "Wait, that's not what I meant."

She looked down at his hand. "Sounded like it."

"Don't go yet," he said.

She inhaled and then shrugged off his grasp. "Okay, but understand that I like to do things my way. Maybe one day I'll take you up on help, but for now I'm content with the decision I've made to come here and raise my son."

"Stubborn, so incredibly stubborn," he said, adding a smile to soften the words. "I admire you for putting your son above yourself. Not many people do that, not when they have talent like yours."

"Who says I'm doing it just for him?" she said, picking up the sweating glass and taking another sip of water. "Is there something wrong with not wanting to set the world on fire? You know, some people are content standing beside the fire and basking in the warmth. Our whole culture makes people feel guilty if they don't aspire to the highest things."

"There's nothing wrong with having dreams and taking chances. Plenty of people live in that fire. It can be done."

"And leave nothing but ashes. I like doing gigs here and having dinner with my son. A million dollars would be nice, and I've always wanted to see my name in lights, but I don't have to be the best at everything I do. Guess that's where we differ."

Summer made his life sound so meaningless, as if she'd made a noble sacrifice by shoving her dreams to the back of the closet and coming to Moonlight. Maybe it was more noble, but did that mean people who made sacrifices in the pursuit of a dream made a mistake? Sometimes people made concessions to get what they wanted. "I don't have to have those things, but I like being good at what I do. I'm number one in my market."

Summer gave him a small smile. "That's good, Rhett. Very good."

Feeling petulant, he lifted a finger at Jenn, who stood talking to several women. Then he tapped the empty tumbler, indicating he wanted another. Sighing, he said, "I sound defensive."

"On the contrary. You were trying to be nice to me and I wouldn't let you. I have insecurities. Sometimes they show more than others. You're not wrong—I have dreams. But I'm not unhappy. I wish everyone would stop implying I am. My mom wants me to move in with her because I can't be happy living way out there alone. My sister pushes me to date, like I can't be fulfilled without a man in my life."

"You don't date?" He was more than happy to shift the conversation away from where it had been headed. No sense in making either of them feel bad for their choices.

"Not since I've been back in Moonlight. I'm not sure there's much of a dating scene, though I sometimes get propositioned at bars with hotel key cards and sleazy pickup lines. My mama swears I can meet someone decent in church, but I've been sleeping in most Sundays."

"Alone," he added. And he didn't know why he did. He just didn't want to picture her in bed with another man.

"Yeah, alone." She downed the rest of her water. "But maybe I should go to church. Try to find a nice guy. Might be nice to go to dinner every once in a while. What about you?"

"Me?" He didn't want to talk about his string of failed relationships. He'd dated casually, had two semiserious relationships with actresses who valued their careers over him, and one serious enough for him to buy a ring at Harry Winston. But none had lasted. Mostly because he was, as he admitted, very focused on his career. Not much was put before his show or his new production venture. "I'm not dating anyone. Things have been too difficult."

"Because of the lawsuit?"

"That and other things that don't bear discussing." Wasn't like he would admit to her, in the middle of a honky-tonk, how haunted he was. Wasn't like he could tell her he doubted everything he'd become in Hollywood. He was afraid to admit he understood what she meant about abandoning her career, looking for a better purpose.

Maybe he'd been building castles in the air. He lived a gilded existence in the Hollywood Hills, covering red carpet events, shopping on Rodeo, doing things that seemed so important but were as fleeting as a puff of cigarette smoke . . . and just as hazardous to his health. Fame and fortune were the cornerstones of his world. But sometimes he hated who he was. So shallow, so fickle. Some of the people he called friends were actually douchebags who would step over a homeless man in order to get to the latest hot spot. It was disgusting, yet it was his reality.

Maybe that's why he was here in a place that had substance. It was his shot of vitamin B, hopefully enough to patch him up and get him back on track.

Summer's brow furrowed. "Why not discuss what's bothering you? Sometimes talking about what we don't want to is exactly what we need to do."

"Yeah, 'cause you *so* wanted to discuss your career a few seconds ago."

"Touché."

"I spent thousands of dollars talking about what bothered me, so I've decided to stop talking and just wait it out. Maybe that's why I came back home. Here there's no overanalyzing who I am. Here I become the person I used to be. Perhaps subconsciously I thought I could get a piece of myself back. Or forget about whatever this is that's been weighing me down. Maybe I thought coming home could fix me or something. And, just like that, I've said more than I wanted to say. How do you do that?"

"Do what?"

"Get me to say things I didn't know I knew."

"I didn't do anything. I sat here. But I do understand. Part of me came back here because it was easier. Sometimes you get tired of trying so damned hard. Some of my friends didn't agree with my choices, but I'm sure here is where I need to be right now. I'm good with my decision to come home." Such earnestness in her face. She looked so comfortable with who she was, small tendrils curling around her face, a few sticking sweetly to her neck. Adorable freckles sprinkled her nose, giving her that genuine girl-next-door vibe he'd always been a sucker for. Her lips looked soft. He wondered how soft they were.

His grandfather's words floated back to him. *Not the kind of girl you mess with.*

But then again, Summer was a grown-ass woman who didn't need an old man to protect her. Besides, Rhett wasn't going to do anything stupid. He liked spending time with her. Was that a crime?

"Go out with me," he said before he could think better of it.

She jerked back, her hand hitting the glass and nearly toppling it. "What?"

He caught the glass before it tipped. "Go out on the boat with me. I've been wanting to take Grampy's boat for a night run. Come with me."

"Oh, you mean . . . yeah, um, you shouldn't go alone. I'll ride with you."

He realized she misunderstood.

She thought he just needed someone with him for safety reasons. He'd meant it as a date.

But this might be better. If she thought it was a date, she would have expectations. Hell, he'd have expectations. He knew he wasn't in the right place for something more than friendship with Summer. After all, she essentially lived with his grandfather and shared a kid with his former best friend. Not to mention, he'd be leaving soon, and the idea of keeping a spark of something going while he was over a thousand miles away was ridiculous.

"Great. The weather's supposed to be gorgeous this weekend, according to The Weather Channel. I should know. Grampy's television is either on The Weather Channel or ESPN. And occasionally Fox News, where he proceeds to argue out loud with the guests there. I am an authority on cold fronts, the Panthers' defensive game plan, and Republican midterm strategy. Come at me with questions."

"I'll keep that in mind," she said, the mood shifting back into something lighter. "David's staying with Hunt this weekend. Something about a new glove. And as long as Maisie doesn't get swamped by several funerals, she shouldn't need me. But let me double-check my schedule to see what time my last lesson is."

"We'll shoot for Friday. Text me when you check your schedule."

"I don't have your number."

"You do. I texted you a few nights back."

Someone called Summer's name and he leaned over to see the bass player motioning toward her.

"Break over," she said, taking a few gulps of water and sliding from the stool. "I'll look forward to Friday night. I haven't been out in a boat in a while."

He caught her hand. "Hey, I'm glad you're going with me."

"Everyone needs a friend sometimes, Rhett," she said. Her gaze fell to their locked hands, so he gently squeezed hers. Summer lifted her eyes to meet his. For a moment they stood, hands linked, gazes locked. Something passed between them. Something warm curling inside of him, suggesting he was still alive.

Nothing he'd done to that point—therapy, acupuncture, sex, running until he puked—had been able to knit together the open wound in his soul. Perhaps the people who knew him, people who understood that beneath the shiny exterior was a man who was good, could help him discover himself again. He needed to be here in Moonlight, tucked into the place that had made him. Here he'd learned to conquer insecurity, overcome whatever came his way, become a man who'd climbed to the top of the ratings of late-night TV. If he could do it before, he could do it again. Moonlight and its people could bring him back from the darkness.

"I have to go. Band's waiting," Summer said.

"I wish you wouldn't. I feel better when you're with me." He meant the words. Even as he acknowledged what they could set into motion. This was Summer Valentine, the girl who'd loved him once.

"Don't do this, Rhett. Don't say things you shouldn't."

"I'm not. I like being with you. I feel more myself than I have in ages."

"I can't fix what's wrong with you. You know that, right? And I won't be your distraction. You can't do that to me."

"I'm not. I just want to be . . . I just like . . ." He, who always found the words, couldn't seem to articulate how he felt. Rhett didn't want to use Summer. He liked her too much to hurt her, but something compelled him to be near her. "I'm not asking you for anything."

Summer pulled her hand away, her face somber. "You're a man I can't play with, Rhett. You know that. I can't be left behind, gutted and gasping."

"Summer—"

"Stop." She held up a hand, her hazel eyes unyielding. "You know the power you have over me, the power you've always had. Don't use that against me. I'll be your friend, but I can't be a casualty. To you, I'm just another woman. One of hundreds. But to me, you're . . . you know."

With those words, she turned and walked away, passing people who'd been staring at them. She smiled at a few, but fixed her eyes on the stage and the band waiting for her. He curled his hand against the emptiness.

He was a person like everyone else. Sure, he was nationally recognized and had star power, or whatever his agent liked to tout when he worked to get him jobs. And sure, he was screwed up from the accident that past summer. Anyone would be. But that didn't mean he would hurt Summer.

But if you tell her pretty things, take her to bed, and let her fall back in love with you and then leave, wouldn't that hurt? Wouldn't that be the very definition of using someone?

He flicked the mosquito of truth away even though the pesky rascal made a damned good bit of sense.

"Here ya go," Jenn said, setting the whiskey in front of him. "I made it a double. On the house."

"No. I'm paying. Let's settle the tab now." He reached for his wallet and withdrew a card. "In fact, let me buy the house a round. Least I could do."

Jenn took the card. "You just made a whole lot of new fans. I mean, we're all fans, you being a hometown boy and all, but this will put you over Cleveland Rennix."

"The guy who did the backstroke in the Olympics in the 1930s? Are you telling me I'm behind Cleveland?"

"Hey, he won silver," Jenn said with a laugh before sashaying away. "Always good to have a Carolina boy home."

Her words slammed into him. Carolina boy? He swung his gaze to the stage, where Summer stood adjusting the mic and thought about the song she'd sung before the break. Was it about him? Bittersweet and full of regrets, the song unspooled the notion of a woman in love with a golden boy she couldn't have.

But what if she could have him? If only for a little while.

That thought warmed him more than the whiskey sitting at his elbow.

CHAPTER SIXTEEN

November, present day

Summer knew she should have made an excuse for not going with Rhett. All day long she'd played around with really good ones. "I have a migraine" had come in second to "I got my period and have cramps." Since she had neither of those two things, and because she really wanted to be with Rhett, she didn't call and beg off. Instead, she'd put on extra mascara and shaved her legs.

Yeah. She was just that stupid over Rhett.

After the last guitar lesson of the day, she'd driven home and taken a quick shower, careful to not get her hair wet. Riffling through her makeup drawer, she unearthed a sample of perfume from some fancy shop in Savannah and dabbed it between her breasts while muttering to herself that she'd lost her damned mind.

She was certain Rhett had asked her to go with him because he needed someone to be with him. It wasn't a date. But then the way he'd looked at her, held her hand, allowed hopefulness to creep into her heart. So she used the buttery lip gloss Maisie had given her on her birthday. And before she left the bathroom, she glanced at herself in the mirror. The woman staring back at her looked like she thought this was a date.

"Dumb ass," she muttered to her reflection before grabbing a tissue and swiping off the lip gloss. Then she picked the container up and painted it on again. Because a girl always needed pretty lips, date or not.

"Why are you wearing makeup? I thought y'all were going out on the boat," David said from the couch. His packed backpack sat at his feet, his phone was in hand. As always. "You know, Rhett's famous and dates really hot girls."

Implication: You're not in his league. In fact, you're not even playing the same sport.

Summer stopped and looked at her son, who was waiting for Hunt to pick him up for the night. "I know that, but I wasn't going to go out looking like a hag."

"All I'm saying is, don't be weird, Mom." David returned his gaze to the phone. He pecked at it and then looked back up at her.

"I don't need your advice, David. You're fourteen and don't know a fraction of what you need to know when it comes to women."

"I know you fixed your hair to go on a boat."

"I braided my hair so it wouldn't get knotted and took a shower so I didn't compete with the shrimp Pete leaves on board. I know who Rhett is and I know who I am. Thanks for the reminder, though." She sounded miffed. She shouldn't. Her son was absolutely correct. She didn't have any business lusting after Rhett.

"I wasn't being insulting, Mama. Just so you know."

She absolutely knew. She'd always known. Rhett Bryan was out of her league . . . even more so now that he was a celebrity. "When's your father picking you up? And are you wearing cologne?" She sniffed the air, catching a hint of something that smelled like Axe body spray.

"He's on his way, and, I know you're going to freak, but there's this party. No, not party. Get-together. Some of the baseball guys invited me."

"Party? No. You're too young for a party."

"Mom, I'm nearly fifteen, and everyone's going. Especially a lot of the guys from the baseball team. I'm trying to get to know them and stuff. There'll be parents around. I think it's a bonfire. Dad knows the people and said it's okay with him if it's okay with you."

"I don't know about this, Dave. You're springing this on me as I'm walking out the door. I know what happens at parties."

"What? You get pregnant?"

He might as well have slapped her. "Are you really going to do this right now?"

David's face hardened. "What? It's hard to make friends here, Mom. Especially when your parents aren't married and barely talk to each other. It's the first party I've been invited to, and I like these guys. I just want to go by for a while. Dad said he'd take me and pick me up. And Lyle Alexander will be there. He goes to church with me."

Summer still smarted from his flippant comment. Yeah, David knew he'd been the result of prom night, but he didn't know that Summer and Hunt had barely known each other. Summer hadn't felt the need to include details, only tell him that she had no regrets. Little white lies never hurt, and she loved that kid like there was no tomorrow. Clichéd as the phrase was. "Will there be alcohol?"

"The parents aren't passing it out or anything, if that's what you mean." He waggled his shoulders and looked at her like he could do nothing about other kids sneaking in booze. Which he couldn't. "I won't drink. I don't even like that stuff."

"You're not making me feel better about this, and I have to go."

"Please, Mom. I want to make friends with these guys. They're cool, and if I make the team, we'll be playing together."

Indecision flip-flopped inside her. "Okay. Fine. Check in when you get there and when you leave. I'll text your father to make sure he's talked to the parents. Next time let's discuss this beforehand. No more ninja attacks." She jabbed her pointed finger at him. "Behave."

"I will," David, said breaking into a rare grin. "I'll be a Boy Scout."

"Yeah, you will," Summer said, pushing out the door into the coolness of the night. She had a lump of apprehension in her gut. David wasn't really ready for parties, was he? Or perhaps she wasn't ready for parties and all they implied. She still remembered prom night, the vodka shots, and . . . what happened with Hunt.

She paused midstep, prepared to spin around and tell David he couldn't go, but just as she made to turn, headlights swung past her. Hunt drove up the gravel path in his big truck. She stood still, waiting for him to pull up.

"Evening, Summer, David ready?" Hunt said as the window rolled down.

"I'm ready," David called out from behind her. He passed her, throwing an arm around her shoulders. "Bye, Mom."

He pocketed his phone, slung his backpack over his shoulder, and hurried to the idling truck. "Hey, Dad. Mom said I can go to the Easterlys for the bonfire."

"You okay with it?" Hunt asked, leaning forward, sounding surprised.

"Are you?"

"I think he'll be okay. I know the Easterlys pretty well. Good people."

"I'm hesitant to let him go because I've not really talked to him about parties. What happens at parties." She tried not to laden her words, but it came out that way.

A flash of irritation zipped across Hunt's face. He hated being reminded of that night fifteen years before. Summer understood. She didn't like remembering it much herself. "I'll talk to him about drinking and girls. I'm prepared to do that."

"Okay," she said, almost smiling as a horrified look appeared on her son's face. "I think he needs a curfew. Ten thirty?"

"Eleven," David was quick to counter.

Liz Talley

"Ten forty-five it is," Hunt said with a smile before shifting the truck in gear. "Don't worry, Summer. He's growing up, but you raised him right."

Summer waved as they bumped off down the driveway, hoping Hunt's words were the truth.

She walked around Pete's house and headed down toward the boathouse. The large boat bobbed gently in the inlet, but Rhett wasn't in sight. Her footfall on the wooden deck sounded somehow profound, like she'd made up her mind about something. Thing was, she didn't know what. No clue where she and Rhett were heading . . . if anywhere.

"Ahoy, mate," Rhett said, emerging from the boathouse.

"Ahoy," she said, giving him a smile.

The man looked like every woman's dream in a pair of khaki jeans that hung so perfectly on his frame it somehow seemed indecent. A Henley clung to his torso, and he'd pulled a University of South Carolina ball cap over his burnished locks. The running shoes should have looked dorky, but they didn't. He looked like he'd stepped out of a catalog for the outdoorsman.

Conversely, Summer looked like she'd stepped out of a gypsy encampment. She wore wide-legged pants with an embroidered hem, artisan clogs, and a tight, light-blue T-shirt beneath her old windproof navy jacket. Big hoop earrings brushed her shoulders, and she prayed the wind on the boat ride wouldn't pull them loose.

"You look fantastic," Rhett said, eyeing her appreciatively.

A warm glow flickered in her belly. "Thank you. Oh darn, I meant to bring some water or something to drink."

"Beat you to it. I've got wine and the makings for a pretty spectacular cheese board. I went to Publix." He untied the rope from the boat and extended his hand to her.

She took it, expecting a tingle just from taking his hand. No disappointment there. She felt his touch down into her very soul.

174

Oh please, sister. Get a grip. Wine and cheese doesn't equate to anything other than possible gas.

But her hopeful, romantic voice trampled the voice of reality.

Wine? Cheese? Moonlight? Ding. Ding. Ding. You're on a date, sister.

"Oh, and how was that? Traffic jam? Old ladies faint in the aisles?" she joked, stepping into the boat and making her way toward the seat behind the windshield.

"Old ladies? Hell, no. I had the young ones dropping like flies," he joked, knotting the rope and securing it on the bow. He walked to the back and did something or another and then appeared beside her, sinking into the driver's seat.

"Like flies, huh?" she joked.

"Doesn't sound so good when you think about the comparison." He handed her a life vest and secured the windshield. "Hopefully, it won't get too cold. I know it's silly, but I love to ride at night when the moon is full. The world falls away and there's nothing but darkness and light."

"Wow, you're a poet," she said.

"Nah. I'm just trying to impress the songwriter." He cranked the engine and motored away from the boathouse and dock, heading out toward the river that would take them to the bay. The glowing orb in the sky created a pathway on the water, seducing them out into the openness, daring them to follow the light.

As soon as Rhett hit the river, he opened the engine up. They skittered across the water, wind tearing at them, the boat rollicking toward open ocean. The feeling of careening into nothingness was exhilarating, and Summer found herself laughing for no reason other than she was alive and could feel that down to her painted toenails.

Glancing over at Rhett, she could see the tension melt away. His gorgeous mouth tipped up in pleasure, and at that moment he looked exactly like the boy she remembered, the one who had no cares, who had everything stretched before him in a bountiful smorgasbord of life.

Summer settled back and enjoyed the ride across the bay, waving despite the darkness when they saw other boats coming in for the night. She wondered if they wondered why two fools were heading out while they headed in. Maybe they thought them reckless. Maybe they were right.

Eventually, they hit open water, but Rhett kept the boat parallel with the shoreline. Large houses glittered against the blackness, and the moon cast a beautiful glow on the inky waters that were capped with lacy foam as the waves rolled over. After several minutes, Rhett veered the boat toward a small, uninhabited island.

"We can 'park' here and open the wine," he said above the whine of the engine. He motored closer to shore, where the waves were lazy, shut the engine off, and dropped the anchor.

A profound quietness encapsulated them, punctuated by the swoosh of the small waves against the beach.

Rhett rose and unlatched the windshield, moving to the front of the boat. He withdrew a basket from the cargo hold and spread an old quilt over the fishing deck. "Come on. Let's open this wine and enjoy the view."

Summer unlatched her life jacket and slipped it from her shoulders. The wind was cool but soft, stirring only the tendrils that had escaped her braid. She rubbed her still-glossed lips together and noted that Rhett uncorking a bottle of wine with the moonlight threading his golden hair did look, indeed, like a date. Maybe this was what he'd intended all along.

Her heart leaped against her sternum.

Moving to the front, Summer accepted a stemmed glass of wine from Rhett. "This looks nice. Thank you."

"Oh, here," he said, lifting the top of another storage unit and bringing out a velveteen throw. "Picked this up, too. Didn't know how cool it would be."

Summer took the plush throw and wrapped it loosely around her shoulders as she sank onto the blanket and crossed her legs. The moon loomed over them, somehow bigger than normal.

Rhett filled his own glass and then lifted it. "To old friends and a Carolina moon."

"Hear, hear," Summer said, clinking hers against his and taking a sip of the crisp white wine. "My gram used to call it a whiskey moon because it was when her folks used to run the moonshine."

Rhett smiled and Summer felt her heart trip. God, he looked so good with the wind tousling his hair, his face so smooth and unworried in the softness of the night. His teeth flashed perfectly white, and every inch of his body begged to be touched. She so wanted to touch him. Just feel his warmth beneath her fingertips. "I like that, but I've always called it a Carolina moon, even out in LA. The moon never seemed as big as it did here. Made me feel so small, but so connected at the same time."

"Yeah, I see what you mean," she said, studying the orb.

"Am I the Carolina boy?"

Summer flashed hot and felt the heat in her cheeks. "What?"

"In your song. I remember you calling me that once in high school."

"Maybe, but it's an homage to every guy from here. Just a song."

"Funny, it didn't feel that way," he said, taking a sip of wine and staring out at the reflection of that moon on the water.

It wasn't like Summer could admit Rhett often floated into her subconscious when she wrote about love, longing, or loss. There were times she'd not thought about Rhett. That was true. She'd been in a few relationships where she'd found love or what she'd thought was love. What she'd felt for Rhett had been an idealized crush, a fantasy conjured by a lonely, plump girl who'd somehow captured the attention of the "it" boy. So, sure, sometimes she summoned that yearning in her songs, but she wasn't in love with Rhett. She hardly knew him.

"Maybe it's just the way you sing it. Felt like it was for me. Guess every guy around here feels that way. You're really good, Funny Valentine. Really good."

His use of her old nickname made her chest feel tight. "Thank you, Rhett."

He reached out and took her hand. "The years blur things, you know. I remember some things so vividly. Silly things like where we buried the senior class time capsule or when Andrea Floyd told Wade Smothers, 'Forget about it, buster,' when he tried to feel her up at the junior high dance, but I don't remember why you were so mad at me."

Summer swallowed hard. "I wasn't mad at you."

"Yeah, you were. I came to your house the day after prom. We went out on the porch and you played your guitar. Y'all had a screened porch, and you told me you didn't want to tutor me anymore."

"I don't want to talk about it. It's all in the past." She pulled her hand away and inwardly pleaded with Rhett not to go there. Not to ruin this beautiful moment with questions about a past she'd tried so hard to put behind her.

"You told me sometimes it helped to discuss things you don't want to discuss."

"What do I know?" she said petulantly.

That made him smile. "I don't know. I guess I feel like that's still between us."

"You didn't even remember me when you first saw me. How can something that happened almost fifteen years ago bother you?"

"I don't know. Like I said, some things you remember. Others you forget. It bothered me that you were so mad. I mean, I know what happened at the party the night before was . . . awkward, but we'd been friends. You threw that away."

Summer felt anger edge out the earlier sweetness. That anger was always there, ready to clamber out and seethe with indignation. "Big deal. You were bothered by the geek who didn't allow you to shellac over

178

ugly stuff with his charm. That's your problem. You think a wink and a smile will make everything better. It doesn't."

He recoiled. "I don't do that."

"Yeah, you do. You've always done it. What happened that night couldn't be erased by your good will, Rhett. Ugly things happen and they can't be undone. And there's no way to fix it. It just is. It exists. It doesn't go away." She lifted her glass and sucked down the rest of the wine. Then she grabbed the bottle and poured herself another glass. Hell, with the way this "not actually a date" was going, she'd need the whole effing bottle.

Rhett sat there, studying her, his face etched with hurt. It struck her that her words weren't merely about her situation in the past, but about his situation. He ran from something he couldn't undo. There were no take backs. No erasing the horror. A person had to learn to live with it. That realization was simple. And the hardest thing anyone could ever endure.

After a few seconds, Rhett took her glass.

"Hey, I want that," she said, reaching for his hand. Rhett set her glass next to his and pulled her to him. "What are you doing?"

He wrapped his arms around her, settling her between his legs. His hand pressed her head against his chest and he just held her.

"Rhett?" she whispered.

"What?"

"What are you doing?" she asked.

"I'm doing what I should have done that day. Just being your friend."

His arms squeezed her and she stilled, sneaking her arms around his waist, inhaling the essence of the boy she'd always wanted. A boy who'd grown into a man. A man who still made her blood race, her body tingle, and her heart ache for what she couldn't have.

For several minutes they stayed locked that way, with Rhett's hands occasionally stroking her shoulder or rubbing her waist. There was nothing sexual in the embrace, but even so, Summer was hyperaware of the desire simmering on the horizon. She wanted Rhett. God, she wanted him.

Summer pushed against him and he released her. "Thank you."

He brushed a tendril behind her ear. "You're so beautiful, Summer."

"Don't do that," she whispered, blinking back the sudden emotion that brought tears to her eyes.

"Why not?"

"Because . . ." She shook her head. "I think before we go any further in any direction, I need to tell you about that night. I need to tell you why I was so angry at you. It wasn't because you rejected me. It was because you didn't save me. You fell off your white steed."

"I don't understand. I thought this was about what happened between us."

"That was part of it, and my anger was irrational. I understand it now. But you'll understand everything better when I tell you what really happened between Hunt and me."

"But first," he said, leaning forward. "I just want this one moment."

His lips covered hers.

Summer inhaled deeply, the tang of the ocean, the scent of Rhett's expensive cologne, and then she reveled in his mouth pressed against hers.

He tasted of wine and moonlight, of whiskey and regret, of hope and redemption. His hands lifted to cradle her face, and she opened her mouth to him, drinking him in.

The moment should have been sweet, reverent even, but it wasn't. It was consuming. Hot. Enveloping all her senses, drowning out anything hard, bad, and ugly. Beauty had come to her, and it was in the kiss of Rhett Bryan.

He broke the kiss and studied her face, which he held in his hands. "God, I want you. And I've wanted to do that ever since I saw you in that bathing suit ready to bash me over the head with a lamp. Not that I would even admit it to myself."

His words stole her breath.

He pressed his lips against her forehead. "That was totally for me, I needed that kiss to tide me over."

Summer closed her eyes. "You really are a poet, Rhett, but I meant what I said last night. You can't play with me."

His light laugh skated on the salty breeze. "I knew you wouldn't forget your convictions."

"I don't want to get hurt."

"Who does?" He handed her the wineglass. "But we're getting ahead of ourselves. Tell me what happened that night. Let's finally put the past behind us."

CHAPTER SEVENTEEN

April 2003

In movies, parties are always portrayed with hundreds of people making out, funneling beer, and hot tubbing in their bras and panties. So Summer was a little disappointed—or was that relieved?—that an hour into Hunt's after-prom party, there were only forty people, and it felt more like a cocktail mixer than a rager.

Of course, the night was young, and a steady stream of people rolling through the door along with the raid on the liquor cabinet ensured it would get rowdier as the night progressed.

She'd kissed Hunt in the limo, but ever since they'd arrived, he'd been hanging with a group of guys, shooting vodka or tequila. He hadn't even glanced her way.

"Summer, taste this. It's Diet 7UP and Malibu," Graysen said, shoving a drink into her hand. "You can have tons of these. Hardly any calories."

Was that an insult? Or just a "one of the girls" kind of observation? She took a cautious sip and found it was pretty good. Way better than straight vodka, which had nearly killed her. Summer kept one eye on the door, hoping Nessa would show up to save her from the popular people and their "light" alcoholic beverages. Her toes were pinched and she had a vague headache. Her bed sounded like heaven.

Katie B wriggled between her and Graysen. "Jace just showed up."

"Sweet," Graysen said, her mouth curving into a crocodilian smile. "I'm about to get lit, bitches."

Summer blinked as Katie tugged Graysen toward the balcony. Graysen looked back. "Come on, Summer. Time for something new. Jace has some good shit."

"Uh, I'll be right out. I need to go to the bathroom real quick. Gotta adjust the Spanx." Summer didn't know why she added the thing about the Spanx. She wasn't even wearing them. Maybe because it established an intimacy between her and the popular girl. God, her AP psych class was showing.

But something told her she needed to avoid Jace and his good shit.

Slipping between a few people talking about setting up a beer pong table, whatever that was, she made her way toward the kitchen. When she pushed into the swinging door, she nearly ran into Rhett.

"Whoa, hey, Sum," Rhett said, juggling four beer cans. "Where you heading? Party's out here."

"I just needed a slight break. Uh, just some fresh air."

"Here." Rhett handed the beers off to some beefy guy Summer didn't know. She thought he was a junior and on the football team. "Give these to Hunt. I'm stepping out with Summer for a moment."

The guy looked at Summer and then shot Rhett a "whatever" look.

"Come out here," Rhett said, opening the kitchen door. "What are you drinking? You doing okay?"

"Yeah, um, it's rum and 7UP. It's good. I just got, I don't know, overwhelmed." Summer felt stupid saying that. Maybe she was slightly overwhelmed and a little drunk, but she had enough sense to know she didn't need to go with Graysen. She was pretty sure the cheerleader and pageant queen was about to get high on marijuana, and Summer wasn't interested in doing that at all. A few drinks? No big deal. Dope was a whole other thing.

Rhett headed down the steps. "Let's go down to the beach. I love the way the moon sits on the water."

If she hadn't already been head over heels for him, she would have tumbled at that exact moment. What eighteen-year-old guy liked the way the moonlight reflected on the water and had enough confidence to say it aloud?

Summer took a huge gulp of her drink. Then another, appreciating how the warmth of the alcohol seeped into her bones and made her feel . . . not quite herself. It made her feel loose, almost as if she was . . . as if she belonged.

Rhett turned and waited on her to come down the steps. Some of the girls had changed out of their prom dresses, but Summer hadn't known to bring extra clothes. Rhett still wore his tux trousers, which he rolled up after toeing off his shoes and peeling off his socks. His jacket had been left behind along with the bow tie and cummerbund. His shirt was open, revealing that delicious indentation she'd contemplated weeks ago in the doorway of Mr. Wilson's class. She had to find out what that spot was called. It seemed imperative to know.

Carefully, she unbuckled her shoes and set them, along with her drink, next to Rhett's on the step. Hiking up her dress and praying it wouldn't get ruined, she followed Rhett to the hard-packed beach. The sand glittered with a confetti of sparkles, and small sand crabs skittered to find hidey holes. The waves insistently pounded the beach, and the full moon tossed its light playfully on the water.

"God, it's gorgeous out here. Sometimes I wish I were Hunt. All that money, this house. One day I'll have it, though," Rhett said, shoving his hands in his pockets, staring out where the waves broke. He looked a little lost, but determination steeled his voice.

"I'm pretty certain you will, Rhett," she said, coming to stand beside him, clutching her filmy gown into two big bunches. She still wore the corsage and wished she'd left it behind, too. She wanted to save the cluster of white roses. Preserve the night by drying it and putting it in the memory box her father had given her. Just like her mother had done.

The sand was hard, not as soft as it looked. She wriggled her toes and tried to pretend it was an everyday thing to stand on the beach beneath a spread of stars with the most awesome guy she'd ever met.

He turned to her. "It's so easy being with you, Summer. You're just comfortable."

She didn't know what to say to that. What did that even mean? Was she like his favorite recliner? Not worthy of even trying? Not even a girl to him? Just a buddy?

Why was she even out here with him, anyway? Her date was inside. His girlfriend was on the back patio smoking weed. They shouldn't be out here alone.

"Are you okay, Rhett?" That was all she had. Maybe he could explain why they walked barefoot on the beach in the middle of a so-called "epic" party, and why he wanted her to go along with him.

"Yeah, maybe I'm a bit overwhelmed myself. California's pretty far, and I don't really know my mother's family well. I've only visited them a few times. This feels like such a big commitment, and so many people tell me I shouldn't go."

"Who tells you that?"

"Graysen. She's pissed I'm going so far away, angry that I want to make a clean break with her. But not just her—some of my friends. Their parents. They think chasing an acting career is stupid. Maybe it is." His words were plaintive and she knew what he wanted. He wanted her to say it wasn't stupid. He wanted her to say he'd made the right decision.

"Or maybe being in front of the camera is what you're made to do," Summer said, drawing a line in the wet sand with her toe. "But it's okay. Everyone has doubts."

"You probably don't. Bet you have everything planned out." His voice held affection. He turned to her and tucked a tendril of hair behind her ear. "You know, you're going to make some guy so happy one day, Funny Valentine. I know you can't see it, but you're truly beautiful."

Summer's mouth went dry. "That's . . . that's not true, Rhett. But you're nice for saying so."

"No, it's true. You can't see it. Some girls hit their stride in middle school. Some in high school. They peak. But I can see what a knockout you'll be someday." He slid an arm around her shoulders and pulled her close to him. She fit perfectly next to him, and she awkwardly looped an arm around his waist, careful not to muss her corsage.

She could smell his warmth, feel him inhale then exhale. The squishy feelings she'd had in the limo when kissing Hunt came back, but this time with a vengeance. His too-sweet words paired with the booze coated her, made her want to . . . be daring. For once.

What would it hurt? To kiss him just once? She could go to her grave being happy she'd had one taste of Rhett Bryan.

So she turned into him. Reached up. Pulled his head down. And kissed him.

She partially missed his mouth but didn't disengage to correct the aim. Because the emotions that swept her, that riveted her to him, couldn't be put off even for a millisecond. She was committed to that kiss.

At first he did nothing, but then she felt it—the straightening of his body, the pulling away. He set his hands on her shoulders and pushed her back.

Summer felt dazed, but then she opened her eyes and saw what she least wanted to see in his eyes—pity.

"Sum, hey, I—" he started, shaking his head, those eyes full of alarm, pity, regret.

"No, don't say anything," Summer pleaded. "Just don't. I get it. I get it."

He looked crestfallen. Disappointed, even. "I'm with Graysen. I'm sorry if I said . . . God, I shouldn't have said all that. I wanted you to know you're such a special girl. I—"

"Shut up," she said, scrabbling backward and nearly tripping over a random piece of driftwood. How could she have been so absolutely stupid? Of course, he was just being nice when he said she was beautiful. That's what Rhett was. Gorgeous, talented, funny . . . and nice. Especially to fat, drunk, loser girls who had infantile crushes on him.

He stepped toward her, stretching out a hand. "Sum—"

"Shut *up*." She turned and hiked up her dress, not even caring if he could see her plump white thighs, and she ran back toward the house. Her body burned with shame, with absolute despair. She'd made a fool of herself with Rhett. A stupid-ass fool.

She felt as if she'd been electrocuted. Her body thrummed with shame. "Oh God, oh God, oh God," she chanted as she scooped up her sandals, leaving the drink, and hurried up the steps. She wanted to go home but didn't know who could take her.

Someone had to because she had to get out of there.

She flung open the door to the kitchen and scared the people clustered around the island lining up tequila shots. Hunt was pouring. "Oh hey. There you are. Want a shot?"

Summer slammed the door and looked at everyone waiting for her answer. "Yeah. I want a shot."

Fifteen minutes later, the room spun a little, but that was okay because Hunt was being nice to her. He'd joked with her, occasionally brushed his hand across her ass, pulled her to him once and kissed her. She'd let him, praying that his lips could erase the kiss she'd forced on Rhett.

Rhett hadn't come inside through the kitchen, thank God. Because she couldn't handle seeing him again that night. She shouldn't have gone to the beach with him anyway. Not when her date was apparently digging her, if his lips on her neck and the way he pressed against her were any indication.

After a couple more tequila rounds, Hunt murmured, "Wanna come see my baseball card collection?" He pressed another sloppy kiss against her neck.

A couple of guys hooted. It was some inside joke. But Summer was angry and hurt and didn't give a shit if they laughed. She wanted someone to fix the raw, throbbing rejection pulsing inside her.

"You have a baseball card collection here? At your beach house?" she asked, trying to flirt and play innocent.

Hunt looked at his friends and grinned. "Oh, baby, I got something you've got to see."

Grabbing her hand and pulling her to him, Hunt walked her backward as his friends laughed. She should have felt embarrassed or outraged or something. But she felt something she'd never felt before at that moment—she felt desired. Rhett didn't want her, but Hunt did.

She could feel Hunt's erection pressing against her stomach, and the way he nuzzled her neck made wicked, molten, loopy loops in her tummy. She felt overheated, but she damned sure didn't feel geeky and awkward. Funny how tequila did that to a gal.

There was a back set of steps that led from the kitchen to an upper floor. Hunt stopped when they got to the top and pressed her against the wall and kissed her.

"Mmm," she murmured, liking the way his kisses made her feel. She'd always wondered how it really felt to be turned on by an actual guy and not just by a love scene in a book or movie. Mindlessly wonderful would be the best description. Mindlessly wonderful.

"Come here," Hunt said, taking her hand and pulling her down the hallway. They passed another couple who barely glanced their way. They seemed intent on finding a dark corner or bedroom themselves.

Hunt opened a door and pulled her inside. The room was empty and held a queen-size bed covered in a navy coverlet. Summer didn't have much time to peruse the décor because Hunt was suddenly all over her.

"You're so much hotter than I thought," Hunt murmured, capturing her lips before moving his lips across her jaw to her neck. "You smell good, too."

"I took a bath," Summer said, before giggling. It was an absurd thing to say to a compliment, but she felt so not herself. Her fingertips felt numb and her thighs heavy. She knew she'd weaved her way up the stairs and now just wanted to sink down somewhere so she didn't have to keep her balance. Wait, where were her shoes? Had she left them on the beach? Or in the kitchen?

Hunt maneuvered her toward the bed. "Let's sit down."

She nodded, but that made the room spin. A lamp on a decorative table across the room gave faint light, making Hunt look sexy. He was just like one of the guys in her books. Strong, silent, somewhat arrogant. But deep down, he was sweet. Who needed Rhett Bryan when there was Hunt, right?

The room tilted again as she plopped down onto the bed. "I feel funny."

"You're not going to puke, are you?" Hunt eyed her with something that was not desire. She didn't want him to look at her like that. She wanted him to want her again.

"Nu-uh, come back over here. Kiss me some more. You're good at it," she said, holding her hand out.

Hunt smiled. "Yeah? I told you I could teach you to be a little bad. Want to be a bit more, Summer? 'Cause I know some bad things we could do." Hunt came to her, wrapping a hand around her waist, clutching her rump, and she could feel his arousal. He nuzzled her neck and she prayed it wasn't sweaty.

"You do? I'm really hot," she said, pushing against him.

"It's this dress," he said, bunching up the fabric. "We can do something about that."

The zipper was on the side. Hunter made quick work of it but couldn't get the hook and eye undone. "I can do it," she said, undoing the clasp. The bodice gaped open and Hunt peeled it from her.

"Damn," he said, once the dress hit the floor. "You are curvy as shit. I like it."

Summer tried to look down at her body, which was cinched into an hourglass with the Lycra bustier with tummy support that her mother had insisted on. Edged in lace and mimicking something French, it was the sexiest undergarment Summer had ever owned. It made her look kinda skinny. Held everything in.

Hunt grabbed her and pulled her on top of him. Then he rolled so they were at the head of the mattress and Hunt was half on her. His hands ran up and down her sides, clasping her butt, stroking her thighs. He kissed her over and over, his tongue thrusting inside her mouth. In the back of his throat, he made little groans that made her pelvis feel achy.

Maybe this was how it felt to fall in love, all molten lava and heavy breathing. She lifted her hands to tangle in his hair because that's what the heroines always did in the movies. Because that's what you did when you were making out.

"Sum, baby, are you on birth control, or do I need to use something?"

"Hmm?" she asked, kissing him but then realizing he needed to understand she wasn't going that far. "No, you won't need to use anything. I can't—"

"Good, good, baby," he interrupted, nuzzling her neck, moving his lips down to where her breasts strained against the cups of the bustier, making her forget she needed to clarify. "How does this come off? How did I not see how hot you were? Holy shit."

Take it off? Summer wanted to keep doing what they were doing. She hadn't planned on going to second base on the first date. Was touching boobs second base? Maybe she could let him do that. She'd always wondered how it would feel to have a guy touch her there. It was prom night and he seemed really into her. He'd said she was hot.

His fingers were already around her back, unhooking the bra part of the garment. Just two little hooks to give extra support was what the saleslady had said. The unfastening allowed the cups to gape open.

Hunt folded the cups down, revealing her breasts. She wasn't huge, but she was a full size C, almost a D, and he looked really happy about that.

"Nice," he murmured, cupping her left breast and kissing the top of the right. Summer felt like she wasn't herself. She'd never imagined letting Hunt do something like this to her, but she sort of liked it. She was supposed to like it. Even Nessa had let the saxophone guy touch her boobs. Everyone did it. Or at least she thought so. She wasn't sure, though.

The rattle of the doorknob made Hunt pause. He flipped her bra back up as the door sprang open. Over Hunt's shoulder, Summer could see Rhett's face. He looked as if he'd discovered a crime scene.

Rhett's mouth, which had been open, snapped shut, and he goggled at them, lying on Hunt's bed. Or what she thought was Hunt's bed. Maybe it was just the guest room.

"What the fuck, bro?" Hunt said, giving Rhett a glare over his shoulder. "You can't knock?"

"What're you doing? Is that Summer?"

"Get the fuck out, Rhett. Seriously, dude."

At that moment, Rhett looked past Hunt to Summer. Shame seared her body, and suddenly she felt pretty damned sober. Wrapping her arms around her now-covered breasts, she struggled to sit.

"It's okay," Hunt said, pressing her back. "He's leaving."

Rhett hesitated. "Sum? You okay?"

She should have said no. She should have gotten up, even though Rhett would see her dimpled thighs, and left the room. But then she remembered the way he'd looked at her on the beach. In his eyes, she could see that same pity sharing space with concern. Did he think she was some baby who couldn't make her own decisions? He'd made her feel like a fool, and now he was making her feel like a child who needed protection. He shouldn't have the power to make her feel like a pathetic loser. "I'm fine."

But she wasn't. She wasn't ready to do what she was doing with Hunt. She'd only had her first kiss earlier that night . . . and it was with the wrong boy.

Get up, follow Rhett, and find a ride home. You don't belong here.

"Lock the door on your way out. We don't want to be interrupted again," Hunt said, impatience in his voice.

Rhett didn't move. He watched Summer, waiting for her to say something. She stared back at him, still angry, still hating the way he'd made her feel. Worthless. Rhett had made her feel worthless. After a few long seconds, Rhett murmured "Okay," clicked the button lock, and shut the door.

"Jesus," Hunt said, tugging her to him. "Way to ruin a mood, huh?"

He kissed her and she tried to recapture the desire by kissing him back. He still tasted like alcohol, and she wondered irrationally if she should send him down for more tequila. She felt like she needed more booze so she could get back into the spirit of things. Pun intended.

Hunt's hands were back on her breasts, kneading and squeezing, as he muttered incoherent things in her ear. He still wanted her.

Then his hands slid down to the silky panties that covered her butt. "Ah, wait, Hunt."

But his hands slipped inside, kneading the globe and pulling her against his erection. Desire mixed with alarm inside her brain. She couldn't go this far even if it felt good.

"It's okay, Summer. I know what I'm doing, baby. Just relax."

Summer couldn't relax because his hand was in her panties. She opened her eyes, and somehow his shirt had come off. His torso was smooth with the smallest gathering of dark hair between his pecs. He looked good, but not good enough to go where he obviously thought they were going. "Stop, Hunt. I'm not sure this is a good idea."

He kissed her nose. "Your nerves are so cute."

He tried to kiss her but she wrenched her mouth away. "Let's go back to kissing and maybe just up-top stuff, okay? I'm not ready for all that."

"I got you," he said, pulling his hand from her panties. Relief pooled inside her. And when he stroked the sensitive flesh between the edge of the bustier and the lace of her light-pink panties, she didn't protest. His mouth found hers and he spent several minutes doing nothing but kissing her.

And it was good again.

Summer touched his face and reveled in the rasp of his whiskers against her fingers, in the thought he was so different from her. Hunt moved away from her mouth and kissed down her neck. It sort of tickled, but she liked the way it made her feel gooey inside. Then he was back at her breasts and she let him nuzzle them because she'd said he could stay up top. He pinched her nipples and then he sucked one into his mouth.

"Hunt," she gasped, trying to sit up.

His hand pressed her back. "Relax. Your tits are incredible."

Those words were like honey drizzled over her. Maybe her breasts *were* incredible. Maybe this was what she needed—to act more like a woman and less like a little girl. So she let him do what he wanted and vowed to enjoy it.

But then she sensed a change come over him. An urgency. She heard the clink of his pants hitting the floor. God, they were almost naked. She struggled against him. "I can't, Hunt."

"Relax, baby, it's okay," he murmured against her breasts, as his hands wandered back to the waistband of her panties. She wriggled against him, but his fingers were insistent. They dipped down, sliding down between her legs, invading her.

"Hunt, no," she said, her body warring with her brain. Because she couldn't deny that it felt good. She'd imagined this before. But she wasn't ready. It was too much, too soon.

"God, you're so wet," he said, his hand moving against her.

For a moment she lost her breath. Her hips jerked because the actual touch of his fingers on her most intimate area felt good. Still, she didn't want this. She wasn't going to have sex with Hunt McCroy on prom night. It was too trite. Too ridiculous. Too wrong.

"Stop, Hunt. I don't want to do this. Please," she said, pressing against his chest as she scooted her bottom away from him.

"Don't be nervous. Just relax. I know how to make it good," he said, kissing her cheek before moving down to nuzzle her neck.

Part of her wanted to let him do what he wished. Her body seemed to like it. But the other part of her knew this was a mistake. "You probably can, but I don't want to have sex. I'm not ready."

"You feel ready," he whispered in her ear as his hands left her body.

Relief burgeoned, but then she realized he'd freed his hands only so he could do something to his boxers.

"Hunt, stop," she said as she felt his penis slap her thigh. He'd wedged his knee between her legs, prying them apart. "I mean it. I don't want to."

"It's okay to be nervous, Summer," Hunt said, nipping her lower lip. "Just relax, baby."

"No, get off me," she said, bucking her hips the way she did when she and Maisie wrestled and her sister tried to sit on her. Hunt didn't move. Instead her motion brought her hips up, allowing his penis to slide against the crotch of her panties. The sensation startled her. Scared her.

"Hey, hey," he said, catching her fists before she could shove him off. "Everyone's a little anxious the first time, but you're going to like it, baby. I promise."

Fear clawed at Summer, making the spit dry in her mouth. Hunt was going to do this. He was forcing himself on her. "Please don't, Hunt. I don't want to. I'm saying no."

"But your body is saying yes. You're so wet for me." He released one of her wrists and pushed the crotch of her panties aside, dragging his finger through the dampness between her legs. "See?"

Then he jabbed his penis into the entrance of her body and pushed forward. And it hurt.

Summer screamed and kicked her legs. "Stop it, you asshole. Get off me."

"Shh! Just relax, Summer. You're working yourself up. You're going to make this worse," he panted as he held one of her wrists above her head and started to move inside her. His torso crushed her, pinning her to the bed.

Panic swept over her. She'd said no. *She'd said no.* But he hadn't cared. He was inside her, moving. "Please, Hunt. Please stop."

"Shit, you're tight. Christ almighty," Hunt groaned, moving fast inside her, like he couldn't hear her. Maybe he couldn't. She couldn't see his face, and her effort to use her right hand to push him back failed. She smacked against his back, but he didn't seem to feel it.

Her wrist hurt from where he'd pinioned it, and his hand on her hip cemented her to the bed. She tried to lift her knee to dislodge him from her body, but her motion only made it easier for him.

"That's it. Yeah," he said, moving faster, his hot breath coating her ear.

"Stop," Summer said against his throat. She head-butted his shoulder. "Please. I don't want to do this."

But Hunt didn't stop. He kept thrusting, the pain searing her, her panic fading away to acceptance. Summer stopped fighting and turned her head from him. The scent of his cologne made her nauseous. Or perhaps that was the stupid vodka coming back up, perched in the back of her throat. The room no longer spun. Maybe being raped sobered up a girl.

Hunt grunted and made strangling sounds before he pumped his hips harder and collapsed on top of her with a guttural, "Oh shit."

Summer lay there as Hunt sprawled atop her, still breathing hard. She couldn't seem to move. Like someone in a car wreck who had an out-of-body experience, she saw herself crushed beneath Hunt, tears staining her face. Her corsage torn, petals scattered, ironic symbolism of her utter loss.

Hunt kissed her shoulder. "You were good, Summer. So, so good."

A terrible sob shook her, and she couldn't stop her body from convulsing under the shock and grief over what had just transpired. "Oh God. Oh God."

Hunt had released her hand and now he seemed to register her reaction. "Are you okay? What's the matter?"

Grief spilled out of her and she pushed him off her. She felt his penis slip from her body and thought she might vomit. Her thighs now felt wet and sticky as she scooted from him, flipping up the bodice of the bustier so it covered her breasts.

"Summer, what's wrong? Don't cry. Sometimes it's a little uncomfortable the first time." Hunt said it like he was a doctor delivering a prognosis. *I just violated you and it might have been uncomfortable. But you were good and tight and wet so it's okay. Happy Losing Your Virginity by Rape Day, Summer.*

Summer wanted to hit him, but she didn't. Because she didn't know him. He might hit her back. So for a moment she just stared at him, tears streaming down her face, her panties bunched in her crack. She averted her eyes because she could see he didn't even realize what he'd done. Or he didn't want to admit what he'd done. She picked up a crushed petal lying on the coverlet, closed her eyes, and sobbed. "Why did you do that?"

"Do what?"

"Do that when I said no? You shouldn't have done that," she said, swiping at her face. "What kind of a person does that?"

He looked baffled. "I didn't do anything wrong. You were into it. It's like I said, sometimes uncomfortable the first time. I tried not to go too fast."

"I wasn't into it," she said, snapping her head around, glaring at him. "I told you to stop."

Hunt moved toward her. "Come here, Summer. It's okay. I tried to make it good for you."

"Stop," she said, holding up a hand. "Don't touch me."

"Come on, Summer," he said, his voice cajoling, lowering to sound as if he were talking to a child. "Don't turn it into something it wasn't. We had sex. People have it all the time. I know maybe I wasn't as patient as I should have been, but you wanted it."

She blinked at him. He really didn't get it. The dude had just raped her and he didn't get it. "No, I didn't. You forced that. You're . . . don't touch me."

Hunt stood up, tucking himself into his boxers and pulling on the pants he'd discarded. "You know what, this is bullshit. You're trying to make it sound like I raped you or something. Maybe it wasn't the best experience and you're upset. Okay, whatever, but don't act like you weren't into it. We both know that's a lie."

His hard words peppered her with disdain, and she stared at the scattered petals and then at the ruined ribbons half torn from her wrist corsage. Something about the destruction made her cry harder. She gathered the petals in her hand, unable to stop the tears, the grief, the shame. "You ruined it."

"It's a corsage," he said, shrugging on his shirt and looking at her like she'd lost her mind. "Stupid flowers."

She didn't respond. Couldn't.

Moments before, she'd thought Rhett had made her feel worthless, but she'd been wrong. Worthless was what she now felt. Thrown away. Scattered, never to be whole again. She closed her hands around the petals, crushing them, twisting them.

"You're right. Stupid flowers."

As she released them, tossing them unwanted onto the bed, it occurred to her that it would have been better to follow Graysen outside to smoke the "good shit" with Jace. Better to have gotten high than raped.

She picked up her dress, sober as a judge, insignificant as the petals beneath her feet, and pulled it on, wishing she could die right there. But then again, maybe part of her had.

CHAPTER EIGHTEEN

November, present day

Hunt had never been as terrified as he was standing in the corner of the emergency room, watching the doctor intubate his son. He felt like a boulder sat atop him, pinning him to some awfulness he never knew existed. He realized at that moment that this was what being a parent was. Loving something beyond comprehension and suffering because of that love.

How had this happened? He couldn't comprehend the last twenty minutes—the call, the ambulance, the swooshing doors of the ER giving way to the stretcher David lay on.

"Mr. McCroy?" someone asked from beside him, but he couldn't pull his gaze from the boy lying on the stretcher. David was pale, his shirt covered in puke, his hair plastered to his head. The doctor ran a clear tube down his son's throat. David didn't move. He was completely passed out.

"Huh?" he managed, turning to look at the woman standing beside him.

She had a clipboard in her hands. "Yes, sir. I need to get some information."

Irritation buzzed. "I can't do that now. My son is . . . I can't do that now."

"We don't have to leave your son. Just let me get some basic facts, okay? Like how old is your son?"

"Fourteen. God, he's just fourteen."

The woman droned on with her questions as he watched a nurse start an IV on his son and cut away the ruined shirt. Another aide mopped his face, cleaning up the foamy froth that had clung to David's chin. The boy was thankfully unaware of what was happening to him.

When the Easterlys had called to tell him his son had drunk too much and he needed a pickup, Hunt had intentionally sat on the news. He wanted to put eyes on David before he scared the hell out of the kid's mother. After all, David had been at the get-together for just over an hour and a half. How he'd drunk enough in such a short period of time to pass out didn't seem feasible to Hunt.

But when he got there and saw David, he knew it was serious enough to warrant a 911 call and leave Summer a message to meet him at the hospital.

According to Hal Easterly's son, someone had given David vodka. Lots of it. When Hunt had arrived and found David passed out against the barn, he'd felt vomit rise in his own throat. The boy had thrown up all over himself. He was barely conscious, his breathing shallow. Foam had leaked from his mouth, freaking Hunt out. He'd called the ambulance and then gotten Hal to help him carry the boy to his truck. The other teenagers had stood around, some weaving noticeably, and watched solemnly as he carried his son away. Hunt wanted to shake them all until their teeth rattled, ask them why they would give a freshman that much booze.

"I'm sorry about this, Hunt. I had no idea they had all that liquor. I tried to do a pass every now and then, but I didn't see nothing. I mean, they had Solo cups, and I thought I may have smelled beer, but hell, they're teenagers. I had no clue they were doing all this," Hal had said, looking freaked out himself.

The older man didn't seem to have a clue what kids did these days, and though Hunt knew some of the fault lay with David, he couldn't help the anger that spilled out of him. "You shouldn't have them out here if you can't watch them. My kid is foaming at the mouth. He wasn't even here for two hours. You need to shut that shit down," he said, fighting against the panic as David moaned.

"I know. I'm sorry. Take the boy to the hospital. I'll clear everyone out." Hal didn't seem overly concerned, but then again, his kid wasn't passed out with puke all over him.

The ambulance met them at the end of the long drive. Hunt lifted David from the passenger seat, and the two EMTs took over, placing him on a stretcher and checking his vitals. David was able to open his eyes and follow the light, but as soon as he did, he rolled to the side and threw up.

"At least he's vomiting. It's the ones who don't that scare the hell out of me," the female EMT said, swiping at his son's face, cleaning the puke from his chin and cheek. "We're going to give him some fluids at the hospital. Follow us to the ER."

They loaded his son into the back of the ambulance and took off, lights flashing. Leaving Hunt standing on the gravel road, wondering how in the hell this had happened.

Summer had been apprehensive about letting David go to the party, but Hunt had assured her David would be okay. He *thought* the kid would be okay, and he thought it would be good for David to hang out with some of the guys from the team. Become one of them. Be accepted by the kids who mattered. So Hunt had picked up David, fed him dinner at the Shrimp Shack, and then dropped him off at the Easterlys'. Hunt had even issued warnings about drinking or doing something stupid like messing with the bulls or jumping out of the hayloft. David had rolled his eyes like Hunt was lame, but he'd promised to stay away from trouble.

And look at what had happened.

"Mr. McCroy, the doctor will talk to you now," one of the nurses said, gesturing him over to the bed.

"Hi, Mr. McCroy. I am Dr. Talton, and I'm taking care of your son," the woman in scrubs said, extending a damp hand.

"Thank you for helping him," Hunt said, running a hand through his hair. "I don't know how this happened. He wasn't even at the party long."

"Unfortunately, this sort of thing happens far too often. I did my residency in Columbia, and we got a steady barrage of alcohol poisonings. These kids don't know when to stop," she said, pulling the curtain and moving Hunt away from the bay. "We went ahead and intubated. It's not as serious as it looks, but complications can arise when they aspirate vomit, so best to keep his airway unrestricted and allow him to get oxygen. We've given him an IV to get some needed vitamins and fluids in him. Dehydration is a chief concern. We're going to watch him overnight to make sure his body processes and rids itself of the toxins. He'll wake up soon and we can remove the tube then."

"Is he going to be okay?" Hunt asked, sounding shaky to his own ears.

The doctor shrugged. "He should be, but there can be some complications, depending on exactly how much he drank. High alcohol levels can damage the organs. But most people recover fine. Young bodies and all that, but I can't promise you anything at this point."

Then she left him standing outside the curtain, feeling like a man adrift in an inner tube on a vast ocean. And a shark coming toward him. Yeah, Summer would be here soon, ready to rip him a new one.

He pulled back the curtain and moved toward David's bed. A nurse punched a couple of buttons on the IV cart and then moved around him, pulling the curtain open again. "Let me know if you need anything."

Then she, too, was gone, leaving him alone with his son.

David's lashes were long and lay in stark contrast to his pale cheeks. He looked so young, so vulnerable. Hunt felt his heart contract and emotion clog his throat. God, how had he failed so badly? He'd encouraged David to go, to hang out with the guys on the team. What kind of idiot encouraged his kid to go to a party thrown by upperclassmen? One who didn't know how to parent. Obviously.

Was this a message from the universe? That he wasn't cut out to be a parent? Why had he thought he could correct the mistakes he'd made in the past with the kid? Same ol' Hunt. Always shitting himself when it mattered.

The curtain ripped back and Summer stood there, her face frozen in fear. "Oh my God. What happened?"

She pushed by him, setting her hand on David's shoulder. Her eyes were full of tears when she glanced back up at Hunt. "Why's he got that down his throat? Oh my God. What's going on, Hunt?"

Hunt inhaled and exhaled. "I dropped him off at the party and went over to Jenny's house to watch a movie. David was only there for about an hour and a half when Hal called me. I warned David about drinking. I had a talk with him, like you told me to."

"How does this even happen?" Summer demanded, her face drawing into anger. "They're all underage. He's just fourteen. Who gives liquor to a fourteen-year-old? My God."

"I know. I couldn't believe it myself." What else was there to say? He was angry, too. And disappointed in David, in himself, in Hal Easterly for not knowing what in the hell had been going on down by that barn.

"It looks bad. Why is he hooked up to all these things?" Summer asked, looking at the machine with the screens, beeping, showing his oxygen rate. She returned her attention to her son, stroking David's cheek. "Oh baby."

"The doctor said it's just a precaution. He had a high blood-alcohol level, so they are giving him fluids. The tube is to keep his airway clear.

He already threw up a bunch, but something about the gag reflex and aspiration, I think."

Summer closed her eyes and tears leaked out, streaking her face. Hunt felt so bad for her. She worshiped their son, and he'd been hurt on Hunt's watch. When she opened her eyes, he could see the hate in them. "I told you he shouldn't go. This is on you."

"Now, Summer, to be fair, I talked to him about this. We went over what happens at parties and how dangerous drinking can be. We remember how easily things can get out of hand, how easy it is to succumb to peer pressure and for things go a little further than intended."

Her hazel eyes snapped with ire. "Yeah, things can, can't they?"

"Summer, let's not go there tonight. Not when our focus should be David."

The curtain ripped back and Rhett stood there, breathing fast, as if he'd run the entire way. "How is he?"

"I don't know. I haven't spoken with anyone other than Hunt," Summer said, disdain heavy when she said his name. Of course she blamed him. That was her thing—blame everyone else for everything that happened. Hadn't that been her MO with him from the beginning?

Rhett turned his gaze to Hunt. "I'm fixing to beat the ever-loving shit out of you."

Hunt stepped back at the hate in his friend's eyes. "What the hell for? I didn't pour alcohol down the kid's throat. I gave him a talking-to before he went to the party. I think we're blowing things way out of proportion here. And I don't even know why you are here. Why are you here?"

"I drove her here. And you're full of shit, but that's your way, isn't it? Always an excuse, nothing to see here, not my fault," Rhett said, his shoulders widening, his hands fisted.

Rhett Bryan itched for a fight, and Hunt was happy to give it to him. Just not in the middle of the hospital. But before he kicked Hollywood's ass for interfering in something that didn't concern him, he wanted to know why his former friend was so pissed. "What's your problem, anyway?"

"Summer told me what you did to her on prom night."

"Oh really?" Hunt said, clueing in to the rage in Rhett's gaze. He'd thought Summer had finally let go of the old accusation, so it pissed him off she'd run her mouth to Rhett. Because, of course, Rhett thought he could set the world right. Rhett had always played Clark Kent and cast Hunt as Lex Luthor. So fucking lily-white pure . . . except Rhett wasn't. Just pretended to be a crusader. "So she told you how she slept with me, regretted it, and then tried to accuse me of rape? 'Cause that's what happened. She didn't want Mom and Dad to know she slept with me, so she played it off as nonconsensual. It wasn't."

Summer shook her head and looked down at David. "You were right earlier. Now is not the time."

Anger flooded Hunt. She always tried to make him the bad guy, delivering her little snide remarks and then taking the high road. Like she was better than him. He figured she liked being the martyr. She embraced the struggling single mother role for her own damned reasons. "Why not? It's obviously been a point of contention from the beginning. I'm tired of you making me feel like I'm a criminal, Summer."

"You *are* a criminal, asshole," Rhett ground out between clenched teeth.

"This doesn't concern you, Bryan." Hunt crossed his arms and glared at his former best friend. "It's none of your goddamned business. We're the parents."

"It may not be my business, but it's time someone ironed you out, McCroy. You never see your faults. Everything is always someone else's mistake. Never your own. You know the truth about what happened that night. Deep down under all your bullshit, under all your 'I've been wronged' pronouncements is the truth—you took what you wanted like you always do. Then you tried to twist everything to make yourself look like the victim. Classic Hunt McCroy."

Hunt didn't say anything because Rhett was fucking delusional if he thought Hunt had raped Summer. True, Hunt had been drunk that night. He remembered the tequila shots, the absolute jealousy he'd felt over Molly hooking up with that asshole she'd brought, and the softness of Summer's body. But Summer had been fine with what they'd been doing, at least up until he'd actually penetrated her. Once it got a little uncomfortable, she changed her tune, but it wasn't like he could stop. He'd tried to explain that when a girl was a virgin, sometimes it hurt a little.

Afterward, Summer had left the party and never talked to him again.

Until she found out she was pregnant, and then it had become date rape. She'd told her parents, they talked to their pastor, and some kind of bullshit mediation took place. The whole thing had been a huge snafu with threats of prosecution and ugliness prevailing.

"Rhett," Summer said, her voice pleading. "Let's talk about this later, okay? My priority right now is David."

Rhett pulled his gaze to Summer and visibly softened. "Okay. Right."

"Why don't you get us some coffee?" Summer said. She looked like she was drowning and looking for someone to throw her a life preserver. Or just get her coffee. "Hunt, you want some?"

"I'm not getting him any," Rhett said, sounding like the petulant boy Hunt remembered from the past. In a snit, the way he'd been the time Hunt had eaten the last of his birthday cookie cake. Or the time Hunt had drunk all the Bud Light and hadn't saved any for Rhett.

"I don't want it anyway." Yeah, Hunt could be just as childish.

Rhett issued a hard look. "Sum, how do you take it? Wait, I know. Black."

Then he disappeared through the curtain. The swoosh of the heavy material sounded like a message being sent.

"What did they say about David?" Summer said, wiping the tears. Her eyes riveted to their boy lying so still in the bed.

"They're giving him fluids and watching him. Essentially the body will detox itself. They'll merely observe him."

"Are they going to keep him here? In the ER."

"I don't know," Hunt said, watching her stroke their son. He watched her hands move, the way she looked so lost. Then he remembered Rhett and his words. Summer and her parents had agreed to not use that word—*rape*. So ugly. And so untrue. "Why did you tell him I raped you?"

Her head snapped back as if he'd struck her. She glanced quickly at David, as if to ascertain he was still out. Her stormy gaze found his. "Maybe because it's the truth, a truth you don't wish to acknowledge, but that's what it was."

"You know I didn't force you. You came with me willingly. You let me do things to you. Stop lying and own up to the fact we were both drunk and irresponsible." He made his words hard. He was so tired of this bullshit. Tired of her frosty looks, disdainful words, and politeness.

"You want to do this? Here?"

"Not really, but I'm sick of this thing sitting between us. I'm trying so damned hard to do the right things, to be a good father, to overlook the way you treat me every day, like I'm some pile of shit you have to step around. My family and I aren't proud of ignoring David when he was younger, but I paid child support . . . and for your college." As he said the words, he immediately regretted them. Too far. He'd gone way too far.

"You think I benefited? Because your family paid my tuition? You raped me—it was date rape, but rape all the same—and then walked away, ignoring me, your child, your mistakes, and you think I came out smelling like a rose? Are you stupid?" She left the bedside and moved toward him. In a very angry way.

He should have kept his mouth shut. But damn it, he tired of this constant wall between them. It wasn't good for David, and it damned sure wasn't good for them.

Summer stopped in front of him. "What don't you understand about that night, Hunt? Are you telling me you thought it was okay to proceed when I said no? Or maybe you think that countering with 'just relax' was enough to make it okay that you stuck your dick inside me when I told you I didn't want to have sex with you?" She vibrated with emotion, her hands fisted. She was a reckoning. Scary beautiful. Fiery vengeance. She believed her words, and that gave him pause.

"You didn't say no." A woman could fake arousal, but Summer hadn't faked hers that night. He remembered the eagerness in her eyes, how wet she was. And surprisingly how good she'd felt in his arms. She'd made him forget Molly and all the bad shit in his life.

She blinked, before tossing another glance at a still-sleeping David. "Are you joking? I said no. I said stop. I said I didn't want to go that far. You didn't listen. You gave me platitudes, told me I was overreacting, but you know, a gal kinda overreacts when she's been violated, you asshole."

"I didn't violate you," he said, sounding less convinced even to his own ears. "We were both drunk, and I get that it might not have been a good effort, but I remember some things, Summer. You could have gotten up and left when Rhett barged in, but you didn't. You stayed. You kissed me back. You gave me permission with your body."

Summer shook her head. "I was inexperienced. My first kiss ever was in that limo earlier. I had no other sexual experience, and I didn't understand arousal, you ass. Fuzzy or not, you know I wasn't into what you were doing. Or maybe the sobbing afterward didn't clue you in?"

He felt like she'd shoved a screwdriver into his eye. "You were emotional. Upset about the flowers."

"The flowers?" Summer shook her head, passing a hand over her face. Her eyes looked bright, the color in her cheeks high. "I can't believe this. I can't fucking believe this. You thought I was crying about the flowers?"

"You went on and on about the flowers. That I had ruined them. I remember that."

Summer blinked against the tears, incredulity reflected in her eyes. "You're the most obtuse man I've ever met. Your emotional scale doesn't register past one, does it? I wasn't upset about a fucking flower, Hunt. I was upset that you'd had sex with me when I emphatically said I didn't want to. I was hurt that you'd discounted me that much. Even if I had given you consent, you slept with me and never acknowledged me again. You essentially told me I was worthless. And even after everything, after the pregnancy, the agreement between our families, me moving back here, you never once said you were sorry about what happened that night. You've never apologized for what you did to me."

Hunt swallowed and tried to come up with something to say to her accusations, but he had nothing. It was true. He'd never called her after prom, averted his eyes when he saw her in the school hallway. Avoidance of Summer became a new game for him. He never understood why.

But he knew.

Deep down in the parts of himself he despised, he'd not considered Summer worthy of him. Taking Summer upstairs that night had been nothing but a desperate attempt to ignore the rejection he'd felt by Molly. He'd been head over heels for that girl, and she'd intentionally hurt him by going out with that lacrosse dude. The whole night with Summer felt like he was getting sloppy seconds with an unpopular, nerdy girl Graysen had practically begged him to take so she could play makeover queen. Summer had been a mistake from the beginning. He hadn't been fair to her. That was definitely true.

Of course, being an asshole didn't mean he'd raped her. That whole consent business was in her head. She'd been anxious, not unwilling. If she hadn't gotten caught by getting pregnant, he would have never heard from her again.

Summer lifted her gaze to him. No more anger. Only sorrow. "At the very least you could have said you were sorry, Hunt. Surely even someone like you could see the wrong in his actions."

A groan issued behind them, and David started moving his legs, lifting his hands toward the tube going down his throat.

Summer hurried to their son. "Shh, shh, David. You're okay. Mommy's here."

Reaching over, Summer pressed the button for the nurse. Then she went back to patting David. "Stop fighting, sweetheart. You're safe. It's just a tube to help you breathe."

David's eyes flew open and he looked panicked. Then he tried to pull on the ventilator.

A nurse shoved by him, and then Rhett arrived, holding two coffees. Setting them on a tray table, Rhett flew into action, rushing to the other side of David's bed, grabbing the boy's arm and restraining him. David convulsed on the bed, making frantic choking noises. Hunt stood there for a few seconds, a horrible feeling building inside him, threatening to explode. He felt like his clothes were ropes, cinching around him, and for some reason he wanted to rip them off. Rip off the guilt, tear through the frustration.

He had to get out. Now. Like before, he felt as if a huge boulder sat on his chest, keeping him from breathing. Something thick and hot expanded inside him. Tearing his gaze away from his son, he shuffled backward. He had to leave before he came apart.

But what kind of father stepped away from his son at a moment like this?

The kind who hadn't asked for any of this, who had never wanted a kid with the high school geek who hated him, disdained him, pitied him.

Fuck them all.

He couldn't do this. Being a good father was like pissing into the wind. Hunt had failed everyone he'd ever come in contact with. All the bad in him would come off on David. It was obvious he'd screw the kid up. All that shit Summer had hurled at him, the naked truths about what an asshole he was. It told him everything he needed to know.

He was exactly what everyone thought he was—a washed-up nobody with nothing in his life. David had been his one glimmering hope at being normal, of being somebody worthy of a great kid. And he'd fucked that up tonight.

Get out.

He turned and walked out, passing nurses, people hobbling around the waiting room, a security officer flirting with a nurse.

The emergency room doors swooshed open and Hunt stepped into the cool night.

Only then could he breathe.

CHAPTER NINETEEN

November, present day

For months Rhett had been consumed with his own issues—the nightmares, the lawsuit, the fallout from his tirade, but nothing now dominated his thoughts like the sound of Summer's voice relaying the tale of her rape.

When she'd finished telling him about that night, he had to swallow the vomit in his throat. His crossed legs felt like noodles, and he felt like someone had assaulted him. He'd been there that night. He'd opened the door and knew something was off.

But he'd done nothing more than pull the door closed.

Sitting there in the moonlight, he didn't know whether to hold her or apologize. He'd just reached for her when the theme from *The Twilight Zone* emerged from under the boat console.

"That's Hunt," she said, wiping the tears from her face and unwinding herself from the depths of the blanket. "I need to get it. David's at a party."

He'd wanted to toss the damned phone in the water. He wanted to punch someone. Cry. Jump in the water and swim until he just gave out. Instead he sat like a stone as Summer pulled her purse from the storage bin.

"Hey," she said to the man who'd raped her. "Wait. Slow down."

Rhett uncurled from his position and moved toward Summer.

"You're where? Beaufort County Hospital? He's what? Oh my God."

"What's wrong?" Rhett mouthed, growing alarmed.

"I'll be right there. It will take half an hour, maybe forty-five minutes, but I'll be there. Call me if anything else happens." She pressed the END button and closed her eyes.

"What is it?"

"David drank too much at the party and they had to take him to the ER. He's unconscious."

"Jesus," Rhett said, grabbing the glasses and tossing out the remainder of the wine. He shoved everything into the basket and stowed the quilt. Taking the velveteen throw, he wrapped a pale Summer in it like a burrito and handed her a life jacket. "I'll go as fast as I can."

They'd made it back to the boathouse in twenty minutes and into town in eighteen. Summer had spent most of the drive with her eyes closed and her lips moving in prayer. Rhett had occasionally squeezed her arm and murmured that it would be okay . . . even though he didn't know if that were true.

"Thank you, Rhett," Doreen, the night nurse, said, jarring him from where he contemplated the numbers on the elevator. "My sister will love having your autograph. She loves your show, and what you said to that horrible Bev woman was something everyone in this country has been thinking."

Rhett smiled. What else could he do? He was a tangle of emotions, trying to keep his cool for Summer's sake and trying not to run after Hunt McCroy and beat the ever-loving shit out of him. Yet, Rhett got paid to play a part. He knew how to paste on a winning smile and make people comfortable in high-stress situations. Rhett Bryan: Total Pro. "You're welcome, Doreen. Tell your sister I appreciate the support."

"You betcha," Doreen said, glowing like the fluorescent lights above the nurse's station outside the step-down unit where David now lay, Summer at his side worrying herself into an early grave despite the fact that David was awake and fairly lucid. The doctor had removed the breathing tube and now he was getting fluids and being watched for any collateral damage. "Guess I should check on my friends."

"Right. If there's anything you or Mrs. Valentine need, just press the button."

He walked back into the room, pulling the Sprite from his jacket pocket. "I found one. Had to go to the maternity floor to find it, but I was victorious."

"Thank you, Rhett," Summer said, rising and grabbing a cup from the rolling bedside table. She poured some soda into the cup, adding a bendy straw. "Here you go, David. This will help your throat feel better."

David glanced at his mother, eyes still glassy and unfocused. He obediently opened his mouth and sucked when she placed the straw in. "Thank you."

His voice was raspy from the insertion of the trach tube and a bit slurred. It would take several more hours before the effects of the alcohol had worn off.

Summer set the cup on the tray and sank into the only chair in the room. "Jesus."

Rhett walked over and rubbed her shoulder. "A scare, but David will be fine."

"I know," she sighed, rubbing her face with both hands. She sounded so tired, and it struck him how hard it was to raise a child. To feel that nagging worry at all stages of their lives. Maybe even more so when they became teenagers. A four-year-old can be managed, a fourteen-year-old not as much. "Tonight was just . . . a lot, you know? I feel wrung out and hung to dry."

David watched them, his brows drawing together. "What's wrong, Mama?"

Summer sucked in a deep breath. "Nothing, baby. We'll talk later."

"I'm so sorry, Mommy," he said, his voice wobbly. "I just wanted to be cool like everyone else. I'm sorry. I'm so sorry." Then he started crying. It was the same thing he'd done in the ER once they'd managed to remove the tube. Distraught, guilty, and reverting to a nine-year-old with a tummy ache, David wanted assurance and comfort.

Summer grasped his shoulder. "No more crying. Close your eyes and sleep. We'll talk about this tomorrow."

"I don't want you to be mad. Where's Dad? Is he mad, too?"

"He had to go home. Now close your eyes," Summer commanded.

David did as bid and Summer jerked her head toward the door. Rhett understood and slipped from the room, slightly down the hall, Summer following.

"You go on home," she said, in a soft voice. "I'm staying with him tonight. The doctor seemed to think he'll be good to go in the morning. I'll text Hunt to pick us up. He needs to help me deal with this situation. He doesn't get the luxury of running and hiding. Not any longer."

"I can stay." Rhett felt compounded irritation at Hunt. He'd slipped out without a word. Bastard.

"There's no need. David will sleep the night. I'll bunk in the recliner."

"That's not very comfortable."

"I've slept in worse. I'll be fine." She lifted her gaze to his. "I'm sorry about tonight. It all started so well and then ended so badly. Thank you for listening to me. I wasn't prepared for you to confront Hunt. I want you to let that go. What happened is best left in the past."

"Why?" he asked, the anger awakening again. "Why do you let him off so easily?"

He'd known Hunt could be a spoiled shit sometimes, but he'd never imagined his friend would force himself on Summer. Sorrow for

Summer pressed low in his gut. He couldn't imagine the helplessness or worthlessness she'd felt at the hands of the guy Rhett had set her up with. So much now made sense . . . and so much did not.

"Because I have David to think about. David doesn't know how he was conceived. And to a degree, neither does Hunt. He's never apologized because he truly believes he did nothing wrong. His ego and the agency he's always had in his life distort his version of what happened."

"How does he not know?" Rhett asked, pushing a hand through his hair.

"Because a lot of guys are products of a culture that sends mixed signals about what girls really want. Kids don't listen in sex ed, and parents assume their kids know better. You think Mitchell talked to Hunt about how to treat women?"

Rhett made a face.

"Exactly."

"But you could have told someone. Made him pay."

Summer gave a wry laugh. "You're not saying something I haven't heard all my life. It's easy to say prosecute, but if a victim is brave enough to bring charges, she has to shoulder the burden of proof. She has to defend what she wore, drank, and allowed to happen in the back seat. It's easy to say 'fight it,' but it's a different reality to live through a rape conviction. Most choose to avoid the struggle."

"Better to try."

Her smile told him all he needed to know—she'd been through this one too many times. "I felt the same way, and I told my parents. But remember what I just told you. I would have to defend what I wore, what I drank, how I acted. Everyone at the party saw me and Hunt in the kitchen doing shots and making out. I went upstairs with him. Even you, if you'd been asked, would have said you checked on me and I said I wanted to stay in the bedroom with Hunt. No prosecutor would take that case and go to trial against a 'good' kid with a scholly to Florida."

Rhett knew her words were true. "Okay, yeah, but Hunt knows the truth."

"Rhett, Hunt doesn't see fault in himself. In his mind, I cried foul when I got caught. Hunt was the hot, rich baseball player who could get any girl, and I was the desperate nerd trying hard to fit in. He would have ended up looking like the victim. I would have been the woman who wanted to ruin his future or worse, a desperate gold digger. Hunt's father told my dad that exact thing—they would hire an attorney who would turn me into the biggest slut in Beaufort County."

"You can still do something about it. You could—"

"Press charges? Dredge it up? To what result? So I can embarrass my son, tear down the fragile bridge I've built with Hunt, drag my name all over town . . . again? I don't want that."

Rhett shook his head. "I know, but he doesn't have to pay for—"

"Publicly accusing Hunt would hurt David. I'm not willing to do that. David's innocent. I can sacrifice the justice so he doesn't get hurt."

"You sacrificed everything. College, a music career, seeing Hunt pay for what he did. Why do you do that?"

"Because I'm a mom. I don't erase me, but I don't shortchange David." Summer hesitated as if she wanted to be careful with her words. "I haven't forgiven Hunt for what he did, but I understand who he is. As you pointed out, Hunt's good at making excuses for his mistakes. He doesn't accept blame for much."

Rhett wanted to argue with her, to make her nail Hunt to the wall on this issue, but he recognized the truth in her words. Hunt wouldn't accept blame, and the only people hurt by bringing up the past would be Summer and David. Still, the injustice seared him.

Rhett vaguely remembered a phone call from Hunt later that fall. His friend had implied Summer had tried to trap him. He'd even blamed Rhett for forcing him to take her to the prom. He recalled his grandfather talking about the girl the McCroy boy knocked up . . . how they'd paid her family off. It was the topic of conversation in Moonlight until someone drove their truck into the bay and was saved by an eleven-year-old who dove in and rescued them.

"I remember Hunt calling me in college to tell me you'd gotten pregnant the night of the prom. He was so angry. You're right. He never said anything about it being his fault."

Summer shook her head. "Some people can't admit their mistakes. I had to live with mine. I couldn't raise a baby in Columbia by myself, so I gave up my scholarship, moved home, and took classes at a community college. Everyone wanted me to give the baby up for adoption, but I didn't. Hunt partied his way through college, got strung out on prescription drugs, and learned to blame everyone else—the coaches, the surgeons, his parents—for every bad thing that happened to him. In some way, he got what he deserved."

"That's a small comfort," he said, eyeing the nurse's station. They didn't need any more gossip for the local coffee shop. "So why let him see David?"

"Because David deserves a father."

The unfairness of it all slammed into him. Hunt had purposefully hurt Summer, and she let it slide. Rhett hadn't intentionally tried to harm anyone . . . and yet a girl died . . . and her family was suing him. "A father like Hunt?"

"Even one as flawed as Hunt." Summer stepped back and sagged against the wall. "Look, I know what you're thinking. You're not the first. People in my therapy group, women who I called friends, essentially cut me from their lives because they felt so strongly about me not letting a rapist into my son's life. I understand how they feel, but I'm not going to let David suffer because I can't deal."

"But he violated you." The bitterness filled his mouth.

Summer flinched. "I'm not defending Hunt. I'm merely accepting that none of what happened was David's fault. I fought against it, but the more I tried to avoid talking about Hunt, the more David wanted to know. He cried because he didn't have a father to teach him to throw a football. He wore the pages of my yearbook out looking at his dad. A year and a half ago he sneaked onto a bus for Moonlight and ran away from Nashville. Didn't take a rocket scientist to teach me that the more I pulled him from his father, the more he wanted to be with him. I knew if I held on to my hate, I would lose. The only other alternative was to tell David he's a result of rape. I couldn't taint him with that. That shit sticks on you."

Rhett knew that was right. He didn't remember his parents, but there'd been an emptiness. And kids were mean. They'd called him "orphan" in grade school.

"So I suck it up and feel grateful that Hunt's trying to be a good father to David. That's what I hold on to—that Hunt is not a horrible person. Just one who made a horrible mistake."

"That he won't acknowledge."

"Have you acknowledged all your mistakes, Rhett?" Summer asked, her eyes almost steely in the dim hallway.

Her words slammed into him. Hard. The mistakes he'd made could fill a dump truck, but there was one that crushed them all. Had he even considered owning up to that mistake?

But it hadn't been his fault. The child had chased a ball unthinkingly into traffic. Still, Rhett knew he'd not had his full attention on the road. There had been worries, stressors, and the wrong smoothie flavor. Everything about that morning had been a mistake, but he'd never owned up to his role in it. "I get that everyone makes mistakes, but some can't be erased."

"I'm not trying to erase what Hunt did to me, Rhett. I'm trying to—I don't know—make a silk purse from a sow's ear. I can't change what happened, but I can change the way I view it. I've had years of therapy. A lot of survivors would have done this differently, but this is what I chose for me. For David. You can be angry as hell at Hunt, but that changes nothing. Only Hunt has the power to change things. Until his eyes are opened—if they ever are—I can only live my truth. May sound like bullshit, but it's all I got."

Rhett focused on the bad neoclassical art hanging in the hallway. Part of him wanted to shake some sense into her, ignite her into doing something. But what that was, he wasn't sure. Yet part of him recognized the truth in her words. It took a strong person to put aside hate and try for love. "You love David more than you hate Hunt."

"Hate's a strong word. It's corrosive and eats at you. I spent many years hating Hunt. I despised him for the glory he got while I rocked a squalling baby and struggled to stay awake in my classes. But now, I pity him."

"Because he didn't make it in baseball?"

She shook her head. "Because he's so incredibly unsatisfied with his life. And I'm not."

Rhett folded her into his arms. "You're pretty amazing."

She shook her head. "Nope, I'm just doing the best with the lot life has given me. Things are still tense between Hunt and me. Sometimes I like that there's still anger there. I'm no saint."

Rhett inhaled, taking in the salty sea and wildflowers tangled in her hair. He wanted to take all the bad away, hide her and give her good things, but he knew her journey had made her stronger. He also knew he wanted her . . . in his bed . . . in his life. But his desires were selfish.

Rhett Bryan should get the hell out of this place soaked in memories, steeped with longing for a woman who didn't belong in his life. His reality wasn't vulnerable single mothers and tangled relationships. The life he led was so far away from the Carolina moon creeping in through the hallway window that it might as well be a distant planet. Here he was the boy he'd forgotten about; there he was a man who held a place among giants.

Thing was, he didn't want to go back to being the man he was.

He wanted to stay in Moonlight, where things seemed somehow easier . . . even if they weren't.

Dropping his hands to Summer's shoulders, he said, "You sure you'll be okay?"

A smile twitched at her lips. "Of course. I'm pretty much accustomed to being alone. Plus, I have that comfy chair waiting on me."

Rhett gave her another quick hug. He wanted to kiss her but wouldn't. "I'll call you tomorrow to check on the kid."

"Bye," she said, giving him a little wave as he started down the dim hallway to the parking garage where he was illegally parked in a physician's parking spot.

His last glimpse of her narrowed in the closing elevator doors.

A heavy sigh was his only company as he pressed the button to the lower level and exited the building. The same big moon greeted him as he backed the car out of the garage and pointed the headlights toward the place where he'd learned to ride his bike, tie a sailor's knot, and catch crabs with chicken legs. The Carolina moon dogged his car, summoning the memory of Summer's face aglow as they bobbed offshore Dog Island, dragging the horror of her story into the light, and eliciting hunger for another taste of this woman who encapsulated him in . . . something.

While Rhett existed beneath a shadow, one he couldn't seem to shake, Summer shone like a lone candle penetrating darkness. Like a desperate moth, he was seduced by the flicker, but a single spark could ignite a dumpster fire.

He couldn't use Summer to feel better about himself.

"Fuck," he said to the darkness surrounding his car. Then he angled a glance up at the moon. "And fuck you, too."

But the moon didn't answer back. It hung steadfast in the sky, watching a world beneath swirl about in conflict.

CHAPTER TWENTY

April 2003

Summer lay in her narrow bed, listening to Maisie play with her Barbie dolls in the next room. The walls were paper-thin, which meant she often heard conversations between Skipper, Barbie, and Ken, who—if her powers of deduction were correct—were embroiled in a love triangle. She should probably tell Maisie that Skipper was only, like, fourteen. She was the kid sister and much too young for Ken.

For a moment, she wondered if there were actual ages on the boxes for the dolls. And then she remembered that they didn't have genitals. Barbie dolls were safe from getting a penis shoved inside them.

Summer rolled over and faced the wall, unbearable grief welling inside her at the thought of what had happened last night. Her head hurt and her stomach roiled as images of the night before popped up like scary clowns in a fun house.

She knew physically she had a hangover, but there was also an ache inside her, a strange discomfort like the first time she'd tried to use a tampon. Perhaps the soreness was her imagination, but still she felt the loss.

And she'd had no say-so in the matter. Or rather, Hunt hadn't listened to what she'd said. The thought infuriated her. That bastard.

"Oh my God, oh my God," she whispered as she flopped to her back, fixing her gaze on the round light fixture above her. A moth had died in the frosted glass bowl, its image nothing but an outline. She knew how the poor thing felt. Fly too close to the light, become a dead, papery shadow.

Last night after she'd pulled on her dress, she'd gone into the guest bathroom and locked the door. Hunt had waited in the room, but she stayed in there so long, sitting on the toilet and studying the rope glued around the shelf that held plush towels, he eventually got the hint and left. Once the outer door snicked closed, she cleaned herself up. There had been a little blood. And semen. Hunt hadn't even bothered to use a condom. The thought she could be pregnant had made her knees buckle.

Even at that moment, the thought froze her, her mouth growing as dry as the moth's wings.

She wasn't pregnant. People tried to get pregnant for months, sometimes years. Her cousin Michelle had to do fertility treatments and still had to adopt a baby from China. No way Summer got pregnant the first time she had sex. That would be a slap delivered to a bruise. Un-fucking-necessary.

Besides, it wasn't real sex.

She knew what it was—date rape. They'd talked about "acquaintance" rape in her sociology class, or was it health class? She couldn't remember. All she recalled was a video they'd watched where a woman suggested a victim make herself vomit to render the sex-starved perpetrator grossed out enough to abandon the rape. Maybe Summer should have gagged herself until she vomited. Maybe Hunt would have stopped saying "just relax" and instead screamed at her for ruining the expensive carpet.

Nessa and Tyler had driven her home. They'd just arrived when Summer had tottered down the stairs and begged them to get out of there. Her best friend had been perturbed to miss out on the party of the year. Supposedly Ben Vermillion and Jack Hamm got into a fight and broke a window. Oh, and Brittany Smith took off her dress and jumped into the hot tub in her bra and thong. So many idiots to watch. So little time. Summer didn't bother to tell her friend that Hunt had raped her upstairs. She didn't want anyone to know she'd even gone upstairs with Hunt. She didn't want anyone to know she'd gotten drunk. And kissed Rhett. And let Hunt touch her boobs. But of course, everyone would know.

Tears formed in Summer's eyes as Maisie yelled, "Help me, Ken. I'm drowning in the pool. Skipper's at the store. I need hellllp. Ahhhh!"

"Hush, Maisie," Summer heard her mother say. "Your sister's still asleep."

"How come she didn't have to go to church? She always gets to miss Sunday school, and I never do."

"Hush," her mother said, closing the door to her sister's room.

Summer heard her door open and she froze, pretending to sleep.

"Summer?" her mother whispered, the door opening wider so Summer could hear snippets of the fishing program on the TV in the living room. Her father was probably in his recliner in his gym shorts with his black-socked feet propped up. It was his Sunday afternoon ritual—church, KFC, and a week's worth of fishing programs recorded on the VCR.

"You finally awake?" Her mother's voice held anticipation. She knew what her mom wanted—juicy details of her prom night.

"Mmm?" Summer asked, totally faking her disorientation. "Mom?"

"You probably need to get up. If you sleep the whole day away, you'll have trouble falling asleep tonight." Moms always said that. Must have been in the hospital instructions sent home with the new bundle of joy. Feed them, burp them, change them, and make them feel guilty if they want to sleep in and not tell you every detail of every moment of their lives.

"Okay," Summer said, struggling to rise, feeling as though a weight pressed her down.

"So . . . ?" her mother asked, easing onto the foot of Summer's bed, trying not to look like a detective going at a suspect.

"What?"

"You know what. How was prom?"

"Fine. It was good. The decorations were really pretty."

"Yeah? Tell me about them. Did you dance? Who had the prettiest dress? Who got prom king and queen?" The questions were like boulders released from the top of a mountain, gaining speed, crashing against all obstacles.

Summer wanted to sink back down and flip the covers over her head and pretend prom had never existed, but her mother wasn't going to let that happen. Answers must be given. It was payment for the shoes she'd thankfully found under the kitchen desk and the chandelier earrings that were still missing. No clue when she took them off. Maybe they'd be in the clutch purse with the empty vodka bottle. Nessa had found Summer's purse in the living room on top of the shiny black upright piano.

"Let's see, I liked Nessa's look the best—pretty and edgy. You know Ness. She wore a bustier, a tutu, and combat boots. And Rhett Bryan and Graysen Hadley won prom king and queen. Of course." Her stomach hurt at the thought. Then she remembered the beach and the way Rhett had looked at her. She closed her eyes against the telltale pain that had to be present in her eyes. "I danced once. The rest of the time, we hung out and watched everyone else."

"Oh, you just watched?"

Summer shrugged.

"Where's your corsage? We can put it in the window to dry. I found some spray that might preserve the color." Her mother looked around.

"Nah, I threw it away," Summer said, trying to sound nonchalant. "It got messed up at the party. I forgot to put it in a safe place."

Her mother's expression fell. "Oh darn. That would have been a great way to preserve the memory. But oh well. Nothing you can do when the thing falls apart. How about some grilled cheese? I can make you one, and we can chat about everything that happened. I can't wait to hear about Hunt and the party. He seemed like such a nice young man. And pretty cute, too." Her mom delivered the last comment with an impish grin.

Ha. If she only knew how nice Hunt was.

"I'm not really hungry. My feet hurt from the heels, and I have a paper due for Mrs. Chatham's class on Monday. The witch is obviously antiprom." Summer rolled her eyes in overexaggerated exasperation. She was a normal teenager. Nothing to see here.

Her mother rose. "Okay, get some work done, and we'll talk later. I know you're tired, but you had fun?"

"Sure. It was great." The words felt like dust caking her mouth.

Her mother tossed a doubtful look her way, but thankfully slipped out the door with a soft, "Later, gator."

Summer sank back onto her bed and stared up at the ceiling. Closing her eyes, she tried to think about anything other than the events of last night. *Focus on college. The comforter you picked out at Belk. The last episode of* Gilmore Girls. *What was Rory going to do? Oh, and what was that funny thing Sookie had said?*

Hours later she woke to an insistent knocking at her door. She'd fallen back asleep and felt like she'd been drugged. Lifting her head was a struggle. "What?"

Maisie flipped on the light. "Hey, there's a boy here."

Fright jumped into Summer's throat as panic seized her. Hunt was here. What was he doing here? Would he tell her parents what they'd done the night before? Her mind raced in cadence with her heart. "Uh, I can't come outside."

Maisie's ponytail was lopsided. "You've been in bed all day. Are you sick?"

"No." Maybe. It felt like being sick. Her body felt heavy, her heart thrummed with ache, and she wanted to disappear into some undiscovered void. Maybe she could live in this room forever. Be a recluse like Emily Dickinson. Or that boy in the bubble.

"You're a lazybones," Maisie drawled.

"Yeah," Summer said, pushing her hair from her face. "Maybe so."

"The boy outside looks like Ken, but his name's Rhett. He's watching *Bass Fishin' Today* with Daddy." Maisie closed the door.

"What the hell?" Summer whispered, licking her lips, which felt as cracked as an African water hole in drought. She eased out of bed, walking to the Jack-and-Jill bathroom she shared with her sister. What was Rhett doing here? Why was he watching TV with her dad? It was like existing in an alternate universe that wasn't parallel but instead flipped upside down and twisted sideways.

She stared at herself in the bathroom mirror. Eyeliner was smudged beneath her eyes, and she looked abnormally pale and drawn. Her brown hair snarled in clumps. Total train wreck. Picking up a toothbrush, she scrubbed the taste of last night from her mouth before running a brush through her hair. Next she pulled on a sweatshirt, not even bothering with a bra, and grabbed a pair of shorts that might have been dirty, or just orphaned from the clean laundry she'd yet to fold.

Pushing out the door, she prepared herself for facing the boy who had driven her to Hunt. Yeah, yeah, it wasn't his fault per se. But . . .

What was he supposed to have done? Kiss her back and declare his love for her? *Get real, Summer.* Or maybe he was supposed to swoop into the guest bedroom and lift her in his arms as his white steed pawed the expensive planking outside the door. *Like he could even lift your fat ass, Sum.*

"What are you doing here?" she asked as she padded barefoot into the living room.

Rhett looked up from the magazine her father had obviously shoved into his hands. "Hey, Summer. You just now getting up?"

Friendly puppy Rhett. At that moment, she almost preferred Hunt's withering dismissiveness. At least Hunt didn't pretend to be something shiny. Rhett was like one of those gold chains you won in one of those crane games. Sparkling, but sure to turn your skin green.

No, that wasn't fair. She wanted to blame someone for what happened. Rhett wasn't responsible for her whoring herself out. He'd been perfectly nice about blowing her off, and he'd tried to save her. Sort of. She had to own that she'd drunk too much, allowed Hunt to kiss and paw her, and climbed the stairs to a bedroom like a complete idiot. Rhett wasn't turning her fingers green. He was exactly who he'd always been—a decent guy.

Still, she had a compulsion to hit him. To make him feel some small measure of the damage she felt. At least smudge him up a bit and make him . . . irritated, ruffled, something more than so damned nice.

"Yeah, something like that," she said, crossing her arms over her breasts. "So why are you here?"

He stood. "Thanks for showing me that bait, Mr. Valentine. I'll try using that color crawfish next time I go freshwater fishing." He turned his baby blues back on her. "Can we go outside or something?"

Summer shrugged. "Sure. We can sit on the porch."

She didn't wait for him. Somehow her politeness had vanished. The porch wasn't wide and held only two worn rockers, but that would have to do. Her guitar sat in one of them, and it struck her that Maisie must have been out here playing and left it unattended. Fury washed over her. She spun back around, nearly running into Rhett. "Dad, Maisie took my guitar without permission again and left it on the porch. She's asking to die a painful death."

Summer turned back around and walked toward the guitar, taking satisfaction in hearing her father ordering her sister to come to the living room.

Rhett looked confused. "Are you okay?"

"Sure. What are you doing here anyway?"

"I . . ." He paused and ran a hand through his hair. "Uh, about last night. I, uh, thought maybe I should come check on you."

"I'm fine." Her words sounded hollow even to her own ears. She picked up her guitar and tucked it beneath her arm, cradling the fret board with her left hand. With her fingers she plucked a few chords as she sat in the rocker.

She wasn't fine. Maybe she'd never be fine. But she didn't want to say that because she didn't want to talk about what had happened the night before. She wanted to forget it happened. Go back to her normal, which was not Rhett Bryan standing on her front porch.

"You say that, but you seem upset. I know what happened on the beach was upsetting and then I found you with Hunt. Uh, I just didn't think you were into him."

She looked up. "I don't want to talk about the beach. That was a mistake. I don't know what happened. Probably the vodka. Not much of a drinker. And Hunt and I were just having fun." The words tasted like poison. She wanted to spit them out onto the porch. Rid herself of the inky blackness covering her soul. *Go away, Rhett. Go find your girlfriend. Leave me alone.*

"You sure?"

She played a few more chords from the song she'd been working on. Somehow holding her guitar gave her protection. The Martin shielded her emotions, preventing anyone from seeing the shredded parts of her. "Absolutely."

Rhett eased into the rocker. "I didn't know you play the guitar."

She strummed a few chords from "Sweet Baby James" and nodded. "I've been playing since I was twelve."

"You any good?"

"Decent," she said, not even bothering to be humble like she would usually be. Yesterday she would have said, "Not really, but I'm working on it." Because that's who she was yesterday. She was innocent, polite, and stupid. Today she just felt stupid. And mad.

"Play something."

"I am." She did a couple of verses.

"I don't know that one."

So Summer sang the second verse and the chorus, thrilling at the beauty of the lyrics. Snow making the world dreamy, frosting the ugly, with miles stretched out like a ribbon. It reminded her of Robert Frost's poem "Stopping by Woods on a Snowy Evening."

"Yeah, I've heard that," Rhett said, his eyes lighting up. "You sing good. Wow, Summer."

She set the guitar down. "Well, you've seen that I'm okay. I have some stuff to do, so I will see you around."

"Summer?" His brow furrowed, the smile falling away. "Something's wrong."

"Nope. Just tired."

"You have some time free this week for calculus?" He stood and looked uncomfortable. She'd never seen Rhett Bryan look uncomfortable. He usually fit his surroundings like an old pair of Levi's.

"Actually, I don't. You can use those practice sheets I gave you. Keep going over those. You'll be okay."

Eyes the color of wildflower and poetry searched hers. She could feel the hurt in him, but she couldn't seem to stop herself from being a total bitch. Okay, not a bitch, but a bit cold. She wanted to yell at him this was how girls were when they have goodness stolen from them. Melodramatic, sure, but she felt every inch of the drama at that moment.

The moment between them rose up and shimmered, like water vapor on hot asphalt. Then it broke apart.

Rhett nodded. "Yeah. That's cool. I think I'm good anyway. Well, I'll be seeing you, Summer. Have a good one."

Then he walked off her porch, leaving her feeling like a shit.

But she didn't call him back and apologize for her actions or words. Because she couldn't. At that moment, she realized she'd been changed, and the Summer who'd walked in sunshine now lived in grayness. She hadn't chosen for it to happen, but just like weather that rolls in and obscures the sun, she could do nothing about it. So she sat on the porch and plucked a few more strings, the sweetness of the vibration the only balm for her that day.

CHAPTER TWENTY-ONE

November, present day

When Sunday morning came, Summer felt like she'd been ridden hard and put up wet. She'd had zero sleep while David was under observation in the hospital, and then once they'd been released, she'd spent the afternoon getting him home—including a stop by CVS for hydration beverages and Tylenol—and fixing a leak under the kitchen sink. Thank God for YouTube and handymen who liked to film themselves. David had spent all day in bed, but she couldn't seem to rest. Her mind kept rolling over the mistakes she'd made as a mother and stutter-stepping when she recalled the confrontation with Hunt in the ER.

Hunt had texted her to check on David, but that was it. No calls or follow-ups.

Something about the way he'd retreated from them worried her. Over the past few years, Hunt had been diligent in pursuing father-hood. His attempts had been almost endearing, and she could tell he'd been reading parenting books by the way he asked questions or made subtle suggestions. He'd never stepped on her toes, always deferring to her decisions, until he'd pressed for David to attend this party. Pair that decision with the horrible scene between them, and Summer was afraid Hunter would head for the hills.

And while she didn't mind seeing less of Hunt, it would be a tragedy for David, who'd grown to count on his father . . . perhaps even love him.

The doorbell rang just as she put the last glass in the drying rack. Summer glanced at the clock on the microwave and realized she'd forgotten to check her son's progress getting ready for church.

"Yoo-hoo, Summer?" Maisie poked her head inside.

"Hey, come on in," Summer said, grabbing a towel and drying her hands.

"Dave ready?" Maisie asked, closing the door behind her. Her sister wore a black sweater and gray wool skirt that hit the top of soft leather black boots. The only concession to the somber outfit was a red-and-black checked scarf. Her sister had taken to wearing dark colors the day her ass of an ex moved out of their four-bedroom house.

"Honey, Maisie's here to take you to church," Summer called toward the small hallway.

No answer.

"He'll be out. Probably sulking. He doesn't want to go. Guilt and all that," Summer said, setting her hands on the counter.

"I understand," Maisie said, glancing down at her watch. Her sister was a stickler for being on time. "In fact, you should understand."

The words were true, but they didn't sting any less.

"Yeah, I do," Summer said, trying to keep the bitterness from her voice. "But the guilty should be welcome at church, right? The people there are supposed to love and forgive, aren't they?"

Not that the congregation had been willing to forgive an unwed teenager who had tried to trick the hometown hero. Summer didn't have a problem with God. She had a problem with hypocrisy.

"I wasn't being ugly," Maisie said, looking contrite. "I just remember that time and how hard it was for you. For all of us."

Of course her sister was right. Summer understood why her parents had bowed to pressure. It hadn't been just about Summer. There was Maisie . . . and their family's livelihood.

Summer remembered the night she'd told her parents about being pregnant. She'd finally summoned up the courage a week after she'd taken the home pregnancy test. The initial explanation of what had happened at the beach house hadn't gone well. When she'd gotten to the part about Hunt ignoring her pleas and forcing himself on her, her father had threatened to kill Hunt.

He'd actually walked to the gun cabinet, his jaw set into stone, his kindly brown eyes turning into rusty bullets, and removed his shotgun. "I hope I have enough rounds for that little bastard."

Summer's mother smacked her hands on the laminate table. "Put that goddamned gun down, Jeremy. Enough violence has been done. We're going to go to the police and tell them what happened."

Her father had snorted. "Yeah, because the kid's going to admit to what he did. Not likely. But he'll talk to the end of this gun."

"Jer, put the gun up. You know good and well that's not going to happen. We're going to figure out what to do and how to make this kid pay for hurting Summer. Put it back."

"Mama?" Maisie asked from the couch.

"Oh my God. How long has she been there?" Carolyn asked, rising from the table. Summer sat there studying the lines in her palms. She felt sick to her stomach all over again.

"What happened to Summer?" Maisie asked, sniffling through tears. "That boy hurt her?"

"Come to the back, sweetheart. Your daddy and I have some things to talk about with Summer. Go play with your dolls, okay?"

Summer's father had set the gun back in the cabinet and sunk defeated to the chair. Over the next half hour, her parents debated what to do, and when they finished, it was decided the first thing was to talk to the McCroys.

But a few weeks later when Summer came home for fall break, her parents had changed their tune.

Their about-face had surprised her . . . or maybe, rather, it insulted her. She'd come in the door and her parents had sat her down, suggesting she think things through before doing something that might be a mistake. Even though Summer was only eighteen, she understood the game afoot.

"I'm not lying," she'd said to her father.

"I know, baby, but there's no physical evidence. You didn't tell us until now. It's your word against his word. You even admitted that you kissed him in front of others and willingly went upstairs with him. That looks bad, baby."

"So you're going to tell the McCroys I was mistaken?"

Her father flinched. "I don't want to, baby, but I have to. Brother Clark was nice enough to mediate this for us. The McCroys are going to pay for the baby, child support, all that. And once we do the paternity test, they'll pay for your school."

"We're selling out." Summer shook her head, incredulous her father had bowed to this asinine agreement. Hunt would be off the hook for violating her, and she'd look like the town whore. "But he forced me. Doesn't that mean anything to you?"

"Of course it does, Sum," her father said, sinking down on the couch beside her. "If this world were fair, then justice would be carried out. But it's not. If we go to the police and pursue this, you'll be dragged through more than what you would . . . well, just having the baby and letting people think whatever they want to think. If we accuse Hunt of rape, our whole family will suffer the consequences. We already have."

"But you said Mom got laid off," Summer said, her voice not even convincing. She knew Hunt's mother was Millie King's best friend. Her mother had worked for the King family for years. When it came down to it, loyalty had meant squat to the Kings.

Her father gave her a flat look. "Even so, the police and lawyers will examine everything we've ever said or done. They'll pry into your life, make you sound desperate and manipulative, and it will go on for years, baby."

Summer swallowed hard at the thought.

"But if you agree to not use the word *rape*, you'll escape all gossip and endless investigation."

"You mean you will."

"I mean us. We're a family. What happened that night affects all of us. Maisie didn't get invited to Juliet Markham's birthday party. Your mother got fired. Brother Clark asked me to step away from being a deacon until things blow over. This isn't about just you."

Summer had felt like she'd stepped off a curb and gotten slammed by a Mack truck. All she thought she was—a good girl with a bright future—had slipped through her fingers. Her virtue wasn't worth her family suffering. "You're saying I should . . . what? Say I willingly had sex with Hunt? That I was some desperate dork craving his body so much I duped him into going upstairs and planting his baby inside me? Because I'm soooo desperate to have a baby at eighteen? Or am I just so money-hungry that I threw my ovulating uterus at him so I could score some cash? That's what you're saying?" Her voice rose to the point of hysteria.

Her father passed a hand over his face. At that moment he looked as if he'd aged a century. "Summer, I'm asking you to be practical. You won't win. You can't. So take the money. Take what you can get because if we go to the police station and press charges against the hometown baseball hero, you'll regret it. Accusing Hunt of rape won't change anything."

Except maybe it would have. Summer may not have succeeded in making Hunt pay for the rape, but she would have at least known that she had value. That her parents recognized that what had happened to her that night was wrong and should be righted.

But then her father said the one thing that made her grow still.

"And what about the baby? Does he or she deserve to come into the world with that stigma?"

At that moment, she'd not actually thought about the child. But he or she wouldn't have to know. Her parents had been urging her to consider adoption. Money was an issue for the Valentine family, especially after her mother lost her job. How would Summer support a baby . . . and did she even want to? Adoption meant she could take a hardship with the University of South Carolina and maintain her scholarship. She wouldn't need the McCroys' hush money, and people who adopted babies often paid the medical expenses. Giving the baby up would be the best solution.

Her father had patted her knee and given her a painful smile. "Just think about this, Summer. Pray on it."

Summer nodded, but she didn't pray about it. She was too damned mad at God. At everything to be humble, mindful, or contrite.

And after the first time she felt David move inside her, she'd wavered on adoption. And then one night while feeling the baby move, she'd had a realization. The only way she could make sure that her child didn't have to go through what she'd gone through was if she kept the baby. He would never be alone, never feel abandoned. She'd spend every waking moment of her life righting the wrong done to the innocent babe. That would be her mission.

And now, looking at her grown sister, a woman who'd been hurt by a man who'd vowed in front of God and family to love and honor her until death they do part, Summer knew she couldn't protect David any more than she could protect her baby sister. "You're right. It was hard on all of us."

David entered the room wearing pants too short and unable to tame the cowlick on his crown. Summer's heart squeezed when she noted how fast he was growing into a man. "What was hard on everyone? What I did?"

"Yep," Summer said, shooting a look at her sister. "But we'll hold our heads up somehow."

"Don't joke, Mom," David said, looking upset. "You know how sorry I am. And I'll never drink again. I swear. Never. Ever."

"Mark this down," Summer said to her sister.

Maisie smiled. "You ready, D?"

"Yes, ma'am," David said, turning to the slender bookshelf next to the mounted television and pulling out the Bible his grandfather had given him right before he'd passed away.

"We're eating at Mom's after church. You coming?" Maisie asked, opening the front door. A cool breeze pushed a few leaves inside.

"If I wake up in time," Summer said, eyeing a stack of mail she needed to sift through. "I'm going back to bed once y'all leave. I'm beat."

David shot her another apologetic look. The kid was getting good at the "I'm so worthless" shtick. Summer was almost ready to stop being disappointed in him. Kids made mistakes, right? At least David had learned early on the dangers of peer pressure. And other than a brutal copay for the emergency room visit, no permanent harm had been done.

Thankfully.

Summer turned off the lights, shrugged out of her jammies, and filled the bathtub, adding some rose petals and Epsom salts. She had a new romance book and a hot cup of herbal tea calling her name. She'd just dipped one foot into the fragrant waters when someone knocked at the door.

"Damn it," Summer muttered, trying not to be aggravated. David had probably forgotten his cell phone or something. She shrugged into her bathrobe, jerked the belt tight at her waist, and padded to the front door.

"Hey," Rhett said when she pulled open the door. He stood framed by the bright autumn morning, dressed in worn jeans, a T-shirt from some surfer bar, and flip-flops. Total Californian.

"Hey," Summer said, suddenly very aware she was naked beneath the robe and that her hair was snarled in a clip atop her head. Oh, and, of course, she wore not a drop of makeup. "I was just about to take a bath."

"Yeah?" he asked, his gaze dipping to the skin showing at the closure of the robe. She could feel a rivulet of water run down her leg. "I saw David get into someone's car."

"My sister. She's taking him to church."

An awkward pause hung between them. Summer didn't know what she should do. She had a tub full of fragrant water and a morning to herself, but she wasn't going to send Rhett Bryan packing. Not when he made her palms sweat and her heart beat triple time. The silly torch she'd always carried for him had found an accelerant over the past week. She'd like to chalk up the insane desire to slide her robe from her shoulders to all the memories dredged up, or maybe it was merely the fact she'd gone too long without sex. Either way Summer felt torqued and primed to toss reservation out the window.

"Uh, you want to come in? I have fresh coffee," she said finally.

He studied her for a minute. "I thought you were about to take a bath."

"I am. Or I was." She cast a glance back to her bathroom door. The water was still running. "But I don't want to be rude."

"Why not?" he asked with a grin, stepping toward her. "I'm butting in on your morning. I'm interrupting your bath. You can tell me to take a hike."

"Take a hike," she said.

He shoved his hands into the pockets of his jeans and turned.

"Wait," she said.

Rhett turned, arching an eyebrow, looking so achingly familiar. "Yeah?"

"Why did you knock on my door?" Something that felt like hope fluttered in her gut. What did she want him to say? How far was she ready to go with him?

"I wanted to see you. Why did you invite me in for coffee when it's obvious I inconvenienced you?"

Good question. "Because."

"You're polite?"

"I wanted to see you, too," she said.

Rhett smiled. "In that case, I'll have a cup of coffee."

Summer stepped back and gestured with her hand like a flight attendant ushering someone aboard. "Come on in."

After she'd shut the door, she stood a moment trying to figure out what to do. Should she excuse herself to pull on clothes? Plop on the couch butt naked beneath her terry cloth robe? Ask him if he wanted to join her in the bathtub? Of course, they both wouldn't fit, and though the image of Rhett Bryan naked, slippery, and smelling like roses was so tempting it made her mouth dry, she'd told herself she wouldn't go there with him. Her heart couldn't handle the trampling.

Her sister's earlier words echoed in her brain. *If you have the chance . . .*

But what if s-e-x wasn't on Rhett's mind? The kiss a few nights before had been incredible, passion had stirred beneath the sweetness, but she made a broad assumption if she thought Rhett wanted to—

His arms came around her and he pulled her to him, dropping a kiss on her nose.

"Oh," she murmured, glancing up at him. "I'm naked under this robe."

A naughty grin tugged at his lips. "Oh yeah?"

She studied his beautiful lips. How many times had she done that over her lifetime? Dozens? Hundreds? Even when she watched him on the flat screen chatting with some celebrity promoting a movie, she'd hungered for those lips. "That was a stupid thing to say."

"But intriguing," he said, sliding a hand down to her butt before giving it a pat.

For a few seconds their gazes hung up, their measured breaths quickened. She was keenly aware of his body hard against hers. Rhett was warm like sunshine and smelled like California—all fresh yet unfamiliar.

"Go get your bath," he said, releasing her and walking toward the kitchen. "I'll pour myself a cup and wait on you."

Disappointment mixed with confusion. What was that all about? They'd been so close to tipping over the edge and plunging into something wonderful, and then he pulled back.

She watched him open a few cabinet doors, looking for a mug. Then he picked up the carafe of the French roast she'd splurged on and poured himself a cup. He turned and crooked that eyebrow again. "You going?"

Summer nodded and headed to the bathroom. The water was almost to the top of the tub. She turned it off and pulled the plug to let some out. As she watched the water lower, she perched on the edge of the tub. Damn, she was so confused. Was Rhett into her? Or not? Did she want him to be? Or not? She remembered the pass she'd made on the beach all those years ago—she obviously couldn't read him for shit.

And anyway, what would be the result of dragging him into her bedroom and asking for the full Rhett Bryan experience?

At best, multiple orgasms. At worst, horrible regret.

Toss-up.

She jabbed the plug in the tub, locked the door, and dropped her robe. The water welcomed her, whispering she should soak her cares away. The clink of the fridge shutting in the kitchen screamed, "The fabulous Rhett Bryan is in your kitchen."

Tell her what she's playing for, Ed.

A brand new . . . mistake!

Summer sighed and made short work of bathing, even touching up her legs with the razor and intentionally avoiding touch-ups on her bikini area. She wasn't going there with Rhett. She'd misread all the signs the same way she had all those years ago. Yeah, he'd kissed her just now, but that was it. And it hadn't even been all that passionate. More flirty and friendly.

She dried off and pulled on her robe, leaving her hair in the clip. Her only concession to a hot, famous guy in her kitchen was the mouth rinse and swipe of lip balm. Oh, and deodorant. Then she opened the door and nearly ran into Rhett.

"Eek," she yelped, nearly running into the cup of coffee in his hand.

"I didn't mean to scare you," he said. Rhett looked genuinely concerned. "I just wanted to bring you some coffee. Are you okay?"

Something clicked in her brain. A sort of "ohhhh."

"I'm not that fragile, Rhett," she said, taking the cup from him.

"I know," he said, following her into the living area, his voice sounding pretty unconvincing. This was what the kiss on the nose was about. This was why he pushed her away. He thought she needed to be handled carefully because of the date rape.

"You think I'm afraid of being with you?" she asked.

"No. I don't think you're afraid of me. I just . . . well, I haven't been with anyone who . . . who . . ."

Summer sank onto the couch. Guess she would go commando under the robe, awkward as it was. She sipped the coffee and looked up at Rhett. "How do you know you've never been with someone who's been sexually assaulted?"

"I suppose I don't."

Rhett ignored the recliner and instead sat down beside her. His hands cradled the mug David had given her for Mother's Day. Pink flowers and a Bible verse decorated the porcelain, which emphasized the daintiness of the mug in Rhett's masculine hands.

"More women than you think have dealt with sexual assault. But I've worked hard to get past any sexual hang-ups I had. What happened to me wasn't easy, but when you combine alcohol, rejection, and dumb decisions, bad things happen. So I don't do those things, and I've had some healthy relationships with decent guys who helped me heal. So if you're worried you have to handle me like a victim, don't. What happened that night doesn't define me. It doesn't keep me from embracing my sexuality."

Rhett took a sip of coffee and then looked at her. "Yeah?"

"Yeah. I mean, if that was what you were doing. I'm not trying to say you wanted to . . . what I'm saying is if you're"—she took a deep breath—"holding back because you think I'm damaged, then don't."

"Maybe I was." He studied her, his pale-blue eyes so intense in the dimness of her living room. "I didn't want to be presumptuous. I also wanted to . . . to . . . I don't know what I'm trying to say. I felt like I needed to give you space or something."

"That's nice of you, but again, Hunt took away my innocence, but he didn't steal the pleasure I take in sex. I'm not saying it was easy the first few times, but I persevered."

"*Persevered* sounds terrible."

Summer gave a light laugh. "Touché."

"So . . . ?"

"So . . ." she echoed, wondering if his *so* meant what she thought his *so* meant. "We have a few hours to, uh, have coffee?"

He stared blankly.

"Please don't make me kiss you, and then you say something about how I'm a terrific girl and I'll make some man a happy man someday, and then you say—"

"I'm not, but I did some research about intimate relationships with rape victims. The author said to allow the victim to set the boundaries. And then there was something about touching exercises," he said, and damned if he didn't look absolutely earnest.

She envisioned Rhett on the Internet trying to find the right way to be intimate with a rape survivor. It was both amusing and touching that he cared so much.

He'd tossed the ball on her side of the net, so she stood, unbelted her robe, and with one wriggle of her shoulders, her robe fell to the floor.

The move could go either way. Rhett had no doubt seen dozens of nude women with tight bodies and high breasts that had never nursed a baby. Summer had a slight belly and her thighs were thicker than what she would have liked, and there was the fact that she'd not bothered to touch up her bikini area. Why hadn't she at least given the area a cautionary swipe of the razor?

Rhett's mouth did a little open/shut thing, but his eyes fastened on the abundance of flesh, his gaze sliding down her body. But he didn't move.

If this was going to happen, it was up to her. "I love the sound of touching exercises, but the boundary is you can touch only what is uncovered."

"I can handle that," he said, pulling her to him.

She fell gracelessly into his arms, but she didn't care much because his lips found hers. Greedily he kissed her, like she was water and he was thirst.

And it was good. Very, very good. As in the man knew how to kiss a woman until she lost her breath . . . along with her good sense. Desire coated her like warm honey. She wanted to stay there forever, yet she wanted to push him harder, drive them both to the point where the real world fell away and there was only pleasure.

"You smell so good," he whispered, dropping tiny kisses along her jawline while his hands explored the hills and valleys of her body. "You taste even better."

His mouth found hers again as she twined her arms around his neck, threading her fingers through the silky hair at the nape of his neck. She'd dreamed of this so many times, but her fantasies couldn't come close to the wonder of actually being in Rhett's arms.

"Bedroom?" he asked after ripping his mouth from hers. Dilated blue eyes lazily searched her for an answer. He looked hotter than anything she'd ever seen. Heavy breathing, tingly feelings, and the erection pressing against her side told her he was as into her as she was him.

"Please," she said, sliding her hand up to cup his raspy jawline. "I want this."

He slid her to the side and rose, pulling his shirt overhead and tossing it onto the recliner. Hewn muscles and golden skin made Summer nearly drool as she shoved off the couch and started down the hall. She heard the clunk of his shoes hitting the floor and the jolting sound of the man removing his jeans as he followed.

When she opened the door to her bedroom, she turned. Rhett caught her against him, his boxer briefs clearly outlining his arousal. He looked like a dream standing in her little hallway.

Rhett looked down at her cradled in his arms. "Are you sure?"

Summer leaned forward and kissed the indentation at the base of his throat before rising on her tiptoes and kissing the cleft in his gorgeous chin. "I've been waiting my whole life to have you, Rhett Bryan. I can't be any more sure."

He kissed her then, a sweet, tender, hot, molten kiss that made her curl her toes against the worn floorboards. Pulling back, he looked down at her body, lightly glancing the curve of her breast before sliding a hand down to her hip. "You're beautiful."

His words curled round her like a tender melody. He'd once told her she was pretty, but this time she believed it. The reverence of his touch, the way his gaze hungrily engulfed her, and those sweet words became the tempo for what would happen on her rumpled sheets.

"I don't want to hurt you, Summer," he whispered against her neck.

She smiled into his golden hair. "I'm not asking for forever, Rhett. I'm happy with Sunday morning."

So he pulled her into the room and she locked the door.

He didn't waste time with checking out her cluttered room or asking her any further if she was certain she wanted this. His arms came around her, his lips found hers, and again she was lost in the music of Rhett.

His body was hard and warm, pure sunshine curving around her. The hands that found her ass hauled her tight to him as he devoured her lips, her neck, her earlobe. Heat pulsed inside, storming her with need.

She wanted him more than she'd ever wanted anything. Her hands could find no rest. She caressed the broad shoulders, the sandy curls on his chest, the broad plain of his back. At that moment Rhett belonged to her, and she would play him like she played her music . . . with utter pleasure.

Rhett pulled her onto the bed, and she fell atop him, finding it a happy coincidence that all the hard places lined up with her soft ones. She kissed the cleft of his chin again, giving a little wiggle to make sure certain parts of him made delicious friction on parts of her that needed . . . delicious friction.

"I want this to be good for you, Summer," he murmured, his fingertips stroking the plump breast resting against his chest. "I want to go slow, but I'm losing it here, baby."

Summer shifted to her side, sliding her hands down, skimming his tight stomach, tracing the erection straining his boxers. "How about we not worry about anything other than pleasing each other? We can go slow next time."

"Next time? You have plans, do you?" His mouth covered hers as he rolled her onto her back. Again the parts lined up. She moved, sighing at how good he felt atop her. Delicious weight, salty skin, and the essence of the boy she'd been waiting for her whole life.

"Mm-hmm," she murmured as he trailed a hand down her side, making her belly jump. He dropped his head and kissed the top of each breast.

"A good performance always deserves an encore."

Rhett groaned his approval against her breasts, filling his mouth with better things than words. Then Summer lost her ability to flirt . . . to talk . . . to make sense of anything other than Rhett making love to her on a Sunday morning. Because it had been a long time since she'd had a man's hands on her, since she'd had a man's mouth on her, since she'd felt the fullness of a man inside her.

And it damned sure would be a long time until she found another man who made her feel so alive. Like a song, the notes fell in place, the harmony unfolded, and when the deafening crescendo came, there was only beauty.

And Rhett.

For Summer, that was enough.

CHAPTER TWENTY-TWO

November, present day

Rhett woke to afternoon sunshine and a strange room. But then he remembered where he was and who the warm lump next to him was.

Summer.

He flexed his toes and stretched his spine, savoring the slight crack of his back. They'd made love until they were exhausted and then dropped into sated, dreamless sleep. He'd not dreamed of blood-slicked roads or silent screams. Instead he'd fallen into a satisfied state of unconsciousness. For the first time in forever, he'd awoken without a pit of despair in his stomach.

He knew having sex with Summer wasn't some magical pill that healed him. He wasn't that corny, but still he couldn't ignore how good he felt at the moment. The sex had been hot, but afterward as they lay there, murmuring funny stories, sweet, warm limbs intertwined, a strange comfort covered him like a blanket from his past.

Carefully, he slid his arm from beneath her shoulders. She groaned and then made a funny little piglet sound before snuggling back into the depths of the down pillow. His arm tingled with numbness, and part of him wanted to roll her onto her back and taste her sweetness again, but a glance at her alarm clock told him her son would be home soon.

And the knot of complication formed.

He climbed from the bed, careful to not wake Summer. The last few days had been hard on her, and a good stretch of sleep was what the doctor ordered. Along with a couple of orgasms. He'd been happy to deliver those.

Rhett picked up his boxers, softly shut the door, and dressed in the dimness of the living room. Before he sneaked out, he picked up her robe and draped it over the back of the dining room chair. As he turned to go, he caught sight of a folder on the table. Several handwritten sheets of music hung out. He lifted the flap and looked at the title. "Carolina Boy."

The haunting song came back to him as he read the lyrics, and he remembered how beautiful and strong she looked up on that stage.

A few words to music execs, a call to a good manager and agent, or even a bug in the ear of a country music artist could net Summer another look. If this song lay in this folder without anyone seeing it, it would remain mere ink on paper. He dug into his pocket and pulled out his phone. There were several messages, nagging reminders of the world he'd left behind. Soon, he'd have to face that world. He couldn't hide in Moonlight much longer.

Spreading the sheets out on the table, he snapped a picture of each of the sheets, his heart warming at the doodles on the side of one sheet. He pushed the sheets back together and tucked them into the folder. Summer had said she didn't want his help, but surely if she could get a shot at doing something more than playing backstreet bars and ramshackle honky-tonks, she'd take it. Writing music and singing was her dream . . . even if it was a deferred one.

At the very least, he could give her a chance. If someone was interested, she could decide whether she wanted to pursue the opportunity or not.

He pushed out the front door into the cool November day, marveling at how pretty the marsh looked when the grasses faded to straw and the hardwood trees preened with fall color. Even the Nest didn't look as tired against the blue sky.

He climbed the back steps to find Grampy Pete sitting in the broken Adirondack chair smoking his pipe.

"That chair looks like it might fall apart at any moment. You should wait for the new ones I ordered," he told Grampy.

"I ain't worried about it. If it falls, it falls."

Rhett headed toward the sliding glass door, intending to fix a sandwich. He felt ravenous. Good sex did that to a guy.

"I told you to leave her alone," Grampy said.

Rhett paused with his hand on the handle. "What do you mean?"

"You've been at Summer's for half the day. Her boy's at church. I can add two and two together. Been doing that for years."

"I like Summer." The words seemed lame for what he felt for her. She wasn't just some lay. She was his friend and he cared about her. And he'd asked before he slept with her. Lord knows he'd never press her for something she didn't want.

"Everyone likes Summer, but they don't sleep with her. You're going to be leaving soon. I'd say probably right after Thanksgiving. Maybe before, since I know the day don't mean much to you. No offense, but you've never been a sentimental boy."

"It's not like that," Rhett said, turning toward the man who'd always been his compass.

"What's it like? She lives here and is raising a boy. You live in LA and you're building a career. You ain't taking her with you. She wouldn't last two months out there. And the kid's dad is here. Summer needs a man who will stay with her. You ain't staying, so you shouldn't have gone knocking on that door."

Irritation rose in Rhett. "You don't know what I'll do. You're making assumptions."

"No. I'm speaking the truth. You're mixed up about a lot of things and looking for answers. You're using Summer as a distraction. Look, I understand. She's pure goodness, and everyone wants to have some goodness in their life."

Rhett sat down on the chair next to his grandfather. The old wood shifted with his weight, and Rhett prepared himself to fall, but the chair held. "I'm not using her."

"Then what are you doing?" The words were little darts finding their target.

"I don't know. I don't want to hurt her."

"But you will."

The words dug deeper into his soul. "I won't."

"There's one thing I know about that woman—she has a thing for you. Always has. Oh sure, she acts like she don't. She don't bring you up, but when the topic of conversation arises, she gets this look before she pretends she don't care nothing for you. But I read people well."

Rhett took a deep breath and wondered how he could explain what Summer was to him. She'd helped him breathe again. Hell, he felt better than he had in forever.

His grandfather puffed on the pipe, letting the silence sit between them. Finally, he cleared his throat. "I don't think you'd intentionally hurt her. You ain't the kind to use and run. You're a good boy, Rhett. I'm not sure you still believe that, but you are."

Something squeezed in Rhett's chest.

"You came back to remember that, to rediscover that part of yourself you hid because being good doesn't always make you successful out there. In that world you live in, being good gets you stepped on, pushed aside, relegated as weak. You came home because you needed to get centered and get back who you used to be. Thing is, you never lost that. That's why that Beverly woman galled you so much."

Rhett rubbed a hand over his face. "Maybe you're right. I wasn't sure why I came home."

His grandfather nodded, and again silence inserted itself between them. Grampy puffed on his pipe, little wreaths of gray against the blue sky.

"What do I do?" Rhett asked.

It was the question that had pecked at him since that morning last summer. Ever since that moment when he climbed from the vehicle and saw what he'd done, he'd been lost.

Grampy looked at him as if he sensed the depth to the question. This wasn't about Summer, but about everything in Rhett's life. Both he and his grandfather knew Rhett was the sort of person who made a plan and pushed forward, like a running back through a defensive line, churning his legs, looking for a hole to get through. Rhett's life so far had not yielded much pushback. In fact, Rhett had reached the end zone time after time. But what happened when there was no end zone . . . or he couldn't find one?

"You put one foot in front of the other. You remember who you are. Where you came from. Who I taught you to be. A man of honor. Everyone screws up and everyone faces hard times. When your father died, a part of me went with him, but I had to keep going. I had you looking up at me with those sad blue eyes. I fought that darkness for you. So what are you fighting your darkness for, Rhett? What is the meaning of your life?"

Darts of realism were nothing compared to the cannonball of doubt that smacked into him. What *was* the meaning of his life?

"I don't know," he said after a full minute ticked by.

"You might want to start with that. Maybe if you figure out what's worth living for, you can start living again."

His grandfather's last words were imparted as a closing argument. Rhett may not have been around Grampy much over the years, but he knew a final word when he heard it.

Rhett rose and went into the house, his head swimming with thoughts chasing more thoughts. He'd gone through months of therapy, but none of the million-dollar gurus pinpointed what he was lacking like Grampy had. His grandfather could make a fortune on the mixed-up West Coasters. Hell, he could pocket a pretty penny on the screwed up East Coasters, too.

His phone buzzed.

Summer.

Where'd ya go?

He texted back. Letting you get some needed sleep.

K. Tell Pete I'll bring lasagna tonight. Need to plan menu for Thanksgiving.

He sent a thumbs-up.

And then he sat down hard on the old barstool his grandfather had gotten at a restaurant supply clearance. The set didn't match, but his grandfather loved that they were sturdy. No flash for Pete Bryan.

Rhett had made a mistake sleeping with Summer. The text was a prime example. Already she'd slipped him into her life. Lasagna. Holiday plans. Like they were . . .

No. She wasn't assuming or implying anything. Just handling dinner plans. Still, the questions Grampy asked hopped from neuron to neuron in his brain, demanding he give them attention. Paired with his grandfather's disappointment in Rhett for messing around with Summer, the confusion about his future had him scrambling to figure out his next move.

His phone buzzed again, jittering on the bar.

His agent.

"Yeah," Rhett said, deciding to answer rather than let another message go to voice mail.

"What the fuck, Rhett? I've been calling you for the last forty-eight hours. There are time constraints on some of this shit, man," Bruce screeched.

"Sorry. I've been out of pocket."

"Why are you still in South Carolina? What the hell is going on with you, man? Your attorney's been calling, the network, there's some serious shit that needs your attention. Jane Townsend called and she needs some quotes from you on the fallout."

"Fallout from what?"

"On the story the *Times* did on the Tavares family. The one that brought out Reis Tavares's criminal record and had neighbors admitting the Tavares kids ran around unattended all the time. You don't have a fucking TV?"

"As you know, I've been avoiding the news for my mental health."

"Well, people are talking. Jane did a good job of casting doubt on this family. The reporter wants to run a follow-up piece. She wants a quote from you. How horrible the accident was, how bad you feel, how you've suffered PTSD. But most importantly how you feel you weren't at fault for that child's death."

"You told Jane to do all this?" Rhett asked, as his gut churned. Yeah, he'd agreed it was the best defense against the suit, but something about it didn't sit right with him.

"She said this is what needs to be done. The judge set the trial for December so he can clear his cases before the holidays. We couldn't wait. You needed damage control. And you disappearing makes it look even worse. You need to get back here. Lionel James called yesterday, and they want to film your cameo in the Will Ferrell movie the first part of next week. And then we have a meeting with the studio execs about the contract extension for *Late Night* the following day. The studio wants an evaluation by some fancy-ass shrink before they negotiate. I'm telling you this Bev shit has done some serious damage if they need you to get the okay of a shrink. I'm up to my eyeballs, Rhett."

Rhett felt everything around him fold in on him. This was why he couldn't handle his world anymore. The career he'd so loved pulled harder on his feet, making the hangman's noose tighten around his neck. At that moment, he couldn't fucking breathe.

"I'll be there Friday."

"You need to get on a plane now."

"I can't today, Bruce. It's not possible. I have things to wrap up here."

"When?"

"Friday's the best I can do. Set up the meetings and I'll be in touch." He hung up before he could change his mind. Dread encircled him, squeezing his midsection.

Rhett closed his eyes.

He had to go back to his world. Grampy was right. He'd come home to find some goodness, but he'd also come home to hide from the hard stuff in his life. Thing was, a person couldn't hide forever. Eventually he had to face what he'd built with the choices he'd made in life.

His phone buzzed again.

Summer.

David going to movies with Maisie. Want to come back over and have . . . coffee?

Yeah, he wanted to have coffee. Again and again. Until the world fell away. But his world wasn't content to sit in the back seat any longer. His world was tapping his shoulder and insisting he turn around and go back to where he really belonged.

Rhett surveyed the large living area of the Nest. Worn furniture sat pointed at the shiny new TV Rhett had bought. Duct tape covered the arm of his grandfather's recliner, the floors needed a new stain and seal, mismatched chairs circled a table piled with mail, and a stack of

Field & Stream magazines spilled out onto the hand-hooked rug where Rhett had once played with his Power Rangers. The lived-in room was an interior decorator's nightmare . . . but yet the sight pleased Rhett.

Part of him would always belong here, but he wouldn't give up the life he'd made in California to stay in Moonlight. His grandfather thought LA too shiny, prefabricated, and commercial, but he wasn't wholly right about the place Rhett laid his head most nights. Sure, there were shallow kooks and narcissistic assholes, but there were truly beautiful people, too. LA had guys who worked beneath hoods to take home the bacon for their families, waitresses slogging through two shifts to afford college tuition, medical personnel working volunteer hours at shelters. Plus, there were the Hollywood Hills overlooking a glittering LA at night and gorgeous beaches to practice his surfing skills. South Carolina would always be in his soul, but he'd made room for the sandy, sunny California. That wasn't just where he lived—it, too, was part of him.

His heart contracted when he thought about Summer. He'd been in some good relationships and some shitty ones, but he'd never held such a tenderness for someone the way he did Summer. He could chalk it up to having a past with her—maybe the shared experiences during their formative years had forged a stronger connection. The thought of doing a no-mess walkaway scene like they do in the movies created self-loathing and . . . despair.

Rhett didn't want to ride off into the sunset.

But he had to.

Because he and Summer couldn't work. Their worlds were so vastly different. Hers was French toast and hamburgers, nagging a kid about homework, and thumbing through a magazine while her son watched the NFL. His was salmon with truffle risotto, nagging a production assistant, and standing on the red carpet reading through production notes while starlets posed for the paparazzi. Worlds away, opposite coasts, staggered lives. Summer deserved someone who would come home to dinner and sit in the stands with her, cheering David on the mound. She deserved someone who was stable, who wasn't always on the go, who wasn't getting sued by the family of the child he'd accidentally killed. Summer deserved love that he couldn't give.

He should have heeded the warning he'd given himself that night at the hospital. He should have stayed on the beach and not have waded into Summer's waters. Walking away from her would hurt.

Before he could talk himself out of it, he called and arranged for airfare and pickup for Thursday evening. He'd have Thanksgiving dinner with his grandfather before flying back west.

"You fixin' a sammich?" his grandfather asked as he slammed the door shut. The scent of his pipe followed him inside.

Rhett looked down at the bread he'd set on the counter earlier and shoved his phone into his pocket. "Uh, yeah. I just made my flight to LA. I'll go back Thursday night."

"Flying the coop, are you?"

"I have to go back sometime, I guess."

His grandfather stomped into the kitchen and slid a plate from the upper cabinet. Setting it next to Rhett, he opened the bag and withdrew four slices. "It's been good having you home. I know I got a little stern with you about Summer, but I'm glad you came home when you needed to."

"It *is* my home," Rhett said, retrieving the turkey he'd picked up when he'd bought the wine and cheese for the date night with Summer. Seemed so long ago that he'd packed that basket and prepped the boat for the romantic cruise around the bay.

"Yes, and you should always come here when you need to remember who you are. You know you're getting everything in my will. I can't leave this place to Carlton or Frank. They'll get their wives in here and have it looking like some show house. Or, hell, they'd sell it and go to Tahiti on the profits. Can't trust those two to keep your grandmother's dream alive."

Rhett didn't want his grampy to talk about dying. He couldn't stomach the thought of losing his only family. His mother's family had treated him like a second-rate Moped when he was in college, but when he struck gold as a DJ on a local station and got syndicated, they suddenly loved their grandson and nephew. When Rhett ended up on television and then hosting a game show, they'd shown up with hands out, requesting loans and posing potential investment opportunities. They weren't horrible people, but they weren't his grampy Pete. They weren't truly his family (though they loved to be called Rhett Bryan's family).

Until the last few weeks, Rhett had never realized how lonely he felt in a place he belonged. Sure, he was busy in LA, but Rhett didn't have many people in his life who were there because they wanted to be. His closest relationships were with his agent, production assistants, and casting agents. He sometimes played basketball with a fellow comedian, and occasionally spent holidays with his costar on the one rom-com he'd made. He could get dates and go to dinner with other artists, but none knew the true Rhett Bryan.

He wanted to go back to California, but he wanted someone beside him. Maybe it was time to think less about his career and more about his happiness.

"Let's not talk about when that happens," Rhett said.

Grampy looked up from slathering mayonnaise on his bread. "Why not? Dying's part of living, ain't it?"

Rhett cut his sandwich diagonally, like they did in commercials, and grabbed a bag of Cheetos. They'd always been his favorite chip, and in four days he'd have to get back to eating healthy again, settling only for a single day of the month to visit his favorite taco stand on the beach. "Yes, but I don't want to talk about it. We've talked about too many heavy subjects this afternoon."

"You're not holding a grudge because I told you to lay off Summer, are you?"

"No."

"Okay, so if you like her that way, why would you give her up so easily?"

"'Cause you're right," Rhett said, sliding his plate onto the bar and snagging a stool. He sat down and took a bite. Damn, there was nothing better than white bread.

"I usually am," Grampy said.

"And humble."

Grampy gave him a rare, snaggletoothed grin. "Apple don't fall far from the tree."

Rhett snorted.

"My pops told me to stay away from your grandmother, too. I didn't listen."

His grandfather didn't say anything else, and instead went about the business of making his sandwich. Rhett gave it a full minute before he said, "What are you trying to say?"

His grandfather shrugged. "You said you liked her."

"I'm seriously trying to figure out if you're being intentionally irksome or if you've succumbed to Alzheimer's. If it's the former, stop. If it's the latter, what home do you prefer going to?"

"You ain't putting me in one of those hellholes. If ever I get to where I need to wear diapers or start talking to the walls, I'll just take the boat out and pull the damned plug. I'll go out with a glub."

"Again, let's not go there."

"What I'm saying is you young folk don't know how to persevere. Your grandmamma waited for me when I was over in Korea. Three years she didn't see me and we were fine. Wrote letters, got a little leave, and met up. Spent all three days in a hotel room. That's how your daddy came to be. We didn't have to have it perfect. Bah, you say you can't be there and here. Sure you can. If you want something bad enough, you make it work. Like I did with your grandmamma. Like your daddy did with your kook of a mother, God rest her soul."

"Summer and I aren't in love. We're just friends who . . . flirted with something. My life is too complicated right now, remember? I've got to figure some things out, and it's not fair to Summer to ask her to wait while I decide what I want in life. Or if I even want to change anything in my life. Things are complicated." He wanted more with Summer. But they couldn't work, so he should start buying the words he was selling to Gramps.

"You think Koreans shooting at my head wasn't complicated?"

"No, I'm not saying you didn't exist in danger, but maybe having things cut and dried—you live, you die—made it easier for you to see what your life was. I can't do that right now. There's too much going on inside of me."

Grampy studied him for a full ten seconds. Then he picked up his sandwich and took a bite. "Want to watch football? Titans are playing."

Rhett blinked, trying to figure out if this was another part of Grampy's Obstacle Course of Finding the Truth in life. "Sure."

"Good. I'm tired of talking about feelings. You gotta figure yourself out. I can't do it for you."

True enough. Rhett picked up his plate and followed Grampy into the living room. The older man turned on the TV, found the game, and settled into the ancient recliner. Rhett sank onto the couch, balancing the old Corelle plate on his knee. The phone jittered against his thigh. He dug it out.

Summer.

Hello? You already blowing me off?

He stared at the words for a few seconds, vacillating between tossing his uneaten sandwich on the coffee table and running to Summer's house or being reasonable. He knew he should tell her it had all been a mistake. Protecting her from the hurt his departure would bring would be wise. That was assuming she'd be hurt. Grampy could hypothesize himself to death, and Rhett could make guesses based on the past, but only Summer knew if whatever she felt was true enough to care when Rhett went back to LA.

No way. Watching Titans game with Grampy. I'll see you tonight.

What would she read into that text? Many women he knew would analyze it seven ways to Sunday. Others would get pissed and tell him to go fuck himself.

Okay. See you tonight.

But not Summer. Because she wasn't like the other women he'd had in his life. Summer lived in the back seat. She was a mother and therefore used to being second. Something about that was both endearing and irritating. Double-edged sword, that. He wanted her to demand he come to her, to give her the attention and respect she deserved. Yet he savored that she didn't get ruffled and bent out of shape that he didn't drop everything and come running for another tumble in her bed.

But why wasn't he running to her bed?

If all he had were four more days of Summer and Moonlight, why was he sitting there watching a game he cared nothing about?

"Hey, Grampy. I need to talk to Summer."

His grandfather stirred, obviously having already started his Sunday nap. "Huh?"

"Enjoy the game." Rhett tried not to look so eager to get away, but he may have run-walked to the front door. He'd tell her he was leaving and then see if she wanted to make the most of the time they had left together. He'd put the ball back in her court. Her choice. God, he hoped she chose four days of goodness.

CHAPTER TWENTY-THREE

November, present day

Hunt would have stayed in hiding forever except his son's tearful apology crushed the wall he'd erected against fatherhood and made him feel like a total asswipe for avoiding the kid for the last two days.

"I'm so sorry, Dad. I was just going to have one drink so I wouldn't look like a total dork, but then they kept giving me more. I didn't want to tell them no. I wanted them to like me. I feel so stupid. Please don't be mad at me," David said when he saw him at the movie theater on Sunday afternoon.

Hunt had gone with Jenny and her daughter to see an animated movie that afternoon even though a Disney feature film was pretty much his version of hell. He'd gone out for popcorn and run into David, who was with his aunt Maisie. His first thought was that God had a sense of humor.

"What are you doing here?" he'd asked his son, casting a look at Maisie. The woman looked concerned to see her nephew at near breakdown.

"I'm here with my little cousins." David jabbed a thumb over his shoulder, but his plaintive eyes never left Hunt.

"Oh," Hunt said, trying not to feel so uncomfortable with all this emotion in the theater lobby.

But he did. Mostly because he didn't know how to feel. He'd screwed up letting David go to the party. That decision had not only scared the hell out of him, but had also been the catalyst for the horrible scene in the ER. Since that time, Hunt had been laid up in his condo, licking his wounds, avoiding texts from David and Summer, trying to convince himself to leave Moonlight. Cut ties and run.

Because he never should have tried to be a real father to David.

Some men weren't cut out for having kids.

"I know you're mad. I mean, I screwed up. This morning in church, I asked God to forgive me. I don't want you to hate me again."

"Hate you?" Hunt flinched. He grabbed his son's arm and pulled him away from the lines forming. "What do you mean by that?"

"Like when I was a little kid and you didn't want me."

Oh shit. That's what the kid thought. Hunt knew he worked hard to please him, but he'd not known the kid thought he had to earn Hunt's love. David thought his father hadn't wanted him. "It wasn't like that, David. It wasn't because of you. It was because of me."

David made a face. "You didn't want me when I was a baby. I never saw you and stuff."

"That's because I was messed up. When your mom found out she was pregnant, it . . . stunned me. I wasn't ready to be a dad, and I was selfish. Then I went to the minors and got tangled up with drugs. I know you know a little bit about what happened to me, but I wasn't in a good place. I couldn't take care of myself, much less you. You had nothing to do with the mistakes I made."

"Oh," David said.

"People mess up. Just like you did with the drinking. I just messed up bigger."

David was like every other kid. He wanted to be accepted. Hunt remembered his own years as a freshman at Martindale Academy. He'd tried to blend in with the other kids, drinking too much, smoking a little pot, trying to get lucky with the girls they met in town. Hunt had had no guidance from his own father except vague warnings to toe the line and make good choices and, for God's sake, throw in the upper eighties or his ass would be benched.

"You sure? You didn't . . . I mean, I haven't heard from you. I texted you." The kid's face turned red, and that made Hunt feel like shit. Hunt had been focused on how terrible a parent he was, and David thought he didn't care. Didn't the kid know Hunt was trying to spare him having a crappy father? Nope. The kid thought Hunt's silence was anger, but the truth was Hunt was scared.

"I'm not mad, David. You made a mistake. But there will be consequences, just like there were for me. I haven't talked to your mother yet. She has the final say-so."

David glanced over at Maisie, who was busy wiping spilled soda off her son's T-shirt. "Because Mom has custody?"

Hunt hesitated and tried to figure out what the kid was getting at. "Mostly."

"Well, you're my dad. You should have an opinion."

"I am your father, but legally I don't."

"Why don't you want me?"

The question might as well have been a baseball bat to the head. He literally stepped back. "I do want you."

"You haven't asked Mom to change anything."

He didn't know what to say. Before all this happened, he'd planned on asking Summer to consider reevaluating their legal agreement. His parents had essentially forced him to sign the legal paperwork once the blood test had come back positive, but he now wanted more. "I'm going to do that, David."

Or he had been.

"Good," David said, holding up a finger to his aunt, who'd started waving him back toward them with urgency. Her two kids had started doing that runaround thing kids did when they got bored and no electronic device was in hand. "I want to belong to you, too. I mean, you know."

Hunt did. He understood wanting love. "We'll talk about it soon. I'll pick you up after lessons on Tuesday."

David hesitated for a moment and then he stepped forward and wrapped his arms around Hunt.

Hunt automatically wound his arms around his son.

It was the first time the kid had initiated physical contact, and Hunt felt something lumpy and suspicious in his throat. He inhaled the smell of his boy—shampoo and salty teen boy. David finally unwound his arms, his own eyes sheened with tears.

"Go on with your aunt. We'll figure stuff out. It's not as bad as it feels right now," Hunt said, looking for the entrance to the restroom. He needed to get himself under control.

"Okay." David gave him a half smile.

Hunt issued a wave toward Maisie and booked it into the men's restroom, where he shut himself in a stall and tried not to cry. He couldn't remember the last time actual tears had come to his eyes. Maybe rehab or therapy. But that kid had undone him.

So on Monday he'd texted Summer that they needed to talk. She'd sent back a text. **Good idea. Wednesday? Can you come here?**

He texted, **I'll be there around 6:00.**

On Tuesday Hunt walked down from the office and to the high school ball field. Rhett had brought David early so he could practice hitting with a few sophomores that Summer had vetted. Don was running late, but Hunt needed to escape from the office. The crisp day and the clink of the bat called him out to the field where David tossed the ball around with guys he'd hopefully play with in the spring.

Hunt leaned onto the dugout wall where the kids' bags splayed, spilling batting gloves, jackets, and empty sports drink bottles. David and the guys hadn't even noticed he was there, which was somehow even better. There was something wonderful about catching a kid being himself.

"Dude, that's a strike," one kid called from behind the plate.

The guy pitching gave a knowing smile, but the batter shook his head. "Bullshit. That was high and outside."

"Caught the corner," the catcher insisted, glancing out at David, who shagged balls. "What do you think, Dave?"

"Caught the corner," David said.

"What does he know?" the batter grumbled, swinging the bat back around to rest on his shoulder.

"You saw him pitch. He knows," the catcher said, adjusting his face mask.

Hunt smiled and enjoyed the next ten minutes or so of the boys arguing as they each took ten pitches and switched around. David looked surprisingly competent at the plate, though he got sucked in on the low-inside pitches, and when he'd pitched, he'd sat them all down. *Impressive* was the word on the tip of Hunt's tongue.

Don's truck pulled into the high school lot and Hunt raised a hand. Don was on the phone and didn't see him. The boys tromped into the dugout, still not seeing Hunt behind the green cinder-block wall.

"Dude, are you punished for life for getting wasted?" one boy asked.

David chuffed. "Yeah. I can't play video games during break, and I have to rake Pete's yard and bag up all the leaves. I'm lucky Mom let me come out here. She's still pissed."

"What about your old man?" another asked.

Hunt felt his stomach clench.

"He ain't that mad. He said it was what kids do."

"He probably got trashed all the time in high school, too."

"Probably," David said.

266

"Oh my God, did y'all see Anna Clair Miller? Landon hit that. She was so drunk, she didn't know her own damned name," one of the boys said, laughing.

"Landon got with her?" another boy echoed.

"He ain't a virgin no more and neither is she."

David cleared his throat. "She was passed out?"

"I guess. She was awake for some of it," the kid answered.

David cleared his throat again. "Uh, well, technically that's rape."

"No, it's not. She was all over him."

He could hear David suck in a breath, then slowly release it. "Actually, it's rape if she can't give consent. If she's passed out, she can't say yes. So technically it's rape."

"How do you know?" Another boy asked. "You teach sex ed or something in your spare time?"

David laughed nervously. "Nah, my mom was a rape counselor. She knew a woman who was passed out and the guy had sex with her. He went to jail for a year."

"Damn," one of the boys said.

"It's called date rape," another boy said.

"Yeah, they talked about it in health class in eighth grade. Some of that is bullshit, though. Girls are always all into it until they get caught with a guy's dick in their mouth. Suddenly they're all 'He made me do it' or 'I was too drunk to know better.' They're just afraid everyone will think they're a whore," the guy who'd been catching said.

Hunt felt heat wash over him. It was like the blast from an oven . . . or a blast from the past. Summer had been drunk and she'd told him no. Well, sorta told him no. She'd changed her mind when they were halfway there. He'd thought she was just nervous. Most guys, including Hunt, didn't know about foreplay when they were teenagers. The first time he and Molly had sex, she'd hit him and told him it stung and that she was bleeding, but eventually it got better. But with Summer, she'd accused him of rape from the beginning.

But it wasn't.

Was it?

"Doesn't matter," David continued, his shyness gone. He sounded like he knew exactly what he was talking about. He was confident. "She can say no in the middle of it. If she says stop, you're supposed to stop."

"But what if you're about to, you know, get there? That doesn't seem fair. She lets you fuck her and then says get off when you're about to come?"

"I'm just telling you what I know," David said.

"I call bullshit on that," another boy said. Hunt heard them moving toward him. He ducked behind the dugout. Don was walking his way.

"Call it what you want," David said, "but you could get arrested for it."

"That's not fair," one of the boys repeated.

Out of the corner of his eye, Hunt watched as David placed his glove carefully inside the beat-up bag Hunt had found in his garage. They were supposed to go to Charleston and buy a new one, but then the kid got smashed and hospitalized.

Hunt leaned against the dugout, his legs actually trembling. When he glanced to his right, he saw his father heading down the hill. Coming to do for David what he'd done for Hunt. And what was that, exactly? Berate under the guise of coaching? Protect him, his arm, his career at all costs? Call Summer Valentine and her parents liars so they didn't jeopardize his son's chance to throw a ball?

What had Hunt done?

What had his father done?

Hunt felt like he'd been hit with a stun gun. Out-of-body experience, mind blown, something crazy happening. Those words his son had said turned him inside out . . . blasted him . . . sent him staggering.

Rape.

An ugly, ugly word. When first uttered, it had seemed an unfounded accusation, dangerous to him and his family. Then it had been a shaky foundation for a relationship with the woman who'd given birth to his child. But rape had been something he'd been convinced he'd never done.

But now . . . now he wondered if he'd been wrong.

"Hey, Hunt," Don said, extending his hand. The older man nodded toward where Mitchell McCroy stood in the outfield, arms folded across the top of the fence. "Your old man must have gotten the message, huh?"

Hunt looked at Don's hand and then took it. "Yeah."

"You okay? You look sick."

"Dad?" David poked his head out from the dugout. "When did you get here?"

The kid looked panicked.

"Just a few seconds ago. I was checking my voice mail," he said, holding up his phone and waggling it. "You have fun with the guys?"

The three other boys came out, each extending his hand and introducing himself. Hunt knew two of the boys' parents. One was new to the area.

"Can we stay a few minutes and watch Don coach David? Van's a pitcher, too," the boy who'd argued with David said, jerking his head toward the taller boy. Hunt had dated the kid's aunt when he'd moved back to Moonlight. He was pretty certain she'd consented. In fact, she'd straddled him in the movie theater.

"Sure. If it's okay with Don," Hunt said, arching a brow at Don.

The older man nodded. "Sure. Nothing I like more than helping kids learn. You guys come on. If one of you is a catcher, we'll give you some reps."

Hunt walked to the bleachers and pulled out his phone. For the first time in his life, he typed *date rape* into the search feature on his phone. Words like *nonconsensual*, *drinking*, and *act of power* leaped out at him. He read an article on one site and then switched to another, almost desperate for one expert to take up for the guy. Surely someone would say that if a woman drank too much, dressed too sexy, or led a guy to believe she wanted sex, it wasn't rape. Some responsibility had to be placed on the woman, but site after site hammered home the fact that anything done against a woman (or man) without clear and full consent was a crime.

Eventually, Hunt pocketed the phone.

Staring out at the boy nodding to Don, Hunt thought back to that night long ago. He vividly remembered his anger at his parents, the hurt he felt at Molly dumping him, and the mounting stress to win every game and go to state. He'd been primed for reckless behavior. Pair that with a drunk and friendly Summer, and trouble was bound to occur. He remembered being convinced she wanted him, which had soothed some of the pain he'd felt. Oddly enough, he recalled trying to make her like him . . . and not like Rhett.

Yeah, he'd known she'd had a thing for his best friend. God knows her gaze hung up on Rhett a million times that night, and something about that had pissed Hunt off. Why wasn't he good enough for the girl who was pretty much a charity date? Maybe he'd devalued her a little. And perhaps he'd used her to make himself feel better. And according to the last three websites he'd visited, it was likely that he'd raped her.

Bile rose in his throat.

He got up and paced, rounding the bleachers, climbing back up and sitting down hard. He felt like a caged beast, trapped by his thoughts and decimated by the realization he'd been lying to himself for over fifteen years.

What was he supposed to do now?

Admit to Summer that he'd been deceiving himself for years? Apologize for not listening to her? Tell her he hadn't known what he did was rape? She'd probably wondered how he couldn't know. When he thought back to that night, he remembered some pushback, tears, and the way she'd carried on about the corsage that had gotten messed up.

And just nights before, he'd seen that same accusation in her eyes. He'd thought he'd left the hospital because he couldn't deal with what had happened to David, but perhaps deep down beneath all the bullshit he'd sold himself, he'd finally seen the truth. David's words to the boys playing ball had been the final nail in the coffin of his excuses.

Hunt had spent his life escaping blame. Not many people held his feet to the fire or told him when he wasn't doing right . . . except his father. His anger at his dad had obscured the truth from Hunt. But his eyes had been opened to his grievous mistake . . . and he could no longer close them and pretend his choices away.

"Hey, Dad," David said, jogging toward the fence. "Don said you can throw the best knuckleball he's ever seen. Will you show me?"

Hunt shook his head. "I'm too old and my arm's not warmed up."

"But I've never seen you pitch." The plaintiveness in the kid's voice weakened his resolve.

"Come on. Please." David gave him a smile.

His son's desires were always going to be Hunt's undoing.

"Okay, I'll throw a few," Hunt said, rising from the bleacher, hoping that doing something constructive would take away some of the fresh guilt pooling inside him.

Hunt walked onto the field, picking up a spare glove one of the kids had left on the dugout bench, and swung his arm in wide circles, warming up muscles he'd not used in many years. He wasn't even sure if he could throw even half as well as he used to. He might end up embarrassing himself or disappointing David. Something about that stung him almost as much as the self-realization he'd had just moments before. He didn't want David to be ashamed of him.

Hunt had screwed up, and he'd have to make that right.

David deserved that much.

"Show 'em what you got, Dad," David said, the confidence he had in Hunt shining in his eyes.

"I'll do my best."

CHAPTER TWENTY-FOUR

November, present day

Summer pushed the grocery cart through the store, trying to remember everything on the list she'd left at home on the counter. Forgetting her list was a rare occurrence, but the last week and a half had been a whirlwind of craziness. At least that was the story, and she was sticking to it.

For the past few days she'd been living a lie . . . and it was about to be over.

Rhett was going back to LA in just over twenty-four hours, and that thought made her heart vibrate with sorrow. Yeah, she'd drunk a glass of stupid and let herself get attached to Rhett. Or maybe she was living out one of her favorite movies—*The Bridges of Madison County.* She'd duped herself into believing Rhett would ask her to come with him, but deep down she knew the only bag packed would be his. Then she'd watch him ride away into the sunset.

Her life was here. His was not.

To her, Rhett Bryan was everything.

To him, Summer Valentine was a pleasant distraction.

End. Of. Story.

"No more Butterballs," Maisie said, placing the bag of brown sugar in the cart. "How can there be a Thanksgiving with no Butterball turkey?"

Summer shook her head. "Travesty. I never thought it could happen."

"Just like I never thought I would be shopping for Thanksgiving dinner with Rhett Bryan. He just sweet-talked Mildred Hodges into a second sample of some kind of new pizza snack. Unheard of." Maisie craned her head toward the end of the aisle where people stared at Rhett . . . but tried to look like they weren't staring.

"That's how he was in school. Everyone gave up their seat for him, loaned him lunch money, and practically lined up to walk behind him. People just want to be around him . . . and give him extra samples." Summer surveyed the cranberry sauces. With or without whole berries, that was the question . . . among other things.

"So how is he in bed?" Maisie asked.

Summer nearly dropped a can on her toe. "What?"

"Oh, come on. You look both flushed and tired . . . but in that good I-just-stayed-up-for-amazing-sex way. I'm not judging. I'd do him, too."

"You would not," Summer said, not bothering to confirm or deny. "And just because I'm tired doesn't mean I'm having sex." But she was. Lots of sneaking around, soul-stirring sex. She was giddy, tired, sad, and resigned to upcoming heartache. She was a woman in love with a man who would close the door on her soon, but she was wringing every moment and locking it away for the lonely times that would come. Did that make her pathetic?

Probably.

Maisie watched Rhett walk back to them, carrying the pizza samples on a towel. "I don't know. My heart's still broken, but I bet he'd go a long way in mending it. He's a free-pass kind of guy."

"Hush," Summer said, grabbing two cranberry sauces and tossing them in the cart. One of each to appease everyone at the dinner table.

"These are amazing. I figured I could only have two if I want to keep my girlish figure," Rhett said, jabbing the napkin toward them. "These extra-cheesy pizza stix are for you ladies. Wave at Mildred so she knows I gave them to you. She's very particular with her samples."

She and Maisie took the bread sticks and waved toward Mildred, who had an eagle eye on them.

"Do you think you can pick out five or six medium-size sweet potatoes, Mais?" Summer asked, hoping her sister got the hint and left her with Rhett, which was selfish of her, but every second that slipped past was like sand through an hourglass. It was a dumb cliché, but so effing true. Those grains kept falling, and there was nothing she could do to prevent it.

"Yeah, I got ya," Maisie said, heading back toward the produce section.

"Having fun playing at being normal?" she asked Rhett, pushing the basket down to where the green beans sat awaiting their place in dozens of upcoming green bean casseroles.

"Hey, I *am* normal. Sort of." He grinned. His cheerfulness felt forced, the way she faked joviality when David was about to receive a vaccination at the pediatrician. Cheesy jokes, silly games, here comes the shot . . . and tears.

"I wish you weren't leaving tomorrow," she said before she could stop herself. Damn it. Why did she say that? It had tumbled from her mouth like a pea escaping her fork at a fancy dinner party. She didn't know whether to pretend it hadn't happened or try to shepherd it back onto her plate. "I shouldn't have said that."

"No, I wish I didn't have to go, either," he said, picking up a can of corn. Such was corn. A great avoider, obviously.

Summer sighed. "This is stupid. I know you're going back and I'm staying here. What do you think about fruit salad?"

"In general or for Thanksgiving dinner?" Rhett said, obviously trying to lighten the mood. An older woman with overly teased hair turned in to the aisle. Her heavily made-up eyes zeroed in on Rhett holding a can of creamed corn. Summer couldn't blame her for looking suddenly hungry. The man made corn sexy.

"You know I'm trying to change the subject from me being pathetic to turkey dinner. Go with it, buddy."

When he looked at her, his eyes reflected . . . pity? God, she didn't want him to pity her. She wasn't some pining groupie or pathetic nerd anymore. She was a strong woman who had never needed a man. She could do power ballads, drink whiskey, and disable an attacker. She didn't need to be pitied because she had feelings, damn it.

"I think fruit salad is always a good idea," he said.

"Me, too," the newcomer said, pausing in front of the canned yams before tossing them into her shopping cart. She gave Summer a curious glance and Rhett a crocodilian smile. "I have a great recipe if you want it."

"Really?" Rhett asked, cocking his head in the most adorable way. Summer felt the older woman vibrate with pleasure. "Is that an innuendo or, like, for reals?"

The woman laughed and waved a big diamond under Rhett's nose. "Now, sugar, I can't say you're not tempting, but I'm happily married."

Oh, this woman was good. She knew how to play hard to get.

"Now you put away those dimples, sugar, or all bets are off. Poor ol' Donald could be just a memory to me . . . though I *have* been married to him for thirty-two years."

"I better not ask for that recipe, then." Rhett gave her a smile that glittered, and Summer nearly stuck her finger down her throat and mocked vomiting.

"Sugar, they should require a license for a smile like yours," she said, giving him a wink before sashaying down the aisle.

Summer didn't know whether to snort in disbelief or laugh.

"She's good," Rhett mused, watching her turn and stroke a display of cans on the endcap with a saucy smile on her face. Gone was the pity. Instead his dimples were out to play.

"She's right. Put away the dimples. I don't need random women trying to make time with you." Even though she was heartsore, it pleased her to see Rhett so relaxed. He'd been sleeping better, laughing more, and avoiding any talk about his life in California.

"Hey, yours is the only coffee I'm drinking," he said, shoving his hands in his pockets and falling in beside her. "You know, I like grocery shopping."

"Weirdo," she said, watching Maisie twirl the bag of potatoes as she headed back toward them.

Maisie dropped the potatoes in the cart. "I've got to get back to the shop. Shelia called. We have a few last-minute orders for table arrangements. I want to get everything wrapped up early this afternoon so I can help you get everything ready tonight."

"You're bringing rolls and squash casserole, right?" Summer asked.

"Right," Maisie said, giving her a quick squeeze. She paused for a moment, eyeing Rhett beside her. "Aren't you two just peas and carrots."

Summer gave Maisie the stink eye. "Bye, Maisie."

Rhett just smiled. Of course.

"Ignore her. She's insane," Summer said, pushing the cart toward the frozen foods. She'd ordered a pie from Etta, but she'd thought about making her grandmother's chocolate pie. If she did, she'd have to cheat with a store-bought crust. Time, sands, and all that.

"Are you the pea or the carrot?" he teased.

Summer didn't answer because she was pretty sure she was the tomato, a fruit trying to pass itself off as a veggie. Instead she headed to the checkout, where she found Rhett's face plastered across the front of the *National Enquirer* with the logline "Late-Night Accusations: Bryan Attacks Family of Girl."

Rhett's face went white when he saw it. "I'll meet you in the car, okay?"

Concerned, Summer nodded. When he'd disappeared through the sliding doors, she picked up the gossip rag. Two people with full carts were before her so she leafed through the magazine, finding the page with the story. Didn't take long to see what it implied. Summer shoved it back in the rack, confused by what she'd just read.

When she got to the car, she didn't say anything. Rhett sat in the passenger seat pecking on his phone, his jaw clenched tight. No element of the flirty, relaxed celebrity remained. He muttered "fuck" under his breath three times before they pulled into the Nest's driveway. Across the stretch of yard in her parking area idled Hunt's big truck.

"What's he doing here?" Rhett demanded, his face no longer stony and impassive. A storm rolled onto the horizon, overshadowing the article in the *National Enquirer*.

"I forgot he was coming. We have to talk about David and where we stand on things like parties and dating. Fun stuff. Can you take these inside? I'm going to do most of my cooking at Pete's. Not much room in my kitchen."

"I don't want to leave you alone with him," Rhett said, unbuckling his seat belt.

Summer snorted. "You realize I've been alone with Hunt more than a dozen times. I've taken more self-defense and martial arts classes than you can imagine. I'm good."

Rhett's expression didn't change. "Fine. I'll take the groceries inside. Got some calls to make anyway."

Summer climbed out and headed toward Hunt's truck.

He rolled down the window, casting a cautious glance toward Rhett, who was likely standing there looking threatening. "Is now a good time?"

Summer glanced back at Rhett. "He's more bark than bite, right? I'm the one you should worry about. I have a black belt."

"So warned." Hunt shut off the engine and climbed from the truck. Walking around to the passenger side, he pulled out a plastic container.

Inside was a corsage of white roses.

Summer's heart did a funny flip. A strange feeling swept over her, but naming what it was seemed too difficult. Hunt held the container out to her, but she didn't touch it.

"I got you this." His voice sounded soft on the early afternoon breeze.

She took the clear container, focusing on the delicate ivory blossoms. The ribbon was the exact blue of her prom dress. Soft, sweet blooms nestled in iridescent blue, innocently unaware of representing what she'd lost.

Looking up at Hunt, she asked, "Why?"

"Because I didn't understand what I had done to you."

Summer glanced to where Rhett unloaded bags from her car. He kept watching them. She couldn't see his expression, but she knew it was aggressive. No need for a scene like this past weekend. "Maybe it would be better if we spoke inside."

Hunt followed her into the dim house. She couldn't remember the last time he'd been inside her place. Usually he preferred to stay outside with his truck idling when he picked up David. She gestured to the couch. Hunt sank onto the edge and looked about as comfortable as she did at the gynecologist.

Summer took the chair and lifted her eyebrows.

"I looked up date rape, uh, on the Internet." He didn't look at her. Instead he focused on the sunflowers in the vase on the table.

She decided to wait to see where he went with this.

Finally, he looked at her. "I'd never looked that up before. Didn't feel a need to."

"Why did you? Because of what happened at the hospital?"

Hunt shook his head. "No, not really. More because of David."

"David?"

"Yesterday I overheard him with the baseball guys at the field. I had walked down from the office to watch him. I stood in the shadows of the dugout because I wanted to see how he looked without knowing I was there, you know? Anyway, I overheard him shooting the shit with the guys. At first they ragged David about the party, but then they moved on to discussing a girl who'd passed out. David pretty much schooled them on how to handle a situation with a girl who's been drinking. He talked about consent and stuff like that."

"I worked as a rape crisis counselor in Nashville for a few years. Some of the jargon sank in, I'm sure." She felt a flash of pride at her son. He'd not only gleaned important information about how to act in situations, but he felt motivated enough to educate others.

"Yeah, I had never heard much about consent and what constituted date rape. They didn't talk about that kind of stuff much when we were in school. David sounded so . . . sure. Those other guys tried to blame the girl, but the kid didn't let them. He told them they could go to jail if they didn't stop when a girl asked."

"In so many words, yes. A guy needs physical or verbal consent. He can't assume a girl who is passed out or incapacitated by, let's say, fear, is willing and consenting to sex."

"Yeah, so I looked up some things and . . . I may have been a bit . . . obtuse."

Summer didn't say anything. She knew from her time counseling that it was best to remain quiet and let the other person tell his or her story.

"For years I assumed you said you'd been raped to save face. I knew it hadn't been . . . uh, good. For one thing, we were both drunk, but I was mad about a lot of stuff around that time. There was a lot of pressure on me, and you were out of your element. I figured when you came up pregnant, you needed an out with your parents. I was mad at you for lying. Then when things like the Duke lacrosse scandal happened,

I validated my opinion by thinking that's how girls throw shade when they get caught."

He paused and sucked in a deep breath. "I figured it was easy for a girl to say, 'He raped me' instead of owning her own mistakes."

"You thought that's what I did?" She couldn't hold the anger from her voice. This didn't sound like an apology. This sounded like the same old Hunt. She glanced down at the corsage she'd placed on the coffee table.

"Yeah. I did. And when my parents paid money to keep you quiet, I imagined that was your family's motive. It worked for me. My dad implied you'd done it intentionally."

"My family didn't benefit from my getting pregnant. Quite the opposite, in fact. My mother lost her job, my sister was shunned, and I had to leave the University of South Carolina so my family could help with the baby. Nobody got rich, Hunt."

"I know that now," he said, his face reflecting an apology. "I know a lot more than I ever really wanted to know, Summer."

He paused and looked down at his linked hands. "What I'm trying to say is that I'm sorry for what happened to you. For what I did. I have a lot of excuses for why I pressed you to have sex that night—"

"Not pressed. Forced," she said.

"Yes, forced. But none is more important than I didn't stop when you said no. I guess I'm a rapist." The last words were said with a catch in his voice.

Summer nodded. "Technically you are—or were—but here's the thing, I had some culpability. I'm not victim shaming myself or buying a load of crap that a girl dressing suggestively or going home with a guy means she asked to be raped, but I gave off a lot of mixed signals that night. My emotional state was unbalanced, and the butt load of vodka and tequila didn't help. Not to mention, I liked how it felt to be held, kissed, and desired. You were young, confident, and drunk, which also isn't the best frame of mind for hearing no in a sexual situation."

"I understand that now," he said.

"But that doesn't excuse you for proceeding when I said no, but it does . . . explain why educating kids about situations like ours is so important. It's why David knew the right thing to say to boys bragging about sexual assault."

Hunt's head hung and he took a deep breath. "I know it's asking a lot, but I hope one day you can forgive me for what happened. That you can forgive me for being such an asshole about how the pregnancy thing went down. I know I have to make up to David the wrongs I did in the past, but I owe you, too. I suppose we'll never be friends, but I want you to know I'm sorry, Summer. You didn't deserve the way I treated you."

This was what she'd always wanted to hear—Hunt to say that he'd been wrong about that night and all that came afterward. Hearing him grovel had been up there on the list with winning the lottery and getting a recording contract. He'd finally done that for her . . . and for her son. He'd taken responsibility for his actions.

"Okay," she said.

"Okay, what?"

"I forgive you for what happened that night."

"That easily?" he asked, looking stunned.

"Yeah. Because, believe it or not, I've healed. I'm not completely over it. Sometimes I have nightmares, but they're rare. Thing is, Hunt, I moved past being sexually assaulted because I didn't want it to own me. It wasn't easy because I still had anger toward you. But eventually I accepted that it wasn't my fault. I've claimed my life."

"Still—" he started.

Summer held her hand up. "Besides, what do I gain by punishing you forever? You came here and expressed regret for your actions. You made a mistake that affected both our lives, but finally you're owning what you did. Look, the silver lining is that ugliness gave us something pretty damned awesome. David's not perfect and can't hold his liquor"—she gave a choked laugh—"but he's a great kid."

"Yeah, he is." Hunt looked around the small living area, his gaze lingering on the pictures of their son. "You've done a good job. I sorta fucked up by encouraging him to go to that party."

"Me, too, but that wasn't solely on you, Hunt. Yeah, maybe both of us should have vetted that party better, but ultimately David made the decision to drink . . . a lot. He has to own his choices, too."

A few seconds ticked by.

When Hunt looked at her this time, tears pooled in his brown eyes. The sight of Hunt crying loosened the knot of hate she'd always had for him. "I also wanted to say that I'm so glad you kept him. I used to be mad at you. I thought you kept him as a pawn against me, but, oh God, I'm so glad you kept him. He's the brightest spot of my life."

"Yeah, he is, isn't he?" Summer said, her own voice breaking. Emotion washed over her, a sort of release of all she'd held tight to for so long. Sure, it wasn't going to be as easy to surrender the hurt created the night Hunt forced her into sex, but his apology went a long way to repair the bitterness she'd lugged around. "Why did you bring the corsage?"

Hunt shrugged. "I couldn't figure out how to fix what I had done. There's no way to go back and undo what happened, but an image of you crying over that corsage stuck in my memory. I didn't do so hot in English class, but I remember studying symbolism. You weren't upset about the flowers but about the rape. That corsage getting destroyed paralleled what happened to you . . . to your innocence. I crushed it. Took the beauty from you. I wanted to show you I was sorry with more than just words."

Summer swallowed hard.

"It's probably stupid," he said.

Summer picked up the container and popped the plastic box open. Lifting the cluster of white roses, she inhaled the waxy scent. "I don't think it's stupid. You're making amends. I appreciate that, Hunt."

He sat for a moment, swiped his eyes, and then stood. "Well, you have things to do. Saw Rhett out there unloading groceries. David said you were cooking a big meal for tomorrow."

She wasn't about to invite him to Thanksgiving dinner. She wasn't that good with Hunt. "Always lots to do around the holidays."

"Yeah," Hunt said, stretching out a hand.

She hesitated before placing her hand in his. It was the first time she could remember voluntarily touching Hunt. His hand was slightly sweaty and enveloped hers.

He wagged her hand, giving it a slight squeeze before releasing it. "Thank you for forgiving me. I will do better. Got a little freaked that night at the hospital, but I'm learning what it means to be a parent in the trenches. I'm done with running from responsibility and my mistakes, Summer. I promise."

Summer smiled. "I can see that. Maybe at the beginning of the new year we can meet and talk about custody and strategies for raising a teenager."

Hunt's lips twitched. "So far it's been an adventure."

"That's an understatement."

Summer saw Hunt out and watched him drive off. Inside she felt odd, like she'd scaled a mountain that had stood in her way for far too long. Euphoric in a way, but also very calm. Like she knew it would come, it did, so now she could move on to other mountains.

When she walked across the scraggly stretch of patchy grass and trees, Rhett was waiting for her. He looked perturbed, his hair sticking up from thrusting his hand through it. The earlier, silly Rhett had disappeared.

"What was that all about?" he asked.

Over the last few days, any mention of Hunt had intensified Rhett's grudge against his former friend. After years of therapy, Summer knew that Rhett projected his anger over the lack of control of his own life onto Hunt. She hadn't wanted anything to mar their last moments together, so she avoided the subject of Hunt. But she couldn't not answer Rhett.

"David, stuff we needed to deal with," she said, looking up the steps to the entrance to the Nest. "You get everything put up?"

"I gave the bags to Grampy. He seemed particular with where everything went. So are you good?" Rhett asked. He asked it in a nonchalant way, but he looked upset.

"Actually, the shouting match at the hospital was effective. Hunt came to apologize. Finally."

"For raping you? Or being a shitty person?"

"Rhett," she chided, climbing the steps, still raw from all the earlier emotion. She didn't want to squabble with Rhett over Hunt. "If you can't let it go, can we at least not talk about it?"

"Are you kidding? He thinks a simple apology erases what he did? But of course he does. That's how he was raised. Throw money at it and act contrite and there are no consequences."

Summer stiffened at Rhett's anger. "This is not yours to decide, Rhett. No wrong was done to you. We've had this conversation already."

"So you forgave him? Just let bygones be bygones?" Rhett looked stupefied. And pissed. Any other day and she might stop to appreciate how intense he looked when outraged. But not today. She wasn't in the mood to appreciate Rhett being overly dramatic.

"Yeah, I did."

"God, you're stupid," he said, shaking his head.

She'd been about to walk inside and leave him sulking, but at those words she spun. "Excuse me? Did you call me stupid?"

He glowered at her but said nothing.

"Using your big words, huh?" she drawled, embracing the anger crackling inside her. He didn't get to belittle her merely because he disagreed with how she handled Hunt. Or because he was going through a rough time himself. "As I said before, this is not yours to forgive. It's mine. Just because you can't control the things happening in your own life doesn't give you license to try and control mine."

"What does that mean?"

"I saw the headline on that magazine."

Rhett went still as well water. "We're not talking about that. We're talking about you . . . and how you let Hunt off easy. I don't understand you."

She perched above him, a winged harpy. "You don't have to understand, Rhett. I handle my life the way I handle my life. Emphasis on *my*, you ass."

"I've seen how you handle your life. You slice away pieces of yourself. You play at being a martyr or, worse, a doormat. Your sister uses you, your kid forced you to give up your career, and now Hunt says he's sorry, and you're giving him what he doesn't deserve. You let things happen to you and don't do anything about it."

His words slammed into her. Martyr? Doormat? How could he say those things about her? Just because she loved the people in her life . . . and willingly made some sacrifices for them? "I am not a doormat, you asshole. Or a martyr. I don't need people chasing me around with Sharpies wanting my autograph to be happy. I'm content with who I am."

"I'm going to ignore the fact that you think that makes me happy," he said, narrowing his eyes. "Let's get back to you. You could be doing so much more, but you settle. It's like you don't think you deserve anything good. You won't even let me help you."

Rhett had lost the dimples along with everything else that made him remotely appealing. He looked like an asshole deflecting his fears onto her . . . and he was sticking his pretty nose where it was not wanted.

She jabbed a finger at him. "You're going to lecture me about excuses? Talk about being scared and running, mister."

He drew back. "Watch it, Summer."

"You watch it. Hunt came to make things right with me. He owned his part in what happened years ago. He can't undo what was done, but he's trying to make things right. Owning up to what he did was big for him . . . and for *me*. It had nothing to do with you. You've got your own restitution to make."

Rhett's eyes turned to ice. "I don't have any restitution to make. What happened to me was an accident. I wasn't at fault."

"Technically, yeah. But you had a role. After all, if you hadn't been there, that girl wouldn't be dead. Have you ever apologized for your part in it all? Or are you just going to do what the McCroy family planned to do to me—use your power to crush that family? Didn't they lose enough without your PR people digging up their lives and making them look bad?"

"That's not what I'm doing. I'm not like the McCroys."

"But you're letting your people smear them. Have you even met the little girl's family? Talked to them? Said you're sorry for what you did?"

"I don't have to apologize. In case you didn't see it, criminal charges weren't filed. Know why? Because the kid was at fault."

"She was eleven, Rhett."

Rhett's breath came hard, his blue eyes hardened to ice. But he said nothing.

"There is power in saying you're sorry. Think about that one day when you're back in LA, preaching to people about taking responsibility for who they are. You told Bev how to treat people, how to respect and value them, and then you allow your people, or whoever they are, to tear down that family."

"That's not fair," Rhett said, clenching his teeth and glaring at her.

"Life isn't fair. Didn't you get the memo? It ain't all sunshine. Rain falls on everyone. You take a cut-through, a kid runs out in front of you, and she dies as a result. It wasn't fair to you, to her, or to her parents. I went upstairs with Hunt and got raped. Wasn't fair to me, either."

"That's different," he ground out.

"Is it? The reason why you're struggling in life is because you've rarely had to deal with rain, Rhett. Outside of losing parents you don't remember, sunshine has always sat on your shoulders. But here's the hard truth—shit happens. Sometimes you have to wipe it off and keep going . . . and sometimes you have to shovel it."

"Thank you, Forrest Gump."

Summer stared at him a few seconds, shook her head, and went up the steps, feeling like her heart was breaking . . . and like she wanted to hit something. Before she wrenched open the screen door, she whirled back to Rhett. "And don't ever insinuate I'm afraid. I'm many things, but a coward ain't one of them."

"So you *say*. But what have you actually *done*?" he asked.

She walked into Pete's house, wondering how the day had turned upside down, wondering if Rhett had intentionally picked a fight with her to make leaving easier, and wondering how much truth lay in his parting words.

She walked through the door without turning around to ask . . . and out of Rhett's life for the second time.

CHAPTER TWENTY-FIVE

California, two weeks later

Rhett had ended up having sushi for his Thanksgiving meal at a restaurant near the Savannah airport. He'd told himself he didn't care about turkey and dressing, that sushi was his tradition and that the crab rolls were phenomenal. They weren't. Instead they tasted of ashes and heartbreak.

On the flight back to LA, he'd given himself a good talking-to. Better that he and Summer end the way they had. They'd spent many good days in a bubble of wonderfulness, but a mean kid with a sharp tack had stood on the perimeter, insuring they would be no more.

He'd hated being the mean kid.

At present he sat in an austere office, doing one of the many things he had to do to get his life back. Dr. Laura Zimmerman had been the studio's choice in psychiatrists.

"So, Mr. Bryan, what's your plan for dealing with a situation like you had last month?" the therapist asked, her blue eyes oddly piercing. The network wanted an "objective" party. Rhett was under the impression that all shrinks were supposed to be objective, but the studio heads mentioned something about safeguarding against Rhett's charm and influence.

Dr. Laura Zimmerman had thus far been unmoved by his dimples and carefully constructed answers.

"I won't go on a tirade. I will smile and go to commercial break. Then I'll let Artie handle anything inappropriate while I drink seltzer water off set," he said. *Good answer, Rhett.*

"Is that how you'd prefer to have the situation handled?"

"No, but I learned my lesson."

She lifted one eyebrow, a trick he'd never perfected. "Yes, but how would you handle it if you had your druthers?"

"Druthers? Is that term still used?" he teased.

Dr. Zimmerman didn't even blink. Obviously, she had no sense of humor.

"I would punch them in the face," he said, before pressing his hands to the air. "Just kidding. I wouldn't do that. I'm actually pretty nonviolent."

"Define *pretty*."

Rhett sighed and tried to remain unruffled. But that was getting harder and harder to do. Dr. Zimmerman seemed determined to see exactly how he would handle a difficult person by *being* that person. Weren't therapists supposed to feel safe and comforting? This woman wouldn't know a warm fuzzy if it smacked her in the face. "I don't use my fists. I'm mostly calm and collected. Most people would characterize me as a good guy."

"Do you use other forms of violence to deal with things in your life that perturb you?"

"Why? Are you trying to find out?" he snapped.

"Hmm," she said, scratching something on her notepad. Her glasses perched on a thin nose. Her cheekbones were high, her complexion milky white. And she wore ugly shoes. He probably shouldn't trust a woman who wore ugly shoes.

"Can I go now?" He gave her a congenial, talk-show-host smile.

"Almost. Tell me about your relationship with your family."

Rhett collapsed back into the chair with a heavy sigh. "My parents were killed in a car accident when I was a small child. My grandfather in South Carolina raised me. I have a good relationship with him. In fact, I just spent nearly two weeks with him."

"Mm," she muttered, scratching some more on her pad. "And how was that?"

Soul-stirring, cathartic, beautiful, wonderful . . . sad. "Fine."

"And what about relationships here in LA? Do you have any significant romantic attachments? Close friendships outside of your career?"

"Sure. Uh, no to the romance. I'm in between. And I have friends." But even as he said the words, he knew he didn't have anyone who filled the role of mentor, confidant, or good buddy. His housekeeper, Marta, probably didn't count since he paid her to be around.

"You said 'in between.' Can you give me more details on what exactly that means?" Her watery eyes pinned him to the upholstery. No blinking. He wondered if she ever blinked.

"I guess that didn't sound right. What I mean is that I just got out of a relationship."

"Okay. Can you categorize that relationship? Was it serious? Casual?"

What he'd had with Summer over those weeks should have been casual, but it felt anything but. Since he'd come home from South Carolina, leaving a day early because he couldn't face sitting across from her raving about stupid turkey, he'd felt adrift. All the good accomplished in Moonlight had pulled away from him, like a tide going out, sucking at his soul. Sound sleep had fled, to be replaced with tossing and turning, and his old friend bourbon had shown back up to mooch off his emotions and numb him to the hard stuff in his life. He lusted for the easy comfort of South Carolina. He thirsted for the warmth

Moonlight and Summer had wrapped him in. "More casual, I guess. She's someone I've known forever, and when I went back home, we sort of fell into something."

"Fell into something?"

"Yeah, but it couldn't last because I'm here and she's there."

"This was sexual in nature, I'm assuming?"

"Yeah, but it wasn't limited to sex. Summer and I go way back. We're friends, too. She's a remarkable woman, really. If things weren't so hard . . ." He trailed off because he didn't know how to finish that. He'd stay with her? Date her? Marry her? He hadn't thought much about what-ifs because he'd had too many have-tos in his life.

Dr. Zimmerman arched the other eyebrow and waited.

"She made me feel like a human again. Like I wasn't merely a made-up person on television. Perhaps I lost sight of myself out here. Pushing myself and keeping my eye on the prize became paramount. Then I got the prize and I wasn't satisfied."

"A common problem in LA," Dr. Zimmerman said, almost sounding human herself.

"Yeah, it is. You asked about relationships, and the truth is that I don't have any outside of work. Sounds crazy because I grew up with healthy relationships all around me. I've worked hard to be this person I thought I wanted, and now I'm somebody I barely recognize . . . except when I went home. There, I felt real . . . even needed. I fixed the railing on Grampy's deck, took Summer's kid to baseball, saw old friends, and—" He paused because he had been about to say he'd fallen for Summer.

But that couldn't be true because people don't fall in love in a matter of weeks . . . even if they had known the person forever. That sounded ridiculous.

"Let's just say I escaped for a while, but it wasn't the real world."

"And this is?" she asked.

He stared at her for a few seconds. "It's my world. Or at least it was."

Dr. Zimmerman looked at her watch. "Our time is about up, but I'm not quite finished with my evaluation. Do you think you can come back next week?"

"I'll have to look at my schedule."

"Are you still seeing"—she flipped through the chart at her elbow—"Angela Goodman?"

"Not any longer."

"I would suggest regular therapy, Mr. Bryan. You underwent a traumatic experience."

"I know, but I'm fine." He wasn't, but paying someone hundreds of dollars to talk about his feelings and then still not being able to sleep or taste food didn't make sense. He hadn't been getting any better, so he'd stopped going.

Dr. Zimmerman didn't say anything to that claim. She merely stared at him.

"Okay, fine. I'll go back to therapy."

"That would be wise. See Denise and schedule something for next week on your way out." Dr. Zimmerman turned in her swivel chair and started tapping on her laptop, effectively dismissing him.

"Bye," he said lamely.

"Goodbye," she said, not looking up.

Rhett rolled his eyes and went out to see Denise. Dr. Zimmerman was weird as shit, but he scheduled an appointment with her for the following Thursday. He told himself it was because the network required it of him, but if pressed he would admit talking to someone who wasn't all "own your feelings" was therapeutic. He nearly laughed at that thought.

Needing some fresh air to clear his head, he headed for the Pacific Coast Highway. Traffic was lighter than normal for some reason, so it only took him an hour. Five minutes after that, he walked along the beach, pants rolled up, collar unbuttoned, wind in his hair.

Gulls pirouetted above him as he let the water roll over his toes. Surfers paddled, the sun shone, and kids shrieked. Quintessential California. There was even the faint scent of pot on the breeze.

He shouldn't have left Summer the way he had. Packing up in the middle of the night and leaving her a lame-ass Dear John letter made him the lowest of low. Their heated discussion had gotten out of control. Rhett had said some horrible things to her, things that weren't even true. Jealousy and some crazy inclination to hurt her before she could hurt him had reared twin heads and hissed that he should strike and leave before love crippled him. So he'd listened to the ugly and spouted absolute trash.

And then ran.

But Summer's words had followed him to LA. Words about forgiveness, owning mistakes, being accountable for his decisions. She'd been right about what he was trying to do to the Tavares family. He'd allowed his PR team to squash them. His lawyer had called, gleeful because their attorney wanted to talk about a settlement. Their plan had worked.

And now he'd done what the McCroy family had intended for Summer. He'd manipulated the story line so the family looked irresponsible, crooked, looking for a payout. To them, he no doubt seemed a rich, callous man who would stomp on any attempt to take from him.

They couldn't know what killing their daughter had done to him.

His grandfather's question came back to him. What meaning did his life have?

Rhett Bryan could be summed up with "host of *Late Night in LA*" and little else. He wasn't a father, a husband, a partner, or a good friend. He'd spent so much time chasing his dream of fortune and fame, he'd forgotten there was more to life than his name in glittering lights. He measured himself by how many award shows he hosted, how many cameos he'd done in films, which actress sat with him at exclusive restaurants. His net worth was measured only in dollar signs.

Anyone standing outside looking in would say the meaning of Rhett's life was his career.

Kicking at the wave, Rhett walked a small piece and then confronted the sun hovering above him. The rays warmed him, but not more so than the softness from the Carolina moon the night he'd held Summer on the boat. He wished he could go back and relive those moments, feel the peace she brought him, taste her soft lips, capture her soft sighs as she tightened around him, finding release. He wished he could take back the hard words, the way he'd pushed her away, content to wallow in his own misery. He needed more than what he now had, but his life still felt knotted tight.

So many thoughts swirled around him, much like the waves pulling at his feet—mistakes, wrongs, consequences, courage, regret, redemption.

How did a man right the wrongs in his life?

Start at the beginning.

The sun sat on his shoulders, bearing down in conviction, as Rhett started back to his car.

Before he could find a new meaning in his life, he had to fix what was broken.

The Tavares family lived in a modest, two-bedroom apartment housed in a brown box building. A tattered awning shielded a glass door that surveyed a scraggly patch of grass out front. Whip-thin palm trees writhed in the background, competing with the surprisingly lush potted plants standing guard outside the entry. A cluster of flowers and crosses sat near the road and took his breath away. But he parked and walked past it, shutting out the images it evoked.

Rhett got lucky—the door hadn't closed completely. He climbed the flaky, wrought-iron stairs to the upper apartment where the Tavares family lived.

Before he knocked on the door, he wrestled with himself again. Once he knocked, he was committed to his path. Rhett sucked in a deep breath, then lifted his fist.

After several seconds, a small boy opened the door. He regarded Rhett with dark eyes, wearing jeans a bit too short. He said nothing. Just stared at Rhett.

"Uh, hello," Rhett said, trying to not look so nervous. "Is your mother or father here?"

The little boy didn't answer.

"*Quem é esse?*" a woman's voice sounded from the depths of the house.

"Some man, Mama," the boy said.

The door jerked wider and Ana Tavares appeared. At first her face was curious, but when she saw Rhett standing there, any politeness disappeared. She tried to close the door.

"Please, Mrs. Tavares, I need a moment of your time," he said, catching the door with the flat of his hand.

"No. Go away," she said, pushing against the door. "*Socorro!*"

Rhett felt someone moving toward the door. Another angry face appeared, wearing a scowl vicious enough to clear a prison yard.

"Please, Mr. Tavares. I just wanted—"

"You have no reason to be here," Reis Tavares said, jabbing his finger toward Rhett. The child scampered back into the depths of the apartment while Ana clutched her shirt, twisting it into a knot. "You've done enough to us. I don't care who you are. You are shit."

"No, I'm not. I swear," Rhett said, taken aback at the violence in the man. Reis looked as if he might murder him on the spot. He remembered the police reports and had a moment of panic. He should have found a different way to do this. "Please, I need to talk to you. I have some things to say. You don't even have to invite me in."

Reis's murderous expression didn't fade. "So talk. I'll give you one minute before I pound your ass into a puddle. I don't care if I go to jail. People already think I'm a thug now anyway."

A neighbor opened a door and stuck his head out. He looked stoned but very interested in what was playing out before him. Reis glanced at the man, scowled even deeper, and said, "Come inside. I don't want more nosy-assed reporters knowing my business."

Rhett swallowed the dryness in his throat. "Thank you."

The apartment smelled of cooking and was filled with mismatched furniture and huge houseplants. A wizened old woman rocked in the corner, her leathery hands clacking knitting needles together. She glanced up and gave him a polite nod.

"So?" Reis said, crossing his arms. There was no offer to sit down.

"Uh, I wanted to come here to apologize."

Ana swiped at the sudden tears coursing down her cheeks. "That's why you came here? To say sorry?"

Rhett sucked in a desperate breath. "For everything."

"Well, our daughter's dead. That can't be fixed." Ana's expression grew fierce.

The knife of guilt twisted inside him. "I know, but . . . but I never said those words. I never said anything to either of you. And then—"

"You sic your lawyers on us. Make us look like we wanted nothing but money. We don't care about the goddamned money. We just wanted you to hurt." Reis's jaw tightened, his fists clenched. "But you're not sorry. You're white. You're rich. You're famous. You don't have to be sorry."

Rhett pushed a hand through his hair. "I am those things. That's true, but your daughter was someone. What happened took her away from you. I need to tell you how sorry I am for what happened."

"You didn't try to help her," Ana said, her voice low. She wrapped her arms around herself in a hug. "You climbed out of your fancy car and stood there. And she died."

"I should have done something—"

"You should have fucking swerved out of the way. You ran right over her." Reis's words rained on him like bullets.

"I didn't see her. She came from the side, Mr. Tavares. I didn't see her." Rhett couldn't stop pushing his hand through his hair. He'd come this far, intent on owning his role, but he couldn't find a way to ease the grief these two people felt. He was making everything worse. This wasn't working. "I wish I had been able to stop, that I could have done something to save her."

Reis looked like an injured bear, his hulking shoulders tense, his expression anguished. "But you didn't. After you ran her over, you didn't even try to help her. Like she was trash."

"No," Rhett said, holding up a hand. "No. Never that. I don't know why I couldn't move. My body shut down and I couldn't make myself do anything. It wasn't because I didn't care or want to help. I . . . just couldn't."

The words were hollow to even his own ears. He should have tried something that day. Drag the car off her, CPR, something.

"Josefina ran out in front of him, *meu filho*," the old woman said from the rocker.

"Shut up, old woman," Reis snapped.

"Do not disrespect me," the old woman said, setting aside her knitting. "I was there."

"You were where, *Avo*?" Ana asked, turning to the old woman.

"I was there. Sitting in the chair Yogi leaves outside when he smokes. I had my eye on the young ones. Josefina ran after the ball, but she didn't look. She forgot where she was. He could not have avoided her. She was very fast."

"Shut up," Reis said, turning his scowl on the older woman. "Josefina played on this street many times."

"You cannot blame others for misfortune," the old woman said, rising from her chair and setting down her knitting. She shuffled from the room, but not before tossing a hateful look at Reis. They all watched her disappear into what looked to be a kitchen.

"Look, I should go. All I wanted was to say how sorry I was. I didn't come here to upset you," Rhett said, inching back toward the door. "Recently a friend taught me about the power in owning one's mistakes. Josefina's accident was unavoidable, but I was there. I made choices that day, choices I regret. I wanted to tell you how sorry I am that you lost your daughter, and that no matter the outcome of the lawsuit, I want to do something. Maybe set up a scholarship in your daughter's name. That is, if you both are okay with that?"

Both Ana and Reis stared at him.

"I'll go now," Rhett said, feeling behind his back for the doorknob. Summer had been wrong. He'd done nothing to make the situation better. Ana and Reis felt worse, he felt worse, nothing had changed.

"Does your lawyer know you're here?" Reis asked.

"God, no. In fact, he'll probably hand my case over to someone else when he finds out. The first thing he told me was to say nothing, to admit nothing. Standard advice from an attorney."

Reis nodded. "A lawyer came looking for us. She wasn't even in the ambulance and they were ringing my doorbell."

Rhett wasn't surprised. There was a death, and a celebrity was at the wheel. "Yeah, well, the lawyers can squabble over the money. They are good at that. But I needed to say this to you. So I can sleep. So I can feel like a person again. I don't care about the money, either. I just want . . . God, I'm a selfish bastard. This isn't about me. I really wanted it to be about her. To honor your daughter in some way." As he said the words, something welled inside him. His throat ached as emotion rolled over him.

Ana walked toward him, easing her husband back. "You mean this? This isn't . . . a stunt?"

"No. I shouldn't have come." Rhett blinked back the sudden moisture gathering in his eyes, aware he needed to get out before he crumbled. Something dark within him unknotted, rising to the surface as he saw firsthand their utter grief. "I'll go now."

Josefina's mother set her hand on his forearm. "You didn't have to tell us that."

He looked into her dark eyes. In the depths he found something so profound, his body began to tremble. He couldn't name it—tenderness, understanding, knowledge of who he was. The grief he'd hidden swelled inside him. He should have left seconds before. "I'm sorry . . . I gotta . . ."

But his body once again betrayed him. A sob tore away, unfettered from his soul. He jackknifed forward, pressing his hands to his torso as if he could hold everything back. And then it engulfed him. "Oh God, I'm so sorry. I'm so sorry."

Ana's hands clasped his shoulders as uncontrollable grief flowed out of him. She murmured words that Rhett didn't register—some were in Portuguese, others English. He was helpless, other than to crumble to the floor and hold on to her. His levee had failed.

After a few seconds of sobbing, he rocked back on his heels, stunned at what had just occurred. He looked up at Ana and Reis, who both had tears sliding down their cheeks.

"I'm sorry. I don't know what happened." He swiped a hand across cheekbones that *GQ* had once described as chiseled, then he struggled to his feet. He felt drained. Altogether, it was the strangest damned thing that had ever happened to him.

Ana pulled a tissue from a box sitting near the worn recliner. Reis had sunk into a chair, his expression void of anything. The man looked gobsmacked.

"Sometimes we need to let things out so we can get better." Ana handed him the tissue. "Like an infection, you know."

Rhett had never been so embarrassed. His resolve to say his piece and slip unobtrusively back into his regular life had disintegrated at Ana's compassion and he'd broken apart. "Maybe so. I have to admit I'm pretty embarrassed."

Reis looked up, tears still swimming in his eyes. "We're good with the scholarship fund. Josefina loved to read. That would have pleased her."

Rhett nodded, swiping again at eyes that felt raw. His head ached, but his soul felt oddly unencumbered. "I'll start the process by the end of the week."

He opened the door, turned to them, and nodded.

Ana stood beside her husband, her hand on his shoulder. They nodded back and Rhett felt something in the universe expand and snap into place.

He'd done what he needed to do.

In more than one way.

CHAPTER TWENTY-SIX

California, two months later

Summer took the keys to the compact car and pushed out into the lot where the rentals were housed. The thought of driving in LA gave her the willies, but she wasn't getting back on the plane to Charleston without doing what she'd come to do. So she brushed her nerves under her doormat of confidence and looked for parking spot 134.

The car was a bright-blue clown car but fuel efficient, a.k.a. cheap. She'd blown her savings on a ticket to LA, so she didn't have any choice. Cheapest rental it was. She clicked open the doors and set her overnight bag in the back seat. Then she programmed her phone for the studio where Rhett filmed *Late Night in LA*. Pete had nabbed her the ticket and sworn whoever he'd hoodwinked into secrecy. Pete had claimed she was an old friend who Rhett would love to see.

That was questionable and possibly only half-true.

Summer had spent the holidays faking good cheer, vacillating between anger at the way Rhett had sneaked out of her life and grief over losing the only man she'd ever loved. Or at least thought she loved.

Then she'd gotten a call from Payne Reynolds. *The* Payne Reynolds with Strata Records. She'd been stunned.

"Wait a sec, Mr. Reynolds. I mean, you're *the* Mr. Reynolds, right?" she'd asked when he'd greeted her like an old friend.

"Yes, ma'am," he said with his trademark country twang. "Seems we got a mutual friend, and now you have a new admirer, Ms. Valentine. And really, you can't dream up a better name for an artist than Summer Valentine. It screams country music."

Summer had been standing in the middle of Publix when he called. She picked up an apple absent-mindedly and put it in a plastic bag. "Uh, yes, sir."

"Is this a good time to talk?"

A woman beside her huffed, impatient to get to her Jonagolds, no doubt. But Summer couldn't hang up on Payne Reynolds. What if he didn't call back? She gave the woman a dirty look. "It's perfect."

"Great. Well, Rhett said you might be a little miffed at him for doing what he did, but he sent me a copy of your song 'Carolina Boy.' Now I'm not one to usually take stuff like that. Favors and all. I learned early on how favors can bite you in the ass. But I told the boy to send it on over, and I gave it to Lynette. She tooled around with it, and she sang it for me. Shit, I nearly bawled like a baby listening to it. That's good stuff, Ms. Valentine. Real good stuff."

Summer bumped into the tomato display, sending two boxes of grape tomatoes crashing to her feet. "Uh, thank you, Mr. Reynolds."

"Call me Payne," he said. "Next, I looked you up on the YouTube, and damned if you can't sing, too. Ol' Rhett knew a good thing when he saw it."

But not good enough. Summer shoved the little tomatoes into the plastic containers, hands shaking, stomach rolling. She couldn't believe what was happening. At Publix. "Thank you. Rhett's an old friend. He saw me play when he was home. I sang that song."

"Yep, I like that boy. He's a southerner. Tries to help out people who need a leg up. You seem like an artist who has the right boots but no horse. Rhett's latched them hands for ya. You wanna ride, Ms. Valentine?"

"I do, Mr. . . . uh, Payne. I've been ready to ride all my life."

He laughed and then proceeded to schedule a meeting in LA with her. He was out working on the country version of *American Idol* and wanted to get her in a studio. The same one Carole King used to record *Tapestry*. He said he had a hunch. Summer hung up and sat down hard in the middle of the produce section.

People stopped their shopping carts and stared.

Rhett had somehow gotten his hands on her sheet music. "That bastard."

Someone gasped.

And then Summer started laughing, probably sitting on a few tomatoes, surrounded by bins of fruit and veggies. Her big break had just come . . . in the produce section.

Summer had reeled over what happened, but kept it close to her vest. Then a week later, David had flopped onto the couch. "What about you and Rhett?"

Summer flinched. "What do you mean? Rhett lives in LA."

"I know. But you're all sad since he left. Like you were into him. He was into you, too."

"He's a celebrity. He lives in LA. Doesn't matter who is into who. That can't work."

"Why not?"

"Because."

"You always get mad at me when I say that," he said, opening a bag of chips and chomping on a few. Crumbs fell onto his T-shirt.

"You're making a mess."

"So? I can clean it up. I know where the vacuum is."

"Do you?" she asked, allowing the sarcasm to drip.

"Pete told me Rhett talked to the family of the girl he killed. He told them he was sorry, like my dad told you he was sorry. Pete says Rhett's turned a corner. That he's ready to find meaning in his life. He said he thought that might be you."

"Who told you that your dad told me he was sorry?" Summer felt her stomach flip over. Surely Hunt hadn't told David about the rape.

"Dad did. He said he told you he was sorry for not helping you, for not being there for you. He said telling you that he was sorry was the best thing he's ever done. Besides me. But, yeah, of course, because I'm pretty awesome."

Summer smiled and shook her head.

"Rhett likes you. You like him. Maybe that could turn into something. He's pretty cool, and you don't have a man in your life. I'm good if you want to make him my stepdad. He comes with amenities," David said with a shit-eating grin and a waggle of his eyebrows.

"Just because you want access to Selena Gomez doesn't mean I'm going to go chasing after Rhett."

"No, I want you to be happy. You were happy when Rhett was here. I know y'all were sneaking around and sleeping together. I mean, I have ears."

Summer turned the color of her lipstick. Bombshell Red.

"Be fearless, Mom. That's, like, a motto for our baseball team. If you want things, sometimes you have to go get them. Something good *came* to you—the whole music thing—but if you want the other good thing, I think you'll have to go get it."

For another few days, she chewed on the words her too-smart-for-his-britches boy had given her. And she thought about the truth behind the ugly words Rhett had flung at her before he ran back to LA. The combined words of the two men who mattered most to her had driven her to pack her bags, max out her emergency credit card on a plane ticket, and roll the dice on making all her dreams come true.

Rhett had come to Carolina to find himself . . . then gone back to fix the mistake he'd made.

Summer had come to California to find herself . . . and she'd come back knowing she'd put herself out there.

Nearly an hour and a half later, Summer pulled into a parking lot, parted with a kidney for the parking fee, and climbed out to stretch her legs. She probably looked a mess because she'd fallen asleep on the plane and drooled on her sweater, which thankfully had dried. Her hair felt dry and frizzy even though the humidity in California was almost zero. She rooted in her purse for some lip gloss and a comb. She couldn't show up to tell Rhett Bryan he was a total dumb butt—and so was she—looking like a hag.

She sucked in her stomach for good measure, too.

Once inside, she went to the Will Call window. The woman inside the office gave her a cheerful smile and a ticket that put her front and center. Perfect.

"Mr. Pete said you're an old classmate of his. That's so fun," she said. She had sparkly eye shadow and blue hair. Her nametag said "Lily" and she looked excited for Summer.

"Yep, we're old classmates."

"That's so cool. What was he like in school?"

"The same as he is now."

"Adorable, right?"

"Yep. Absolutely." No need for Lily to know her boss was an ass. Though technically he wasn't her boss. He was the talent. And technically he wasn't an absolute ass. He was a man. Which said everything.

The line to get into the studio was long and boisterous. She seemed to be the only person flying solo, but got a great seat up front. She didn't see Rhett at first because the production assistants or whatever they called them were so engaging. She found herself laughing in spite of her nerves. She could see why people wanted to be in the studio audience—they became an integral part of the show.

"Now, ladies and gentleman, we present your host for the night . . . Rhett Bryan," the announcer said.

The people around her went nuts as Rhett walked onto the set.

He smiled, pressing his hands up to quiet the audience after a good twenty seconds of cheering and people calling out stupid things like, "We love you, Rhett," and, "Rhett for President." Summer wanted to snort at that one. Did they really want him to tell other countries they were doormats and accuse them of letting people take advantage of them . . . and then leave? Can you say World War III?

"Thank you for being here," Rhett said, boyish charm firmly in place. "We have a terrific show lined up, but you already know that. I know Andrea went over what we need from you. You're an important part of the show. First, I'm going to run through some stuff, a sort of rehearsal. Feel free to let me know if my material sucks."

Rhett talked for a few more seconds before his gaze found hers.

The expression on his face was comical and he stumbled over his words.

But like the professional he was, he completed his monologue before waving and disappearing off set. Cameras moved, the crew adjusted mics, and set decorators or whatever they were called filled coffee mugs and set up cards and stuff on Rhett's desk.

One of the people who'd given them instructions bounced over and tapped her on the shoulder. "Excuse me, miss, would you follow me?"

"Why?" Summer asked.

"Mr. Bryan would like to see you," she said.

The woman to her left squealed, "Oh wow, you get to do something. Is she doing 'Name That Leftover'? Or 'Oopsie Daisy'?"

The assistant merely shrugged.

Summer knew what she was about to do and it had nothing to do with guessing songs, naming characters, or doing silly tricks. She scooted out, some people around her clapping their hands and patting her on the back.

Jeez.

The assistant led her to the back, where she passed Liam Neeson (who was tall, craggy, and not as brooding as she'd have guessed), a gaggle of people running around doing "things," and a man who narrowed his eyes at her in a measuring way. He didn't smile when she nodded at him.

The assistant knocked on a door and it opened.

And there was Rhett.

"What are you doing here?" he asked as soon as the door closed behind her. He sounded rattled.

"Seeing your show?"

"What are you doing here?" he asked again, crossing his arms. His blue eyes projected anxiety, irritation . . . hope? Maybe she read too much into that, though. After all, he'd been clear that his world and her world were not the same. And all those people out there applauded him, adored him, would maim and destroy to be standing where she stood in his dressing room.

"Becoming your stalker? You don't have one already, do you?" Her nerves demanded she use flippancy as a diversionary tactic.

"Knock it off. I don't have time to play games. I have a show to do in"—he looked at the clock in the dressing room—"fifteen minutes."

"We left things unfinished," she said.

"I wrote you a letter." He had the grace to look contrite.

"So nice of you."

"Why now, Summer?" He ran his fingers through his hair, scowled, and then tried to make the tufts lie down again when he obviously remembered he had to go on set. "And why here? At the studio? Before a show?"

"I knew you'd be here, and I sort of wanted to see you in action."

A knock sounded on the door. Rhett frowned, walked over, gave a few short words to whoever knocked, and then shut it again.

"Okay, the way we left things wasn't good. But things were getting too . . . too much," he said, turning toward her.

"So you said ugly things to me, pushed me away, and left town?"

Rhett's face reflected guilt. "I didn't mean those things. Jealousy and fear are two things I'm not used to."

He paced the breadth of the room. She'd never seen him so unsettled. Of course, she'd never seen him in any light other than being her ideal. "Some things you said were *somewhat* true. I have sacrificed parts of myself for others, and, yeah, success scares me. Maybe I quit Nashville too soon. Maybe I put others before myself. But that's who I am. I'll never regret putting my child first. That's the deal I made with him the minute they placed him in my arms."

Rhett paused in his incessant pacing and looked at her. "You didn't have to come all the way to LA to say that."

"Maybe not, but I have other reasons, and I'm practicing not being doormatty."

He had the grace to look chagrined. "Payne called you?"

"Yes, and I have a meeting with him. But this isn't about Payne, it's about me and you."

"What me and you?" he asked.

Those words pierced her heart. "I guess I got my answer. Good luck with the show tonight." She turned toward the door and forbade herself to cry. He didn't want her. She'd known there was a fifty-fifty chance he'd tell her to hit the road.

"Don't. Wait." Rhett grabbed her arm and spun her toward him. "You can't do this to me, Summer. I'm trying to get over you."

She studied him. "Why do you *have* to get over me?"

"Because you live in South Carolina. You have a life that isn't like this." But even as he said those words his gaze dropped to her lips. Rhett looked hungry, anguished . . . not the dazzling man who'd told jokes on set a few minutes before.

This was her Rhett. Raw, authentic, conflicted.

"So we're done because I don't live here?" she asked.

He pulled her to him. "You don't know how thin my control is right now."

Summer let him hold her, felt the beat of his heart, the steel in his arms, the softening of his body. "Why do you try to control things you can't?"

He set his head against her hair. "I don't know."

Summer pulled away from him. "I came here because we have things to say that can't be said over the phone or, God forbid, a text."

"I have ten minutes, but after the show we can go back to my place. We can talk about . . . whatever it is you have to say."

Summer shook her head. "I can't wait any longer. Sixteen years ago, I kissed you on the beach and it didn't work out. It *so* didn't work out. I left things undone, and you walked out of my life. Gone was the chance to tell you how I felt or even try to salvage what was left of our friendship. I assumed I wasn't worthy of a guy like you. Even now, I feel pretty unworthy. You're a star. I'm a music teacher, billed by *Nashville Music Today* as 'old-fashioned and reticent.'"

"You know that's not true," Rhett muttered.

"But right now, I'm being brave. I love you. I've always loved you and probably always will. I know that likely doesn't change anything, but I'm not standing outside the fire any longer. I'm all-in even if I get burned."

Rhett stood close to her, so close that she could see he'd missed a few hairs along his jawline when he'd shaved. She inhaled the familiar smell of his cologne and felt the deep breath he took at her words. "You love me?"

"I do. As stupid as that makes me. We spent a week and a half together, and that's all it took to tip me back over the edge," she said against the softness of his gingham shirt. "It may be fast but . . . it happened for me."

309

"Ah, Summer," he said, pulling back. "I can't tell you what you do to me, but how can this work? I can't stand the thought of pulling you into something that would hurt you. This isn't an easy life."

"So you're going to stand outside the fire? Why would you be scared to . . . love me?"

Flying to LA and asking Rhett Bryan to love her was the biggest gamble of her life. When she really thought about it, it was crazy. Hollywood celebrities didn't engage in relationships with small-town music teachers. And if they did, it was for a silly fling. But she'd done it, and on the next day, she'd meet with the head of a record company to discuss a potential record deal.

Call her the gambler.

Rhett stared at her for a few seconds, his gaze searching every inch of her face before returning to her eyes. "Because I'm damaged."

"We're all damaged, sweetheart," she said with a smile.

Rhett's lips covered hers and he emitted a deep sigh, wrapping her back in his arms. He lifted one hand and cupped her jaw, as he nudged her lips apart and deepened their kiss.

The door opened behind them, someone yelped, and then it shut again.

Rhett laughed then before pulling away. A tender flame of something wonderful danced with amusement. "I always tell them to knock. What if I were in my undies?"

"Someone would get a treat," she said, pressing her fingers against her lips.

"You're a brave woman, Summer Valentine," he said.

Inside her heart dropped. He was telling her no. This was the way a guy ended a relationship. This was the way Rhett had dashed her hopes on that beach years ago. *You're a great girl, but . . .*

"But . . ." she managed through the sudden emotion clogging her throat.

Rhett smiled. "Is there supposed to be a but?"

"You tell me."

He shook his head. "When I came back, I felt like hell again. Couldn't sleep and the nightmares started again. The network made me go to this shrink who was . . . like someone Glenn Close could play. Creepy but compassionate. I don't know . . . just different. She didn't offer platitudes, she listened and asked pointed questions that had me examining my life. A part of me hated her, but she was damned successful."

"A good therapist doesn't always give you warm fuzzies. Sometimes we need tough love," she said.

"She gave it, and I realized I'd spent my entire life chasing fame and fortune as if only that could define me. I had few friends, a nonexistent support system, and an ulcer that flared up on occasion. My life looked full, but it was smoke and mirrors. It was sobering."

"And that led you to seek out the Tavares family?"

"I thought about what you'd said, what Hunt's apology meant to you, and the courage it took for him to admit he was wrong. So I went."

"And?"

"I cried like a baby." He gave a sheepish grin. "Crazy, huh? I guess I'd never truly grieved about that child's death. I'd kept all the trauma associated with that day inside. It just came out. I think I scared that poor family."

Summer grabbed both his hands and held them. "I'm so proud of you. That had to be cathartic."

He clasped her hands. "You don't know. It was like I had finally ripped the bandage off, and I knew how you felt, why you had to let all that anger and hurt go. I couldn't heal until I faced the monster in the room."

For a few seconds, they stood, holding hands.

"Will you stay with me tonight?" he asked.

Her heart sank again because he'd still said nothing about why he couldn't love her. She wanted to share his bed, but even more so, she wanted to share his life. "What are you asking?"

A knock sounded on the door. The grumpy man she'd passed in the hall popped his head in. "They're waiting on you."

"I'll be right there."

"Now, Rhett."

He pressed his lips together. "I have to go, Summer. We'll have more time to talk after the show."

Summer tried to tamp down the disappointment. She hadn't planned to talk to him before the show. Instead she thought she'd catch him afterward. Now she had no answers to where she stood in his life. "Okay."

Rhett checked himself in the mirror and hurried toward the door. She blinked and he was gone.

"God," she whispered, sinking onto the chair sitting in front of the dressing table.

The door opened again and Rhett whooshed inside, grabbed her from where she sat, and kissed her hard. "I was wrong. Instead of asking you to stay the night, I meant to ask you to stay forever."

Summer's heart surged against her ribs. She couldn't control the tears that sprang into her eyes. "Seriously? Forever?"

He kissed her again. "We have things to work out, logistics and stuff, but I want you in my life. I ran because I was scared of you, scared of loving you. But I'll stand in the fire with you, Summer . . . even if it's in South Carolina. We can make this work."

He kissed her again, this time the sweetest kiss she'd ever had. Because in his kiss was a promise, and she knew that when Rhett Bryan wanted something, he got it.

"Yes," she breathed when he broke the kiss. "I'll stay with you."

Someone in the hallway shouted for him. Rhett kissed her hard again. "After the show, we'll have coffee."

Summer laughed. "With cream."

He turned and leered at her. "Are you doing dirty talk, Funny Valentine?"

And that made Summer laugh harder. "Maybe."

Smiling, he said, "This is about to be so good. I love you. I'll see you after the show."

Summer gave him a smile, her heart expanding with love so intense she thought she might burst. She'd heard people talk about what it was like being in love, but she'd never known how truly profound, wonderful, invigorating, and half the adjectives on the Do Not Use list in her creative writing class it could be. It was complicated, but Rhett Bryan loved her.

"It's a date, Carolina boy," she called after him before collapsing onto his dressing room couch in a state of euphoria.

She'd rolled the dice on Rhett and won the jackpot. Now all she had to do was get Payne Reynolds to offer her a recording contract.

But first, coffee.

CHAPTER TWENTY-SEVEN

South Carolina, spring

The month of April still clung to winter, so Rhett pulled on the jacket he'd bought in the Savannah airport. California already boasted of warm days and balmy nights, and he hadn't expected a forty-eight-degree night when he'd gotten off the plane.

David was getting his first start as a pitcher that night, and Rhett had promised the kid he'd be there. Red-eye be damned. He'd take something and sleep on the plane. But not before he got to kiss Summer good night . . . and maybe climb in the bed with her for a little snuggle.

Or a lot of snuggle.

The game was in the bottom of the first inning, and he spied Summer in the stands sitting with her mother, sister, and Grampy Pete. He felt her anxiety as she twisted her hands and watched with utter concentration the gangly kid on the mound. He understood the nerves. He had them himself.

Hunt sat not far from Summer, and he looked equally enthralled by the boy on the mound. Hunt's folks sat in front of him, and a pretty blonde woman sat at his side. Rhett assumed she was the kindergarten teacher Summer had told him Hunt had been dating.

Rhett patted his pockets, smoothed his suit pants, and slid onto the bench beside Summer. She gave a start when he brushed against her cheek.

Her eyes went big. "You came! Oh my gosh, I thought you wouldn't make it."

"I promised David I would. Wasn't easy, but I'm here."

Summer gave him a hard hug, and then redirected her attention to her son warming up on the mound. Rhett chuckled as he slid into the back seat of her mind.

"Hey, y'all, I brought bubble gum," the blonde sitting with Hunt said, holding out a hand with several pieces of wrapped gum to everyone sitting around her. "My mama used to always bring bubble gum to the ballpark when my brother played. She said it helped her jitters."

"I'm not nervous, Jenny," Hunt said, looking nothing but nervous.

Jenny stilled his bouncing knee. "So I see."

Rhett still didn't have warm fuzzies for his former best friend, but he'd tried like hell for David's and Summer's sakes to get past the anger. The resentment might always be there. Instead of dwelling on it, Rhett took Summer's hand and turned his attention to David, who stood on the mound wearing the familiar red and gray. The kid looked loose, but every now and then, his eyes darted to where his family sat in the bleachers. Hunt gave his son a nod of confidence, and when David saw Rhett, he smiled.

Rhett gave him a thumbs-up. *You got this, kiddo.*

Mitchell McCoy leaned back and said, "David's looking good, but I still think he needs to rotate—"

"Don't. We talked about this," Hunt interrupted.

"I know I said I wouldn't meddle, but—"

"No, Dad. Nothing. You sit and watch. Enjoy watching your grandson play a game. This is not life and death. He'll be fine even if they pull him in the first inning. It's a game."

Mitchell made a face but latched his lips together.

Rhett slid a glance to Summer, who smiled at the firmness in Hunt's voice. She'd told him Hunt had gone to his parents' house after he left Summer's house back in November and confronted them about how they'd treated Summer and David. He'd also broken down and told them the truth about what had actually happened prom night. Eventually, he'd gotten his parents to talk to Summer, to apologize for what they'd done to her family.

The situation was tenuous at best, but everyone agreed to be adult about it and consider David. He was worth biting one's tongue and pretending to get along. After all, that's what most families did. Of course, Rhett thought *family* was a loose term for what they were, but David didn't seem to care. He'd blossomed into a more confident, outgoing kid.

"After the game we could go to the Rib Hut to celebrate the win," Jenny said, looking at all of them.

"I'm Rhett," he said, extending his hand to her.

"I know," she laughed. "God, I'd have to be dumb and stupid to not know that. I'm Jenny. Hunt's girlfriend."

Hunt didn't flinch at the title she gave herself.

Huh. Interesting.

"But we don't know if they're going to win," Maisie said.

"Of course they will." Summer smiled at her sister. "David's on the mound, and he's a natural."

"Like his father was," Mitchell flung back.

"Like his father was," Summer agreed.

Hunt looked over at her and gave her a grateful smile.

"I didn't think I'd be so nervous, but I think a hive of bees has taken up in my belly," Summer said.

"I wasn't this nervous when I pitched in the state game," Hunt added.

Grampy Pete slid down and eyeballed Rhett. "Glad you made it. The kid was sure you wouldn't."

"Luckily, we wrapped production early. I have to be back in LA tomorrow, but then I'll be back next week for Easter."

Summer squeezed his hand. "Shh! Here we go."

"He's ready. Don't worry." Hunt leaned forward as the batter walked to the plate and tapped it.

The first pitch was a perfect cutter for a strike. Everyone released their breath at once, making Summer laugh.

"Now you know how I felt," Mitchell said to Hunt.

The inning ended with David retiring two batters before a ground-out to short for the third out. As David walked off the mound, he glanced into the stands at his family . . . his very big family. The kid's smile could have lit up Fenway.

Rhett leaned over to Summer. "This is so weird."

She nodded. "He went from just me and him to . . . all this." She jerked her head toward the motley crew to her right.

"No, I meant being at a baseball game, watching your son pitch, sitting here with my fiancée."

Summer jerked her head around. "I'm not your fiancée."

"Oh, I was sure I asked," he said with a wicked smile. "Will David get to hit?"

"What?" Summer said, her attention now all on Rhett. He didn't mind sharing her with her son, but it was good when her attention was all on him. "Um, no. He's a PO."

"Right."

"That's pitcher only," she said, her gaze still on him.

"I know. I played ball."

She was waiting on him to clarify the fiancée thing, but he let it sit for a while. A few long seconds ticked by as the other team trotted onto the field. Maisie fussed at her twins, Grampy Pete moved down to talk to the McCroys, and Jenny tapped on her phone.

"Rhett," Summer said.

"Yeah, babe?"

"You said fiancée. I'm not."

"Oh, well. I must have forgotten to give you this." He reached into the jacket pocket and drew out a small box.

The way she sucked in her breath made his heart smile.

"What's that?" she said, sounding shell-shocked.

"Check it out," he said, keeping his eyes on the field. He couldn't look at her and hold it together. This was probably the worst time to do this, but once he bought the ring, he had to get it on her finger. David wouldn't mind sharing his special night with his mother. The kid could have his baseball diamond, and his mother could have hers.

"Oh my God," she breathed as she opened the box to the ring sparkling inside. "Are you . . . is this . . ."

"Yes and yes," he said, finally looking at her. He wanted to laugh and cry at the same time. Her face was comical, but the tears welling up in those beautiful hazel eyes made his heart clench. "I know things are crazy right now, but I want you to be mine. We'll work around recording your album and my work schedule, and find the perfect date."

She couldn't seem to take her eyes off the diamond. Okay, so he went overboard with a six-carat, emerald-cut diamond, but he wanted to spoil Summer a little. Someone *should* spoil Summer. More than a little.

"It's huge," she breathed. "I can't possibly—"

Maisie leaned over and looked at it. "If you don't want it, I'll take it."

Summer snapped the lid shut when her sister reached for it. "No, you won't."

Maisie laughed and elbowed Summer's mother. Carolyn, who'd been talking to Jenny about kindergarten, turned around. Her face shone with pure love.

In fact, everyone stopped what they were doing and watched Summer.

She turned to Rhett. "You're serious?"

He tapped the box. "That says I am. Oh, wait." He slid off the bleacher and got down on a knee. "Funny Valentine, will you do me the honor of becoming my bride?"

Summer covered her mouth with her hand as tears dropped onto her cheeks. She nodded. "Yes. A thousand times yes. A million times yes."

Everyone in the stands started clapping. A few had started filming the proposal with their phones, but Rhett didn't care. He wanted the world to know he was in love with this woman. The baseball team on the field ceased their warm-ups, and the Mangham High School Bucs leaned out of the dugout, curious why everyone was applauding. Seeing Rhett on his knees in the stands and Summer crying, David came to the fence.

"Sorry to steal your thunder, Ace," Rhett called out, after sliding the ring on Summer's hand. "I couldn't wait any longer."

"Does this mean I get to meet Selena Gomez and Lil Wayne?" David asked, laughing.

"I'll invite them to the wedding," Rhett said, rising and kissing the starting pitcher's mother.

David's laughter rang out above the buzz of the crowd surrounding them. Women flocked to Summer's finger like bargain shoppers rushing a sale on Black Friday. He moved back, catching his grandfather's eye. Grampy Pete winked at him.

At that moment, Rhett Bryan knew he'd found the meaning of life.

It was in the curve of her cheek, the touch of her lips, and the hope she brought for a new future.

This Carolina boy had found his home.

With his Carolina girl.

ABOUT THE AUTHOR

Photo © 2017 Courtney Hartness

A finalist for both the Romance Writers of America's prestigious Golden Heart and RITA Awards, Liz Talley has found a home writing heartwarming contemporary romance. Her stories are set in the South, where the tea is sweet, the summers are hot, and the porches are wide. Liz lives in North Louisiana with her childhood sweetheart, two handsome children, three dogs, and a naughty kitty. Readers can visit Liz at www.liztalleybooks.com to learn more about her upcoming novels.